# THE DISAPPEARANCE

## David W. Roberts

SILVERBIRD
**PUBLISHING**

Published in Australia by Silverbird Publishing
& David W. Roberts

First published in Australia 2025
This edition published 2025
Copyright © David W. Roberts 2025
Cover design, typesetting: WorkingType (www.workingtype.com.au)

ISBN: 978-0-6459162-2-5

# About the Author

**David Roberts** migrated as a qualified teacher from the United Kingdom. After seventeen years working as a teacher, deputy principal and principal in country New South Wales, he became a university academic. University appointments and consultancies enabled David to travel widely and broaden his horizons. Now retired, he lives with his wife in Adelaide.

This is his eighth novel.

# Other titles by David W. Roberts

*One Thing Leads to Another*

*Easytimes*

*Graham's Story*

*Eve*

*Murder on the Heysen Trail*

*White Rose*

*Scrubber McDade*

# PART 1
## (1959)

# Lucy

A gentle breeze fluttered my floral curtains and a pair of blackbirds somewhere out in the garden chortled contentedly. I squinted at my trusty alarm clock and slowly registered it was only a few minutes past nine in the morning. Turning over, I closed my eyes and snuggled back under the bedclothes. I knew it was a Saturday and no school today. But then it slowly dawned on me I had promised to meet Betty at the end of her lane at ten o'clock. We're going "boy-hunting."

Betty's my best friend and we're in sixth form together studying for our "A" levels at St Anne's Catholic College for girls. Betty's a real brain-box studying mathematics, chemistry and physics whilst I struggle along with the so-called "soft" options of geography, English and history. I don't know how Betty handles such difficult subjects that are totally mumbo-jumbo to me. Betty is determined to go to university and become a scientist, whereas I'm quite happy just to learn basic secretarial skills. I figure that with reasonable shorthand and a decent typing speed; I'll land a useful job with a firm of lawyers or accountants or perhaps even a medical practice. I can be earning real money within a few weeks of leaving St Anne's, while poor Betty slogs away at university for three years or more and in that time earns zilch.

There isn't time for a bath so I wash my face and hands in warm soapy water. Mum still refuses to let me wear any make-up which annoys me intensely. 'When you are eighteen, dear...' she keeps saying. Returning to my bedroom, I slip out of my PJs and stand naked in front of my full-length mirror. I like what I see. My breasts are still small but nicely shaped and definitely still developing. I have what the boys call "an hour-glass figure." I wiggle my hips about in a sexy way and then look at myself sideways. I once saw a movie where there was a female pole dancer who did this sort of thing and all the men sitting about were absolutely glued to the show. Men are fascinated by the naked female body. Come to think of it, I get a thrill from seeing a strong, strapping male physique.

There's a sudden knock at my door. I grab my pyjamas and hastily cover my private parts.

'Are you awake, dear?'

'Yes Mum, just getting dressed. I'll be down for breaky in a jiffy.'

Actually, it's a bit more than a jiffy because I have to think carefully about what to wear. "Boy-hunting" is a pastime that Betty and I engage in every few weeks whenever the boys are playing a serious footy match in our village. We don't want to look like sluts, nor do we want to appear like snooty private school girls. It means trying to find something to wear that's in between. To be honest, there isn't much choice in my wardrobe since I don't own many clothes. In the end I select the bottle green blouse I've worn a couple of times before because it's colourful and a bit tight so it shows off my neat breasts. I wonder what Betty will be wearing?

Breakfast at our house at weekends is always a bit crazy. Mum goes "on strike" and lets us kids get our own food; on condition we clean up afterwards and don't do anything drastic like setting fire to the place. On school days it's very different. Mum is well and truly in charge then and cooks us all a proper breakfast. She doesn't have to worry about lunches during the week though because our school provides a cooked main meal and desserts.

My two younger brothers, Rodney and Derek, go to different schools. Rodney's at Dryton co-educational comprehensive school because the stupid numbskull failed his eleven plus exam to get into a grammar school and Derek is at West Dryton primary. Derek will sit his eleven plus next year. If Derek passes, he'll go to grammar school; if he fails, he'll join Rodney at the comprehensive. The eleven plus is a make-or-break test, but I reckon Derek has learnt from his older brother that you need to work hard if you want to escape ending up at a comprehensive school. Betty and I both passed our eleven plus exams which is why we're at St Anne's, a school for the academically gifted.

Mum is sitting at the end of the kitchen table behind a large bowl of steaming Uncle Toby's oats and a cup of tea. The tea-pot is there too, sitting on a mat and hidden under an ancient tea-cosy shaped like a hen. Mum enjoys at least two cups of tea on Saturday mornings, the only day when she has time to fully relax. Derek has burnt his toast again and Rodney is teasing him relentlessly about it. He stops his harassing when he notices me standing in the doorway.

'Hi sis.' He looks me up and down as if deciding how many marks to give me out of ten. 'Going boy chasing again today, then?'

Immediately I feel my face colouring. Rodney has this amazing ability to know exactly what I'm planning. He must be psychic. I had told mum last night that I was going over to Betty's so we could study together.

'Don't be stupid Rodney. If you must know, I'm meeting my friend Betty so we can do a bit of studying together.' This deliberate lie makes my face go even redder.

'Studying "A" level boys more like...'

'That's enough you two,' mother interjects, firmly.

Rodney smirks smugly into his baked beans. He knows he was on the money.

I have just enough time for a couple of bits of Hovis bread, covered in lashings of butter and Robertson's chunky marmalade and slurp down an orange juice. I grab a Coxes Pippin apple on my way out.

# 2.

....

# Malcolm

It's a freezing day mid-January, 1959. The green bus, number 44B from Abingdon, pulls up outside the gates to an austere early Victorian drab sandstone building. 'Culham College' announces the driver dispassionately. I shoulder my backpack and scramble to the front of the bus to collect my battered suitcase from the luggage hold. Four other blokes are doing the same. As I reach the bus-steps, lugging my ancient, over-weight, over-sized suitcase, the bus door swings open and cold air blasts me full in the face. I can see my warm breath streaming out of my nose and mouth.

Five of us have arrived on the 3.18 from Abingdon and we regard each other warily as we stand, shivering, with our assorted pieces of luggage on the side of the road. Four of us are clearly lads more or less straight out of school, but the fifth man is much older, mid-forties probably. The older man takes the initiative.

'Major Tom Pratt,' the older man declares, extending his hand to me first with a broad grin.

'Err...Malcolm...Malcolm Entwistle.'

*What the hell is an army major doing here? He must surely be one of the lecturers?*

Major Pratt greets us one by one with a firm handshake, then heaves what looks like a khaki army swag onto his right shoulder and heads off smartly along the short road that leads to the main entrance of Culham College. Without another word, the rest of us follow along behind the major struggling to control our ungainly suitcases that constantly bash up against our legs. It's only about fifty yards to the entrance but it seems far more by the time we have swapped hands several times and our arms feel ready to drop off. Above the main door there's an inscription writ large, "Honi Soit Qui Mal y Pense." I have no idea what this means, although I do recognise it as being French.

Without stopping, the super fit Major reaches the heavy timber double doors and turns the sizeable metal ring that serves as an elaborate door handle and enters an extensive high roofed hall, replete with massive dark timber beams and rows of long narrow lancet windows stretching along both sides of the building, reminiscent of those found in Norman churches. Like sheep, we four younger men follow the major relieved to be out of the bitter cold. In front of us is a green banner strung across the hall that says, "Welcome New Students to Culham College for Schoolmasters." The place seems full of excited people, almost all male, a cacophony of noise arising from the combined chatter of a score of conversations. Somebody calls us over to a long trestle table where we are welcomed, have our names checked off, handed a room key, a campus map and a small booklet entitled, "Rules and Regulations." We are instructed to assemble in the gymnasium at five o'clock when the College Principal, Dr Venables, will address the new intake of students. Dinner, we are informed, will be served in the Dining Hall at six. It's strongly suggested we find our study/bedrooms straightaway before it gets dark.

Looking at my room key, I see I'm in study room 209. According to my campus map, this room is to be found in a strangely named residential block called "Montessori." (Later, I discovered that each of the eight unattractive red brick residential blocks has been named after a prominent educationalist). It takes me another painful five minutes of puffing and heaving my luggage to reach "Montessori" by which time my arms feel as though they have been torn out of my shoulder sockets. Finally, I stumble through the entrance to Montessori as the light is fading and a cold sleet starts to fall. My troubles are not over yet, however. According to the directory, room 209 is on the fourth floor at the farthest end of the corridor. There are no lifts!

Thankfully, my large metal key works and the door of room 209 swings open with a squeak to reveal a spartan room with two single beds, two small school sized desks, one large beaten-up wooden wardrobe and a tired waste paper basket. On the end of the beds are thin white towels with "Culham College" printed on them. The bed I would have preferred by the window has been taken. Somebody's luggage has already been dumped there.

The lighting is inadequate. A single forty-watt bulb hangs morosely from the high ceiling in the centre of the room and no other lighting is provided. The room is miserably cold, although I notice my unknown roommate has had the good sense to turn on the central heating radiator before leaving. So far, the heater appears to have had little or no impact on the icy temperature. The room is so uninviting I decide not to unpack and heave my suitcase onto the spare bed together with my backpack. Remembering to take my key with me, I set off to find the toilets and washing facilities which are situated half way along the corridor and, not surprisingly, are equally unappealing. Basic is the word that comes to mind. There are four showers, four sit down toilets in cubicles, a smelly urinal and a row of eight white china basins positioned beneath a long ancient mirror that's cracked and damaged. At least there is hot water, I discover, if you can find a tap that has a handle that works.

Welcome to Culham College for Schoolmasters, my home for the next two years!

# 3.

# Lucy

Although Betty and I study totally different subjects and are destined for divergent careers, we share a fascination for boys. Being at an all-girls school, we are starved of any contact with males. There are, of course, a few male teachers at St Anne's but they are old and crusty and of no interest to two lively teenagers. Betty is an only child. Her parents decided she should attend an all-girls school because she was academically gifted and they didn't want her to be distracted by boys highly charged with testosterone. My mother's reasoning for sending me to St Anne's was quite different; she felt guilty because she's a lapsed Catholic. Sending me to have a Catholic education was a feeble attempt on Mum's part to make amends for her non-committal to Catholicism. My mother doesn't feel quite so bad, she once told me, if at least one of her offspring keeps in touch with the faith by attending a Catholic college.

I have to admit that going to St Anne's is no more than a token effort to become a "good" Catholic on my part. With regard to my "faith" I do only what the school requires of me and nothing more. Daily school assemblies are mandatory. I'm constantly amused at such events by one of the prayers that comes up with astonishing regularity. The school principal always seems to be looking directly at me whenever she intones, 'let us pray for all those who are *not* one of us.' The old bat must know that my mother and I don't come to mass on Sundays. Of course, there are other kids at the school who are not even "tykes." The "Prots" are welcome, as long as they pay their school fees on time. I still remember how thrilled my mum was when, in fifth form, I surprisingly topped the class in Religious Studies. I often wonder whether Mum bragged about this to her Catholic friends.

Mum rarely speaks about my father, who left us suddenly nearly ten years ago when I was only seven. Mum was pregnant with Derek at the time. I have fond memories of my dad and there's still a cavernous empty space in my life where he should be. I still remember the little things we used to do together; him pushing me on the swings down at the park, helping me climb trees, reading stories to me and Rodney by the crackling open fire before bed time. Dad, I recall, smoked a pipe and had this tobacco aroma about him that was curiously attractive. His favourite tobacco was called "The Three Nuns." In the evenings, after I was supposed to be tucked up and asleep in bed, I would sometimes sneak downstairs and see him relaxing in his chair in the sitting room with his newspaper, puffing away contentedly on his beloved pipe, with his tobacco pouch and a box of matches beside him. There are still several nuns teaching at St Anne's and I sometimes wonder what they would think if I told them my dad smoked a tobacco called "The Three Nuns"?

It's as if my mum has tried to erase every memory of my father. There are no photographs of him about the house; even the chair he used to enjoy so much in the evenings is long gone. Sometimes, if I'm cleaning for mum, or looking for something in the back of a cupboard, I can still smell faint traces of his tobacco. After dad's departure, Mum's bedroom quickly became a totally female domain. Any reminders of the man she was married to for nine years were hastily expunged. Out went the heavy drapes to be replaced by softer, prettier curtains with a floral design. Removalist men turned up with cardboard boxes and carted off dad's clothes and personal belongings. Mum even had their bedroom repainted and dad's office, next door, converted into an extra bedroom for the new baby.

I remember watching all this activity around the house in a state of frightened confusion. Where was dad? Why had he left us so suddenly without any explanation? Didn't he love us anymore? Was he ever coming back? Most distressing of all was the thought that if dad could disappear overnight without warning, would mum do the same thing one day and leave us children alone in the world? Rodney was barely four at the time and took it hard. I tried my best to be brave for him and stay cheerful. At nights I often crawled into bed with mum where I would cry myself to sleep. Whenever I asked questions, she would simply cuddle me close and make fatuous comments such as, 'Dad didn't want to stay here anymore.' When I asked 'why?' her answers became vague and unhelpful, 'He's got other things to do' or 'he's busy doing something else.'

Rodney certainly changed after dad left us. If anything went slightly wrong, he would fly into a temper and stamp and rage about the place. It would take him a long time to calm down and he'd end up sulky and uncooperative. Almost every night he wet the bed. The teachers at his kindergarten were alarmed at the deterioration in his behaviour too. Nowadays, all these years later, Rodney still has a chip on his shoulder and can become aggressive about silly little things. He continues to get into trouble at school too. I take great care not to provoke him.

Now that I'm nearly eighteen years old and about to sit my "A" levels, I reckon I'm mature enough for mum to open up and tell me exactly what *did* happen ten years ago. Parents don't just walk out on their families overnight without warning and not come back. I have a right to know. I've stressed this to mum on a couple of occasions but she just smiles sweetly and tells me she'll tell me when the time is right. In my opinion, the right time is now!

Understandably, I've often pondered what happened to dad. There are several possibilities. The most likely explanation is that after nine years of marriage mum and dad simply separated. I was only seven at the time dad left but I'm surprised I didn't pick up the vibes then that they were not getting along. Little children can be hyper-sensitive to what's going on around them.

At one stage, I wondered whether dad had suddenly died. But that didn't add up for a couple of reasons. Firstly, mum wouldn't have tried to forget he ever existed by removing everything associated with him and then not speaking glowingly to us kids about him. Secondly, every month a mysterious item arrived in the mail. It was always in a long light blue envelop delivered by the postman in the first week of the month. On the back of the envelope was the address of a company of solicitors who called themselves, "Gregory, Basham and Price, Family Solicitors." Mum once divulged that inside there's a monthly cheque which provided enough money to keep the family going with most of our expenses. If these light blue envelopes kept coming, I reasoned, it must mean dad was still alive somewhere.

Of course, there are other less savoury possibilities for dad's disappearance. Perhaps he was secretly living a life of crime and is now cooling his heels in some desultory prison somewhere? To remain at her majesty's pleasure after ten years suggests it must have been a pretty serious crime. Murder? Rape? Maybe he was the gang leader of some major crime network? Could it be, that behind the loving dad I remembered so fondly, there was a sinister scheming master criminal?

I have never ruled out the likelihood my dad is permanently hospitalised in some sort of a medical institution. Perhaps he had a mental breakdown and for his and everyone else's safety, he has been ensconced in a hospital for the mentally insane? We have been studying "Hamlet" as one of our "A" level texts this year and the part where Ophelia goes insane, I found quite devastating. Could my father have succumbed to something just as awful? Many people are ashamed to admit that one of their family is mentally unstable. Could this, perhaps, be the reason for my mum's long silence?

From time to time, I hear about somebody in the neighbourhood who has suffered a traumatic medical event that kills them, or leaves them permanently disabled. Old Frank, at number forty-seven, had a massive stroke and within two weeks was dead. And then there was Aunt Sally who had a heart attack and is now so disabled she is being cared for in a nursing home. I remember also, there was a young man called Alex in the next street over who wiped himself out in a car accident. "Severe brain damage" was the verdict and Alex ended up as a complete vegetable. Could a horrific medical event have befallen my poor dad so that he's lying in a coma somewhere? If dad's disappearance is due to medical reasons, then surely mum would have told us about it.

The most likely explanation is that either mum, or dad, were unfaithful and this ended their relationship. But which one? I've always thought young Derek looks different to Rodney and me. He has fair, almost blonde straight hair and pale skin, whereas the rest of us are more coffee coloured with darker, curly hair. Derek is also shaping up to be two or three sizes larger than the rest of us. He is only ten but definitely larger boned and a heavier build than I or Rodney. His blue eyes are atypical too. Could it be that mum is the guilty party and she had an affair which resulted in the conception of Derek? It seems feasible. Alternatively, perhaps dad played away from home and mum kicked him out?

All these theories have rolled about in my head over the years, with no conclusive answers. I'm determined to press mum to give me the whole story soon and certainly before I leave St Anne's. Dad's disappearance cannot remain a mystery forever.

# 4.

# Malcolm

After using the ablutions I wandered back to my less than inviting study room number 209. I reckoned I had half an hour to kill so I might as well sort out some of my gear and stake a claim to one half of the battered old cupboard provided for our personal belongings. There was no way everything was going to fit into my half of the cupboard, which meant I was obliged to keep the rest of my stuff crammed up in the suitcase under the bed. As I stowed my clothes away, I reflected on what had brought me to the start of a two-year full-time teacher training course in the heart of the English Cotswolds.

The life we are born into is a matter of pure chance. In my case, I grew up in a relatively privileged environment. My parents liked to describe themselves as "gentlefolk" and came from one of the many echelons of "upper-class" British society. Within these upper classes there were many layers, or sub-classes, rather like the strata piled one on top of another in a sedimentary geological formation. There were distinct and precisely defined boundaries between the numerous layers of the British privileged classes such that you were likely to be cruelly snubbed should you dare to think, or act, above your station. To fall from grace and end up in a "lower" class layer than you were born into was considered unforgivably demeaning.

My family is a "military" family. My father, a professional soldier in the Royal Artillery, retired in 1947 with the rank of major. Both my grandfathers, however, rose to far higher office. One was a major general and my mother's father made it to the dizzy heights of lieutenant-general. Such senior army rankings placed them high up in the pecking order of British society. They lived grandly in gracious houses surrounded by domestic servants and enjoyed the cultural and social delights afforded only to those of equivalent social standing. Sadly, my grandparents have passed away.

At the turn of the twentieth century Britain virtually ruled the world. A quarter of the world's landmass was coloured red in the atlases of the day depicting the vast reaches of the British Empire. This position of almost total dominance in world affairs was strongly reflected in the arrogant "superior" attitudes of the British people, particularly among the wealthy and powerful upper classes. Britain ruled the waves and London was recognised as the greatest city on earth. Britain's world status seemed unassailable.

Now, my father is hyper-sensitive about class and class distinctions. There are good reasons for this. For several years my father woed my mother before finally managing to persuade her parents that he was worthy of their daughter. At the time of their romance, my father was a lowly captain and the general and his wife expected their daughter, Joan, to marry a much higher ranked officer. As it turned out, my father struggled to make it up one more rank to become a major. Consequently, he was particularly sensitive about class distinctions because he had never been able to meet the general's high expectations.

Unfortunately, there was more ignominy to come. My father retired from the army a youthful forty-seven-year-old on a major's pension at the end of the second world war. The two catastrophic world wars (1914-1918 and 1939-1945) virtually bankrupted Britain. After World War two the world was a very different place. The United States was emerging as the new world leader whilst the population of battered and bloodied Britain was left to lick its wounds and struggle to rebuild and recover from the smashing it had received at the hands of the Nazis. No longer able to maintain or finance its colonies, the British Empire steadily crumbled as colonies aggressively sought their independence from the broken mother country. The allies had been victorious, but for Britain it had been at a crippling cost.

The austere financial straits that Britain found itself in during the late 1940s and 1950s severely impacted many people, my parents particularly. Pre-war, my parents had enjoyed a generous salary, comfortable living conditions and domestic help. My mother organised the servants, never went to work (ladies didn't need to) and enjoyed a fulfilling social life. This ideal world rapidly faded away after World War two. My father's army pension was "fixed", which meant that year after year it never increased despite the fact that the cost of living was rocketing up. He realised too late, that he had retired far too early. Soon my parents were forced to down-size, to let go their domestic help and my mother found it necessary to learn how to shop, cook and take care of the house herself. She never complained but it must have been hard and at times humiliating adjusting to this new humbling social order.

I'm their only child. They were determined to send me to private schools, even though it was a heavy strain on their steadily declining resources. Father came out of retirement to take on a lowly office job to help pay my school fees. We had remained throughout this challenging time a proud military family, despite our change in fortune, and it was made clear to me from a very young age that I was expected to carry on the family's noble military traditions. It was assumed I was destined for the Royal Military Academy, Sandhurst as soon as I turned seventeen and a half. My successful entry into the British Army as an officer would, in my parents' eyes, go some way towards maintaining a semblance of their "upper" class status. My parents would still be able to hold their heads up high and say, 'Well young Malcolm is at Sandhurst, you know...' and later, 'Malcolm has now joined his regiment as an officer.'

Sadly, I let them down!

Like many seventeen-year-olds, I didn't know what I wanted to do. I had performed well at school ending up as the school's vice-captain and winning my sporting "colours". School "colours" were highly sought after and only a handful of boys qualified to wear the coveted "colours" tie. I was enormously proud of this achievement, which had come about as a result of my many appearances in the school's top athletics, fives, rugby, tennis and swimming teams. I had also performed well in the school's CCF (Citizens' Cadet Force) finishing with the rank of company sergeant major and second-in-command. In my final term at school, I sat the entrance examination for the Royal Military Academy, Sandhurst and passed. My parents were thrilled and my school achievements augured well. Their only son appeared destined for a successful career as an officer in the British Army and would continue the family's proud military tradition.

So far though, I had simply followed the path the family had set out for me. Sandhurst, a career in the army and as a result of this, acceptable status in Britain's class society. To be perfectly honest, I had been so busy enjoying all my sporting exploits that I had given scant thought to any other possible careers. It had been a case of just doing what everyone expected of me.

The next step, after passing the written examination to enter Sandhurst, was attendance at a three-day War Office Selection Board assessment and it was here that things began to seriously unravel.

# 5.

...

# Malcolm

I'll never forget the three torrid days I spent at the War Office Selection Board attempting to meet the high standards required for acceptance into the Royal Military Academy, Sandhurst, Britain's elite training program for regular officers entering the British army. For the first time in my life, I was forced into some serious thinking about my future. Did I really want to be a soldier or did some other profession have greater appeal? I was a touch over seventeen and a half years old when I nervously reported to the Guard House at the formidable looking entrance to Sandhurst.

On arrival, I was required to strip down and undergo a thorough half hour medical check. This done, I was fitted out in jungle greens together with army boots and a folder containing notes and regulations to be read that evening. I signed a statement expressing my willingness to participate in all the activities over the ensuing three days and gave my consent to do so entirely at my own personal risk. This, I thought, sounded ominous! Next, I was handed two white bibs to be worn at all times during the day, one for my front and one for the back. From henceforth, I was to remain totally nameless, except for the number on my bibs which was thirty-six. I never really got accustomed to the sergeants yelling, 'Move it thirty-six', 'push harder thirty-six', 'get your bloody arse over here thirty-six' and so on, for three long and painful days.

Dinner that first night was held in the officers' mess. We were told to wear "mufti" (civilian clothes) and our bibs. The forty officer-cadet applicants were seated at meticulously laid out tables, as if we were in a high-class restaurant, and were served by junior ranks, whilst the assessing officers watched us hawk-like from the sidelines with their clip-boards and pens at the ready. It was a formal dinner. Starched white tablecloths and serviettes seemed too good to use and the cutlery, perfectly positioned, shone as if polished. I remember looking around at the other seventeen and eighteen-year-olds in the group and sensing immediately that I was probably inadequate in this company. I felt rather small and puny in comparison and lacked the confidence and boldness most of these more rugged looking characters displayed. What the hell had I got myself into, I wondered?

The food was excellent though and after our desserts had been cleared away, we were addressed by a Colonel Roseman, the officer in charge of our three-day assessment. No less than eight other army officers, in impeccable dress uniforms, formed a semi-circle around the colonel as he spoke.

'Good evening gentlemen. My name is Colonel Roseman. Welcome to the Royal Military Academy, Sandhurst, one of the first, and most respected officer training establishments in the world. Only the best officer cadets will successfully graduate from here. Sandhurst, as you know, has been the training academy for countless distinguished British army officers over many years.

During your stay gentlemen, you will be treated as officers and will be expected to behave as such. Unsavoury, vulgar behaviour will not be tolerated.

You are here to try to impress us. Unless you are an abnormal group, only about half of you will meet the demanding standards required for entry to the academy. You will receive notification of your results about one week after completing the three-day program. There are only three gradings: pass, deferred for a second attempt and fail. There is no avenue *for appeal. Those that make the grade first time will commence training here at the July intake. Those of you who qualify to try a second time must do so within six months and before you turn eighteen and a half. If you are deemed to have failed gentlemen, it means you have been assessed as not officer material. You are, of course, welcome to then try to join the army but as a non-commissioned officer.*

*Standing behind me are the distinguished officers who will be responsible for assessing you in every activity you undertake over the next three days. Deliberately, they do not know your names. We do not wish to be accused of bias or favouritism. Like it or not, you are only a number to us for the next three days. Failure to display your bib, front and back, at all times will be regarded as a serious offence. You are not to speak to any of these gentlemen. They will, however, be giving you orders and instructions from time to time. Remember, don't speak to the officers unless spoken to.*

*Breakfast will be served at 0700 hours. Punctuality at all times is essential. Dress for breakfast is army fatigues. You are to be seated in the Drill Hall, ready for the day's activities by 0800 hours. Any questions?'*

There was no way I was game to ask a question in that highly charged atmosphere but one silly idiot couldn't help himself and jumped to his feet. No doubt this twit was hoping to make an impression from the outset.

'Yes, sir. Could you give us a run down on the kind of activities we'll be engaged in over the next three days please?'

'You will be fully briefed in the morning,' was the curt reply. I noticed one of the assessors squinting at the questioner, probably already noting his bib number and recording something on his clip-board.

I remember wondering at the time how this game fellow had been regarded by the assessors. Was he marked down as being a precocious opportunist or marked positively as a young man displaying unusual initiative and courage? After all, potential officers would surely be expected to have both these attributes. It was a quandary that worried me throughout the next three days. Should I try to display leadership and initiative or demonstrate that I was an excellent team member willing to cooperate and contribute at all times?

That evening, I retired to my private bedroom straight after dinner to read up on the rules and regulations so that I would be adequately prepared in the morning. As I approached my bedroom, I was accosted by a smart young soldier in uniform with two stripes on his arms.

'Good evening, sir, Corporal Jones. I'll be serving as your batman during your stay with us. Should you have any soiled clothing sir, or want your footwear cleaned, kindly leave such items outside your door before you retire for the evening. They'll be laundered, or polished and ready for you first thing in the morning.'

I was taken aback by this. My father had spoken occasionally of having a "batman" who, apparently, had the job of being a sort of personal servant for serving officers. The colonel had said that whilst at Sandhurst we would be treated like officers and here, already, was proof.

'Thank you, corporal. I will indeed leave out some gear for you,' I replied, rather shyly.

'And will you require a wake-up call in the morning, sir?'

I had not thought to bring an alarm clock so this was a more than welcome offer.

'Oh...yes please. Six-thirty will do nicely.'

'Very good, sir.' Corporal Jones clicked his heels and marched smartly off down the corridor. I discovered later that the unfortunate Corporal Jones must have had to endure virtually sleepless nights, since there were twelve of us in his corridor and each night every one of us left out piles of dirty clothing to be washed, dried and ironed, together with shoes or boots for cleaning to be ready again in a few hours' time when we emerged for an early breakfast.

Anyway, I remembered to put out my walking shoes and "mufti" soon afterwards and was pleasantly surprised to find said items awaiting me at six-thirty next morning when Corporal Jones knocked politely on my door. The clothes were clean and pressed and my battered old walking shoes looked the best they'd ever been. Perhaps, I mused, an army officer's life wasn't so bad after all…

\* \* \*

The three days that followed were extraordinarily intense and demanding. On several occasions I was sorely tempted to "throw in the towel". Had I enjoyed ready access to a car, I probably wouldn't have stuck it out. We were involved in assessment activities from eight in the morning until around eight in the evening each day with only a short break of half an hour for lunch and another short tea break in the afternoon. Clearly, the course was designed to "break" anyone with any weakness. Not surprisingly, at least four of my peers did drop out and went home. The forty who started the program were divided into five sections with eight cadets in each. We rotated through a string of set activities over the three days according to a tight timetable. Half the activities were out of doors and went ahead whatever the weather. My section endured three long outdoor activities in cold, drenching rain! Whatever we were required to do, the ubiquitous assessors were there observing silently and making copious confidential notes. It was a group of aggressive sergeants who supervised every event and issued the orders or instructions. I really got to hate those guys!

Almost thirty-six hours of assessment activities to determine who was officer material struck me as excessive. To explain every activity would take me ages, so I will limit myself to describing a few only, enough to give you some sense of what we endured. The outside activities were designed to test teamwork, leadership, initiative, problem solving ability, physical fitness and agility, courage and endurance. How well we scored for these various attributes was never disclosed. We had to complete a number of assault courses within a given time. I managed to finish most of these but was clearly outclassed by some of the tougher more agile fellows. Challenges included scrambling through narrow rat races, climbing rock walls and rope ladders, swinging on ropes to cross over deep water, jumping off high walls, swimming across a swollen river in full army fatigues and crawling through dark, muddy tunnels. I soon discovered I suffered from weak arms and shoulders. Towards the end of the three days my arms, wrists and fingers stiffened and cramped up so painfully I was forced to withdraw from the final physical test. This refusal, I'm sure, cost me dearly.

The indoor activities were designed to find out more about us as people. I remember there was an intelligence test, a long session on my own with two psychologists and later with an interview panel. One activity I found most nerve racking was having to give an impromptu five-minute speech in front of about twenty people. Two sections were combined for this activity, together with four assessors. When your number was called you had to leave the room to collect your topic. You then had five minutes to prepare a five-minute speech before returning and delivering it from the centre of the stage using a lectern and microphone. My topic was "The Loch Ness Monster." I don't think Nessie would have been particularly impressed with my performance!

I have never been so relieved to leave an establishment as I was at the end of those three gruelling days. I was physically and mentally exhausted and slept the whole way home with my father driving our old Morris eight.

A week later, as promised, an official looking letter arrived in the post. I had had plenty of time to reflect on my three challenging days at the War Office Selection Board and had arrived at a disturbing decision; I definitely did *not* want to join the British Army as an officer. My main reason was the kind of young men I would have to mix with socially and with whom I would be required to work throughout my career. These guys were different to me. I sensed a ruthless streak, a lack of compassion, a tough determination to get things done at all costs. These qualities were missing in my own make-up. I felt I was more sensitive, more considerate, more questioning about what was right and wrong. Some of the young men I'd met at Sandhurst couldn't get enough of the physical demands placed upon them; they relished the challenges, the sweat, the pain and discomfort. They were tough and uncompromising and made of sterner stuff than me.

I nervously carried the unopened letter upstairs to our second floor flat, knowing my parents would be anxiously awaiting the result. My acceptance at Sandhurst would be a huge red-letter day for them. All their dreams for their only child would be realised and they could proudly telephone relatives with the exciting news. Somehow, I would then have to break the awful news to them that I was not going to accept the offer of a place at Sandhurst. Failure, on the other hand, would be devastating. I honestly didn't think I was going to be accepted; the best I could hope for was an invitation to appear again before the board in six months' time. If this was the result, it would at least give me more time to determine how best to tell my parents of my decision to never join the army.

I entered our sitting-room, a large, airy room, pleasantly furnished with antique furniture passed down through proud military generations. My parents were sitting where they always sat for afternoon tea. My mother always occupied the easy-chair closest to the blazing open fire with the tea-trolley in front of her. As the lady of the house, she dispensed the cups of tea always pouring the milk in first. A silver bowl, replete with silver tongs contained the white sugar lumps. The silver tea-pot was enclosed in a pretty hand-knitted tea-cosy, one of several my mother treasured. The open fire burned brightly in the grate spitting out occasional sparks when a lump of burning coal shifted position. The copper coal-scuttle beside the hearth was still half full of lumps of shiny jet-black coal.

My father sat facing the open fire in "his" arm chair, replete with side-table and his blue angle-poise lamp. A side-plate with an untouched chocolate marsh-mellow and a half-consumed cup of tea awaited his attention. My parents considered it poor manners to start talking before everyone was sitting comfortably with their cups of tea and side-plates containing whatever was on offer for afternoon tea. We were the epitome of reserved English gentry. Displaying one's emotions was strongly discouraged. It was stiff upper-lip and all that...

'Would you like your cup of tea now, dear?

'Yes, please.'

I waited while my mother poured the milk from the fine-China milk jug, then carefully strained the tea-leaves and handed me my matching plate, cup and saucer complete with a teaspoon.

'And what can I offer you to eat, dear? There are fresh cucumber sandwiches?'

Being only seventeen, I was constantly hungry and definitely had hollow legs. Mother placed four of the small delicately cut, decrusted white bread cucumber sandwiches on my plate and passed it across to me. I sat on the spare easy-chair with my cup of tea and plate of cucumber sandwiches safely resting on the side-table. I could feel my parents looking at me expectantly for they had seen me enter the room holding an official looking letter from this afternoon's post.

'Sugar, dear?'

I took the sugar bowl and plopped two white sugar lumps into my cup. I returned the sugar-bowl, stirred my cup gently and realised I could delay no longer. I reached for the letter and tore it open.

'Perhaps Malcolm, you would like to read the letter to us?' suggested my father, doing his utmost not to appear impatient. The letter was typed, short and horribly official looking.

*Dear Mr. Entwistle,*

*Thank you for participating in the recent War Office Selection Board's three-day assessment programme.*

*The officers responsible for assessing you have carefully considered your performance.*

*We wish to remind you that there are three grades that the assessors can give.*

*Grade 1: Deemed acceptable for immediate entry into the Royal Military Academy, Sandhurst.*

*Grade 2: Deemed unacceptable for entry into the Royal Military Academy, Sandhurst.*

*Grade 3: The Selection Board remains undecided. This grade entitles you to appear one more time at the War Office Selection Board, provided your appearance occurs within six months of the date of this letter and is prior to you turning eighteen and a half.*

*You have been assessed as Grade 3.*

*There are no avenues for appeal.*

*Would you kindly advise us, within two weeks of the receipt of this letter, whether or not you wish to appear a second time before the War Office Selection Board.*

*Yours faithfully,*

*Colonel Roseman (Commanding Officer)*

# 6.

# Lucy

It's a pleasant April morning. The sun is warm and welcoming, no need for jumpers, raincoats or umbrellas. I can stay dressed as I am and show off my neat little figure. As I hurry along a grey squirrel bounds across my path, stops for a moment, looks back at me inquiringly, then hurries on as if on some urgent mission. There's a joyful chorus of blackbirds, sparrows and thrushes chortling away in the garden hedges trying to out-do each other. Looking ahead, I can see Betty is already there, waiting patiently for me under a leafy elm tree at the end of her lane. We share a hug.

Betty and I have been best friends since arriving together at St Anne's Catholic college for girls almost six years ago. Over the years we often found ourselves in the same classes as we studied the broad range of subjects available for our "O" (Ordinary) levels. Although our academic interests have been different from the start, we discovered early on that we shared a fascination with boys. We are, of course, deprived of their company at St Anne's so have had to seek their company out of school. Betty has met a few Catholic boys at church but my family rarely attends mass, so this opportunity has been denied me. Together, Betty and I have persuaded our parents to let us attend Scottish dancing classes on Friday nights and this was the best thing we ever did. On a decent Friday night there are well over forty of us teenagers going through our steps, learning reels and flirting mercilessly. It's great fun and full of romantic intrigue.

Betty is cleverer than me. Anyone who can handle the "A" (Advanced) level subjects she has selected to study has to be a brain-box. What I lack in brains, however, I make up for in personality and looks. Coming from a quiet and strictly religious family background, Betty is predictably rather shy and lacking in confidence. She's also an only child which doesn't help. Sometimes I know I shock dear Betty. I suppose it's because I'm an extrovert and she's an introvert. Nevertheless, I'm sure I'm good for Betty because I "bring her out" and encourage her to do things she would never attempt if left to her own devices. I have to admit occasionally Betty has a calming effect on me and this helps me moderate my behaviour when I get too carried away. They say that opposites attract and I guess that's the case in our long-lasting relationship.

'Hello Lucy, lovely day.'

'Perfect weather for boy hunting,' I smirk.

'Are we going anywhere special?'

'Yes, of course, we are. Yesterday, I found out from Mrs. Adams, my PT teacher, there's a football match this morning starting at ten-thirty down at the village playing fields which should be full of delicious young men.'

'Oh, really? Which teams are playing?'

'It's our village team taking on Culham.'

'Culham? Do you mean the village or the teachers' training college there?'

'The teachers of course. Just think of all those spunky young blokes. And... they're just the right age for us, Betty. I can't wait. Come on...'

We linked arms and giggled mischievously as we crossed the road and headed downhill towards the village's one and only quality soccer pitch located on the grassy river flats. We arrived a few minutes before the game was due to start and the players were still milling about doing stretches and warm-ups. The pitch has been freshly mown; the lines marked with black creosote and the nets hooked up into position around the goal posts. The smartly clad referee was already out in the centre of the pitch with his foot resting on the match-ball and his whistle poised.

As we approach through the ring of greening deciduous trees that encircle the ground, we can't help but admire the beauty of the location. Along one side of the football pitch flows the river Hars, a favourite haunt for fishermen, hikers and romantic couples. Today the water is moving sluggishly through the reeds with the occasional duck paddling slowly around before diving for some tasty snack. On the other side of the river are verdant pastures broken up by hedgerows and, in the far distance, gentle hills fold into each other like pillows. Light brown guernsey dairy cattle graze contentedly in these lush fields showing no interest in the frantic activities on our side of the Hars River.

Half a dozen wooden benches have been placed, seemingly randomly, along the touch-line with most already occupied by chattering village supporters. At one end of the ground there's a collection of ancient swings, see-saws and a broken-down round-about that has attracted the attention of several young children who are racing about yelling and squawking. At the opposite end of the ground there's a car-park containing a dozen or more cars and a small bus with "Culham College" emblazoned across its side, together with the college crest and the words, "Honi Soit Qui Mal y Pense."

Betty and I know most of the village players. They're a mixed bunch ranging from a few lads from the local high school to the die-hards in their forties who stubbornly refuse to accept that they are getting too ancient for ninety minutes of strenuous soccer. There's nobody in our village team that interests us. But the spunky young men from Culham College offer a fresh lot of faces and all sorts of romantic possibilities. As we near the sideline, the referee gives an impatient blast on his whistle and the two teams run, somewhat haphazardly, onto the field. With pre-game nervous chatter the players take up their positions.

The Culham lads are smartly kitted out in red tops and matching socks with clean white shorts. In contrast, our village team looks somewhat daggy in their tired faded blue gear. The antiquated scoreboard at the end of the ground proudly welcomes spectators and players to the "C" grade match between the home team, West Dryton, and the visitors, Culham College. Unfortunately, whoever is in charge of the scoreboard has forgotten to remove the number "4" from the last team to visit, so that it reads as though Culham College is already leading 4-0 before the game begins. Once the spectators notice this oversight they start yelling and screaming at poor old Fred who has been faithfully looking after the village scoreboard for more years than anyone can remember. Finally, the hapless Fred realises his error and grumpily makes amends. The score is corrected to show 0-0. With another blast of the whistle the game is finally underway and we girls settle down to do some serious assessment of these Culham boys.

Betty and I agree that the Culham lads offer us the best chance of finding a potential boyfriend. To have made it to Teachers' College means the student teachers must be reasonably intelligent and therefore likely to end up with secure jobs and salaries above that of the average worker. If we can find a couple of young men we like, they might be a good "catch." Culham College for Schoolmasters is only five miles from our village and there's a regular bus service that goes past the college on its way to Abingdon. Young as we are, we two girls are already looking out for potential life partners, who might provide us with the security and comfortable living we crave in order to one day raise a young family.

It's one thing to get down to watch the local football match; it's far more difficult to find an excuse to actually "meet" any of the Culham boys. The game is in progress and the players are concentrating on tackling, marking their opposite number and chasing after that elusive ball. The combatants pay scant attention to us spectators. So, for a bit of fun, Betty and I decide to pick out the Culham lads we most like the look of and worry about how we will ever get to meet them later. We've done this a couple of times before; once when a men's basketball team arrived in the village to play a demonstration match and again when a boys' high school sent us a choir to sing at last year's Christmas carols. Interestingly, on both occasions, Betty and I selected different boys. I think Betty's looking for the "brainy" ones, whereas I'm looking for the "brawny" lads.

There are only eleven players in a soccer team so spotting the best of the bunch is not too challenging a task. Culham has a couple of reserves sitting on a bench near us but Betty and I don't see anything to recommend either of them. After ten minutes of observing, we have both picked out our first choices and, giggling, put our heads together to compare notes. True to form, Betty has selected a pleasant looking fellow who's wearing glasses and looks brainy as her first choice. I've chosen an athletic guy on the wing who's handsome, plays hard and is clearly one of the most dangerous players on the field.

A few minutes after making our personal selections, Culham scores. Amazingly, it's the young man I like who is the one who dribbles the ball down the touchline and centres it beautifully for one of his team mates to hammer home. I knew then, I was on to a winner. Betty and I have already turned traitors to our village and start clapping the successful Culham boys enthusiastically.

'Ere, wot you clappin 'em for?' a rough voice demands, 'them's the bloody opposition.'

'Ain't yous from the village no more?' snarls a second sneering voice.

We turn to find two of the rough village lads glaring at us. One is Glen, the baker's teenage son, the other is Nigel who's from one of the local dairy farms. Glen is dressed in the village team's gear and is obviously a reserve waiting to go on to play. We both feel horribly guilty for our disloyalty to our village and realise the boys' criticism is well deserved. Shy Betty apologises immediately, but not me.

'Sorry Glen, sorry Nigel,' Betty mumbles.

'It's the sporting thing to do to clap good play whichever team it is,' I snap back, defiantly.

'No, it ain't,' Glen retorts.

Thud! Suddenly, without warning, a soccer ball smacks into the side of Betty's face so hard it knocks her off her feet.

'Shit! Where'd that come from?' exclaims Nigel, as the three of us hurry to help Betty back on her feet.

Betty's sobbing and scrabbling about on the ground trying to find her glasses. She told me once she's as blind as a bat without her "gig-lamps" as she calls them. I get to Betty first and help her up, whilst the boys retrieve her glasses that have miraculously survived the impact. Betty has a nose bleed as well as a dirty face. I fumble for the handkerchief I always keep up my sleeve and hold it to Betty's nose as I offer comforting words.

The incident has caused quite a stir. The ref stops the game and a number of other spectators come over to see if Betty is okay. One man offers a much larger handkerchief for Betty's bleeding nose and there's a chorus of sympathetic voices.

'I *do* apologise...I'm *so* sorry.'

Keeping one hand on Betty's nose, I turn to find my number one choice from the Culham team standing right next to me with an anxious expression on his face.

'Was it you?' I ask.

'I'm afraid so,' he replies.

I now have a close-up view of my number one choice. He's taller than I thought, a good head and shoulders above me and is sweating profusely. Small beads of perspiration dot his forehead. His hair is darker than I had originally noticed and he has strong hairy legs with mud covered knees. His socks are both at half-mast. What I like most about the young man is his pleasant face. It's one of those honest, kindly faces, belonging to a person who means no harm to anyone or anything. He's not smiling now though and is showing genuine concern for Betty, who still seems to be trying to work out what actually happened to her.

'It *was* an accident,' the young man assures Betty. 'I was trying to kick the ball down to the centre forward but I sliced it hopelessly. Trying to be too clever, I guess. I'm so sorry.'

'We know you didn't mean it,' I say, putting my hand instinctively on his arm. 'We'll be fine,' I add.

He looks at me full on for the first time and I just love his eyes. Some people's eyes are devoid of life but not this young man. There's a sparkle there that gives me goose-bumps. It's not so much the colour that I notice but the intelligence and warmth. His eyes are immediately engaging and I don't want to look away so I hold his gaze for as long as I can without being rude. Then the whistle blows. He flashes a brilliant smile at me and is gone. I'm left wondering what his name is?

# 7.

...

# Dorothy

It's half past ten and I finally have time to sit down and relax. As a single mum with two teenagers and a precocious eleven-year-old, life is frenetic. Anyone who tries to tell me it's harder when the kids are very young doesn't know what they're talking about. Teenagers are far more complex, unpredictable, moody and, at times, plain stupid. They think they know everything and refuse to listen to us wiser grown-ups. Eleven-year-old Derek is not actually a teenager, of course, but he already behaves like one. I seem to spend my entire life lurching from one disaster to another and always of the kids' making.

It's more than ten years since Tom, my beloved husband of nine wonderful years, suddenly disappeared. I still find it unbelievable that a presumably happily married man can just vanish overnight and seemingly without trace. Tom has become just another statistic, one of thousands listed in Britain as "a missing person." I'm sure the police have given up trying to find him; they've not been in contact with me for a long time. If I had a few thousand pounds to spare, I could perhaps put up a decent reward for anyone to come forward with helpful information. But, as a single financially struggling mum, there's no chance of that. I can barely keep our heads above water as it is. There's no money for holidays, family outings or anything vaguely luxurious. Fortunately, I inherited a few thousand pounds from an aunt which has helped keep up with the house mortgage payments and to send Lucy to St Anne's.

The day Tom disappeared is as vivid in my mind now as it was back in 1949. I literally woke up one winter's morning to find his side of the bed cold and empty. Usually, I was first up in the mornings with three youngsters to care for and Tom needing to leave for work before eight o'clock. To find him up before me was a surprise, I reasoned he had gone to work early and forgotten to tell me the night before. Like all busy families there was a set of routines we went through every morning. I dressed the children and prepared the breakfasts. Tom put on the washing machine and hung everything out to dry before he left. During winter he also cleaned the grate in the lounge and set the fire-place up ready. Fixing the fire often necessitated chopping wood out the back and bringing it in to dry by the fire-place. If everything went to plan, Tom left in his car by five to eight and would be at work no later than a quarter past eight.

Tom was a nuclear physicist employed at the nearby Harwell Atomic Energy Research facility. Obviously, his work was top secret and he could never divulge any information about the laboratories in which he worked. My husband deeply respected the need for total secrecy and never discussed anything with me. I still have no real understanding about what actually happens inside Harwell.

Tom and I met at Oxford where he was doing his doctorate and I was completing a Bachelor of Arts with a major in British Medieval History. He was my senior by three years and clearly endowed with a brilliant brain. There was no way I could comprehend the scientific theories and mumbo-jumbo he was grappling with, but he was more than pleased to share my love of medieval history and together we would tramp around innumerable historical sites whenever we could.

Because of Tom's vitally important research at Oxford University, he was exempt military service. He never explained to me why he was excused, but I guessed his research had something to do with the war effort and most likely with the production of more powerful armaments.

Tom and I had enjoyed a passionate physical relationship. Amusingly, Tom sometimes described our intimate times together as being like his research; "volatile and explosive." I miss those exciting nights together terribly.

Before we tied the knot, I had to undergo a thorough character review with two female officers from MI5. 'We need to have a full security clearance,' they said, 'to make sure you're not an enemy spy.' Tom and I married in 1941 when Britain was increasingly suffering the unwelcome attentions of the Luftwaffe.

Sometimes, when we were making love, and Tom was getting to a point where he was desperate to climax, I would deliberately delay proceedings. It was at such moments that I knew I could almost definitely wheedle information out of Tom had I been a foreign agent. My husband's defences were down and I knew I could easily pop a question while he was in such a vulnerable state. But I never took advantage of him that way. Delaying was delicious anyway, because then we sometimes managed to reach our orgasms together.

The morning Tom disappeared I was, as usual, flat out with the three kids. Lucy was seven and had to get ready for Infants school, four-year-old Rodney was destined for kindergarten and baby Derek needed personal time with me to enjoy his breakfast. To be perfectly honest, it never occurred to me that morning that Tom might have gone permanently missing and I carried on normally. It wasn't until five o'clock that evening when Tom was usually home, that I started to wonder if something was amiss. When there was no sign of Tom by close to six o'clock, I decided to ring one of his mates at work. He gave me the surprising information that Tom had not shown up for work and everyone had presumed he was home, indisposed. This news was alarming. It was not like Tom to leave me in the dark; if there was some kind of a problem he would always ring me.

For the sake of the kids, I kept my cool. After tea Lucy asked where dad was and I brushed it off saying he was going to be late home and I would read the bedtime stories to them tonight. Inside, however, I was far from calm and a number of awful scenarios began to flash across my mind. Tom had crashed the car and was lying helpless down an embankment somewhere, undetected. Perhaps he had had a massive heart attack, or a stroke and was lying desperately ill in some hospital too sick to tell the staff who he was or how to contact me. Worst of all, Tom could have been involved in a massive car accident and been badly injured or even killed. I kept telling myself not to be so dramatic, so pessimistic, Tom would probably walk through the door at any moment. Then I thought it might be my telephone. Perhaps it was not receiving phone calls. I hung desperately to this idea until I had the kids safely tucked up in bed earlier than usual and before seven o'clock so I could listen to the BBC regional news on the wireless. The seven o'clock news is a fifteen-minute bulletin, but there was nothing remotely helpful reported.

As soon as the news ended I switched off the radio, checked on the kids and rang Tom's boss. It had occurred to me that Tom might have been sent to some hush-hush top-secret conference at very short notice and my panic was simply a silly over re-action. Professor Grant Zeidler was a terrific bloke and Tom and I got along very well with him. He had been most encouraging of Tom's work and had hinted that a promotion could be in the offing soon. As I rang Grant's number, I kept saying to myself, 'Stay calm Dorothy, breathe deeply and sound relaxed.'

'Good evening, Mrs. Zeidler speaking.'

'Oh, hello Mrs. Zeidler, it's Dorothy Hardvale here.'

'How nice to hear from you, Dorothy.'

'I do apologise for disturbing you but I was wondering whether I could have a word with Professor Zeidler please?'

'Yes, of course, my dear. He'll be delighted you rang because I have him busy doing the washing up. I'll go and get him.'

'Thank you so much...' I waited as patiently as I could.

'Good evening, Dorothy. How are you?'

'Oh, good evening, Professor.'

'Please call me Grant.'

'Grant, this may seem a bit of a silly call but Tom hasn't returned home tonight. I'm wondering if something may have happened at work today?'

There was no answer for a moment or two.

'Dorothy, I've been running all over the place today but now I come to think of it I don't remember seeing Tom in the laboratories. As you know, there are over sixty of us working at Harwell, so it's quite possible he *was* here all the time and I missed him. Can you leave it with me for a few minutes and I'll ring Mike? He's in charge of the project on which Tom is working. I'll ring you straight back.'

'Thank you so much, Grant.'

A few minutes later Grant rang back with the devastating news that Tom had not even arrived at work!

*   *   *

I rang the Oxfordshire Police. The young constable on duty took me agonisingly slowly through a lengthy series of questions that were obviously asked of anyone reporting a missing person after normal business hours. Worst of all, he sounded bored and disinterested! The plethora of questions included a detailed description of what Tom looked like, where he worked, the type of car he drove, whether Tom had been behaving in an unusual manner recently, particulars about our family and the route Tom usually took to get to work. The only time Constable Brown allowed himself to digress from the set script was when I told him my husband was a nuclear physicist employed at the Harwell Atomic Power Research facility. Half an hour later, with the barrage of questions finally answered to Constable Brown's satisfaction, he came out with a whole lot of crap about not worrying too much and advised me to go to bed and get a good night's sleep! Funny ha ha!

Constable Brown must, however, have spoken to the officer-in-charge because around eight-thirty that evening I received a call from London. The caller did not disclose his name but said he was ringing from the headquarters of MI5. The man explained Tom's disappearance was of enormous concern to MI5 since he had been working on a highly sensitive research project. It was top secret and MI5 feared foul play. When I asked what he meant by "foul play" he was not very forthcoming. It was quite obvious to me that MI5 was concerned Tom had been taken by enemy agents.

I barely slept that first night. I imagined poor Tom being interrogated in an old barn somewhere by unsavoury characters and even tortured if he declined to respond fully to their questions. Tom was a plucky sort of fellow, but I had no idea how well he would stand up to rough treatment. I knew him only as a loving husband and father to our three children. He was warm and friendly to everyone around him and well liked. A popular member of the village cricket team and, like most Englishmen, fanatical about his football. In every respect, he was well grounded and regarded as a contented family man.

On our last night together, we had made love. Usually, we waited until the weekend when we both felt less stressed but Tom was keen on his last night even though it was a Wednesday. I knew he was interested because he had opened a bottle of red wine and made sure I enjoyed a couple of glasses during the evening. Tom also went out of his way to be helpful that evening and whenever he thought the children weren't looking his hand would come exploring. I love sexy foreplay and Tom didn't disappoint.

With the children safely asleep we showered together. Tom has only to see me naked to get an erection and we spent time luxuriously soaping each other down until we were pink and zinging. I enjoy looking at Tom. He's well-built and still without any unnecessary fat. We dried each other down lovingly, lingering over the most interesting parts. I couldn't help looking down at Tom's pride and joy and started massaging him there gently until he begged me to stop. Next, he opened the bathroom door and with a light kiss to my neck asked me to walk slowly towards the bed while he watched. Arriving there, I turned, pulled back the blankets and lay stark naked on my side of the bed pleading with my eyes for Tom to come to me.

I could see the hunger in his eyes as he lay down beside me and his hands began to rove over my body. After nine years of intimacy, he knew exactly what I wanted as his hands moved teasingly over my stomach, my face, my neck and shoulders before gradually moving in closer and closer to my breasts. With heightened anticipation, I reached between Tom's legs to fondle his firmness. He settled on my breasts initially with his fingers and then his mouth while one hand caressed my most private parts. After a few minutes with my nipples erect and glistening between my legs, I was beautifully ready.

'Come on Tom, give it to me.'

'Not yet, darling,' and he lifted me up so that I was kneeling on the bed and positioned in front of the bedroom mirror. For a moment or two he allowed his eyes to wander ravishingly over my body and then he looked longingly in the mirror before he gently rolled me back down on the bed.

'How do you want it?'

'Any way you want it, Tom. Just do it. I love you. Please, please give it to me.'

# 8.

# Lucy

etty was plucky about her unexpected encounter with a football and bravely put up with the smart-arse jibes that came from some of the spectators, 'Best bloody header of the match, darling' and 'try using the top of your head next time sweet heart.' Someone eventually produced a towel to wipe off any remaining mud from Betty's face and her nose stopped bleeding within a few minutes. I offered to walk her home but she insisted she wanted to stay.

Half time came and the uncouth Nigel ran out with a plate of quartered oranges for the village team. The two teams dutifully changed ends which meant my self-appointed "heart throb" was now playing on the far side of the pitch. However, the brainy looking lad that Betty liked, was playing left back on our side of the field. There were no more unintended incidences during the match and Culham went on to win a tightly fought game 3-2. We two girls decided to hang around for a short time afterwards in case there was an opportunity to properly meet the two young men we liked.

Our patience paid off. The lad who kicked the ball that accidentally connected with Betty's head, was still feeling guilty about it and came trotting over to apologise a second time. He was accompanied by the brainy looking bloke that Betty had chosen. Later, we found out fortuitously they were best mates.

'Hi girls! So sorry about that accident. Are you okay?' asked the tall striker of the misdirected ball, still with a concerned look on his face.

'Yes, I'm good thanks,' Betty replied. I glanced at her; there was barely a sign of the ordeal she had endured an hour earlier.

'You owe me a new handkerchief though,' I declared, holding up the well bloodied cloth I had used to stem the flow of Betty's nose-bleed. I looked at the tall Culham man with a broad smile on my face and wondered how he would respond.

'No problem,' he smiled back, holding my gaze with those gorgeous eyes. 'This gives me the perfect excuse to ask for your address so I can post you a replacement.'

My heart leapt; this young man wasn't wasting any time. I like that in a person, decisive and no messing about.

'Happy to oblige,' I laughed, 'do you have a piece of paper and a pen?'

At this juncture, the lad who Betty liked grabbed his sports-bag. 'I've got a notebook and a pencil in here,' he offered.

Things moved quickly. We properly introduced ourselves, hurriedly exchanged addresses and phone numbers and, as the boys climbed onto their Culham bus, they both promised to be in touch again soon.

We waved the bus off and excitedly started to walk back to Betty's house. We couldn't believe what had just happened. Incredibly, it looked as though we might have landed our first real dates!

\* \* \*

Betty and I tried guessing what our first date might entail. We presumed it would be the two boys taking us two girls out together to make up a foursome. That would be less scary than being invited to go out with the boys individually. We now knew the boys' names and tried to get used to their sound. Unbelievably, Betty's boy was called Michael Brain; mine was Malcolm Entwistle.

Betty thought they would take us to the flicks. The nearest cinema was in Oxford so, unless one of the boys owned a car, we would need to travel there by train. I was not so sure. Paying to take us on the train, and then buying tickets for the film might be too expensive for the two students. My guess was that they would catch the bus to West Dryton and take us out somewhere in the village. The village boasted four places where you could have a drink or something to eat. There were two pubs, The Red Lion and The Hare and Tortoise. Being only seventeen, we girls would have to limit our drinks to something non-alcoholic which was a bummer. The boys, we were sure, were eighteen and allowed to drink.

Then there was the village bakery which stayed open at weekends and served up quite an array of tarts, cakes and buns. The bakery had a number of chairs and tables for their customers use. It was, however, owned by Glen's parents, the lad who had been so rude to us at the football. Finally, there was the Copper Kettle Tea Rooms which was the only posh place in the village. Run by Mr. and Mrs. Sprightly, the tea rooms catered mostly for tourists who frequently visited our picturesque Cotswold village. The Copper Kettle served traditional English afternoon teas; scones, cream and strawberries in season, yummy-looking tea-cakes, a wide range of delicate sandwiches and even hot buttered raisin toast in winter. The Copper Kettle was forever popular and you sometimes had to wait half an hour just to get a table.

It was all very well us girls musing about where we might be taken for our first date but there was a far more serious problem haunting Betty; would her parents even let her go out with a boy? I have to admit the thought had passed through my mind too, however, I was confident I could persuade mum to let me go. After all, the boys were teacher trainees and surely could be trusted. It was different for Betty though, being the only child of a conservative Catholic family. She feared her father would put his foot down and tell her to wait until she had finished her "A" levels. Getting to University, he would probably say, was far more important than going out with boys.

On our way back into the village we crossed over the road to look more closely at The Copper Kettle. I had been into the tea shop only once, as far as I could remember, when Aunt Maud had stayed for a week and Mum was desperate to find something to do with her. Aunt Maud was the classic snob. Although she never actually said so, I reckon she looked down on our family as being rather infra dig. She only stayed under sufferance, I'm sure.

The Copper Kettle was, as usual, bulging at the seams and there was even a smattering of people standing outside waiting to be invited to come in to be seated. The establishment was similar to thousands of others scattered throughout the highways and byways of Britain, quaint and cosy with everyone terribly squashed up and speaking in hushed, subdued voices so as not to be overheard by other people sitting close by. We put our hands up to our faces and peered through the thick glass windows only to be rewarded by an elderly couple who glared back at us for being so rude. Staring through windows at feasting customers was clearly considered impolite.

'Let's go in,' I suggested, 'just for fun.'

'No way,' responded my cautious friend, 'anyway we haven't any money.'

'I've got two pounds in my purse.'

'That's not enough Lucy. Come on let's go.'

'We ought to go in and have a quick look, Betty. You never know, the boys might bring us here for afternoon tea.'

Betty had had enough and was already storming off. The wind had picked up and the large Copper Kettle sign that hung above my head began to swing gently back and forth emitting a weird groaning sound.

Clearly, a Devonshire tea wasn't going to eventuate today!

# 9.

# Malcolm

The college bus that brought us back to Culham College for Schoolmasters trundled slowly up the driveway around five o'clock. It had been a great day. Not only had we won our game after a closely fought contest, but because of my one poorly directed pass, I had ended up meeting an attractive girl. My best mate, Michael Brain, seemed excited about the lass he had met too. Together, we resolved to follow-up with Lucy and Betty over the next few days.

My first semester was coming to an end and I was starting to feel more at home at Culham. My academic timetable kept me busy with lectures and tutorials. First-year students were required to study Child Psychology, Educational Theory, Teaching Methods and at least three "academic" subjects. After a bit of chopping and changing, my three academic subjects ended up being Art Methods, English Literature and History. Sadly, I had never been attracted to the sciences because the science teachers at my public school had been so hopeless.

Extra-curricular activities were encouraged at Culham. During the semester I had joined the College's Country Dance Club (a great place to meet girls) as well as the Football Club. Unfortunately, there was no rugby club at the college because most of the students at Culham were from state high schools and not from public (private) schools, the home of rugby union. Best of all, living at

Culham College had already become a sort of sanctuary from the troubles I was experiencing at home.

Breaking the news to my parents of my decision not to re-apply for the War Office Selection Board was the hardest thing I had ever done. My father, in particular, was unforgiving. He said little at the time but I knew that inwardly he was seething. Somehow, he managed to contain his emotions and remain civil but his anger was undeniable and he gave expression to this anger in a financially crippling way.

Having rejected an army career, I needed to find an alternative profession. My "A" level results were not good enough to get me into a university so most of the major professions were automatically closed to me. Nursing looked interesting, but was almost exclusively a female domain; teaching presented itself as a genuine possibility. I began pouring through stacks of brochures for the many teaching colleges scattered about the country and finally applied to half a dozen located in the midlands. Entry requirements were less stringent than for the university sector and I was pleased to soon be offered a place at four of my chosen colleges. I selected Culham because it was in the attractive Cotswold countryside, offered full student accommodation during semester time and was sufficiently far away from my parents that I would not be expected to visit them at weekends.

When my parents discovered I was planning to embark on a teaching career, it was the last straw. In my father's view, teaching was a lowly occupation and not worthy of his one and only son. He never said this to me in so many words but he showed it by his actions. The cost for a student to board for two years at a residential teachers' college was considerable. The parents of students selected to attend were means tested and expected to contribute whatever the government deemed they could comfortably afford to pay. The government would then pay the balance. My parents were assessed as being financially able to contribute around eight hundred pounds towards my teacher education over the ensuing two years but chose not to honour this. This meant it was left to me to try to find the eight hundred pounds, an almost crippling burden.

Apparently, my parents were within their rights to refuse to make any financial commitment, so the government never pursued the matter further. Instead, I received a letter informing me that I must find the eight hundred pounds to cover costs. I didn't know of any other students at Culham who were in a similar predicament to me. Most students chose to earn extra money during their vacations so they had the wherewithal to go to parties, the cinema, to court girlfriends, buy extra clothes, or invest in more expensive items such as second-hand cars or motor-bikes. For these students, getting a job during vacations was quite simply extra pocket-money, but for me, finding paid work was a matter of survival.

My parents felt I had let them down badly by not pursuing a military career and I suppose I had a bit of sympathy for their point of view. After all, they had struggled to keep me at boarding school since I was seven years' old. School fees for a period of ten years represented a huge financial burden when they were managing on a single fixed income. The cost of my private education had meant a significant sacrifice for them. Nearly all the other students at Culham had enjoyed a free state education so my parents were justified in feeling ten years of private school fees had been largely wasted on me.

When I first arrived at Culham, my parents and I were barely on speaking terms and I had no desire to stay with them during my vacations, even though it might have been a way of getting free accommodation and meals. They probably wouldn't have wanted me in their house anyway. In addition to trying to earn eight hundred pounds to refund the government over the next two years, I now had to also find, and pay for, cheap accommodation during my vacations as well as feed myself. It didn't seem fair that I had all this financial pressure on me when still only eighteen years old. I was determined to manage somehow, because deep down, I wanted to prove to my parents that teaching was actually a noble profession that could be both rewarding and respected. I guess I still wanted my parents to feel they could be proud of me.

*  *  *

After our soccer match, Michael and I chatted briefly with the two girls standing on the sideline and before we knew it we had promised to get in touch with them again, with a view to taking them out. But I'm virtually destitute! There's no way I can spend any money taking out girls! I'm really drawn to Lucy though; she's attractive, seems to have a strong, fun personality and I'd love to get to know her better. On the incredibly tight budget I've had to set for myself there's no way I can do more than phone her.

We have a shop on campus that serves as a general store and educational bookshop. Apart from the text books we need for our studies, the shop sells toiletries and an amazing array of horribly tempting snack foods. Young men are always starving and the shop owners know exactly what to put out on display that is irresistible. However, I resolved never to spend a penny at the shop, except on absolute essentials and I relied entirely on the college food supplied in the dining room to satisfy my hunger. The college food is nothing to shout about but I could always load up on bread or left-over cold vegetables. Three somewhat stodgy, over-cooked meals, are provided every day, including weekends.

Before dinner I trotted down to the students' phone booth on the ground floor clutching the scrap of paper on which Lucy had neatly written her telephone number. Dinner was served between six and six thirty so I had about ten minutes to make my call. This, I felt, would be more than enough since public telephones gobble up money at the alarming rate of a precious shilling every two and a half minutes. I had decided I must be brutally honest with Lucy and explain that I would like to see her again but I was destitute

48

and couldn't afford to take her anywhere. As far as building any sort of a romantic relationship with Lucy, this approach seemed totally doomed. I mean, seriously, how many girls would be interested in pursuing a relationship with a man who's virtually penniless?

Nobody was in the phone booth so I dragged out my last two-shilling coin which would buy me about five minutes. I dialled Lucy's number and watched my precious coin rattle down the money slot. It was ringing!

'Good evening, Dorothy Hardvale speaking.'

A moment of panic hit me. I'd been so focused on speaking with Lucy that it hadn't occurred to me that she's surrounded by her family and someone else in her household was likely to answer the phone call. Furthermore, Lucy didn't tell me her surname. So, who the heck is this Dorothy Hardvale? Have I rung a wrong number? Could this Dorothy be Lucy's mother, or perhaps an aunt, or even a visitor?

'I...I...I wonder if ...I could...er... speak to Lucy please?' I stuttered out feebly.

'And who are you, may I ask?' demanded Dorothy Hardvale. She sounded like a grisly sergeant-major from the War Office Selection Board.

'Um...I...er...met Lucy...er...today, at the football,' I said, hesitantly.

'What football? My daughter was studying with a friend this morning. She has her "A" levels coming up very soon.'

At least I now knew I had rung the correct number and had reached Lucy's place. The person I was speaking to, presumably, was Lucy's mother and she sounded a formidable woman. Had I spilt the beans? Was Lucy really supposed to have been studying but had decided against the idea and went down to the soccer instead? Had I opened my big mouth and landed Lucy in trouble?

'Are you still there?' came the dragon at the other end of the line.

'Er...yes. I...'

'Well, young man, perhaps you'd like to explain just exactly where you met my daughter?'

'I met her...today...at the soccer,' I mumbled.

'Do you play for the village?'

'No... I play for Culham.'

'Culham? Do you mean Culham village or the college?' I sensed a slight softening in Mrs. Hardvale's tone.

'I'm a student at the Culham Teachers' College.'

'Wait a moment,' she snapped and I heard the phone being clattered down onto a hard surface.

'Lucy...Lucy...telephone...'

To my relief, Mrs. Hardvale appeared to have decided I was not an immediate threat and that her daughter could at least speak with me.

There was a long pause. I could hear a dog barking in the background somewhere and then the sound of footsteps approaching. Somebody grabbed the phone and Mrs. Hardvale announced, disparagingly, 'There's some man on the phone for you, dear. I have no idea who he is, except he's at the college.'

I wondered how much of my precious two shillings' worth had already been gobbled up before I managed to speak to Lucy.

'Hello?' came a hushed, cautious voice.

This whole phone call business was turning out to be a total disaster and I'm tempted to replace the phone right now and abort. I'm interested in befriending Lucy but she might not wish to reciprocate. Quite possibly she gave me her telephone number never expecting me to bother to ring.

'Oh, hello. This is Malcolm, the bloke you met at soccer today.'

'Oh, hi Malcolm. You're very quick to ring me.'

'Lucy, first another apology. I think I may have got you into trouble with your mum. I told her I met you at the soccer today and she said I couldn't have because you were at a friend's place studying for your "A" levels.'

There was a short silence and then a bit of a giggle.

'Malcolm, do you ever stop apologising? This morning you

apologised for kicking a soccer ball into the face of my friend, Betty. Now you're apologising for possibly getting me into trouble.'

'Oh, Lucy, I'm so sorry...'

'There you go again...' she laughed.

'You won't believe what I'm about to say, Lucy. I would really like to take you out but I don't have any money. It's a long story and now my phone money is about to run out.'

'Then, how about you come here and have tea with us? You'll have to put up with my stupid younger brothers though. I'll ask mum when you can come. Can you give me another ring later this evening?'

'That's very kind of you Lucy. I've only thirty seconds left. Please say thanks to your mum for me.'

'I will. Don't forget. About seven o'clock is a good time.'

'Where do you live?'

'We're at number 47...'

The phone clicked twice and went dead. My money had expired.

# 10

## Betty

In many ways Lucy and I are poles apart, yet we are best friends. She's outgoing, extroverted and great fun to be with. Everyone thinks she's personality plus and she's hugely popular at school. Lucy is terrific at sport, plays in the school's hockey first eleven and is a mean tennis player too. I often wonder what she sees in me because, in comparison, I'm quiet, rather timid and hopeless at sport. I know I'm cleverer than Lucy (twice I've won the award for the best academic results in my year) but I don't boast about it. I asked her once why she thought we were close friends and she just said, 'Betty you are my rock. Whenever I'm going off the rails, you pull me back.' That's probably true. I suppose most kids see me as being boringly dependable, plain to look at but loyal and caring.

Our friendship goes back years now, ever since we started at St Anne's Catholic College together. On a number of occasions, I've managed to extricate Lucy from a sticky situation. I've often helped with her homework. I even covered for her one day when she wagged school to go to a jazz concert with a boy. Another time I made her see sense when she had had a massive argument with her mother and was determined to run away. I'm sure Lucy misses her father, who took off so suddenly and mysteriously. Lucy was only seven when her dad scarpered. Occasionally she says things that make me realise she still feels cheated with only the one parent at home.

I'm the academic one; Lucy's the sporty one but we both adore boys and get quite infatuated with a few of them. Mind you, we *are* selective and pick out the boys we admire very carefully. Until now we have done nothing more than fantasise about them. Neither of us has actually been out on a proper date, although Lucy went with this boy once to a jazz concert. She said she didn't like him much but he had a free ticket so she went along just to hear the music.

Sometimes, as girls do, we talk about the boys we've met and whether or not they might measure up to our lofty ideals about a future "perfect" husband. I know we're only seventeen but rapidly approaching eighteen, yet we have both already formulated an image of our "Mr. Ideal." I'm looking for a gentle, sensitive man, highly intelligent, caring, calm and dependable. I want someone who's prepared to travel the world because, as a university academic, which is what I expect to be, I'll be doing research overseas and attending innumerable conferences. A well-respected research scientist with these attributes would be perfect for me.

Lucy, on the other hand, says she wants someone who is "spunky" (her words, not mine). He has to be terrific at sport, handsome, with a physique to match, decent, hard-working and honest. She's not looking for a "brain-box," but Lucy's "Mr. Perfect" needs to be an outdoors person, happy to go camping, mountain climbing, canoeing and always adventurous. Lucy has also confided that she wants her man to be "sexy" and provide her with several athletic little off-spring.

Sometimes we chat about our respective family situations. Once again, our backgrounds are surprisingly different. Lucy has to put up with two younger brothers who gang up on her and enjoy playing silly practical jokes. She often complains about their stupid hijinks, but deep down I know she loves them dearly. Rodney is fourteen and crazy about football. He plays left wing for the Brocklehurst Wanderers under fifteen team and skites like mad if he ever scores. Lucy's younger brother, Derek, is nearly eleven and a cricket nut.

According to Lucy, he's forever going on about his heroes in the English test team and will sit for hours glued to the radio listening to the test cricket commentaries. Derek's small in stature but has already made up his mind to be a world famous off-spinner. Lucy is happy her brothers are sports-mad but it really annoys her when they boast, ad infinitum, about their sporting prowess.

I've always been a bit scared of Lucy's mother though. She's almost forty, strikingly handsome with a beautifully symmetrical face and lovely olive skin. She's a fine tennis player and this has helped her keep a very respectable figure. When she puts on make-up she looks quite glamorous. Sadly, she usually comes over as being stern and rather formidable. Lucy reckons her mother has never recovered from the sudden disappearance of her husband all those years ago, which has left her angry and resentful. If there was a new man in her life, Lucy believes her mother would soften and see life more positively. Unfortunately, no eligible men ever come to their house and, as far as Lucy can tell, her mother has totally lost interest in men. Mrs. Hardvale has a fulltime job as a doctor's receptionist and her salary, together with the monthly payments that continue to arrive from her "ex," means they manage to get by financially.

I woke up this morning with a sore face where the soccer ball hit me yesterday and gave me a nasty nose-bleed. After the incident, I actually wanted to go home but I knew Lucy wouldn't approve. Instead, I kept watching out for the boy I had picked out as my first choice in the Culham team. As it turned out, Michael Brain was close mates with Malcolm, the bloke who Lucy liked. As always, Lucy was pushing for more and now, quite unexpectedly, Michael and Malcolm have our telephone numbers and say they want to see us again.

To be honest, I'm feeling stressed about this whole business. I'm worried what will happen if Michael Brain asks me to go out with him. One part of me is saying, I'm nearly eighteen and should willingly accept any invitation that comes from Michael. The other part of me, though, makes me feel guilty. I'm desperate to get into university and need three top "A" levels in Mathematics, Physics and Chemistry if I'm to be accepted into the science faculty at Oxford. I study long hours well into the evenings preparing for these examinations. If I start dating it might negatively impact my studies. Anyway, I very much doubt my parents will let me go out with a boy at this crucial stage in my schooling. It's a conundrum. Most likely the boys will forget all about our meeting and never get around to inviting us out.

Of course, I haven't been entirely honest with my parents. Yesterday, they were under the impression Lucy and I had been meeting at her place to study together. We have done this a few times before and they seemed quite happy about the idea. Once, dad asked how studying together was helpful for us since we were taking totally different subjects. He accepted my answer that it was just pleasant to enjoy each other's company and when it was time for a break, we could share a drink and a snack together.

I still have a red mark on one cheek where the ball hit me. When I came down for breakfast this morning, my mother noticed it and inquired whether I was feeling well. She thought I was looking flushed, she said. Anyway, everything blew over and no more was said.

Dad is a family doctor and has a practice in the village. He's one of the old-school family doctors who provides a "holistic" approach to the health of his patients. This means he limits the number of families he is prepared to consult with so that he can provide the quality time and attention they deserve. His surgery is open every morning from eight till one o'clock and then he has lunch and begins his visiting rounds in the afternoon. Because he is so conscientious, he sometimes doesn't get home until seven o'clock in the evening by which time he's exhausted and often grumpy. It's best to steer clear of him in the evenings. After dinner, his normal practice is to go into the drawing-room to enjoy "The Times" with a relaxing port or a whisky. More often than not, he simply falls asleep.

We live in a rambling early Victorian house with two storeys and a large attic. Our research shows the house was built in the 1840s and has been extended a couple of times over the years. It's far bigger than we need and several of the rooms are virtually unused. We employ a house-keeper, Maggs, who struggles valiantly to keep the house passably clean and habitable while organising and often cooking our meals. There's a gardener too, old Ned, who's employed two days a week. Ned is well past doing two hard days of physical work and barely manages to keep things around the immediate vicinity of the house neat and tidy. Dad doesn't have the heart to give Ned his marching orders, even though it's rumoured he's over eighty. Ned's the typical old retainer, always polite and respectful with a ready smile and an appropriate comment as he potters about doing his chores.

We also have a black Scotty (a Scottish terrier) called Boots. Dad's favourite author is Rudyard Kipling and he owns a complete set of his literary works. He told me once that it was in one of Kipling's books that he found the name "Boots." Boots is also getting a bit long in the tooth being fourteen years old, but we love him dearly. Sadly, walks are beyond Boots now, so he settles for a daily amble around our extensive garden.

Because dad earns a good salary mother has never had to go to work to earn money for the family. She's still a busy woman though. Her days are filled with church affairs and charities, the church choir, supporting the local Conservative party meetings, garden parties, fund raising events, the local rambling association as well as running our home. She's the typical died-in-the-wool, English lady of leisure. Traditions are important to mum and must be faithfully observed at all times. She's loving towards me in a distant, reserved sort of way. We rarely embrace or touch, yet she is kind and considerate. Mother is also fiercely protective of dad and always makes a fuss over him when he comes home tired and grumpy. She's fifteen years younger than him and it shows. At fifty-five dad is struggling to keep up with his heavy work-load, whereas mother is bursting with energy and always dashing off to do something or other.

I can't imagine them ever making love. Perhaps that explains why I'm the only child, born barely nine months after they married. Perhaps they only managed it once? Neither of my parents has ever talked to me about the "birds and the bees" and I have to admit I know precious little about that sort of thing. St Anne's Catholic College ran two "special mornings" for us girls and both were a total giggle. The first morning was all about periods (already too late for some) and the second was about staying a virgin. The emphasis was on remaining "pure" and how purity was God's command. A few of the girls in the upper sixth have openly boasted they've already "done it" with boys, although I have my doubts.

My dear friend Lucy has her antennae out there twitching for anything to do with boys and sex. Recently, she heard about a Swedish film director called Ingmar Bergman who's famous for his "adults only" films. A few locals in the village have been talking about two of his recent films, "The Seventh Seal" and "Wild Strawberries." Some of his films, Lucy claims, actually show men and women doing it! There's a cinema in Oxford that shows Bergman's films and Lucy desperately wants me to go with her to see one. Perhaps we can go after my "A" levels and when I've turned eighteen? I've seen dogs doing it so I suppose that's what humans do too. Lucy reckons it's not like that though. She says there's lots of different ways to do it. I'll never be game to ask my parents how they did it.

I've been in my bedroom for over an hour now, sitting at my desk pouring over my physics textbook. The teacher has recommended certain topics to concentrate on as being the most likely questions to come up in this year's "A" level exams. One of the things we have been busily doing recently is completing old "A" level exam papers from the last ten years or so. It's excellent practice. After a time, it becomes clearer which topics the examiners concentrate on most. After an hour's studying this evening, however, my mind starts to wander and I lose concentration. I reach into the top drawer of my desk and pull out my 1959 W.H. Smith's desk diary. I'm conscientious about my diaries and try to jot something meaningful down for every day. Sometimes it's personal, at other times it's topical.

As I thumb through my personal diary a few major events of 1959 jump out at me. March 30th and 20,000 people demonstrate for nuclear disarmament in Trafalgar Square; a cause I strongly support. August 4th Barclay's Bank becomes the first bank in the whole world to install a computer. As a potential university mathematician, I find this really thrilling. Mark my words, I predict we will see many more computers in the future. 1st September, dad buys the latest British car sensation. It's called a "Mini" and has a revolutionary transverse engine. I love it. On October 8th we had the general election and Harold MacMillan and the Conservatives were returned to power with an increased majority. Mum is absolutely chuffed about this because she works hard for the Tories. I'm not sure where my political leanings are just yet.

I turn on my transistor radio to tune in to the top twenty and am pleased to hear that Cliff Richards and the Drifters is still number one. Several other of my favourite artists are still there on the charts; Chris Barber, Russ Conway, Buddy Holly, Elvis Presley and Shirley Bassey. If Lucy is listening, she'll be pleased too.

Next, I hear the telephone ringing downstairs and mum answers. A moment later she knocks gently on my door and enters.

'It's for you dear,' announces my mother with a puzzled look on her face. 'I think it's a young man called Michael Bain?'

'It's Brain, mum.'

As I scurry downstairs, I wonder what thoughts are racing around in mum's head. I've said nothing to her yet about our hurried invitation to go out with the boys, anticipating the boys would have second thoughts and most likely forget the whole idea.

Now, suddenly, I've got some explaining to do! I lift the receiver and give mum a huge glare because she seems intent on standing there and listening in on my conversation.

'Hello,' I say tentatively, as if I don't know who's on the other end of the line.

'Hello Betty, it's Mike here. I hope this is a good time to ring?'

'Oh...yes...yes, it's fine,' I reply, giving mum another dirty look which she studiously ignores.

'Now, are you doing anything next Sunday evening Betty?'

'Err...no...I don't think so.'

My heart starts pounding. Heavens, he's really going to ask me to go out with him. I'm totally unprepared for this. I know I'm almost eighteen and most of the girls in my class at school have started dating, but I've been a bit of a laggard. What are my parents going to think? Will I even be allowed to go out?

'Well, Betty, it's strange how things have worked out. Malcolm's really keen to see Lucy again but he doesn't have a car and he reckons he's destitute. There's no way he can afford to take Lucy out anywhere. When he rang her up he explained his sad predicament and Lucy's mum solved the problem. She invited Malcolm to come to dinner at their home next Sunday night. Although she didn't quite solve the problem because there's no way Malcolm can get there and back. He doesn't have a car and there are no buses late on Sundays. So, I offered to drive him over and then pick him up later.'

'Why didn't he just borrow your car for the night?'

'No way! My car's an old bomb with a terrible double-de-clutch problem. I would never let anyone else drive it. It's just too dangerous. Anyway, Lucy's mum then said I could come to dinner as well and to bring you if you would like to come.'

'That's four of us then!' I exclaimed.

'Your maths is verging on the brilliant, Betty. Apparently, Lucy had told her mum that I wanted to take you out, which is why she invited you as well. I believe you and Lucy are best friends?'

'Yes, we are. That sounds great, Michael. Hold on a minute and I'll ask mum if it's okay.'

Mother is still listening intently and has picked up the gist of our conversation. I cover the phone with my hand to prevent Michael hearing what we say.

'Mum did you hear that? I've been invited to go round to Lucy's next Sunday evening for dinner. Is that okay?'

'This is all very sudden. You haven't been totally honest with me, Betty. Who's this boy on the phone?'

'He's at Culham College, training to be a school teacher.'

'Well...you can go but you and I now have a few things to discuss, my dear.'

I didn't like the sound of this, but at least mum had grudgingly agreed.

'Are you there, Michael?'

'Yup.'

'Mum said that's all right. What time will you pick me up?'

'We've been invited for six-thirty, so about twenty minutes past?'

'Fine. I'll be ready. Thanks so much. Bye.'

I was really excited; I hastily replaced the receiver before Michael could add anything more. Now it was time to face the music with my suspicious, annoyed mother.

Mother has an uncanny way of making herself look larger when displeased. She comes closer towards the offending person, thereby invading their personal space. I was her height now so we stood face to face with only a few inches between us. I could almost feel her body warmth. I had only been on the receiving end of this frightening phenomenon a few times before, but had witnessed it once or twice with dad. It was truly intimidating.

'Betty, would you please explain exactly what's been going on? I don't think you have been straight forward with me and your father.'

Mum was right. I had not mentioned the encounter at the soccer match yesterday and had been deceitful with regard to my studies. I had also lied when mum queried how I had managed to get a red splodge on the side of my face. Now, I had to explain how Michael Brain had met me and had decided he wanted to take me out. I resolved to tell part of the truth only; just enough to get me out of this immediate awkward situation.

'Lucy and I needed a short break from our studies yesterday afternoon, mum, so we went for a quick walk down to the soccer game down on the river flat and that's where we met the two boys from Culham. We only spoke to them for a few minutes and they asked us for our phone numbers. We never thought they were serious.'

My mother's mouth firmed and the pupils in her eyes contracted. It was not looking good.

'Are you telling me that instead of studying with Lucy, as promised, you both went off to watch a game of football instead?'

'Not the whole game, mum.'

'Long enough to meet some boys and get invited out!'

Something in me suddenly snapped. I was almost eighteen, virtually an adult and I didn't see why I had to be treated like a child any longer. For the first time in my life, I answered my mother back. The words came tumbling out; I couldn't stop them.

'I've been studying hard for my "A" levels for almost two years. I'm top of my class in Maths, Physics and Chemistry and expect to be dux of the school. Sometimes I just need a break and so does Lucy. We'd had enough studying yesterday so we decided to go and watch the soccer. Most of the girls in my class have boyfriends. You can't stop me seeing boys. In a few weeks' time I'll be an adult anyway, and can do what I bloody well want.'

Mum was totally shocked at my outburst and for a moment or two simply stood there, aghast. I held my ground and realised I had my hands on my hips in a display of angry defiance. At the same time, I experienced a massive release of pent-up tension. This was a critical turning point in our parent-child relationship. I was, at last, standing up for myself. No longer was I prepared to always do as I was told.

Mum was sort of spluttering and still having difficulty coming out with a meaningful sentence. I remained rooted to my spot, looking daggers and daring her to challenge me. Finally, mum found her tongue.

'Don't you dare swear at me! Nobody ever swears in this house. I expect a full apology.'

With that, she swivelled round and disappeared into the kitchen leaving me alone, but feeling triumphant.

# 11.

# Dr. Brindleton

During the second world war I served as an officer in the medical corps and was based in hospitals in the south of England established specifically for the treatment of wounded servicemen evacuated from the front. It was incredibly demanding work. Many times when a new batch of badly injured men were ferried in, I would work throughout the night without a break. Time was often a critical factor. The quicker we could attend to the most severely damaged men, the better their chances of survival.

It was during this torrid time that I met Glenis. We were both based at a military hospital called Limpley Stoke Manor, outside Bath, in the west country. I was one of the junior doctors and Glenis a volunteer orderly. My job was quite simply to save lives. I had qualified as a doctor at the start of the war in December 1939. Treating trauma victims at Limpley Stoke Manor was a harrowing experience but at the same time deeply rewarding and undoubtedly the best way to hone my skills as a medico. I admit I made mistakes there. Thankfully, I don't think any of the men I treated died as a result of my inexperience. In that high pressure environment I probably learnt in six months what a peace time doctor might take six years to absorb.

Glenis lived with her family in the pretty village of Limpley Stoke and volunteered to help at the Manor shortly after it was converted into a hospital during the winter of 1939. Glenis had no medical training whatsoever, but was a compassionate young woman, who willingly threw herself into whatever was needed in a hospital struggling to cope with the never-ending stream of bloodied patients coming through its doors. The tasks Glenis willingly took on were not always pleasant ones, cleaning up and disposing of soiled sheets and bandages, comforting men in great pain, talking to distressed relatives, writing letters for men unable to do so. It was stressful work but Glenis was determined to do her part to assist the war effort.

Being an attractive blonde with a more than adequate bust, I noticed Glenis was never short of male admirers. Walking through the wards usually provoked a whistle or two, perhaps a compliment or even a blown kiss. The men were never crude or rude and Glenis accepted their interest as being well intentioned and their way of showing appreciation for a pretty woman doing kind work about the place. Naturally, romances sometimes developed between nurses, volunteers and the wounded men.

As one of the youngest doctors at Limpley Stoke Manor and still unmarried, I was well aware that I probably had the pick of the young eligible ladies working at the hospital. Unfortunately, punishingly long hours and many challenging surgical procedures exhausted me most nights and all I wanted to do at the end of a long day was get back to my digs, cook a quick meal and collapse into bed. Some nights I was too fatigued to undress and simply fell asleep fully clothed sprawled across my bed.

Towards the end of 1941 things at the hospital settled down somewhat and the medical staff were at last scheduled to have one evening off each week. It wasn't much but that evening off became something special, a time I looked forward to all week. My evening off was always a Saturday evening, the most prized day of the week. Orderly Glenis, being a volunteer, was allowed to work more flexible hours and if she wanted evenings off it was nearly always possible, unless a large intake of wounded soldiers was due to be admitted.

I'm not sure what it was that initially attracted me to Glenis. She was pretty and always cheerful with an engaging smile and an easy, natural way with her. Being a volunteer, she didn't have to dress in the starched uniforms worn by the registered nurses. She was free to wear what she wanted. Glennis had a commendable dress sense and always looked well groomed. A natural blonde, she skillfully made a feature of her hair. Glenis usually wore simple jewellery, tasteful and never ostentatious.

I suppose I must have been quietly noticing Glenis's attributes for many months. I remember during those crazy busy days and nights, thinking that I liked her and should try to see her socially sometime. Life was so full of urgent surgeries, seeing patients on my rounds, prescribing medications, attending meetings about patients, talking to patients' families, that I simply didn't get around to organising anything. Then, one Saturday night, when I was about to leave the hospital I spotted Glenis, arm in arm with one of my colleagues, walking through the hospital carpark and jumping into his car. It was the wake-up call I needed! If I didn't move fast, Glenis and I might never meet socially.

Next week, I deliberately skipped the first part of the weekly planning meeting when I saw Glenis working alone in the hospital laundry. I walked boldly into the steamy room, wearing my clean white coat and my stethoscope dangling about my neck. It was horribly hot and noisy in the laundry with two large industrial sized washing machines churning away emitting loud sloshing sounds, as well as several driers purring away on the other side of the room. It was hardly a pleasant environment to strike up a stimulating conversation with an attractive girl I had never spoken to before.

'Hello, I'm doctor David Brindleton,' I announced in a loud voice, as I approached the unsuspecting Glenis with my arm extended ready to shake hands.

Glenis jumped.

'Oh! Sorry, I didn't hear you come in doctor...'

'That's okay. It's Glenis, isn't it?' We shook hands.

'That's right... Glenis, Glenis Broughton,' she smiled, shyly.

I had obviously put her ill at ease by barging in and surprising her.

'My apologies for giving you such a surprise. I should have knocked first.'

'That's all-right doctor. Is there something I can do for you?'

For the first time I noticed her intensely blue eyes and how delicately she had applied mascara to her long eye lashes. Up close she was stunning.

'Yes, there is,' I said brazenly, 'please will you come out with me on Saturday evening?'

My invitation hit her like a bombshell and she was clearly lost for words. I filled in for her by blabbering on.

'I know this is all very sudden, but I've noticed you working about the hospital and have been meaning to ask you out for months. I'm so busy I never seem to have time to speak with you. I get Saturday evenings off now...and when I saw you in here...I thought I would grab the chance. I'm sorry, this is not the way I would normally ask an attractive woman out for a date.'

Glenis blushed and looked at me intently with those soft blue eyes.

'Doctor...that's very kind of you. I don't know what to say...'

'It's easy, just say yes!'

One of the machines in the laundry began beeping loudly, imploring its operator to come and switch it off. Glenis turned to deal with the matter and I didn't hear her reply. The machine shuddered to a halt and she returned.

'I'm sorry about that,' she smiled.

'So...Glenis...what do you say?'

'Thank you, doctor, I'd love to go out with you.'

*   *   *

Next Saturday evening I drove through Limpley Stoke with my headlights appropriately dimmed. The blackout had been in operation since the start of the war and was one of the war time deprivations I had never quite become accustomed to. Shops, businesses and homes had to ensure that after sunset there was no light escaping through any windows, doors or rooftops to assist the enemy aircraft to navigate their way towards their bombing targets. People used all sorts of devices to blacken their places; thick cardboard, black sheets and heavy curtains, wooden shutters and, if all else failed, black paint. Failure to stringently observe the blackout regulations landed you in serious trouble with the night wardens who patrolled the streets fiendishly, and were empowered to impose heavy penalties on the spot for any miscreants.

Hitler had made it abundantly clear that when the time was right he would invade the British Isles. The intense Luftwaffe bombing raids were designed to "soften us up" and break our fighting spirit, so we would surrender meekly when the time came. One of the actions taken by the British government was to order the removal of sign posts throughout the land to make it harder for the Germans to find their way about. Tonight, this action was creating problems for me! I knew I had to take a turn to the left about a mile after Limpley Stoke but without street lights or sign posts, I was uncertain of my whereabouts and which turn I needed.

Fortunately, a gibbous moon was shining and after taking a couple of wrong turns, I eventually saw on my left a house that fitted the description Glenis had given me. She had described a two storeys Tudor place standing out on its own and set back from the road on a large property surrounded by a drystone wall. Squinting out of the car window, I could just discern the name of the house, "The Poplars." Not many poplars remained but I was relieved I had successfully arrived at my destination, albeit nearly half an hour late. The car scrunched its way along the gravel driveway and I pulled up outside the front door. Glenis was standing there waiting for me, clutching a small handbag and looking as pretty as ever in the moon light. I apologised profusely for my lateness as I held the car door open for her.

I had booked a table at the local pub that rejoiced under the unlikely name of "The Three Idiots." Nobody seemed to know for sure who the three unfortunate folks were after whom the pub was named. Numerous colourful stories circulated about the three that were generously exaggerated whenever the beer flowed and worked its magic. There was general agreement, however, that they must have been three males because the pub's sign, swinging outside, depicted three rustic, jolly looking fellows with bright red cheeks and silly hats. Since no lighting was permitted, it was difficult to observe the three idiots with any clarity on this particular evening.

I opened Glenis's car door and enjoyed another waft of enticing perfume that had so exquisitely scented my car as we motored in to Limpley Stoke. Together we slipped through the door to the restaurant as quickly as possible to prevent too much light escaping and were shown to our seats. I had asked for a 'quiet table' away from the noise.

The meal was nothing to rave about. If I remember correctly, I had "Toad-in-the-Hole," with one rather measly sausage and Glenis ordered "Roast Beef of Old England" which came with one small, almost see-through, slither of beef. Rationing was in full swing, so we couldn't complain. Desserts were similarly limited and we both ended up having Rhubarb Fool. Bulmer's Cider was on tap; a drink Glenis had already acquired a taste for by the tender age of nineteen. However, it was not the food we had both come for, but the excitement of making a new acquaintance.

We got along famously. After the meal we retired to the lounge where we enjoyed another half pint of Bulmer's and chatted on until closing time at eleven o'clock. I knew I was smitten and I was sure Glenis was too. We agreed to do the same thing next Saturday but would try the other pub at the opposite end of Limpley Stoke known as "The Green Bullfrog."

And so began a whirlwind romance. At the end of three months, we were engaged and after another three months, married! The uncertainties of war time encouraged short, intense romances. At the back of every young couples' minds was the awful fear that something unspeakable might suddenly happen. Even in quiet little Limpley Stoke, in the heart of England, there was always the nagging fear that one night the Germans might bomb us out of existence. And what might happen if the Germans really *did* invade and occupy the country?

Glenis and I stayed on at Limpley Stoke for another year after our marriage and it was there that Betty was born in November 1942. After two years at the Limpley Stoke Hospital, I was promoted to Captain and transferred to another military hospital in West Drayton in the Cotswolds. At the age of thirty-five I was the senior medic there and had to assume additional administrative responsibilities. Glenis stayed home to look after Betty. My workload became almost unbearable. My medical work was no less than I had been doing at Limpley Stoke, but now I had a heavy managerial role as well. In June 1943 I suffered a mental breakdown and required six months off work to recover. During January 1944 I was abruptly invalided out of the army medical corps and found myself suddenly out of work.

My luck was in, however. West Dryton's elderly, well-respected family doctor, Peter Giles, was pushing eighty and decided he'd had enough. He contacted me when he heard of my out-of-work predicament. In effect, he offered me "first refusal" as his successor. Peter's West Dryton practice was somewhat run down and he was the first to admit it. A number of his patients had drifted away, or died. Privately, Peter confessed to me he had not kept up with some of the medical advances as he aged. Nevertheless, he was confident that with a young enthusiastic doctor at the helm, the practice would pick up and again be busy and successful. Glenis and I decided to take on the challenge and I took over Peter's practice in March 1944.

Fifteen and a half years later we are still enjoying peaceful West Dryton. The practice has steadily grown and some of the locals who drifted away during Peter's time have returned. The population in the village and surrounds has increased steadily too with the area becoming a popular tourist destination. I believe I've established a reputation for being a caring, well-informed and hardworking general practioner. Our only regret is that we have not had more children.

Glenis and I are both practicing Catholics and attend mass regularly. Glenis is also involved in a number of voluntary initiatives to assist the smooth working of our parish. Failure to have more children was not for want of trying. When there was no sign of a sibling for Betty after five years we arranged to have medical check-ups. Apparently, I was firing blanks! There was no medical procedure to assist me so we had to accept the situation. For a while we contemplated adoption but in the end never got around to it. Now we feel we're too old to adopt a young child.

Of course, we are immensely proud of Betty. She has thrived at St Anne's Catholic College and even been dux of her year on two occasions. Like all parents, we'll be hugely relieved when these wretched "A" levels are finally out of the way and we know Betty has been accepted at Oxford. We had hoped she might follow me into medicine but she has her sights set on being a research scientist. Betty's marks in Physics, Chemistry and Mathematics have been excellent so the future is looking bright. This year Glenis and I have done everything we can to keep Betty focused on her studies. Apart from attending mass every Sunday and Scottish dancing classes on Friday evenings, she has had no distractions. Fortunately, there's no boyfriend around. Plenty of time for that sort of thing later.

# 12.

# Glenis

etty's defiant outburst has shocked me to the core! Never before has my daughter answered me back so rudely when I've spoken to her. What's more, she swore! I didn't know she even knew that horrid word. I have retreated to the kitchen to get a cup of tea and lick my wounds. My daughter has challenged my authority and I have no idea how to respond. I need to sit down with a cup of calming tea to think about our nasty altercation. Why on earth did Betty blow up like that?

I open the kitchen cupboard and remove the tea caddy. Following the accepted rules of tea making, I place one spoonful of tea leaves in the teapot for myself and one extra for the teapot. Next, I fill the faithful old kettle half full with water and place it on the gas-ring. I select my usual cup and saucer and pour in the milk. No need for sugar as I'm still trying to lose a few pounds. While I go through this routine, my mind is drumming away trying to make sense of what happened a few minutes ago.

Perhaps Betty is not herself because of exam pressure? It's a well-known fact that some children fall apart when getting close to important events such as sitting their "A" levels. Until now, Betty has not shown any signs of trepidation and appears to have been going about her daily tasks perfectly normally. She's a quiet, reserved girl by nature though, and may not have wanted to tell us if she was feeling a high level of anxiety about the upcoming examinations. The more I think about it, the more plausible this explanation becomes to explain Betty's sudden abhorrent behaviour.

Anxiety always increases my need for comfort food so I walk over to the biscuit cannister and grab not one, but two Mars bars. Settling back on the stool at the kitchen table, I check the kettle which has yet to boil. There's time to attack the first Mars bar. A moment later the kettle whistles its high-pitched song and I turn off the gas and pour the boiling water into the teapot. Three turns anti-clockwise and the tea has drawn and is ready to pour. As I do this, a second possible explanation for Betty's wild reaction comes to mind. This one is equally troubling!

Perhaps Betty has genuine feelings for a boy and this is making her behave erratically? David and I have always told Betty that her studies are the most important thing in her life right now and not to even think about the opposite sex. This was a big reason for why we sent her to St Anne's Catholic College for girls in the first place. Too many young girls get silly crushes over some teenage heart throb and then lose their direction and focus. If this is the case for Betty, then David and I must take steps to stop this nonsense immediately. Betty has already admitted she and Lucy met two boys at the soccer match yesterday. Is it possible that she's been having a clandestine relationship with a boy for some time?

This alarming idea is so worrying that I eat the second Mars bar without even realising. Two discarded wrappers now look accusingly at me. But, what to do next?

Three things come to mind. As soon as David arrives home from work, I must tell him what has happened. He is so level headed, he'll calm things down and will know how to handle the matter. Then, of course, we must speak with Betty. We are both owed an apology for her deceitfulness in going to the football when she had assured us she would be studying. And, thirdly, I want a personal apology for the disrespectful way Betty spoke to me and for using the "B" word. It might also be wise to ring Lucy's mother to ascertain what she knows. Betty and Lucy are close friends and the two girls are surely in this together. It's possible that Lucy's mother, Dorothy, can shed further light on this whole sorry business.

I look at the kitchen clock. David probably won't be back until seven o'clock or even later. The house-keeper made a casserole for dinner tonight and I place it in the oven and start preparing vegetables. Perhaps Betty will come into the kitchen and apologise? However, David surprises me by coming home early.

'Oh David, dear, how wonderful to see you home early for once. It's only five-thirty.' My husband advances into the kitchen and gives me a peck.

'The last two appointments for the day both cancelled so I took an early mark.'

'Now, my dear, can I get you a cupper?'

'No thanks. I think I'll take the extra time to finish off the letter I'm writing to the council.'

'David, before you do that, I need to talk to you about something rather urgent that has just come up.'

'Oh...nothing serious, I hope?'

'Well, I think it is.'

David pulls out a chair, sits down and crosses his legs as if he's about to listen to yet another patient's woes. I pull out another chair, opposite David, and tell him of my disturbing discussion with Betty as accurately as I can remember. Of course, I don't actually use the "B" word. David listens intently. Although he doesn't interrupt me, I can see he's becoming increasingly angry. I finish off by saying I have had no apology from Betty and I think we should ring Dorothy to find out what, if anything, she knows about the girls wagging their studies.

David doesn't comment for a moment or two and sits there strumming the fingers of his left hand on the table. Then he stands up and walks over to the oven where he stays warming his back-side.

'I'm so sorry you have had to put up with such bad behaviour,

Glenis. Whenever I'm confronted by a difficult situation like this, I always start by making sure I have all the facts at my finger-tips. In this case, I think you're right, we need to hear what Dorothy Hardvale knows about all this. Why don't you give her a ring straight away?'

'Good suggestion. I'll ring her now.'

Dorothy and I have been friends for almost six years now as a result of our daughters becoming so chummy. I've always felt a level of sympathy for her. The sudden unexplained disappearance of her husband, Tom, about ten years ago must have been so hard to bear. Dorothy rarely speaks about it nowadays, but it would be unnatural if she didn't still wonder what has become of him. Presumably, he's still alive, since monthly payments keep coming into her bank. Theories abound. Sadly, it seems the authorities have given up on the case. The trail has, by now, gone stone cold.

Dorothy picks up after the third ring.

'Good afternoon, Dorothy speaking.'

'Hello Dorothy, Glenis here. How are you?'

'I'm well thanks. This must be telepathy...I was just about to ring you!'

'I expect it's about the same thing, then?'

'What our girls were doing yesterday instead of studying?'

'Correct. I found out from Betty a little time ago that she was down at the soccer and meeting boys. A boy called Michael something has just rung up and asked Betty to go with him to your place next Sunday evening. This is all a bit sudden, isn't it?'

'Yes... Lucy never told me about going to the soccer until a young man from Culham College rang her this afternoon. He sounded pleasant enough. Apparently, he wanted to take her out but said he couldn't afford to. What do you think of that? Anyway, Lucy didn't miss a trick. She immediately invited him to come to dinner here! No flies on her!'

'And did you agree to this, Dorothy?'

'Well, the girls are almost adults now and boys are going to come on the scene very soon, whether we like it or not, so I said that's fine. This way I'll have a good look at the young man which is much better than the two of them meeting in secret.'

'That's very wise of you Dorothy. Is Betty correct when she tells me you have also invited her to come for dinner along with this Michael boy?'

'Yes, it should be fun. Four young people sitting around the dinner table together. My problem is trying to keep Rodney and Derek under control. As you know, they can be quite stupid at times. I do wish Tom was here to discipline them.'

'I should tell you, Dorothy, that David and I are not happy about this sudden liaison between Betty and Michael. We have to keep Betty totally focused on her "A" levels and not distracted. Boyfriends, in our view, can wait until another couple of months once these wretched exams are out of the way.'

'Yes, I can understand your feelings about this Glenis. Of course, our Lucy is not aiming to get into university so she has a more casual approach to her studies. If Lucy picks up one or two "A" levels she will be more than happy, whereas Betty needs three top "A" level passes.'

'Well, I've agreed to let Betty come to your place just this once with this Michael boy, but that's where it will have to stop.'

'Of course, my dear. As parents, we all know what's best for our daughters and I totally respect your wishes. I may be a bit more flexible with Lucy though because the stakes are not so high for her.'

'Thank you, Dorothy dear, for your understanding. I hope you all have a lovely evening together. Would you like me to contribute something...a dessert perhaps?'

'That's very kind of you, but I'll be fine thanks.'

\*   \*   \*

David was listening attentively and had picked up the gist of our conversation.

'What now?' I ask, as I turn the potatoes down and check on the carrots and parsnips.

'I think I'll go and talk to Betty. She certainly owes you an apology for her rudeness and the swearing is totally inexcusable.'

'Don't be too hard on her, dear. She's probably feeling pretty awful right now. I'm worried that the exams are stressing her out. The last thing we want is for her to have some sort of a breakdown when she's so close to sitting these "A" levels. I fear we might be walking on egg-shells.'

David gives me one of his mysterious little smirks, which after almost nineteen years of marriage, I still can't interpret correctly. He leaves the kitchen in a pensive mood and walks slowly up the stairs to Betty's bedroom.

I still love him to bits. He's middle aged but the heavy and unrelenting workload he has endured since graduating as a doctor has aged him prematurely. Despite his long hours, he's over-weight because most of his working time is spent in a sedentary manner. Every morning, including Saturdays, he sits at his surgery desk seeing patients. Then he usually has a packed lunch that I make for him before going out on his rounds in the afternoon to visit house-bound patients. Sometimes, he'll be driving around the countryside for a couple of hours in his beloved old Jag. Finally, there's a late afternoon surgery that starts around 4.00pm and keeps going until he has seen everyone who wishes to see him. He is so conscientious and caring of his patients.

I worry about David's never-ending commitment to work and the toll it's taking on his health. The only days we have together as a family are Sundays and public holidays. I can't remember when we last had a proper holiday together. He's reluctant to appoint a locum to look after the practice so he can have a break, for fear he or she will not properly understand his patients. David believes he's indispensable and that's not a realistic way of thinking. In the evenings he's exhausted. We eat together as a family, then he retires to the lounge to read medical journals or "The Times," and inevitably falls soundly asleep shortly after finishing his port or whisky. He apologises profusely every night when I wake him up to go upstairs to bed. Next morning the alarm sounds off at six-thirty and he's at work by eight o'clock. And so it goes on, month after month, year after year, without a decent break.

I suppose I've built my life around David's work routines. I'm fortunate I don't have to go to work because David's income is more than enough to keep the three of us living comfortably. St Anne's school fees are reasonable and Betty is only a day-girl. We don't entertain much and holidays are virtually non-existent so we save money by living quietly. There's enough money to employ a part-time house-keeper and dear old Fred, our ancient gardener.

We are a devout Catholic family and rarely miss attendance at weekly mass. We have done everything to encourage Betty to follow in our footsteps and to practice Catholicism. Having time to fill in, I often work in the garden, although tactfully always under Fred's supervision. Fred loves his vegetables and mowing the lawns so I concentrate on the flowers. I enjoy tennis twice a week, weather permitting, and am a keen member of several organisations in the village. I have never been trained as a nurse or a nurse's aide, but I do voluntary work helping a few elderly folks in the village with their shopping, appointments and just keeping them company. And, of course, I work hard for the Conservative party. All in all, I keep myself busy and generally contented.

My greatest disappointment is having only the one child. As good Catholics, David and I planned to have four or five children, but it was not to be. Quickly I fell pregnant with Betty and she was a cuddly, adorable baby. We resumed our sexual activities as soon as possible after the birth. However, despite our best efforts, five years after I had fallen pregnant with Betty there was still no sign of a little brother or sister. We began to wonder if something was amiss and arranged to see a specialist. Six months later, after a series of invasive and often embarrassing tests, we were advised that David's sperm was the culprit. David took it hard. He saw himself as a feeble, inadequate male, incapable of producing offspring. I did my best to persuade him otherwise but his lack of virility still haunts him.

Worried about David becoming overly depressed, I secretly sought the advice of a psychologist. Dr Randolph Dreggan had a practice in Oxford and agreed to see David if I could persuade him to come to an appointment. David flatly refused and was furious with me for trying to set up an appointment behind his back. Nevertheless, I had a second private appointment with Dr Dreggan specifically to find out if there was anything I could do to help my husband overcome his feelings of inadequacy. The doctor was very helpful. He explained male infertility was not an uncommon ailment and he had treated many cases. In David's case, he suggested over-work could be the problem. If David could be persuaded to ease off, take annual holidays and find ways of relaxing, it might improve his sperm count.

I was surprised at Dr Dreggan's other advice. In a nutshell, he urged me to have lots of sex with David. His reasoning was that a more loving physical relationship would relax David and then, with time, things might start to happen. I explained to the psychologist that since David's unfortunate diagnosis, we had virtually abandoned any sexual activity. David seemed to have completely lost confidence in his ability to perform. We still slept in the same bed but he was always too tired or simply disinterested. Dr Dreggan's response was that I must *make* him interested! I must have looked blankly at him at this point because he started to describe the sorts of things I could try. It was all horribly embarrassing.

'My dear lady, you are an attractive woman, thirty something years old and at the prime of your sexual being. Use your imagination…dim the lights, dress seductively, wear perfume, fuss over him, play some romantic records, say sweet things to him and don't be afraid to let your hand touch him around his private parts. It's called foreplay. Usually, it's the man's job to seduce his partner, however, in your case the roles must be reversed. I'm sure an intelligent woman like you, Mrs. Brindleton, will know how to seduce your husband. If you can re-kindle his interest in physical love, you will both enjoy your lives much more, and, just possibly, something magical might result too.'

That advice from Dr Dreggan's was nearly ten years ago now. I tried hard to follow the psychologist's suggestions. I went to Oxford on my own, found a shop frequented by young female undergraduates and purchased some incredibly sexy looking garments. Then I planned to set things up for the next Sunday evening when David would not be quite so tired. I cooked his favourite meal, made sure we both enjoyed a second glass of sherry together and put on a record of famous romantic opera songs. As soon as Betty was upstairs and asleep, I went to our bedroom, changed into my new sexy under garments with a silk bath-robe, applied some perfume lavishly and returned to the lounge. David was asleep!

Undeterred, I knelt down at the side of David's lounge chair and moved my hand lightly over his privates. He awoke with a start and looked at me as if he couldn't believe what was happening.

'What the devil are you doing, Glenis?'

'David, I'm longing to go to bed with you. I adore you and I want us to make love.'

I kept my hand on the job and leaned over closer so David couldn't miss my open top and could feast his eyes on my more than ample breasts.

David appeared stunned, unsure what to do. However, I detected the beginning of a hardening in his privates and knew I was getting somewhere.

'Please David. I need you. Take me to bed,' I purred. I lent in closer and gently kissed him on the mouth. My breasts dangled in full view while my hand rubbed his penis more firmly now as my own desires heightened.

He could resist no longer. Without saying a word, he got to his feet and headed for the stairs. I followed him closely and embraced him as soon as we reached the safety of our bedroom, while I rubbed myself up against his organ. I wasn't going to let him go now.

We managed it that night. At last!

As I lay back on my pillow afterwards, I thanked Dr Dreggan for his advice.

Sadly, our new found love-making didn't last.

# 13.

# Betty

I'm not going to put up with my parents telling me what I can and cannot do anymore! In six weeks' time my "A" levels will be out of the way and I'll leave school. Two weeks after that, I'll have my results and should be receiving a letter from Oxford University advising me I have been accepted to read Science. I'll then move into one of the five famous ladies' colleges and start my undergraduate life. It will be a life of freedom and no more parental control. I will eat what I want, do what I want and nobody will be able to stop me.

I love my parents dearly, but they can be stifling with their obsessive attention. Dad never stops working and mother is stuck in all her daily routines. You should see her calendar! Every day is mapped out with things to go to and it's the same week after week. When not out, their attention is totally focused on me and my bloody "A" levels. They're obsessed. If I don't get into Oxford, I reckon they'll go mad. I know I'm going to do really well in my exams; not because my parents want me to, but because I actually love science and mathematics and have decided to become a research scientist. We have great teachers at St Anne's and I'm the best student in the school. I'm looking forward to receiving Dux of school again on graduation day.

Half an hour ago, Mum and I had a nasty falling out. She got all steamed up just because Lucy and I met a couple of boys who invited us out on a date. What's wrong with that? Michael seems a decent enough sort of a bloke. All he wants to do is pick me up in his car and drive me round to Lucy's place to have dinner there on Sunday. At the end of the evening, he'll bring me home. Mrs. Hardvale will be there all the time. A night off from my studies will be good for me. They should be encouraging me to go out and have some fun sometimes.

Perhaps I went too far when I swore at mum? I've never done that before. Wow, you should have seen her face! She went ashen white. I thought she was going to faint. Anyway, I'll apologise for that.

I'm feeling angry still so I ignore my science texts and reach for one of my Winnie-the-Pooh books. I love these silly stories and I'm looking for the funny picture of Pooh and Piglet following a heffalump around a tree, when there's a knock on my door.

I quickly close the book and put it under my desk. 'Come in,' I call, as nonchalantly as I can manage.

To my surprise, it's dad who's standing there. He must have come home early.

'Betty, dear, may I have a word please?'

'Hi dad. You're home early?'

'I was given an early mark.'

'Here, have a seat,' and I transfer my heavily marked and annotated physics textbook from the only spare chair on to the side of my desk. Dad sits down, looking awkward and clears his throat. There are heavy grey bags under his eyes and he's more over-weight than I realised. It looks as though he didn't shave very carefully this morning and his thinning unruly hair needs trimming. We live in the same house, yet I'm not sure I really know him at all well. That's what results from his lifestyle of "all work and no play," I suppose.

'Err...I've been speaking to your mother.' Dad is avoiding eye contact, 'she's rather upset.'

'I'm sorry I swore at her, I was angry.'

'I think you had better apologise to her.'

'I will.'

'What's more worrying is that you have not been entirely honest with us, Betty. We were under the impression you and Lucy were going to spend yesterday morning studying together. Now, mother tells me, you were meeting a couple of boys down at the football ground.' Finally, dad is brave enough to look me in the eye.

'That's right dad, so what?' I'm surprised at the abrupt tone I have used.

Dad is taken aback also. Never before have I dared to answer back like this and I can see he doesn't like it. There's a long silence before he continues.

'Betty, I don't understand what has got into you? First, you're rude to your mother and now you're being impertinent to me. Your mother, against her better judgement, has already agreed to let you go with this Michael fellow to Lucy's place on Sunday night so I can't stop that happening. However, I'm grounding you until you have sat the last of your "A" level exams. This means you can leave the house only to go to school and attend mass with us on Sundays. Should you decide to sincerely apologise for your dishonest and surly behaviour to us both, then I will be prepared to reconsider the length of your grounding.'

'That's not fair! You can't go on treating me like a child. In six weeks, I'll be eighteen and an adult. Then I'll be old enough to get married if I want to and you can't stop me. I'll be old enough to vote or serve in the army. You and mum should start treating me like an adult. Now, please leave my room!'

I don't know where all this venom is coming from but it sure feels good to express it. Sticking up for myself is positively therapeutic. I stand up and glare at my father with my hands on my hips. I can see he's livid and finding it hard to control himself. A couple of years ago he would have smacked me but now that I'm a fully developed woman he thinks better of it. Dad is speechless. Then, like a lamb, he gets to his feet and shaking his head, walks to the door and leaves without another word.

My feelings of elation don't last long. I sit back down at my desk, but find doing any more study is out of the question. I'm too upset and I can't concentrate. I'm proud of myself for sticking up for my rights, but now I've upset my parents and been grounded. I'm blowed if I'm going to apologise though because that's a sign of weakness. I guess I'll just have to put up with being grounded. The only things I'll miss out on are Friday nights at Scottish dancing and going round to Lucy's. There's nothing to stop Lucy coming here instead though.

Then a *really* mischievous idea surfaces. Perhaps I could sneak out at nights and do whatever I want? Lucy and I might meet somewhere? That would be *so* adventurous. Sneaking about the village late at night would, of course, be horribly cold and we couldn't go to one of the pubs because somebody in the village would be bound to recognise us. What else could we do? As I'm racking my brains, I hear mum calling from below. 'Betty, dinner's ready.'

This is going to be one heck of a tense meal! For a moment I think of saying, 'Thanks, but I don't want to eat tonight.' Then I realise I'm really hungry and, anyway, it would be cowardly to stay away. I decide to go downstairs to have my dinner and face up to whatever is coming.

\* \* \*

Our spacious dining room has lovely old furniture passed down to us from dad's family. A splendid oak table, large enough to comfortably seat eight people, is the central feature. A handsome sideboard occupies one side of the room and proudly displays a range of Victorian china pieces, ornaments and wooden artefacts. In one corner stands the ancient grand-father clock with its aged clock-face that chimes every quarter of an hour. I have always loved the melodious "tick-tock, tick tock, tick tock" sound this clock emits. On the other side of the room is a long serving table where dishes are laid out if we ever have guests. We actually have a real electric chandelier hanging over the centre of the dining table which gives us plenty of light and looks grand, although mum complains it's difficult to clean. To be honest, I don't know why she complains about it because it's the house-keeper who does the cleaning.

On the rare occasions we have a tableful of guests, mum sits at one end of the table and dad at the other. On the floor, where mum sits, there's a foot button and mum discretely presses this with her foot to let the kitchen know when she's ready for the next course to come in. It works a treat. Tonight, though, we are sitting in our normal places at one end of the table with dad in the middle.

When I enter the kitchen to collect my meal there's a strained silence. Tonight, the usual easy-going banter about the day's events is absent. I try to pretend nothing has happened and help myself to casserole and vegetables. Mum and dad are in front of me and walk through to the dining room with their plates and sit down. The unnatural silence continues while dad pours himself a glass of red wine and pours my mother and I some water. The gentle ticking of the grandfather clock is in stark contrast to the cutting and scraping of our eating utensils. We eat our meals without a word, avoiding eye contact and the silence is painful.

It's mum who breaks first. 'I've prepared chocolate mousse for desserts,' she announces. It's hardly a provocative statement likely to inspire further comment, but her attempt at making conversation is met with a half-hearted grunt of approval from dad. The grandfather clock chimes half past the hour. Normally, I seldom notice the chimes but tonight it's like listening to Big Ben. I'm determined not to weaken and be the one to start talking, although I do feel I should apologise to mum for swearing at her. We eat on...silently.

Finally, mum can stand it no longer. 'We can't go on like this...it's awful! It reminds me of when we were put on silence at my boarding school. This has never happened in our family before. We need to talk things through. Betty what do you think?'

85

I feel trapped and obligated to answer.

'I'm sorry I swore at you, mum.'

'Thank you dear, that's a good start.'

I sense my parents are hoping I'll go on and apologise for everything else I've said and done but I'm not prepared to do this. The deathly silence descends again and mum is looking distressed. I have to admit this stand-off is beginning to get to me too. I finish my main course and wipe my mouth with the napkin. Dad refills his glass. When mum finishes eating, she picks up our plates and departs for the kitchen leaving dad and I together. Somehow the awkwardness intensifies.

'How long are you going to keep this up?' he asks.

'I don't know but it's not just me, is it?'

'Well, I think a full apology from you would be a good way to start to improve matters.'

I remain silent and mum returns with a tray on which there are three dessert bowls of her chocolate mousse and a container of thick whipped cream. As we finish our dessert, the grandfather clock chimes seven o'clock. It's my turn to do the washing up tonight so I pick up the plates with a quick, 'Thanks mum for the mousse' and with a sigh of relief leave for the kitchen.

It takes me half an hour to do the dishes and put everything away. My parents must have decided to leave me alone because they don't venture back into the kitchen. When I'm done, I throw the wet tea-towel in the laundry basket and go back upstairs to my bedroom. I sit down at my desk with my chemistry text book and turn to the chapter I was last revising. For ten minutes I look blankly at the same page but nothing seems to be sinking in. I'm too upset to concentrate. I keep trying for a little longer, then close the text book and flop down on my bed.

I'm feeling miserable. I've been grounded until my exams are over, my parents are not communicating and now I can't even concentrate on my science revision work! The only bright light on the horizon is that I'm still allowed to go over to Lucy's place on Sunday night.

After another half hour moping on my bed, I can handle it no longer. I know I wasn't honest with my parents when I tripped off to the soccer instead of studying with Lucy. If I apologise to them I might be able to put that matter to rest and then I'll feel like studying again. I rise, tidy myself up and make my way downstairs.

As I reach the living room, I can hear my parents engaged in earnest conversation. I stop at the open door, and unbeknown to them listen to what they're saying. They have no idea I'm eavesdropping.

'I'm not sure you should have grounded her David. It seems much too harsh a punishment.'

'I don't agree. Betty has to be pulled into line. She has the most important exams in her life coming up in five or six-weeks' time. If she goes traipsing off to football games to meet up with boys, she may well lose her motivation to study. We have to put our foot down Glenis and nip this business in the bud.'

'I understand how you feel dear, but this is the first time she's ever done something like this. She's always been totally honest with us until this one unfortunate occasion.'

'How do you know this is the first time? For all we know, she may have been seeing this Michael fellow for months.'

'I don't think so. I'm just worried that if we are too hard on Betty something awful could happen.'

'I don't see why. She's not been honest with us and there have to be consequences for that.'

'Couldn't you just give her a talking to? Perhaps you could give her a warning that if it happens again, *then* she'll be grounded?'

'Too late! I've already told her she's grounded until after her "A" levels are done. I can't retract that. What's done is done!'

'Well, I don't see it that way. I think you should be more flexible. Suppose Betty gets really upset about this and refuses to study?'

'That won't happen. She's desperate to get to Oxford. She wants to be a scientist for heaven's sake. She'll work her little butt off. You'll see.'

'I do hope you're right.'

# 14

## Lucy

I'm sitting at my desk in my bedroom ostensibly to study my notes on physical geography. Actually, I quite enjoy physical geography as it has to do with the shape of the land and how it ended up that way. I'd love to travel to remote and exotic destinations because then I might actually see these physical formations in real life, instead of only seeing photographs of them. I would love to go hiking in the Himalayas, riding on camels across the deserts of the world and exploring volcanic craters. I'm starting to day-dream about skiing in Iceland, a land of snow and fire, when the telephone rings downstairs. Mum is home and always pounces on any phone calls since nearly all of them are for her. This time I'm pleasantly surprised to discover it's my best friend, Betty.

'Hello Betty, how are you?'

'Lucy, I'm feeling awful. I've been grounded for weeks.'

'Why?'

'Because we went down and met the two boys when we were supposed to be studying. Dad's furious with me. This is his punishment for my dishonesty.'

'Oh Betty, that's awful. Mum was angry with me at first, but she's over it now. Are you still allowed to come on Sunday night for dinner?'

'Yes, but only because Mum agreed to it before dad got to hear about it. He would have cancelled it as well, I reckon.'

'Betty, I'm so sorry for you. What will you do?'

'I don't know. I'm sick of being treated like a little child. I'm considering leaving home.'

'What do you mean, Betty? You've got your "A" levels soon. You want to go to Oxford, don't you?'

'I don't know. I'm so angry about how my father's treating me that I can't concentrate on my studies any more. I'm all churned up inside and I can't sleep. I hate being here at home. I just want to get away from this stifling environment.'

'Betty, please don't do anything before Sunday when you come round here for dinner. We can talk about it then, when my mother's not around.'

'Okay. I promise I won't do anything before Sunday. I'll see you around half past six, then.'

I couldn't believe what I had just heard. My normally placid, calm, unadventurous best friend was seriously threatening to abscond from home!

*    *    *

Mum is a traditionalist when it comes to food. She's expecting seven hungry young people to be sitting around our dinner table on Sunday evening, all noisy and ravenous. Apart from her family and Betty, who she knows well, there will be two complete strangers, Malcolm and Michael. On the menu will be roast beef, potatoes, carrots, Brussel sprouts and parsnips served with gravy made from Oxo cubes and mint picked fresh from our garden. Dessert will be apple and rhubarb crumble served with custard and cream. Mum is sure she's on a winner with this meal because her family love it, and anyway, who doesn't enjoy roast beef of old England? War rationing is over at last but it's still difficult to get a decent joint from the butcher. Intriguingly, our butcher has "a bit of a thing" about mum which is why she can always charm a quality cut of beef out of him whenever she wants one. Mum knows how to keep him interested, but also on a leash!

Since speaking with Betty on the phone, I've been thinking about how rotten she must be feeling and what she may decide to do. She's so clever it would be a tragedy if she up sticks and leaves home. What a terrible waste of a brilliant brain! Betty is usually the mature, sensible one, who pulls *me* into line when I'm being irrational, but now the tables have turned. I'm thinking I need to reason with *her* when she comes round on Sunday night. It's time for me to step up and be the sensible one.

"A" levels are tough. Every subject is assessed by a do or die final three-hour examination. Two years of intensive study comes down to a paltry one hundred and eighty minutes of almost unbearable stress as you regurgitate your hard-won knowledge across page after page of special examination exercise booklets. Some students can't hack it and break down before the exam or arrive at the exam centre virtually incapable of putting pen to paper. Some employers argue that if a student is unable to handle the stress of an examination, then they won't be able to cope with the ordeals of the workplace. I'm not so sure about that.

About ten percent of the school population qualifies to go to university. Only the top ten percent of that ten percent make it to Oxford or Cambridge. Everyone at school has been tipping Betty to be accepted into Oxford this year. There's a special honour board in the entrance hall at St Anne's that lists the duxes of the school since the school was founded in 1860 and there's a second honour board that lists past students that have made it to Oxford or Cambridge. Many of us are anticipating these two honour boards will soon be inscribed, "1959 Betty Brindleton."

Sometime ago I abandoned all hope of making it to a university. Universities are not for me anyway. I still want to scrape a couple of "A" levels though, to get me into a decent secretarial college. All I want is a crash course in a broad range of secretarial skills and then I'll be out in the workforce earning an income. With mum struggling financially, I don't want to be a burden on her.

*   *   *

Sunday afternoon is here at last and I'm in the kitchen helping mum prepare the vegetables. We have dragged out the better china set and dusted it down. It's Royal Doulton replete with a few small chips and blemishes. Mum always sees to it that any chipped china ends up in her place. Keeping up appearances is important. My first jobs are to wash and peel the parsnips and then lay the table. Mum has pulled out Tom's favourite table-cloth which depicts famous old locomotives charging around the edge. Fortunately, they are all travelling in the same anti-clockwise direction. 'With four young men around the table,' mum says, 'it will be good to have a "manly" sort of a table-cloth displayed.'

'Lucy dear, what do you know about these two young men coming tonight?'

'Not much, I'm afraid mum.'

'Well, how did you get to meet them in the first place?'

It took me a couple of minutes to explain what had happened at the football match. Feeling expansive, I even told mum how Betty and I had selected our preferences from the Culham team and that Malcolm and Michael just happened to be the ones we later met up with at the end of the match.

'That was very clever of you,' mum remarked, as she placed the joint carefully into the roasting pan.

'It just happened that way.'

'So...,' mum paused before placing the roasting pan in the oven, 'do you know where this Malcolm lad is from or how old he is?'

I shook my head. 'Sorry, mum. We didn't have much time. They had to catch the bus back to college.'

'Well, all I can say is they're fast workers! Tom took nearly six months to get around to asking me out the first time. These young men needed only a few minutes!'

Mum was right.

*   *   *

A few minutes past six-thirty the doorbell rings and I skip down the hallway. Mum and I have had time to get dressed and put on a little make-up. Mum looks terrific. She turns forty in a couple of months' time and still has an excellent figure. If only dad was still around....

We have even managed to get Rodney and Derek to look reasonably presentable despite some grumbling and whining. My brothers are at a stupid age and are an embarrassment. I'm hoping like mad they don't make fools of themselves in front of our visitors.

It's only a ten-minute drive from Betty's place, but in that short time the three have quickly become better acquainted and more relaxed as if they had known each other for years. I make them feel welcome, take their coats and walk them through to the lounge which has been spruced up for the occasion. Mum has even rustled up some flowers from somewhere. We are going to have "drinks" before the meal. What to serve for drinks was something, Mum and I had discussed at some length. I argued that because Betty and I were nearly eighteen we should be allowed to drink something alcoholic. But mum stubbornly refused. She agreed that she and the two Culham lads, who we presumed were over eighteen, could partake of alcohol. So, there were bottles of beer and cider in the fridge and soft drink (punch) for the rest of us. Mum had placed a plate of selected savoury biscuits and cheeses on the table and I had been instructed to pass this plate round whilst mum took the drink orders.

Michael and Malcolm both opted for beer and mum stayed with

her favourite, Bulmer's cider. My brothers had been given strict instructions to stay away until mum rang a bell for the start of dinner.

Conversation flowed surprisingly easily and we covered several topics: schools, exams, soccer, music, cars, Culham, even a bit of politics. Mum popped in a couple of times but was mostly pre-occupied with the final preparation of our meal. Michael and Betty appeared to have hit it off instantaneously and Malcom was wasting no time making eyes at me.

We enjoyed pre-dinner drinks for half an hour before mum rang the bell for dinner. This time had given me plenty of time to observe Michael more closely. Personality-wise, he came over as good fun, entertaining, sincere and intelligent. From our discussions, I gleaned he was enthusiastic about all forms of sport and had a powerful sense of adventure. He had already been mountain climbing in the Cuillins on the Isle of Skye, completed Outward Bound courses and travelled overseas. I liked him immediately and quietly congratulated myself for picking him out from the rest of the Culham lads. He was good looking too! I could fall for this guy, if he was seriously interested.

Dinner was a hit. Mum was in great form, the meal expertly cooked and served and the discussions around the table lively and stimulating. Amazingly, my brothers behaved like angels. They were polite, kept their mouths shut and actually volunteered to help clear the dishes. Malcolm sat across the table from me and kept looking at me whenever he had the chance. By the end of the meal, I knew I'd be more than happy to go out with him if he asked. The Culham boys even enjoyed a second beer under mum's watchful eye.

When the meal was over Malcolm and Michael offered to do the washing up and we girls agreed to dry-up. Mum, considerately, disappeared with my brothers for half an hour to help them get their homework done. I have never enjoyed doing the dishes so much! We flirted unashamedly and I felt a sense of exhilaration unlike anything I had experienced before. Malcolm and I even brushed hands as we passed dishes and utensils between us.

After the chores were done, we four returned to the lounge and played cards for an hour until mum started to make "time-to-go-home" noises. Mum can be pointedly blunt when she wants to and the boys quickly got the message not to overstay their welcome. Mum has a knack of remaining polite but being abundantly clear in her messaging.

As the boys picked up their coats, I realised something must happen if Malcolm and I were to ever meet again. In a few minutes Michael, Malcolm and Betty would be driving off together leaving me at home alone with my family. Mum was happily receiving generous thanks from her visitors meaning a quiet private word with Malcolm was impossible. I took the initiative and told mum I would go outside to see them off. I think my mother sensed the situation, but much to her credit made no objection. Relieved, I scurried out into the front garden. Malcolm wasted no time.

'Lucy, that was a great night. May I take you out sometime?'

'I would love that, Malcolm.'

'How about I give you a ring?'

'Sounds good.'

I glanced across at Betty and Michael who were also having their own tete a tete.

It was drizzling and cold and the three of them soon jumped into Michael's old bomb of a car. It took two or three starts before the engine coughed reluctantly into life and they pulled slowly away. I waved them off and hurried back indoors. I wasted no time in telling mum that Malcolm had invited me out. 'That's nice dear,' she said, 'he seems a pleasant lad.' I wasn't sure how she really felt about the idea.

That night, as I prepared for bed, I wondered how Malcolm was going to manage to take me out when he was supposedly destitute. Was it just wishful thinking on his part? This whole evening had come about because Malcolm had professed to having no money. He had been perfectly honest with me about his pecuniary problems but having no money was going to make the development of any sort of a romantic relationship truly challenging.

Nevertheless, I went to sleep that night with pleasant thoughts about my first ever boyfriend.

# 15.

# Malcolm

I'm smitten! Lucy Hardvale is gorgeous and I just have to see her again.

Michael goes through his painful de-clutching procedures and the car lurches its way towards Betty's home on the other side of the village of West Dryton. I'm sitting in the back on decaying upholstery trying to avoid an unforgiving broken spring. Rain is teeming down and I'm watching the interplay between Michael and Betty in the front. These two are getting along famously. I'm delighted to see this because Michael and his bomb car might again become the means whereby I can visit Lucy in the future.

The heavy shower stops as quickly as it began as we pull up outside Betty's home. I can see Michael and Betty want a few minutes together on their own, so I stay put and they disappear along the driveway. They are only gone a short time before the rain starts up again and a moment later a thoroughly damp Michael comes charging back to the car. I move into the front passenger's seat and with another round of clumsy de-clutching we set off for Culham College.

'That Betty's a really interesting lass. Do you know Michael, she's been dux of her school twice and she's hoping to get into Oxford to read bloody science? She must be a clever girl. And it's not just her brains you admire, is it Michael?'

'To be perfectly honest I've never felt keen on a girl before but there's something rather special about Betty. I don't quite know

97

what it is. Believe it or not, we just had a quick kiss in the wet bushes. It was horribly clumsy; neither of us had ever kissed before.'

'You're kidding? I can't believe you've never kissed a girl before?'

'It's true. What about you, Casanova?'

'Quite a few times. I've had crushes on heaps of girls but only snogged five or six.'

'Oh, that's sick Malcolm. Are you some sort of a sex maniac or something?'

'No, certainly not. It's natural to want to kiss a pretty girl. You're the freak for waiting this long before you got around to it.'

'How far did you go with the girls you kissed?'

'Hey, that's none of your business.'

'Oh come on, you can tell me Malcolm. I'm a total amateur with all this stuff. I need some tips.'

'Kissing and petting only. None of the girls wanted to go any further. One girl let me feel her breasts for a few seconds through her clothes, but then she gently and firmly pushed my hand away.'

'Some of the guys at college brag about their conquests. Do you think they're kidding?'

'Sometimes. It's hard to know what to believe. Personally, I still think it's best to wait until marriage before you sleep with a girl. I guess that's my religious upbringing.'

'Yes, same with me, Malcolm.'

We lapsed into a comfortable silence for the remainder of the short trip back to college and the "old bomb" cooperated.

*       *       *

Meals at Culham College for Schoolmasters are basic, usually over cooked and poorly presented, but at least they are guaranteed to fill us up. I have a hearty appetite but it's nothing in comparison to one of my African friends who's at the college on a Colombo Plan scholarship. I make a point of joining Alex

Dobrila almost every Sunday morning for breakfast just to watch him devouring his meal. There's only a skeleton kitchen staff on duty on Sundays; labour is kept to an absolute minimum and breakfast is always a simple affair. Half the students don't bother to front up anyway because they're nursing troublesome hangovers or relishing long sleep-ins.

Sunday breakfasts at Culham traditionally consist of finger foods only. You turn up at the dining room anytime between 8.00am and 9.00am and pour yourself a cup of strong tea from one of the ginormous silver coloured tea-pots which hold enough hot water for thirty or more cups. It's then a simple matter of deciding where to park your back-side. Alex Dobrila is as black as the ace of spades, six foot eight inches tall and therefore dead easy to spot. He's some sort of a chief back in Uganda and has told me that shortly before arriving in England he had paid thirty prime cattle for another new wife. Sadly, he laments, she has not been permitted to travel to England with him.

This morning, Alex has positioned himself in the middle of one of the long wooden tables immediately in front of a large bowl of hard-boiled eggs. I'm just in time to join a small group of like-minded students who also enjoy Alex's company and watching his unique skills in disposing of his breakfast. Alex doesn't disappoint. He selects a clean brown hard-boiled egg and with a rolling twist of his long dark fingers removes the entire shell in a second almost as one piece. With a laugh for his admiring audience, he pops the entire egg into his mouth. A minute later he repeats the process while his spectators start counting. One... two... three... four... five eggs disappear in as many minutes. Alex contemplates a sixth. Urged on, he obliges, then laughs at the hearty applause of his small band of admirers. Those in the know recall Alex's record is actually seven hard-boiled eggs in the one sitting!

The other finger food on offer for Sunday breakfast is bread, or toast, if you want to risk your life using the ancient and temperamental eight slice toaster. There are bowls of butter and marmalade on hand and even a large Marmite jar. Alex has developed a liking for toast since coming to England and loves the stuff. Today, the six hard-boiled eggs do not suffice so he disposes of several pieces of toast generously spread with butter and marmalade. Marmite, however, is one step too far for my African friend.

There are several other Africans at Culham studying under the Colombo Plan. There's Peter Tanyashi from Nigeria and Reuben Scott (not a very African sounding name) who hails from outside Cape Town, both of whom I get to know well. Coming to England has been a massive cultural shock for these African guys and I enjoy giving them a helping hand. I have become a sort of mentor to them. Particularly difficult are the assignments they are required to complete. Their spoken English is sufficient to make themselves understood but writing in grammatically correct English they find challenging. Fortunately, the lecturers who mark their work, seem reasonably understanding.

One evening I'm in Alex Dobrila's study helping him with an assignment about Piaget and his ground breaking research into the stages of development children go through, irrespective of ethnicity, and we get talking. Alex is intrigued with Piaget and begins to speak about his own children and where they should be, according to Piagetian theory. It transpires that he currently has three wives, four children so far, as well as fifty head of cattle.

'Cattle are money, man,' Alex says, wagging a long fore-finger at me. 'Thirty cattle will buy me one more strong working wife.'

'But how many wives do you need?' I ask.

Alex shrugs his shoulders. 'Many wives give me status. I'm a chief, man! People look up to a man who can keep many wives happy.' He laughs raucously. 'You English are stupid; one wife can't keep a man happy at night.'

I'm unsure how to respond to this assertion and remain silent. As someone who has never kept one woman "happy" for even one night, I feel hopelessly out of my depth.

Alex stood up and fished a battered brown wallet out of his back pocket. Then he pulled out a couple of photographs.

'Look at these, man...'

One newish photograph depicted Alex's three wives and four children, the youngest one still hanging off a generous breast. The second photo showed a herd of wild looking horned cattle standing in the shade of a couple of large trees.

'That's wonderful Alex.' I respond, handing the photos back.

'Get yourself a wife man,' Alex urges, giving me a friendly punch before stuffing his photos back into his wallet.

'I'll see what I can do,' I reply tamely.

An hour later I finish checking Alex's essay on Piaget. He's definitely improving, but it's hard work. At least this time he has started the assignment a few days before it is due so there's time to work on it with him. As I'm leaving, Alex has one more comment to make.

'Don't forget to find a wife, man. They keep you warm at night!'

\*   \*   \*

Alex is twenty-eight years old and already a chief with three wives, four children and a sizeable herd of valuable cattle. I'm approaching nineteen, almost destitute after falling out with my adopting parents, but keen to begin a relationship with a girl called Lucy Hardvale over in West Dryton. I fear I have a lot of catching up to do.

I've been doing reasonably well with my studies. Usually, my assignments are graded as a "B". I have yet to score an "A" for any work and occasionally, I must admit, I slip down into the "C" grades. Anyway, I'm doing okay. Nothing to boast about but at least I now know I can cope with the academic demands placed upon me by the Culham College for Schoolmasters.

One of my most interesting subjects is Educational Psychology. We have been learning about "nature" and "nurture" and the importance of a loving, supportive family environment for children as they grow up. Research is showing that children deprived of nurturing environments are the ones most likely to become poorly adjusted teenagers and to end up as dysfunctional adults. These unfortunate children are more likely to turn to crime or later mistreat their wives. I'm alarmed to discover that adopted children, like me, frequently end up in this group. This finding leads to a period of serious introspection on my part. As an adopted child, could I be "damaged goods"? Am I destined to become a criminal? Will I be a failure in life? I have been haunted by these unsavoury ideas for several weeks now. Sometimes, I lie awake at night for hours trying to deal with these nagging negative thoughts.

Today, I received some good news though. The Brighton Post Office has agreed to employ me again for a minimum of two weeks just before Christmas. The huge increase in Christmas mail requires extra staff and students like me are taken on to help sort and deliver the Christmas cards and parcels. I have been doing this work for the last three Christmases so the Post Office knows I'm trustworthy. The pay isn't marvellous, but if you're fit and strong you can do extra night shifts which will be a great help for my worrying financial situation. Female students are also employed to do the mail sorting and their company is an added and attractive incentive.

I'm tossing up whether or not to read the next chapter in my history text book when there's a knock at the door. It turns out to be Michael Brain.

'What are you doing on Sunday afternoon?'

'Not much. Why?'

'Well, I rang Betty earlier this evening, I really want to see her again. Her parents have invited me to stay for an hour on Sunday afternoon. Betty's not allowed out but she can have visitors for a short time. Her parents seem to be horribly strict with her. Anyway, I'm driving over to see her and I wondered if you'd like to come too?'

'Absolutely! I'll give Lucy a ring tomorrow. This is great Michael. Many thanks. Can you drop me off at Lucy's on the way?'

'Sure.'

'You don't have a spare two bob on you by any chance?'

Michael delves into his pockets and comes up with a stick of chewing gum and a handful of loose coins. He knows I'm totally skint and kindly leaves two and sixpence on the edge of my desk.

'Thanks Michael, you're a really good friend. What time will you be leaving?'

'Two-thirty. I'm invited for three.'

I went to bed that night thinking of the lovely Lucy and hoping like mad that she'd be pleased to have me call in to see her on Sunday afternoon.

# 16.

......

# Dorothy

Friends still sometimes ask questions about my husband, Tom, who so mysteriously disappeared over nine years ago. At the time, the story even hit the national news. The BBC, in addition to the police, spent a considerable time and effort trying to find out what happened to him. Despite some of the BBC's most persistent investigative journalists pursuing a number of potential leads, Tom's disappearance remains to this day a total mystery. The police still say Tom's disappearance is regarded as being an "active" case, but I've heard nothing from them for years.

I miss him dreadfully. Tom, quite literally, disappeared into thin air without trace. It's as though he was whisked into space or exterminated, like in Dr Who. I still find it hard to believe that he left no clues or signs or messages. Nobody has yet uncovered anything to shed light on what happened to him. Somebody, somewhere, must know something, surely? I'm still plagued with so many unanswered questions. Is he still alive? Is he well? Where is he? Will he ever return to us? Why did he leave?

Once a month, I receive a more than welcome cheque from Lloyd's Bank. The first cheque arrived a few days after Tom left and they still come regularly and without fail. Neither my solicitor, nor Lloyds is able to furnish any details except to say that there is an account in Tom's name that contains a significant sum of money, large enough to keep paying out monthly cheques until the last of our children reaches the age of twenty-one. The account was opened two days before Tom went missing by a person, or persons unknown, with a massive lump sum that has been attracting interest ever since. The police were all over the bank to begin with but they have never discovered the origin of the money. I'm so grateful to have this lifeline though. As a single mum with three kids, it would have been almost impossible to survive without these monthly cheques.

I'm not divorced; this is an involuntary separation. Legally, I don't think I can re-marry unless my marriage to Tom can be officially declared null and void. A few friends have urged me to "move on" and look for another person to share my life with. I must admit, as the years go by, this idea has started to take hold. In another seven years my children will most likely have moved away and I'll be left with a house far too large for my solitary needs. For nine long years I have faithfully and patiently awaited Tom's return. I'm sure many deserted wives by now would have found another partner. I guess I'm slowly becoming more open to having a new relationship. At almost forty, when dressed up I can still turn heads and several men in recent years have subtly put out feelers. So far, I've not encouraged any of them.

Speaking about romance, Lucy appears to have a crush on this young Malcolm from the teachers' college. This is the first time she has wanted to bring a boy home so she must be keen. Sometimes Lucy has mentioned some boy she has met at dancing or tennis who she likes but nothing leading to an invitation to come to have a meal. I must say, Malcolm seems a decent enough lad, very polite and respectful and good looking into the bargain. I guess we'll see what transpires, it may fizzle out just as quickly as it started. Lucy and I have never really talked about love and sex. Apparently, St Anne's provides some sort of a program about the birds and the bees but Lucy dismissed it as "a joke." Perhaps, I should organise myself to have a proper chat with Lucy sometime soon

The ironing is awaiting me downstairs. I gather up the garments requiring my attention and set up the ironing board. I'm about to start when the phone rings.

'Good afternoon. This is 467982, Mrs. Hardvale speaking.'

'Good afternoon Mrs. Hardvale. This is Malcolm Entwistle here.'

'Hello Malcolm. Nice to hear from you. Would you like to speak to Lucy?'

'Yes please, but before you get her may I say thank you again for the splendid meal last weekend. You're an excellent cook.'

'It was a pleasure to have you here.'

'One more thing Mrs. Hardvale, please. My friend, Michael, can drop me off at your home for an hour or two next Sunday afternoon. Would it be okay if Lucy and I go out for a walk together?'

'I don't see why not, if Lucy wishes to and the weather's agreeable.'

'Thanks Mrs. Hardvale.'

'One moment and I'll find Lucy for you.'

Lucy's face lit up when I told her the call was from Malcolm and she was thrilled to find out he was coming to take her out on Sunday afternoon. Predictably, Lucy then went through the typical dramas over what she should wear which most girls go through on their first dates. It brought back fond memories for me.

Seeing the delight my daughter is experiencing with the excitement of her first date finally makes me realise what I might be missing out on. However, for me, a mature, married woman with a family to care for, finding another partner interested in having a relationship will be far more challenging. Men will, rightly, be hyper-cautious about dating me. I have a history with the unexplained disappearance of my husband, Tom. I'm no longer a stunning young woman, although at forty I can probably still have children. Anyway, how many men of the right age are still out there and eligible? I certainly don't want to get into a messy relationship with some married man. The greatest barrier is, of course, the financial one. Would eligible men be seriously interested in me when they discover I struggle financially and still have three children in tow? Any man worth having will need to be prepared to marry me and wholeheartedly accept my family too. And then, what happens if the children don't like my suitor? Oh dear, It's all so horribly complicated!

One of the theories the police worked on when dear Tom left me, was murder and it didn't take long for outrageous rumours to surface about who the murderer might have been. Tom had no known enemies, so the accusatory finger of blame was quickly pointed directly at me. I endured torrid grilling at the Oxford Police Station on several occasions. One detective, in particular, convinced himself I was a murderess and proceeded to make my life hell. The newspapers never missed a chance to sensationalise Tom's disappearance and swooped on the allegation I had murdered him following a domestic argument. Most bizarre was a suggestion, which floated about for some time, that Tom had actually died as a result of extreme sexual games we played that had gone horribly wrong and I had somehow then managed to dispose of his body. All this talk of my being a murderess is absolute nonsense.

Everything has quietened down now. Thankfully, almost all my friends stood by me at the time. People have long memories though, and any man who shows an interest in me is bound to eventually hear these old rumours and wonder what he's letting himself in for.

It's time for me to take Lucy out for her next driving lesson. She's doing well so far. It's not easy being a parent, trying to instill good driving habits, when your daughter keeps saying, 'But, *you* don't do it that way, mum.' Unfortunately, I can't afford to pay for an authorised driving instructor which would be the best way for Lucy to learn. So, she's stuck with me. I'll get Lucy to take the car down to the sports ground where her two brothers are playing football.

# 17.

......

# Betty

I'm fed up with being grounded. I'm angry with my parents for being so totally inconsiderate. I feel trapped and this is making me rebellious. Every time I see my parents there's tension in the air. I'm sure they don't trust me anymore. We barely speak to each other nowadays and when we do it's about some trivial, safe topic such as the weather, school or my studies. Thank God for St Anne's. At least there, I have some friends and teachers who treat me normally.

For a couple of days after I was grounded, I was so upset I couldn't study. I'm over that now and I spend my spare time in my bedroom alone with my books. I just love Science and Mathematics. Going to Oxford University will be so fantastic and I just can't wait to become an under-graduate. I'll have digs of my own in one of the women's colleges and I'll feel free. Oh, so free! My parents won't be able to control my life anymore. I'll go to parties, let my hair down, learn to drink and have sex. I've spent my entire life so far in a sort of cocoon, sheltered from real life and all the fun that most other young people enjoy.

Michael Brain rang yesterday and wants to come and visit me on Sunday afternoon. Apparently, being grounded means I can't go anywhere, except school and mass on Sunday mornings but friends are still allowed to come and see me. Last Sunday night, Michael kissed me on the lips in the rain. I didn't expect it; he just did it. I really like him and it's great to think that for the first time I can boast to my friends at school that I have a boyfriend. Michael knows I'm grounded and that we'll not be allowed to go out anywhere. I guess I'll invite him up to my bedroom. That could be fun. If he gave me a quick kiss out in the rain last Sunday, what will he try to do in the privacy of my bedroom? I reckon I need to explore stuff about sex before I go to Uni.

Lucy and I often have lunch together at school. The dining room is huge and about two hundred of the senior girls from fourth, fifth and sixth forms have lunch together between noon and twelve-forty when the juniors arrive. We seniors have to be ready, standing behind our chairs, in time for the teacher on duty to say grace right on the stroke of mid-day. If we're late, we're in trouble.

Lucy can't believe it when I tell her Michael kissed me on the lips. Usually, she's the adventurous one who does everything well before I do. She wants to know what it was like. Was he a good kisser? To be perfectly honest, I was so taken aback when he kissed me, I can't answer her questions. 'Was it a French kiss?' she asks.

'What the hell is a French kiss?'

'It's when you put your tongue in,' Lucy says, pleased she knows something about kissing that I don't know.

We discuss Michael and Malcolm during the remainder of lunch and decide we have landed a couple of really nice guys who we should encourage. 'You never know,' adds Lucy, enthusiastically, 'many romances that start when you are still at school end up with wedding bells.'

'That's going a bit far, Lucy.'

'It's true.'

'Maybe, but we hardly know anything about these guys. They might seem decent fellas but behind their nice faces they could be criminals, or perverts or something else.'

'Oh, come off it, Betty, you're a better judge of character than that. You can tell they're genuine blokes just by chatting to them.'

The five-minute warning bell sounds. We barely have time to

finish, clean up our places and pack everything away before the juniors start streaming in. Classes resume in ten minutes which leaves us little time to visit the toilets and get to our respective classrooms.

\*   \*   \*

I arrive just in time. It's double physics with dear old Mr. Schneider. There are only eight girls at St Anne's doing "A" level physics. For some reason most girls steer clear of the "hard" subjects like maths, physics and chemistry. Some do biology. The great majority of girls stick to the arts subjects like my best friend, Lucy. There's this entrenched idea that girls can't do the "hard" subjects and its boys who have the best kinds of brains for the sciences. In the seventy-year history of St Anne's only two girls have ever made it to Oxford or Cambridge to read science, whereas heaps have qualified for arts. I intend to be science graduate number three!

The girls really like old Mr. Schneider. He's been teaching physics and chemistry at St Anne's since before the war. Believe it or not, when World War two broke out the police came and arrested him because they said he was German. Well, he was born and bred there but he moved to England with his family when he was in his twenties. He has lived here for over sixty years and has twice been bundled off to live in internment camps when there's a war with Germany. He's philosophical about this shameful treatment though and never seems bitter or resentful. His wife is English and she's had to endure her husband being locked up as well as the associated stigma for a total of nine years altogether. Most importantly, Mr. Schneider's a wonderful teacher. He really knows his stuff and takes a personal interest in the progress of each of his students. Nothing is too much trouble. He's happy to help anyone who is struggling with some extra private tuition. I don't need any additional assistance but a few times Mr. Schneider has asked me to stay back after classes to offer me extension work. At these times he really challenges me to think more deeply about what we have been studying. 'Good preparation for university, Betty, my dear.'

There are rumours Mr. Schneider will retire this year, so I'm lucky to have had his tutelage. I know he has high expectations for me and he'll be as proud as punch when I make it to Oxford. He also has high hopes that two or three others in our small class will make it to less prestigious universities or teachers' colleges.

One of the girls in physics is wild Gloria McFane with her shock of flame coloured hair. She's an Irish lass and bags of fun. She sometimes has the class in stitches with her jokes and stories. I don't believe half the things she says but I really enjoy listening to her. Gloria and I would never mix socially; she thinks I'm a stuffy old bore. Very occasionally, I see Gloria at mass on Sundays. She's also a terrific Irish dancer and has danced at school assemblies several times over the years.

Gloria also loves to boast about her numerous boyfriends. At the start of almost every week, she has another story about what she and her latest heart throb got up to over the weekend. I can't believe how open Gloria is about her activities. According to her, she drinks regularly, smokes at least a packet of cigarettes over a weekend and often enjoys sex. It's no wonder she finds me a bore; I don't do any of these things. I suppose I lead a very protected life and don't have access to the temptations Gloria revels in. Of course, this may all change when I start at Oxford in a couple of months.

One thing about Gloria McFane I do envy is her driver's licence. Her parents run the only garage in the village and know all about cars. It was easy for them to find a quality second hand car for Gloria and they encouraged her to get her licence as soon as possible. Now that Gloria has "wheels" she's independent and goes anywhere she wants. Her parents seem perfectly happy about this. I know Lucy would love to have a car and go places too but her Mum doesn't have the money to purchase a second car. In my case, I've never been particularly keen about driving and my parents have done nothing to encourage me. I've heard that students at Oxford University ride these university bicycles everywhere to get to their lectures and social events. There are literally thousands of these bikes parked all over the city. They are there for anyone to use and are free. You just jump on, go to where you want and leave the bike there. When you emerge, there will be other bikes lying about there for you to use. What a great idea! No need for a car to get around at Oxford and you keep fit into the bargain.

\*   \*   \*

It's Sunday afternoon and I'm in my bedroom waiting for Michael to arrive. My parents are insisting we all have afternoon tea together. They're keen to get to know him better, they say, but I'm really worried he won't meet their demanding standards. Never before have I brought a young man home so this is a new and rather terrifying experience. First and foremost, my parents will want evidence that Michael is a good practising Catholic. To be honest, I have no idea what his religious leanings are and we haven't even discussed this. Next, they'll want to see that Michael is a "gentleman" and knows how to conduct himself in polite society. All in all, the next hour or so promises to be more worrying than sitting my "A" levels.

I offered to help mum make the scones but she graciously declined. I think she wants to handle everything on her own. I've taken a bit more time with my appearance and put on the prettiest dress in my wardrobe. Michael said he hoped to arrive around half past two, however, according to my watch, he's already ten minutes late. Dad's a stickler for punctuality and this is not an auspicious start.

When the front door bell does finally ring, I scamper downstairs as quickly as possible to be the one to welcome Michael at the door. He has dressed up for the occasion in a smart tweed jacket, a modest tie and there's even a handkerchief peeping out of his top pocket. His brown brogue shoes are clean and shiny and I feel quite proud of him. In the looks department Michael should be well received by my parents. I lead him into the lounge where my parents are waiting. They stand up to greet him and I make the introductions. Then there's an embarrassing silence before the four of us all start speaking at once. I cringe...this is going to be *so* painful. Finally, dad takes the initiative.

'Michael, do sit down. I understand you are training to become a school teacher?'

'Yes, that's correct sir.'

'At Culham College for Schoolmasters?'

'Yes, sir.'

My mother politely excuses herself to take the scones out of the oven and collect the tea trolley.

'And... tell me Michael, what do you think of the college?'

'I'm enjoying it, thank you sir.'

'More to the point, do you think they are preparing you well for the teaching profession?'

'I think so.'

'That's not really a fair question to ask, is it? Because, how could you possibly know?'

Not waiting for a reply, my father abruptly changed tack.

'Does your teacher training include religious studies?'

'Religious Studies is an elective which is offered for anyone who wishes to study the subject.'

I realise now where this conversation is heading and I know my father and Michael are on a potential collision course. Quickly, I try to think of something to say that might move the conversation elsewhere, but I'm too late.

'I hope *you* have chosen that elective, young man?'

'No, sir.'

'Why not?'

'I guess the subject doesn't really interest me, sir.'

My father's face registers a look of anger mixed with disappointment. Then comes the question I'm dreading.

'So, Michael, does this mean you are not religious at all?'

'I'm afraid not, sir.'

At this moment Mum enters behind her tea-trolley. She is all innocent smiles, having heard nothing of this conversation. She's proud of the afternoon tea she has carefully prepared and intent on creating a pleasant, homely atmosphere. After dispensing our cups of tea, she reveals the freshly baked warm scones and asks me to pass them around together with the cream and strawberry jam. I must say they taste excellent but, as far as I'm concerned, the afternoon is already ruined. My father's body language shows his strong disapproval of Michael and he is certainly not going to condone any further contact between Michael and me. According to father's narrow parochial views, a boyfriend who is not religiously inclined is unfit for his only daughter.

Mum soon picks up there is tension in the room and tries valiantly to make amends. Of course, she has no idea what transpired before she entered the room. The scones are followed by a platter of delightful small tea cakes which I'm also asked to pass around. Despite the tense feeling in the room, Michael enjoys his afternoon tea, a luxury never enjoyed at Culham. He catches my eye as I pass him his third cake but I don't know how to interpret his expression. We spend about three quarters of an hour together as a family group, pretending that all is well. Mum engages Michael several times in conversation but father remains silent. He has made up his mind about Michael and sees no reason to prolong the agony. Eventually, he excuses himself, muttering about something he needs to attend to in his study and thereby breaks up the gathering.

With dad out of the room, Michael offers to help with the washing up and the three of us wheel out the trolley and start on the dishes. Mum probes to find out what the disagreement was before she entered the lounge. Neither Michael, nor I, are prepared to talk about the matter. With the dishes out of the way, there's only ten minutes left before Michael has to leave to collect Malcolm. He politely thanks mum for her hospitality and the two of us go out through the front door and walk down the driveway to his car. Dad doesn't come out to say good-bye. As soon as we are alone, Michael opens up.

'I'm afraid that was a disaster, Betty. Your father obviously has no time for me.'

'Oh, Michael I'm so sorry. I felt so embarrassed.'

'Are *you* religious, Betty?'

'I go through the motions. I'm at a Catholic school and my parents expect me to go to mass every Sunday, which I do, but I have to confess I don't feel anything. I've tried to believe. I enjoy some of the sacred music and I have some good friends who are Catholics. To be quite candid, I see the organised church as just that. A whole lot of people over the last couple of thousand years who have set up this world-wide massive bureaucracy with a hierarchy of men running the show. Put simply, did God create mankind or has mankind created God?'

'Very profound! I have to go, Betty. I had really hoped this first meeting with your parents would have been a success and then I might be welcome to come and see you again. Then, after your "A" levels, I'd be allowed to take you out.'

'That's not going to happen, Michael. But I really do want to keep seeing you.'

'Same with me, Betty.'

'I don't think you can even ring me now. They won't allow me talk to you, even over the phone. So, how can we arrange something?'

'How about I come over late at night after your parents have gone to bed?'

'Oh, Michael, that would be really exciting!'

'How about Wednesday night? I'll bring my torch and flash it up to your window when I arrive.'

'Yes, oh yes, let's do that!'

'What time?'

'They're always in bed before eleven, so make it mid-night and we should be safe.'

'It's a date.'

Then he pulled me gently towards him and we kissed. It was better this second time. We were both expecting it to happen and I was more responsive. We kissed and cuddled for a few minutes before he climbed back into his old bomb, cranked it up and waved me a fond farewell.

I felt exhilarated. At least we'll be together for a short time late on Wednesday night.

# 18.

# Glenis

Michael Brain seems such a pleasant lad and he and Betty appear in many ways to be well suited. I am so annoyed I was out here in the kitchen when some kind of an altercation happened in the lounge. I could have cut the air with a knife when I entered the lounge wheeling my tea-trolley. The atmosphere was icy. Afterwards, neither Betty nor Michael would divulge what had occurred. I must talk to David but he has retired to his study in a grumpy mood and closed the door. It's a sure sign he doesn't want to be disturbed. I always respect his wishes because he works such long hours and tires easily. Anyway, a man needs some quiet time occasionally. I know he's working on a medical paper about general practice in rural locations. Quite likely he'll be bailed up in his study until dinner time. He won't be able to avoid me when it's time to go to bed, though.

Ten minutes later Betty skips back in in a surprisingly ebullient mood. This is mystifying since any kind of a relationship between her and Michael has probably been irretrievably quashed as a result of the mysterious disagreement in the lounge.

'Betty dear, can you spare a few minutes please?'

'Sorry Mum, I need to get on with my revision.' With that, my daughter scurries back upstairs as if a special treat awaits her there. It's not pleasant being the only one left in the dark about what happened earlier.

We always have Sunday dinner promptly at seven. David insists on regular times for his meals on Sundays. He claims the crazy, unpredictable meal breaks he has to snatch during the remainder of the week plays havoc with his bowels, which makes it essential that on the one day of the week when his stomach can have regular intakes of food, it should be respected.

David's mood doesn't appear to have lightened. He has little to say until I serve the dessert, spotted dick, cream and custard, normally a favourite of his. What he then abruptly says to Betty stuns me.

'Betty, I'm sure you are aware that that young man you invited here this afternoon is not an appropriate friend for you. I hope you understand that he is not welcome here. When your grounding is lifted, you are not to see him again.'

Betty looks at her father in silent amazement and I can't hold myself back any longer. 'David, perhaps you could let me know what it is about Michael that has upset you so much?'

My husband glares at me, presumably forgetting I was not present in the lounge when the difficulties arose.

'Please remember, I was out in the kitchen dear, and didn't hear your conversation.'

'Ah, yes, so you were. Let me explain, then.'

'Please do...'

'It transpires that the young man is a non-believer, a heathen, an atheist. We have raised Betty as a practising Catholic and I have no desire to see her religious beliefs destroyed, diluted or ridiculed through associating with such a person. He may appear on the surface to be a pleasant enough young lad, but he has no belief system and therefore is lacking any kind of moral compass.'

'But dad, he could be a humanitarian.'

'Bah... what's that may I ask? What sort of moral fibre underpins a person who says they are humanitarian? Where's the set of scriptures or sacred writings that guide and inspire such people? There are none. They don't exist! If he claims to be a humanitarian, then I rest my case.'

'This seems a bit harsh, dear. He's only a young man and probably still finding his way. Perhaps he has only lapsed in his faith and will return to it soon?'

'Fiddlesticks! A person with no faith floats in the world like seaweed on the tide. Remember what Jesus said in John, chapter six, verse four, "I am the way, the truth and the life. No man cometh unto the father, but by me."'

I look across at Betty, whose face has reddened markedly, although I'm unsure why. Is it shame and guilt that she has not lived up to her father's expectations or is she livid with him? My daughter scoops up a last mouthful of custard, and without another word leaves the room.

'Was that strict ruling really necessary, David?'

'I don't know what's got into Betty recently. First, she's dishonest and goes galivanting around at a football match, where she's picked up by this Michael boy. Next, she has the audacity to bring him here, where he openly admits he's not a practising Christian.'

'Well, at least give him credit for being totally honest.'

'In a few weeks' time our daughter will, hopefully, be going up to Oxford to read science. I know what temptations there are for young students attending university. If Betty doesn't strictly adhere to the Christian principles we have instilled in her, then anything could happen to her there. A university education is wonderful but it is fraught with dangers too. When I went to university, I saw behaviour from some students that verged on debauchery. There was excessive drinking, promiscuity, even drugs. Like it or not, you are exposed to all sorts of radical ideas. Betty's strong Christian background should provide her with the moral strength and fortitude to resist the work of the devil.'

'As you know, I never went to university, so I didn't witness the things you're talking about. But I do think we have to cut Betty a bit of slack.'

"What on earth does that mean?'

'If we set unreasonably high standards for her, she may rebel. We certainly don't want that to happen.'

'Expecting Betty to adhere to a Christian code of ethics is certainly not asking too much. I think we have inculcated a set of values that will stand Betty in good stead. I want to keep her protected from the likes of boys like Michael.'

'I was talking to a few of the mothers of other pupils doing their "A" levels last week after the Parents and Friends meeting. They had some interesting things to say.'

'And what were they, Glenis?'

'Some professor has been doing research into how well students handle their studies at university as a result of the kind of schooling they received.'

'Oh yes, and what were the findings?'

'Rather surprising, actually. It seems that students coming from state high schools settle down to university life and perform better academically than their counterparts from the private sector.'

'I find that hard to believe. Does this professor suggest why he thinks this may be happening?'

'Yes, he believes it's because the high school students are more worldly and better adjusted to life than private school pupils, who come from a more sheltered, protected background. Apparently, many private school students can't handle the sudden freedoms they experience when they arrive at university, whereas the state schoolers are used to the freedom. The state schoolers are also more self-motivated. Private school pupils are pushed and cajoled, and subject to greater imposed discipline, so they don't learn self-discipline.'

'I'd be interested to see this research sometime. About 80% of all university graduates are from a private school background and that's impressive. I have my doubts about what that professor is claiming.'

'I'll clear all these dishes away and have a bit of a chat with Betty before she turns in.'

David returns to his study to work on his paper.

\*   \*   \*

I knock gently on Betty's bedroom door, uncertain what sort of a mood she will be in.

'Come in mum,' she sings out cheerfully. I find her busily practising algebraic problems. She stops what she's doing and gives me a welcoming smile.

'Do you have a few spare minutes darling, for a chat?'

'As long as you're not going to give me another lecture about my religious principles.'

'No, of course not.'

'That's good,' she says, twiddling a pencil with a well chewed end.

'I'm sorry dad was so abrupt with you at dinner time. He gets stressed from over work and he's so anxious that you get to Oxford and make a success of your life.'

'I know. He's not being fair about Michael though. Michael's a lovely man. Just because he doesn't hold the same religious beliefs as dad doesn't make him some sort of an ogre. Many people are not religious, but they're still decent folk. What about Mrs. Hardvale and my best friend, Lucy? I have hardly ever seen them at mass. Is dad now saying I shouldn't be friends with Lucy? Quite a few of the girls at school are only nominal Catholics.'

'I think it's a bit different with Michael because you two could become romantically involved. Dad is probably worried you might pick a partner for life who doesn't share his view of the world.'

'Oh, come on mum. I've only met Michael three times. It's not as though we are about to announce our nuptials!'

'Of course not, dear. This is your first boyfriend and dad is just trying to lay down some sort of a framework for the future.'

'Get real mum. In a few weeks I'll be leaving for Oxford. There are communists there, homosexuals, lesbians, republicans and all kinds of crazy religious nuts. They're going to be studying beside me. My best friends could be lesbians or men that believe in free love. I might share a Bunsen burner with an African witch doctor or someone from Fiji whose parents were cannibals. Part of going to a university is to broaden your horizons, to see the world through the eyes of others. Dad won't be able to control who I see, or who I befriend at Oxford.'

'Oh Betty, you make it all sound rather scary.'

'No mum, exciting!'

I stop to think about what Betty has just said. I can see she is animated about what the future holds and has already put to rest any anger she may have felt towards her father for his narrow views.

'Betty dear, are you very disappointed about not seeing Michael again?'

My daughter blushes deeply, a sure sign there is something she's hiding from me. Ever since she was a toddler her face would redden if she told a fib, or did something she knew to be wrong. I wonder what it is this time?

'Yes, of course I'm disappointed. I really like Michael and he wanted to ask me out on a date. I'm only grounded until I finish my exams, remember. I don't see why I can't see him before I go to university if I want to.'

'It would be like waving a red flag at a bull, darling. Dad would be furious and it would be awful if you went off to university leaving an unhappy father behind. He'd be impossible to live with!'

Betty gives a mischievous giggle, her face still a light shade of beetroot. My motherly instinct is bristling. I sense something is not right and I'm being left in the dark. Betty is definitely hiding something from me. What's more, she knows, I know she's not being entirely honest.

'Is there something else you want to tell me, dear?'

'No thanks, mum,' she says firmly.

I know when I've hit a brick wall with my daughter; there's no point in pursuing the matter further.

'Sleep well,' I say, and quietly take my leave.

*   *   *

David's sour mood appears to have lifted by the time he is ready for bed. He's progressing well with his medical paper and hopes to complete the first draft before next weekend. Our going to bed routine is as uneventful as always. There's little conversation; I get a peck and a disinterested, 'good night, dear.' Any intimacy between us is a thing of the past. My husband is asleep quickly but my mind is still active and I lie on my back ruminating about my chat with Betty.

What was it about her and Michael that made her blush? Clearly, she has developed some feelings for him even though they have only known each other for a short time. Perhaps they have secretly arranged to meet again once Betty's "A" levels are completed and she didn't think it wise to tell me? Maybe they are going to secretly write to each other? I'll keep an eye open when the post arrives each day to see if Betty starts receiving letters. It's hard to think what else they can do in the circumstances if they want to stay in touch.

To be perfectly candid, I don't have a problem with Michael and his lack of religious beliefs. If he's a decent young man, then Betty should be allowed to see him again. But David is dead against it and certainly won't change his mind. It's rather exciting my daughter has a budding romance, her very first one! I vividly recall my own first date and the short romance that followed. I fell head over heels in love with Gerald, a boy down the end of my street, only to discover he was dating another girl at the same time. I found out the hard way that there are people in this world who are known as "two-timers." I don't think Michael is like that though. I really hope Betty has a happier time with her first romance than I did and *I* won't be standing in her way if she wishes to see him again. In fact,

I might turn a blind eye if his letters begin to arrive. I'm always the person who collects the mail in this house, although that might change if Betty is expecting special mail to arrive.

# 19.

# Malcolm

Michael drops me off at Lucy's place a bit before two-thirty on Sunday afternoon and promises to pick me up around four-thirty.

Lucy Hardvale's home is large, Victorian and starting to look run down. I guess it's to be expected since Mrs. Hardvale's husband disappeared over nine years ago and their financial situation has been precarious ever since. Mrs. Hardvale has three children to feed and the upkeep of an extensive home with the considerable expenses that entails. The garden is a mess. There is a lawn-mower, but the blades are blunt and the machine needs servicing. The bushes and trees are over-grown and the handful of fruit trees in the backyard haven't been pruned for years. The Hardvale's can't afford a gardener. Exterior paintwork is shabby and starting to peel away in a few places. The front-door bell doesn't work either so I'm obliged to use the door knocker.

Almost immediately the door swings open and Lucy is standing there smiling and looking great. Her two younger brothers are carrying on with a chorus of wolf whistles and silly comments at the far end of the long hallway until Mrs. Hardvale chastises them and they slink off, still sniggering.

'Hello Malcolm. Let's go out for a walk. I don't want to stay here and put up with those two idiot brothers of mine.'

Lucy's dressed in a light green coat, a darker green scarf, strong walking shoes and is armed with an umbrella.

'That's fine with me,' I reply, 'you're looking pretty,' I quickly add.

'Thanks,' she says and flashes me an enticing smile.

'Where are we going?'

'Down to the football field where I first met you. There's a nice path that follows along the river. I've sometimes seen kingfishers down there too.'

'Sounds good.' It's chilly and I shove my hands deep into my duffle coat pockets as Lucy closes the door behind her.

Lucy is never short of something to talk about and she strikes up an easy, relaxed conversation that includes which songs are currently in "The Top Twenty", the never-ending stupidity of her two brothers and her take on last Sunday evening when we all enjoyed dinner at her place. Then she wants to know more about me and my background. I open up about the difficulties I'm having with my parents, how my decision not to enter the army devastated them and why I'm now so financially embarrassed.

By now, we've walked across the football ground and started the picturesque path that winds its way along the riverbank. A pair of ducks are diving and paddling about, watched over by a lonely blue crane standing resplendent on the opposite bank. It's shady here and the path narrows forcing us closer together. We stop talking so as to better enjoy the beauty of the moment. Lucy is so attractive and I want to take her in my arms and kiss her but something tells me it's too early to make such advances and that Lucy may not be receptive. The last thing I want to do is spoil the development of a potentially exciting new relationship. Then Lucy surprises me.

'Malcolm, do you know what the villagers call this path?'

I look at her and shake my head.

'Guess.'

'How would I know what the path is called? I haven't seen a sign post or anything else to give me a clue.'

'Come on, Malcolm, guess.'

'Riverbank path?'

'That's not very imaginative,' Lucy smiles sweetly and moves closer, at the same time taking hold of my right hand. An intoxicating scent wafts across my face.

'Try again,' she teases.

The famous book, "The Wind in the Willows" flashes into my mind; the story of Ratty, Mole and Toad of Toad Hall who all lived along a riverbank something like this.

'Wind in the Willows?'

Lucy laughs. 'Come closer and I'll whisper it in your ear.'

I bend down so she can reach my ear and she flings her arms around my neck and I feel her hot breathe in my ear as she whispers, 'it's called "Lovers Way."'

No further invitation is needed. We kiss deeply and I hold myself away from her lest she feels my massive erection.

'Oh Malcolm, that was lovely. Do you know you are the first boy I've ever kissed properly?'

'Really?'

'Yes, really. How many girls have you kissed?'

I don't want to answer this question. There are a few but I'm not sure it's wise to tell her. It could ruin a magic moment. So, I gently pull her towards me and we kiss again. Some girls tense up when first kissed, fearful of what may happen next. Not Lucy. She's hungry for more and leans her body seductively against mine. I can't hide my hardness any longer and she's happy to feel it pressing against her. I'm dying to move my hands about her body and fondle her breasts. Lucy's so willing and we seem to mould together perfectly. If we go any further, I'm going to find it difficult to stop.

Lucy is sensing this too. Abruptly she pulls away and stands in front of me, a little out of breath with a whimsical smile playing around her lips. Now, I'm exposed and my erection feels as if it's bursting out a mile through my trousers. It's horribly uncomfortable.

'You didn't answer my question, Malcolm?'

The magic moment is gone, finished as quickly as it flared up.

'Umm...a couple perhaps.'

'Come on Malcolm, be honest.'

'Well... five, I think.' I can feel myself reddening.

'Come on, it's time for us to head home. Michael will be at our place soon. If we're late, I'll tell him you've been fast asleep all afternoon.'

She grabs my hand and gives it a squeeze. As we emerge from "Lovers Way" she quickly drops her hand and moves away because two girls from her school are sitting there on the ground having a picnic. The three girls exchange pleasantries but we've been seen together. Undoubtedly, a new and infectious rumour has just been hatched.

Lucy tells me she wants to see me again but it's impossible to plan anything definite without transport. Girls are strictly forbidden at Culham College for Schoolmasters, so I have to be the one to find a way to travel to West Dryton. With no car and no money for bus fares I'm as good as grounded.

'When we get home, I'll give you the money for a return bus fare, Malcolm,' she promises.

She's as good as her word. When Michael's car crunches to a stop outside her home, Lucy gives me a quick peck and a gorgeous smile. I think I might be falling in love! The money for return bus fares is safely in my pocket.

\*   \*   \*

Michael is furious about the way Doctor Brindleton treated him at their afternoon tea and wastes no time unloading on me. I listen and share his sentiments.

'The bloody doctor's totally intolerant of anyone who doesn't hold the same religious views as him. He's mad! In a few weeks Betty will be off to Oxford University and then she'll be free to go out with whoever she wants. He might be able to keep her caged up until then but after that Betty will be totally independent. He's an absolute drop-kick!'

'So, what have you two decided to do? Are you going to wait until she goes off to Oxford and then date her?'

'No bloody way!'

'But the doctor's banned you from seeing her. You can't go round to her place now. What's more, she's grounded!'

'There's more than one way to skin a cat, Malcolm.'

'What do you mean?'

'If Betty and I want to see each other, we'll find a way.'

'Are you going to try to see her at St Anne's? You can't just lob up at a private Catholic school bristling with teaching nuns and ask to see her there.'

'You'd be surprised what we're going to do. Her father's a total bastard. Betty and I get along famously and we are going to get together anyway.'

There was something strange about the way Michael had answered me. I had the distinct feeling it wasn't as straight forward as he was making out but he didn't elaborate on how the two of them planned to meet again. My friend was so pre-occupied brooding over the impossible Doctor Brindleton during the remainder of the short journey back to college he almost forgot to ask how my afternoon had been.

'We had a good time, thanks. I'm going over to see Lucy again next Sunday.'

'But I can't drive you, Malcolm.'

'That's okay. I'll catch the bus.'

'You said you haven't any money?'

'Lucy gave me some.'

Well... she must be keen!'

'She is...'

\*  \*  \*

The start of the week proceeded as usual. There was the normal string of lectures in Educational Psychology, English Literature (Romantic poets), Physical Training, Practical Art and British History. In the evenings I slogged away at my assignments and devoted another couple of hours working with Alex Dobrila on an essay he had to submit on Shakespeare's Hamlet. I remember asking Alex how he felt about having to study Shakespeare. Surely, I suggested, the great bard is hardly relevant to the kids he would end up teaching in Uganda? Wasn't learning about Shakespeare culturally irrelevant for Ugandans? His answer surprised me. He explained that high school children in Uganda did "O" and "A" levels like their English counterparts, therefore, it was essential Ugandan kids learnt what English kids learnt. And, he added, If the English educational authorities decided Shakespeare was not relevant for Ugandan children and omitted it from the curriculum, the English could be accused of racial discrimination!

When I wasn't fully engaged with my studies, I found myself thinking about Lucy. I'd had girlfriends before but there was something about Lucy that was different in the nicest possible way. Everything about her fascinated me; her little mannerisms, the way she moved, her lively conversations, quick sense of humour, her positivity and of course her good looks. Having to wait an entire week to see Lucy again seemed an eternity so I decided to ring her on Wednesday night. Culham College boasted only two public telephones for over 250 students and they were constantly in use until around ten o'clock at night. If you spent more than a couple of minutes in the kiosk during these busy times somebody would start banging loudly on the door and telling you to hurry-up. This was hardly the ideal way to connect romantically with Lucy.

The post office in the small market town of Abingdon was nearly three miles away. I had noticed there were three telephone booths in front of the post office and I felt confident I could use one of these for ten minutes undisturbed. I reckoned I could easily run there in half an hour. My problem, of course, was lack of money to make the call. Lucy had given me enough for the bus fare but no more. I decided to call in on my Ugandan friend, Alex Dobrila. He was always flashing pound notes about the place and bragging about the money he received as a student on the Colombo scholarship program.

I knocked on his door.

'Come,' came the booming voice of the Ugandan Chieftain.

'Hey man, what you doing?'

'I've come to ask for your help, Alex.'

'You're kidding me, man. You don't need no help from me!'

'Well, actually I do. I've got woman problems,' Alex's eyes widened like saucers, 'hey, that's serious man. Don't you know what to do with a woman?' Alex burst into a hearty laugh that lasted a minute or two.

'Yes, I know what to do, thanks.'

Alex couldn't help himself and made a rude gesture with his arm that crudely indicated what you do to a woman. I ignored him.

'You'll be pleased to know, Alex, I *do* now have a girlfriend.' My remark was met with another long peel of laughter and my friend slapped his knee several times with glee.

'You going to take her for a wife?'

'Hey, steady on, Alex. I've only known her for a couple of weeks.'

'Back home, if I like the look of a woman, I go and negotiate with her family. She's got to be strong and handsome and a good childbearer. If we agree on the price, we get married. Simple!'

'It's different here Alex. Anyway, I was wondering if you could give me a couple of shillings please so I can telephone her?'

Alex pulled a bag of coins out of a desk drawer and scattered them all over his desk with a couple rolling on the floor. There must have been a couple of pounds worth of coins.

'Take what you want, man.'

'I only need two or three bob.'

'Bobs? Which are bobs?' Alex asked, surveying the assortment of English coins widely dispersed across his desk.

'A shilling is a bob. See... this coin is one shilling or one bob; this one here is two shillings or two bob...'

'Man, just take as many bobs as you need. It's play money to me. I only use the paper money and the shops keep giving me back all this small, heavy stuff.'

I laugh. Alex, and his weird use of money, is a story in itself. I pick out three one shilling coins and gratefully pocket them.

'You're a good friend Alex.'

I leave his study with a big smile on my face and approximately ten minutes of telephone romance safely stowed away in my pocket.

# 20.

# Lucy

Geography is my first "A" level examination next Monday morning. I've been doing some studying but not fanatically like my best friend, Betty. She, poor girl, is living the life of a hermit. Grounded and not even allowed to see Michael if he comes to her house anymore. This final week before the exams we don't go to school unless we have a problem and want to talk to one of our teachers. The idea is that we stay home and revise the whole week. I find this totally boring. I prefer to be out and about, seeing my classmates, not sitting on my backside studying at home all day. I have done some work though. If I scrape one "A" level it will be a real bonus because I'm going to Tech College to study secretarial studies and "A" levels are not a pre-requisite for entry.

As I sit here looking out of the bedroom window, my mind wanders all over the place. More often than not, it ends up with Malcolm. He's a good catch for my first ever boyfriend. There's so much to admire about him. I actually like it that he's vulnerable. Wow, Sister Norah, my English teacher, would be impressed I'm using such a big word. But he is! He's told me all about his problems with his parents, how they have refused to pay his college fees and that he's adopted. To some extent I can identify with Michael's concerns because our father walked out on us when I was only seven and we've struggled financially ever since. We can't afford holidays, tickets to the Christmas pantomimes or trips to London.

Compared to other girls my age, my wardrobe is meagre. I won't have any special clothes or jewellery to wear when Michael comes over next Sunday.

I like it that Malcolm is going to be a teacher. That's a caring profession and a well-respected occupation. The pay's not marvellous Malcolm tells me, but teachers are always in high demand so unemployment is virtually unheard of. He's a good marriage prospect but it's far too early to think seriously along those lines yet. I'm sure he really likes me though. I just loved being out with him on "Lover's Way" last Sunday. I hope he didn't think I was being too forward by taking the initiative and giving him a passionate kiss?

Mum has told me a bit about how women fall pregnant but she avoided details. She just told me that the man puts his penis inside a woman's vagina and it feels nice. Some of the girls at school, who are far more worldly than me, told me the man has to get an erection to have intercourse. I didn't know whether to believe them but I found out along "Lover's Way" on Sunday. When I snuggled up against Malcolm, I felt his penis pressing into me. I'm sure he had an erection. How exciting was that!

Mum seems happy I'm going out with Malcolm. I told her we would be going out again next Sunday. I also told her the poor man is destitute, which is why he can't afford to take me anywhere special. She just said, 'he can join the club.' I guess I'm lucky mum's reasonably easy-going, not like the tyrannical parents who control poor Betty's life. To be honest, I don't know how Betty copes with them.

I put away the notes I've been reading and pull out the text-book on human geography. As I'm thumbing through the pages, the phone rings downstairs. A moment later mum calls from the bottom of the stairs. 'Lucy, dear, it's for you.' I skip down the stairs and take the receiver from mum who gives me a wink and tells me it's Malcolm. I feel my heart jump. I wasn't expecting him to ring so soon.

'Hello Malcolm, it's Lucy here.'

'Hi Lucy. I hope you don't mind me ringing you when you're probably studying?'

'No, it's lovely to hear from you.'

'How's the studying going?'

'I'm afraid I'm not a good student. I find studying a real bore, but I've done a bit of work.'

'Good for you. I've been checking the bus times for Sunday. The 142 stops outside Culham at 1.30pm and gets into West Dryton at 1.52. I'm not sure where your bus stop is so I don't know how far it is to walk to your place?'

'All the buses stop at the village green. It's then about a ten-minute walk to our house. Would you like me to meet you at the bus stop? Then we could go for another walk. Or, if you prefer, we can come back here?'

'I guess it depends on the weather. I would so much like to be able to take you out somewhere Lucy but you know why I can't.'

'I understand Malcolm. Don't feel bad about it. I just like being with you.'

'That's sweet of you. I've been missing you Lucy and can't wait for Sunday.'

'Me too.'

We chatted for a few more minutes. Malcolm told me how he had scrounged some money from his African friend for the phone call, scored a goal in a match played between the first years and the second years at the college and was ringing me from a phone in Abingdon so we could talk longer and in peace.

'My money's running low Lucy so I better finish up.'

'Thanks so much for ringing, Malcolm. I'll meet you at the bus stop, unless it's raining.'

'Great. Be good; don't do anything I wouldn't do.'

'I don't know you well enough to know how to answer that.'

'Then you must get to know me better.'

'I'd like that.'

'Bye, Lucy.'

And he was gone. Back to the drudgery of my geography books. At least I have something super to look forward to on Sunday.

# 21.

# Michael

I'm the first person in my family to ever go on to do tertiary education. Dad's a council worker, employed to work on local roads and footpaths as a labourer. Mum takes in ironing whenever she has the time but still has my four younger siblings at home to fuss over. Dad's a rough diamond and swears like a trooper but underneath all the bluster he has a gentler side. He's forty-five now. Working outside in the cruel English climate has started to take its toll. He reckons he's got so many aches and pains all over his body there isn't room for any more. Mum, who has given birth to seven children (she lost two) usually tells dad that there's one part of his body that's still working far too well so he can bloody well stop complaining. Mum's forty-four and she's dead set against having any more kids. Our youngest has just turned two.

Despite my parents working class attitudes, they're hugely proud I've made it to teachers' college. I can just imagine what they're saying to their friends. Dad, shovelling dirt into a hole somewhere and yakking away to one of his mates...

'Me son's doing bloody book learnin' at one of them fancy colleges. Got brains 'e 'as. 'E be bloody teachin' your kids soon.'

Mum, chatting over the fence to the neighbours...

'Our Michael's at one of 'em posh colleges, yer know. Goin' to be a teacher 'e is.'

I love them both dearly. They've always struggled to put food on the table and were forced to rely on the council for cheap council housing. As the family increased in size, we moved from a two-bedroom place to a three-bedroom and finally we're crowded into a four-bedroom council house. Now mum's starting to worry that as the kids move out, the council will downgrade us back to a two-bedroom pad again.

I'm not sure where my brains came from but I always found school quite easy. I particularly liked maths and the sciences. I didn't have much time for the humanities and the arty-farty stuff, though. There were only a few scrappy books for us kids at home and my parents could barely manage to read the Sunday papers. Mum and dad left school at fourteen and found work straight away.

The first time my parents realised I had some brains was when I passed the eleven-plus exam and was offered a place at the local high school. Thankfully, the school ran a second-hand uniform shop so mum managed to clothe me. My school uniforms were always too tight or flopping all over the place, never fitting properly. Whilst at high school, I used to help dad with his hobby; repairing cars. It was a helpful sideline because he would charge any neighbours who had cars for the parts and his labour. This is how I learnt about cars and why I'm now the proud owner of an old Morris eight that still splutters along well enough.

For a time I dreamt of going to university to become a scientist, but too many things conspired against me. It was so cramped and noisy at home I found it difficult to study and do my homework. The family also needed me to get a part-time job to help pay the bills. I did a paper delivery every day before school and sometimes in the evenings as well. I sat my "A" levels and managed to scrape low passes in Maths and Chemistry but, sadly, not good enough to qualify for university. I had given it my best shot. Anyway, getting to Culham is an excellent consolation prize. Now, I'm training to be a maths/science high school teacher. Watch out kids!

My state high school was co-educational. I had a few good

mates that I knocked about with during recess and lunch times but rarely saw any of them outside of school. I was too busy with my paper deliveries or helping dad with his repairs. Dad was well known locally for his skill with cars and certainly trusted. Not many locals could afford a car. Those that did had to make do with vehicles virtually destined for the scrap-heap. Dad had a shed at the back of the house to keep his tools in and we would throw the necessary tools into the back of his old truck and drive round to the neighbour's place to fix their car on the side of the road often with a small audience of interested onlookers. Nobody had the luxury of a garage in our neighbourhood.

There were girls in all my classes, although not many doing mathematics and the sciences. Girls didn't interest me then. Sometimes one of the girls would make eyes at me and try to engage me in conversation. I'd be polite but never encouraged any of them and soon they'd turn their attention to some other poor bloke in the classroom. Mind you, there were a lot of fellows who spent most of their spare time hanging around the girls and the girls lapped it up. Jewellery and make-up were not allowed at school, nevertheless the girls found plenty of other ways to interest the fellers.

I'm enjoying life at Culham College for Schoolmasters. I was dreadfully homesick for the first month but then became good pals with Malcolm, who soon introduced me to his soccer team. I played a bit of football as a kid and have a few basic skills. Now I'm playing right back on a permanent basis. I was surprised to discover only a few of the students at college have cars. When dad heard I was going to college he spent hours doing up this old Morris Eight and then presented it to me the day before I was due to leave. Having a car gives me real status at college and increases my popularity no end.

I'm doing well with my studies. I know it's nothing like being at a university, however, the courses in mathematics, physics and chemistry are probably nearly the equivalent of first year at university. I'm really looking forward to getting into schools as a qualified maths/science teacher. When I'm a practising teacher, I might be able to continue my studies through part time evening classes and one day achieve my aim of becoming a university science graduate.

Unexpectedly, romance has popped up in my life. When we were playing football in West Dryton a few weeks ago, Malcolm and I met up with a couple of the local girls there. One was a pretty lass by the name of Betty Brindleton. This is the first time I have had feelings for a member of the fairer sex. Betty is incredibly clever and, like me, loves maths and science so we have much in common. Next week she sits her "A" levels and is hoping to get into Oxford University. Wow!

Betty's parents are ridiculously strict. Apparently, she watched our football match without permission and for that her father grounded her for weeks until her exams are over. They allowed me to visit Betty for afternoon tea last Sunday which turned out to be an absolute disaster. Betty's father doesn't want me to associate with his daughter, ostensibly because of my lack of any religious faith. However, I think it's a class distinction thing as well! I try to speak "The Queen's English" but sometimes I can't help myself and slip back into my working-class accent. Being a well-heeled doctor, Dr Brindleton believes I'm not good enough for his daughter because of my working-class roots. It's snobbish class distinction of the worst kind!

Betty and I get along famously. She doesn't appear to have any of the hang-ups her father suffers from and is open to having a romantic relationship with me. Amazingly, we actually kissed on our first date! Now we are planning a secret rendezvous at midnight on Wednesday. Somehow the romance seems all the more exciting because we are forbidden to see each other. I can't wait...

\*   \*   \*

My alarm clock rings at 11.15pm on Wednesday night, but I'm already wide awake. I went to bed at nine to try to get some sleep but the anticipation of a secret rendezvous with Betty has resulted in a restless couple of hours with little or no shut eye. I feel fully energised now that I'm out of bed. Opening the window, I notice the weather is kind for this time of year. The sky's clear and the moon's shining brightly. There's a light breeze rustling the leaves of the trees outside my study. I dress appropriately and pull the top blanket off my bed in case we need extra warmth when sitting in the car together. I grab my car keys and tiptoe to the door without waking my roommate. There's no one about and in a couple of minutes I reach my car which I had deliberately parked at the far end of the student car park.

It's a relief when both headlights come on, especially since one has been playing up recently. I think it's only a loose connection. The roads at this time of night are virtually deserted, a great time to be driving. On my way to West Dryton the only vehicles I see on the road are a road sweeper and a police patrol car at the crossroads. The policeman observes me with some suspicion as I pass by. What's a young man doing driving about at this hour of night in such a bomb of a car? I breathe more easily when I check the policeman is not following.

I arrive at Betty's house at five minutes to twelve and, to be safe, park a hundred yards farther down the street. Will Betty be waiting? Perhaps she has had second thoughts and decided this whole idea is just too risky? There's a street light directly outside the short driveway into Betty's home casting a bright light across their gated entrance. Betty will have to run the gauntlet there. There's no other way she can come out to meet me because the property is surrounded by a high stone wall.

I decide to remain in the car, hoping like mad the policeman doesn't drive this way on his rounds. It seems a safer option to stay in the Morris than to lurk around the entrance to the Brindleton's place and look distinctly suspicious. I glance at my watch; it's midnight and no sign of Betty.

At five past twelve, I decide to wait only until ten past and then leave. Goodness knows how many times I look at my watch over the next few minutes. The time drags terribly and still there's no sign of Betty. Something must have gone seriously wrong. I hope she wasn't discovered trying to leave the house or been heard crunching her way along the gravel driveway. At ten past, with a sigh of disappointment, I turn on the ignition and suddenly, there she is, shielding her eyes from the glare of my headlights. Not knowing who has shone their headlights on her, she immediately turns and bolts back in behind the stone wall. Now I've scared her. I turn off the ignition, jump out of the car and hurry down the road fearing Betty has panicked and retreated inside.

The gate is ajar. Cautiously, I call her name. No answer. I call again. Still no response. Gently, I push the heavy wooden gate open and stop on the driveway admiring what I can see of the front of Betty's house. It's deathly quiet except for the sound of my laboured breathing.

'Betty?'

There's a sudden flurry of movement and next moment Betty's embracing me.

'Oh Michael, I didn't know who was in that car just up the road. I was too scared to come back out.'

'Only little old me,' I assure her, 'come on, let's get in the car, it'll be warmer.'

I take her hand and together we half walk, half run the hundred yards to the relative comfort of my faithful Morris Eight.

'Get in the back. There's a warm blanket there.'

And we scramble in, giggling and excited, ignoring the damaged springs and torn upholstery. I pull the blanket over our knees and we snuggle down expectantly.

Betty doesn't waste any time. She leans over, throws her arms around my neck and kisses me firmly on the lips.

'I didn't think you'd come,' she whispers.

'Why ever not? The chance to meet a pretty girl in the back of a car in the middle of the night is not to be missed.'

'Kiss me, Michael.'

'I'm not very experienced, Betty.'

'Nor am I,' she giggled.

This time we linger over the kiss, exploring and enjoying. Things down below are getting very uncomfortable and I need to reorganise myself. Then I become conscious of Betty's hand feeling for me. Crickey, how far is this going? I had thought we might have some kisses and cuddles but that was all. Betty's definitely asking me for more but I'm totally unprepared. I've never been with a girl before and I'm full of mixed emotions; strong desire, surprise, embarrassment because I don't know what to do next and panic if we are caught.

Suddenly the front of the car is bathed in bright light. There's a car heading towards us. We don't know whether to duck under the blanket or sit up and try and look innocent. We pick the former. The car pulls up immediately in front of us with its lights on high beam. A door slams and someone is coming towards us shining a powerful torch. Whoever it is, shines their torch into the car, first in front and then on us crouched down in the back.

'Having a bit of fun are yer?'

No point in hiding any longer. We pull back the blanket and squint at the torchlight. To our horror we see what appears to be a policeman with a nasty smirk on his face. I'm the first to gather my senses.

'Errr...yes thank you, officer.'

'We're not doing anything wrong, officer,' adds Betty.

'Haven't yer got somewhere better than this to carry on?'

'Not really, officer.'

'Ow old are yer, darling?' the policeman asks, looking at Betty.

'Almost eighteen.'

For a moment the officer contemplates Betty's answer as if he doesn't believe her. Then he sniffs and says, 'Orright,' and without another word returns to his car. We sit in silence and watch him drive slowly away.

'Is he the local copper?'

'No,' replies Betty, 'thank our lucky stars. If the local bobby had seen us it would definitely get back to dad and I hate to think what would happen then.'

'Same here,' I reply. 'I think it's too dangerous meeting out here on the road.'

'So do I.'

'So, what are we going to do?'

'Meet somewhere else, of course. Somewhere we won't be disturbed,' Betty declares.

'You must tell me where, Betty. I don't know West Dryton.'

The place she suggests takes my breath away. She has taken my hand again and is looking at me with the loveliest pleading eyes.

'My bedroom.'

'What! Your bedroom! You don't mean that, surely?'

'Why not? It will be lovely and warm and... there's a bed. Mum and dad never come in to my room after they say goodnight.'

'But Betty, it's so risky. How could I possibly creep in and out without being seen or heard?'

'It's easy. The stairs don't creek and we have lovely thick carpet. I can let you in at the back door which will be safer.'

'Oh Betty, I don't know?'

'Come on Michael. Next Wednesday night. Promise me?' Betty was moving her hand under the blanket again making it abundantly clear what she expected.

'Betty, I'm a virgin.'

'So am I. I think it's time we both found out what it's all about.'

I suppose we could have found out "what it's all about" there and then, in the back of my trusty old Morris Eight, however, the incident with the policeman had put the wind up us. Who knows, he might come back again! So, we enjoyed a long, loving kiss and I saw Betty safely back to the gate. She blew me a kiss as she disappeared into the gloom of her house.

# 22.

....... 

# Dr. Brindleton

It's Thursday evening and I'm off to my Rotary Club; the Rotary Club of West Dryton. It's only a small club with around eighteen members, all men of course. We have a diverse membership in accordance with Rotary International's stipulation that only the most senior representative from each professional occupation should be invited to join. As the only medical practioner in the village, I'm a shoe in. Several of my Rotary colleagues run businesses in West Dryton and there's a sizeable group of members who are, what might best be described as landed gentry. Club members wear a name badge that also displays the name of the club and their occupation. The landed gentry have selected different occupations such as orchardist, equine stud farmer, sheep breeder and forestry manager so they can be classified as being involved in varying avenues of the farming industry. I enjoy our weekly meetings and only miss one or two a year. We meet at the best pub in town, "The Red Lion."

This Rotary year I'm responsible for organising our guest speakers. Tonight, I'm thrilled I've been able to attract a professor of physics from Oxford University to be our honoured guest. The professor will be speaking about some of the exciting new developments in quantum physics but, personally, I want to also hear about the life of Oxford undergraduates these days, since Betty will be going there in a few short weeks. I left Oxford's medical faculty back in 1939, just before war broke out, but I understand things have changed for students considerably since then. As the organiser of guest speakers and responsible for formally introducing the guests to the club, I always get to sit next to the guest speakers during dinner. Tonight, I'll have the perfect opportunity to pick the professor's brains.

Professor Karl Stenhauser is a bean-pole of a man, bald on top with a bushy white beard, grown perhaps as some kind of compensation. Most captivating are his intense blue eyes that seem to dance and sparkle when he speaks. Clothing-wise, he gives the impression he hasn't changed out of his shabby laboratory gear for weeks. The professor speaks with a distinct German accent. Interesting, since we were still at war with the Hun only fifteen years ago. Nevertheless, he's a sociable chap and appears to enjoy a good chat. I settle him down next to me with a pint of Guinness and fire a few questions at him as we wait for the main course to appear.

'Professor, when did you start lecturing at Oxford?'

'1946. Not long after the ending of hostilities. During the war I'd been working as a professor in experimental physics at Bonn University. I guess I was fortunate because the British Government recognised my talents and snapped me up once they had ascertained I wasn't a die-hard Nazi. They quickly offered me work here in Britain.'

'You were fortunate indeed! My daughter's going to Oxford to study science next semester if her "A" levels are good enough.'

'Well, that's good news. She must be a bright lass?'

'Yes, she certainly is. I'm a bit worried though about what life is like for neophyte undergraduates at Oxford these days?'

The professor laughs heartily.

'Doctor you should know. You went to university, did you not?'

'Yes, of course.'

'Students go to university to grow up. They learn a lot more than what their lecturers and professors try to instill.'

'When I went to university there was some drinking and stupid

147

behaviour but most of us were well behaved.'

'Well, my friend, you would be hard put to find any students these days that don't imbibe, smoke, take lovers or experiment with drugs. All tempting extra-curricular activities,' and the professor laughed knowingly again.

'Is it really that bad? My daughter's a respectable young girl and we've kept her protected from anything unsavoury.'

'She's in for a shock then,' and the professor slapped me on the back. 'You'd better have a word with her, so she's forewarned.'

The professor's words hit home hard. Glenis and I must do everything we can to prepare our sweet innocent Betty for the degrading things she will encounter at Oxford. At least, I comfort myself, she has a strong religious faith and, therefore, the moral fibre to resist the temptations.

The evening proceeds well. We have a few notices, a hilarious fine session, that realises nearly three pounds for charity and then it's my job to introduce Professor Karl to the club. He proves to be a particularly entertaining speaker and we depart for home at the end of the evening having enjoyed some excellent Rotary fellowship.

As I drive home, I think about how the professor described the behaviour of undergraduates at Oxford these days. I made up my mind to have a long father-to-daughter talk with Betty as soon as possible.

\*   \*   \*

My first opportunity to speak with Betty at length occurs after dinner on Sunday evening. My wife asks me to postpone my talk, however, because Betty's first "A" level examination starts at 9.00am tomorrow morning. When I insist, she pleads with me to go gently and not antagonise our daughter in any way. I don't believe my fatherly talk, given in Betty's best interests, will upset her and I arrange for Betty to join me in the lounge in half an hour after she has finished helping with the washing up. I pour myself a port and settle down with the paper to await Betty's appearance.

I must have nodded off because the next thing I remember is a voice gradually getting louder.

'Dad...dad...wake up dad... you wanted to talk to me...'

'Oh, hello dear, sorry about that. A good meal and a port can be so relaxing.'

'So, I see,' she observes.

My daughter is perching on the edge of an armchair opposite and looking at me inquiringly.

'Now, make yourself comfortable because I want to give you some fatherly advice about Oxford where you'll be going in about four weeks.'

'I'm so excited about going to Oxford dad, but I'm not there yet. I have three vital exams over the next five days that I have to excel in!'

'Well, I have complete confidence in you, dear. I'm sure you'll do brilliantly.'

'Thanks, dad.'

'At Rotary on Thursday night, I sat next to a Professor of Physics from Oxford. He was our guest speaker.'

'How exciting! I wish I'd been there.'

'Yes, I agree. He was an excellent speaker too.'

'What did he speak about?'

'His physics research. The subject of his talk is not what I want to talk to you about, though. I had a rather alarming private discussion with him about students at Oxford University these days. What he had to say was quite horrifying. Apparently, a large percentage of students nowadays get involved in smoking, excessive drinking, promiscuous behaviour and even drugs. There was some of this sinful sort of behaviour happening when I was at university twenty-five years ago, but today, apparently, it's rampant.'

I wait for an appropriately shocked reaction from Betty, but she just sits there waiting for me to continue. I had expected her to register surprise or concern or even disgust.

'Your mother and I have brought you up as a devout Christian girl, so we know you will reject these abominations. However, when you see some of your colleagues succumbing to the ways of the devil you may occasionally be tempted. The purpose of this little talk is to forewarn you. Universities are wonderful places of academic learning; sadly, they can also be places of evil doings and debauchery.'

Betty's looking at me now with a slither of a smile, but still offers no comment. Have I not got through to her? Does she not believe me? Have I not made myself clear? Most oddly, why hasn't she reacted? So, I wait patiently until finally she feels obliged to say something just to break the silence.

'Thanks dad.'

Is this all she can say? Her whole time at university could be ruined if she falls into these unfortunate ways. It could even spell the end of a potentially brilliant career as a leading scientist. Perhaps she's naïve? Think of the shame on our family if she goes away as a God-fearing lass, but ends up rejecting her fine Christian up-bringing.

'Well, dear, I hope you'll go away and think prayerfully about what I have spoken to you about tonight?'

'Yes, of course, dad.'

Without another word Betty leaves the room and goes upstairs. I'm given to thinking it has, perhaps, been a bit too much for her to take in. I hope I haven't discouraged her from going to university by painting such a bleak picture. As with my patients, I always insist on telling them the truth. There's no point in sugar-coating disquieting news. Betty needs to know what to expect at Oxford University and now she's more aware and better prepared. I hope Betty will thank me one day for my fatherly advice.

# 23.

# Malcolm

I have spent Sunday morning in the college library completing background reading for my next history assignment. I enjoy the hushed atmosphere of respect for books and learning that emanates from good libraries. Culham's library is not in the same league as the libraries of the great learning institutions of the world, nevertheless, it's a place for serious, scholarly reflection. Thick carpeted floors muffle the sound of footsteps and any talking is restricted to the occasional quiet respectful whisper. Anyone who dares to shatter the peace with a loud sneeze or an exaggerated cough immediately attracts disapproving stares and is made to regret their thoughtless action.

It's a quarter past twelve, time for me to grab some lunch before catching the bus to West Dryton. Closing my books quietly, I pad over to the history section and after checking the Dewey numbers on the spines, return my borrowed books to their rightful places on the shelves. Smiling at the only attractive female librarian on duty, I pick up my satchel and leave the building, heading for the Dining Room.

After collecting my main course and dessert I sit down with a few of my football team mates. Somehow, they have heard I'm off to visit my girlfriend this afternoon. I don't remember saying anything about this; it must have been Michael who told them. I have to endure a bit of ribbing, mostly good-natured stuff, although a couple of the rougher characters in the group can't resist making uncalled for crude comments. I do my best to ignore them. As soon as I'm finished, I return to my study, spruce up a bit and carefully pocket the few precious coins Lucy gave me. The bus to Oxford, travelling via West Dryton, is on time and I grab a window seat.

As we chug along country roads, passing through a handful of small villages, I wonder what, if anything, Lucy has got planned for the afternoon. Once again, I feel the frustration of being virtually destitute and without the wherewithal to take Lucy out anywhere. Most girls, knowing the dire situation I'm in financially, would have dropped me by now which only goes to show what a terrific person Lucy is. But, how long can I expect her stay with me? At any moment some other guy is going to come sailing along with enough money to take her out, blessed with a car perhaps and leave me for dead. It's just not fair! Lucy's a lovely girl, faithful to me for the time being, but surely it can't last.

West Dryton is an attractive village snuggled comfortably into the valley of the Thame River. The twisting main street consists of a jumble of small family businesses, some of which may have been there since the village first materialised in the sixteenth century. There's a small general store, a butcher, a green grocer, a bakery and a couple of men's and lady's outfitters. There was a sweet shop but it has now reinvented itself as a small gift shop to tempt the increasing number of tourists. There is, of course, a Lloyd's Bank, a Post Office, a couple of pubs, a garage, a cafe and the Anglican church up on one hill and the Catholic church atop another. The village green is just off the main street, a verdant area surrounded by ancient chestnuts and oaks. The bus pulls up at the West Dryton bus stop and my pulse quickens; Lucy is there looking so pretty and waving enthusiastically.

I help an elderly lady with her three bulky shopping bags down the steps and next moment I'm in Lucy's arms. I love the lithe firmness of her body, no doubt the result of her sporty interests. We kiss briefly on the lips and hold hands. I couldn't ask for a more lovely welcome.

'So, what are we doing, Lucy?'

'Well, it's good and bad, I suppose. I hope you won't mind but my brothers have been insisting all week they want you to join them for a game of monopoly. They've set it all up. Perhaps we can play for an hour or so and then go for a walk? What do you think?'

'Okay by me. I'll be going flat out for Mayfair and Park Lane, nothing but the best investments with piles of hotels. It will be exciting to handle all that money even if it is fake.'

Lucy laughs. 'Seriously, it must be awful, Malcolm, trying to make ends meet. I feel so sorry for you. I get a little pocket money each week. Not much because mum can't afford it. I have a bit saved up if it would help you to have some?'

'That's very sweet of you but I would prefer to try and muddle along on my own as best I can. I don't buy stuff at the college shop, unlike most of my fellow students. I stay away from shops so I'm not tempted to spend money that I don't have. And...good news, I've just landed a casual job working at a Schweppes bottle factory at the end of this semester.'

We are nearing Lucy's house now and she gives my hand an extra squeeze. 'Thanks for agreeing to play monopoly with the boys.'

Mrs. Hardvale greets me warmly at the front door. Before long we are enjoying the cut and thrust of buying and selling properties, paying fines, winning beauty competitions and collecting two hundred pounds for passing "Go". True to form, I manage to purchase Park Lane and Mayfair and start adding houses and a hotel, but somehow, most inconsiderately, everyone avoids landing on my top-notch properties.

Monopoly usually goes on for hours. However, Lucy and I had negotiated with the boys before we started, that whoever had the most money and properties at the end of an hour would be proclaimed the winner. And that person was me!

\* \* \*

Once again, we are fortunate with the weather when Lucy and I leave for our walk. This time she heads in the opposite direction from "Lover's Way" and we enter a beautifully wooded area providing dappled shade and a path that winds slowly uphill. Nature is at its best in these wooded landscapes. There's a scattering of mushrooms and other indeterminate fungi while several grey squirrels cavort about in the upper branches. The air is crisp and cool. I can't believe I'm walking through such a magic place with a girl I've well and truly fallen for.

Lucy tells me she has a secret place in the woods that she sometimes escapes to if in need of a break from her family. We walk on, stepping carefully, to avoid slippery tree roots and muddy patches. It's quiet, except for the occasional bird song and our slightly laboured breathing. Lucy is a few feet in front of me and I long to stop and take her in my arms. A few times she glances back to see if I'm still following. The track is too narrow to hold hands and walk side by side.

After about ten minutes we emerge from the woods and make our way gingerly around some massive rounded boulders. These are well eroded granite tors standing powerfully against the elements and forming bizarre shapes. Without another word Lucy takes my hand and leads me on between the boulders until we happen upon a grassy area almost totally surrounded by rocks and forming a sort of private enclosed garden. There are daisies and buttercups flourishing here amongst the lush clover and well protected from the winds. As we enter this little wonderland, we surprise a rabbit that takes off in alarm flashing its white tail. *This* is Lucy's secret garden.

Lucy makes herself comfortable leaning back against a large flat-sided tor warmed by the sun and invites me to join her. We sit close together like two peas in a pod holding hands and overawed by the beauty of this special place.

'What do you think of my secret hideaway, Malcolm?'

'It's a lovely place. I can't believe I'm sitting here next to such a beautiful girl. Who needs money when you can share special places like this with someone you...?'

'Go on, finish the sentence.'

I know I've already said too much. Embarrassed, I look down at my feet. How could I have been so stupid.

'Malcolm, you must finish your sentence.'

Lucy moves suddenly so that she is kneeling and facing me full on, her hands on my thighs.

'Come on, what were you going to say?' she teases.

I can't help myself. Clumsily, I scramble up and reach out for Lucy, but my weight and quick uncontrolled movement surprises her and she topples over onto her back pulling me on top of her like a sack of potatoes. We burst out laughing and awkwardly disentangle ourselves until we are lying more comfortably side by side on the springy grass. Still giggling, Lucy rolls on to her side so she's facing me.

'I think we can do better than that,' she challenges.

No need for any more talking; I lean over and we kiss. Lucy's skin is smooth and inviting and I start kissing her around her face, neck and ears. She is so responsive, so giving, so wanting. My hand starts to roam over her neat firm body and then I come to her breasts. Feeling Lucy's breasts through her dress and bra is frustrating and I start fumbling with her buttons. Lucy's hand comes up and she gently opens up her blouse revealing a pretty pink bra. Then she sits up and unsnaps her bra letting it slip slowly down. I stare for a moment unable to believe how beautiful she is, before she takes my hand and places it where it's desperate to go. She lies down and allows my hand to lovingly fondle her breasts all the while watching my face with her lovely eyes.

This is it. This is where I'm going to lose my virginity in the arms of a sweet and willing virgin. We are lying together in a safe and lovely wild garden hungry to explore each other's bodies. Lucy's hand is groping around my waist trying to unbuckle my belt. I'm as hard as a rock.

Suddenly, I stop and sit up.

'What's the matter Malcolm? Come on... Don't you want me?'

'Oh Lucy, I'm so sorry. Yes, of course I want you! I'm in love with you! I just don't know if this is the right time and place for us to make love for the very first time?'

Lucy sits up and starts scrambling around for her bra. She doesn't say anything and I don't know how she's reacting. I go to embrace her to apologise again but she pushes me away, angrily. Now she stands and hurriedly does up her blouse buttons. Our beautifully intimate time together is shattered.

'Why?' she demands, 'what's wrong with you?'

'I want our first love-making to be special, out of this world, spiritual if you like. I've never slept with a girl before and I don't want to until it's the right girl at the right time and in the right place. I know that sounds terribly old-fashioned and probably stupid but I can't help how I feel.'

Lucy looks at me intensely, searching my face to see if I'm telling the truth. Then she takes both my hands and with a wan smile says, 'It's all right Malcolm. I respect your feelings. You're probably right. Now I'm feeling like a slut for bringing you up here and leading you on.'

'Don't. Please don't feel that way Lucy. I desperately wanted to make love too but something just clicked and made me stop before it was too late. I'm not religious or anything. I suppose giving myself to someone, heart and soul, is very special and I want it to happen in the most perfect way possible. It's as if it's something sacred to be treasured until the right time.'

'Malcolm, what you've just said is beautiful and uplifting and

I do admire you for it. I'm not sure I'm worthy of you after my inexcusably loose behaviour. Please forgive me? You are absolutely right. Giving ourselves to someone isn't just for sex it should be much more than that. But I *do* love you, Malcolm. I suppose that's why I felt it was okay to bring you here. This is a special place for me that I've treasured ever since I lost my dad. I've never brought anyone else here. Honestly...'

Lucy's words move me deeply. I take her in my arms and we stay locked together for several minutes enjoying the warmth and closeness. Then we walk slowly back down the winding track to the bus stop in a sort of a trance. What has happened this afternoon already seems unreal.

Lucy sees me off tenderly at the bus stop and presses half a crown into my hand from her pocket money to pay for my bus fare next Sunday. We kiss and I'm on my way.

# 24.

.......

# Dorothy

This afternoon the four young ones enjoyed their game of monopoly; after a slow start there was much hilarity and fun. Thankfully, Rodney and Derek were on their best behaviour. I provided lemonade and fruit cake for everyone mid-afternoon and stayed for a few minutes to watch. I couldn't help noticing the furtive looks, winks and smiles that passed between Lucy and Malcolm. Clearly, in the space of a few weeks, they have fallen for each other. Is it just a teenage crush for Lucy or is this more? I think it's getting serious. After an hour of monopoly, Lucy and Malcolm are desperate to get out of the house to have time together. I wonder where they are going for their walk?

Lucy returns two hours later looking strangely flushed and in a peculiar mood. I have a sudden panic attack that she and Malcolm may have done more than just kiss and hold hands. I guess I must expect this now that she's almost eighteen and young Malcolm a grown man of nineteen or twenty. I remember being head over heels in love with Tom at the age of eighteen and we slept together several times before getting married. It's amazing what you can manage in the back of a car when there's nowhere else.

Young Malcolm is a delight and I'm fond of him already. If he's the man for Lucy, I'll be more than happy. He seems calm, mature and level-headed and a teaching career is a safe secure occupation, although I have heard the pay is ridiculously low. Like nursing, teaching is considered to be a "calling," or a "vocation". Those that enter the caring professions do so because they love what they do. There's a general consensus in this country that those that work in the vocations derive so much satisfaction and reward from their work that they can get by on the smell of an oily rag. I'm not sure that's fair; everyone deserves a decent wage. In my view, they're being exploited.

Lucy sat her first "A" level last week and felt she did "okay." The other two exams are this week. She has been doing some studying, although not as much as I would have liked. I'm glad though she seems to be taking her exams in her stride, because I've heard of girls at St Anne's who have buckled under the extreme pressure. Betty, Lucy's best friend, appears to be relishing her exams but she's brilliant and surely bound for Oxford.

'Lucy, darling, can you spare a few minutes to help me in the kitchen please?'

'What do you need doing, mum?'

'Those spuds need washing and peeling please. Better do at least five of them as we all have healthy appetites. How was your walk?'

'Good thanks.'

'Where did you go?'

'Oh, just walking around the village...'

'For two hours?'

'We were chatting.'

'You two seem to be getting into quite a serious relationship?'

'Yes, I suppose so.'

I feel I must warn Lucy about what may happen and the dangers of an unwanted pregnancy. I should, perhaps, have talked to her about this earlier but the right time never seemed to come round. I decide I must broach the subject now.

'Darling, a kiss and a cuddle is fine but you do realise that things can suddenly escalate and get out of hand, don't you?'

'Yes, mum,' she replies, in a condescending tone of voice.

'I've never spoken to you before about contraception. There are ways to prevent anything happening, you know.'

'Mum, you don't have to give me a lecture. Malcolm and I are virgins and we plan to stay that way.'

'I'm pleased to hear that dear, but men can be very persuasive you know. You should be prepared for anything to happen.'

'Thanks, mum. Anything else you want me to do in the kitchen?'

'I'm only trying to be helpful dear. I was in the same situation as you myself once, remember?'

Lucy looks at me with increased interest. 'Did *you* wait until you were married, mum?'

I've never been good at hiding the truth and I feel myself blushing heavily. Lucy senses my embarrassment and presses me.

'Come on, be honest with me mum. Did you do anything with any of your boyfriends before you got married?'

There's no escape, I'm trapped.

'It was war time, darling. Things were different then.'

'Come on, tell me the truth, mum.'

'Well, I did sleep with your father a few times before we married.'

'Any others?'

'Yes, there was one other but it was only once. He was killed.'

This stops Lucy in her tracks and she pauses for a moment. 'That's really sad,' she remarks. Then, without another word, she exits the kitchen and races upstairs to her bedroom.

My attempt to give Lucy some sound advice about contraception is a disaster. Somehow, she has managed to turn the topic around and get *me* to confess to something I've never told anyone before.

\*   \*   \*

Next morning, after the children have left for school, Glenis Brindleton telephones. She invites me to join her for a morning coffee at her home. It will, Glenis suggests, be a chance for us mothers of children currently sitting "A" levels to de-brief and unwind. Glenis and I have occasionally met for a coffee ever since the time our girls started at St Anne's six years ago. We are not close friends; I find her strong faith and conservative attitudes somewhat overwhelming, but nevertheless, I do enjoy catching up from time to time.

The Brindletons are well off and arriving at their lovely home reminds me how my children and I might have been living today, if Tom hadn't left us. Tom was earning an excellent salary as a nuclear physicist at Harwell Research Station all those years ago and was, I'm sure, destined for the top echelons of the British nuclear industry. It's only when I visit the homes of people such as the Brindletons that I feel envious for what might have been.

Glenis is as welcoming as always and before long we are sitting in her loggia at the back of the house looking out on the expansive back garden. They have an excellent grass tennis court (no ugly netting surrounding it), a variety of rhododendrons and camelias that obscure the tall perimeter fence and a sunken rose garden immediately in front of us. In the centre of the rose garden, on a marble plinth, is a life-sized statue of a naked Eros. I have to admit Eros, the Greek goddess of love, looks stunning. At the far end of the garden are several mature leafy deciduous trees. The Brindletons can afford to pay a full-time gardener to maintain their little bit of heaven.

Glenis busies herself with serving the beverages then moves from general polite chit-chat to her main reason for inviting me to her house.

'Well, my dear, how are you handling the "A" level jitters?'

I avail myself of a couple of the delicate cucumber sandwiches Glenis is offering before I answer.

'No problems really, Lucy seems to be taking it all in her stride. But of course, it's not essential for her to excel because she's not trying to go on to a university. How's Betty managing?'

'Well, I think. She's been happy with the papers so far. We've had boyfriend problems though. Betty seems to have a silly teenage crush for this Michael lad. He's been over to your place for dinner, Dorothy. What did you think of him?'

'Very pleasant lad, well-mannered and he even came out to help with the dishes.'

'Oh really? Well David won't have him in the house. He took an instant dislike to him and has ordered Betty never to see him again.'

'That sounds a bit drastic. Why?'

'Well, you know what David's like. Apparently, Michael's not a church-goer and freely admits he's a non-believer. That's like waving a red rag in front of my husband.'

'At least he's honest, Glenis. What did *you* think of him?'

'Like you, I found him to be a nice enough lad. However, we have tried to bring Betty up as a good Christian girl and we want her to find a boy with the same strong faith. Preferably Catholic, but we would have no objection to a good Anglican.'

'How do you feel about Betty going on to Oxford? She'll meet all sorts there and you won't be able to keep a close eye on her?'

'Yes, we realise that. We are praying that her strong faith will guide her and steer her away from any undesirables.'

'Is Betty still planning to become a physicist?'

'Very much so, Dorothy dear. In fact, she has decided she wants to become a *nuclear* physicist. There is so much happening in the world of nuclear energy nowadays. Just this last year two more nuclear power stations have opened up in Scotland, Britain has begun building its first nuclear submarine, HMS Dreadnought and the Americans have launched the world's first nuclear powered submarine called the USS Scorpion. Even the French are getting in on the act exploding massive atomic bombs in Africa somewhere.'

'It's truly amazing what scientists are achieving these days. I sometimes wonder what Tom would be doing now if had he not disappeared.'

'Of course, Dorothy dear. I had forgotten he was a nuclear physicist. It's so sad that he left you.'

'Yes, I often wonder what has happened to my Tom.'

'Of course, being in the nuclear industry has its dangers too. Apart from handling uranium and everything else, you can get caught up in spying. Did you hear they've just released Klaus Fuchs?'

'No, remind me, who was he?'

'Fuchs was arrested back in 1950 on espionage charges. He was found guilty of passing our nuclear secrets to the Soviet Union. He was given fourteen years, but released in June this year, for good behaviour, after serving only nine.'

Yes, I remember now. It was about the same time my Tom disappeared. Fuchs was German, but had been naturalised as a British citizen. Rotten traitor!'

'And then of course, nuclear physicists have to put up with these crazy campaigners for nuclear disarmament. There were 20,000 of them demonstrating in Trafalgar Square recently!'

'Why doesn't Betty think about using her scientific gifts in some other field of exploration or research?'

'What did you have in mind, dear?'

'Space perhaps? The space race is really thrilling. Every few months something new is achieved. What about those two monkeys the Americans sent into space this year and brought back safe and well?'

'Yes, wasn't that great. What were their names again?'

'Miss Able and Miss Baker.'

'Of course.'

'Another great British invention this year is Christopher Cockerell's Hovercraft. It hovered all the way across the English Channel in around two hours. Could Betty get interested in that sort of thing?'

'I doubt it. I think her mind's made up. Nuclear physics is where she's headed. We already have her booked in to one of the five "women only" colleges at Oxford.'

'Well Glenis, I wish her the very best of luck. She's worked so hard; she deserves all the rewards studying at Oxford can give her.'

'Thank you, Dorothy, dear. And I do hope Lucy gets to secretarial college and does really well.'

# 25.

# Betty

Oxford University, here I come! I'm waiting for mum to pick me up from school having just come out of mathematics B, the last of my "A" level papers. My friends think I'm mad but I actually love doing exams. I feel it's a contest between me and the examiners and I love such challenges. I'm hoping to score almost 100% on this last paper, although I didn't have quite enough time to double check all my answers. Most of my fellow "A" level mathematics friends have been milling around me asking what the answers were to some of the questions and or what the correct formula was for question four. I'm the person they come to for help. I'm happy to assist as much as possible, although it's too late now. The "A" level results are expected to be released in a fortnight's time and I can't wait to hear how I've fared.

I can see mum parking the car in a vacant spot down the street. Grabbing my bag, I start making my way down to meet her. She's delighted to hear I loved my final "A" level paper and suggests we go down to "The Copper Kettle" to celebrate the end of exams. Mum loves this rather snobby place and meets her friends here from time to time. I just hope she's not going to embarrass me by saying silly things about me in front of whoever else happens to be there. Mum's in an expansive mood and with a generous smile, ushers me in through the front door with its jingling bell announcing our arrival. We wait a couple of minutes to be seated. A pretty lass, who left St Anne's a couple of years ago, welcomes us and seats us by the window. Apparently, mum had pre-booked this spot.

Mr. and Mrs. Chadwick, joint owners of "The Copper Kettle" have a nice little business going. The café consists of two seventeenth century houses with the wall between them knocked out to provide a large enough space to squeeze in about fifteen tables. Each table is covered with a delicate table-cloth, a small posy of fresh flowers in the centre, side plates, napkins and mats placed in readiness for the anticipated tea-pot and its clutch of cups and saucers. The walls are decorated with water-colours depicting quaint thatched cottages in romantic English gardens full of lupins, holly-hocks, roses, forget-me-nots and snap dragons. It's all very cute. Mum orders a full afternoon tea for two, which will materialise as freshly baked date scones with strawberry jam and full cream followed by a generous selection of English tea cakes.

I tell mum about the mathematics B exam paper for a few minutes, although most of what I'm saying is double-Dutch to her and her eyes soon glaze over. Enough said. The pretty girl returns, wearing a dainty apron covered in colourful fruits, a dimply smile and carrying a tray containing everything we need for mum to dispense the cups of tea. Mum asks a surprising question.

'Betty dear, I was talking to Father Thomas yesterday in the vestry, and he asked me a question about you that I didn't know how to answer.'

'Really, mum. What was it?'

'He asked me where you stand in the faith versus science dichotomy?'

'And what exactly did he mean by that?'

'Well, he tried to explain it to me. He thinks there are two possibilities with regard to what you might believe in. I have to confess, I'm not going to be very good at explaining them to you.'

'Perhaps it would have been more sensible if Father Thomas had spoken directly to me, rather than asking you what *you* think I believe?'

'Quite so, dear. Perhaps he'll ask you after mass next Sunday. At least you will now be forewarned. What I think Father was getting at was that some people think everything in this world can only be explained by a belief in the almighty. Only God could have created the universe and all that's within it. Then there are others, the non-believers, who subscribe to the notion that science will eventually explain everything in the universe and how it has been created. I think Father Thomas was interested to know whether you believe God created everything or whether you are so enamoured with science that you believe a complete understanding of science is enough to eventually explain our existence within the universe.'

'Whew mum, that's a bit heavy, isn't it?' I slosh a generous spoonful of cream and jam on the still warm scone sitting temptingly in front of me, while I think how best to answer. Mum sips her tea, watching me carefully.

'I reckon there's a middle path, mum. It doesn't have to be faith *or* science; it can be faith *and* science. Science will never explain everything, so there's a powerful argument for believing in some other super natural being as well. Does that make sense to you?'

'I think I understand, dear. I'll try to explain your views to Father Thomas. Now, do have another scone before I eat the lot.'

\* \* \*

It's Wednesday evening, my exams are finished and tonight Michael is driving over to be with me at three o'clock in the morning. I'm doing my best to contain my excitement and behave normally. The dishes are washed and dried and I even helped put everything away. Dad asked how well my last exam went and positively bristled with pride when I told him I think I might have scored 100%. I'm also relieved Mum didn't mention our tete-a-tete at "The Copper Kettle" to dad, who, if he had heard my response, would want to give me another lecture. I'm retiring to bed early in the hope I'll get some decent sleep before Michael's arrival. My alarm clock is set for ten to three and placed under a cushion to muffle the sound.

I must have fallen asleep soundly because the buzzing of my alarm clock barely penetrates my hearing. Floundering about on the floor, I press down the alarm button on top of the clock and switch on my bedside light. It's five to three. I pull on my slippers and winter dressing gown and leaving my warm bed unmade, tiptoe to the door and ease it open slowly. I pause there for a moment, listening intently for any signs of life. It seems my parents are sound asleep. We are fortunate not to have squeaky floorboards like many other older houses and I make it safely to the top of the stairs. Still no sounds, so I continue my journey down the stairs and along the narrow passage way that leads to the back-door. I'm conscious of my heart pounding like a hammer in my chest as I carefully ease the back-door open.

A blast of cold air hits me as I close the heavy door behind me. I feel safer outside the house in our large back garden bathed in the eerie light of a waning gibbous moon. Choosing the grass verge, rather than the noisy gravel path, I skip quickly round the side of the house and make my way through the bushes to the gate at the front of our place. So far, so good, I have escaped without any problems. Now comes the trickier part; getting Michael to be as quiet as me as we make our way up to my bedroom.

He's there, anxiously pulling on a cigarette which he flicks into the gutter as soon as he sees me. We embrace and he gives me a smoky kiss. Yuk! I don't like the taste of a cigarette mouth. He feels cold so I grab his hand and lead him back through the garden the same way I came. We're startled by an animal that hurtles across our path and disappears into the nether regions of the garden. 'A cat?' mouths Michael. We continue to make our way quietly through the back door, along the passage, up the stairs and safely into my bedroom. Then with a relieved, controlled giggle, we embrace again and this time linger over our kiss.

Michael and I have never talked about sex but I'm up for it, if he is. I feel like being irresponsible and throwing caution to the wind now that my exams are out of the way and I'm confident my marks will get me to Oxford. Besides, the stories I've heard about what students get up to at Oxford encourages me to do some sexual exploring before I go there. I'm sure Michael has never been with a girl before, so it will be fun to experiment together. I turn on my light and the radiator to warm the room up a bit and look at the young man I'm going to invite to take away my virginity. Is he, I wonder, thinking the same as me?

I haven't thought through my moves with Michael. The heroines in the few films I've seen are sometimes the instigators of romantic scenes, so I reckon it will be okay for me to initiate something. I know precious little about sex and intercourse. Mum has never discussed sex with me, and I've never asked her anything that might embarrass her. Apart from a couple of useless "talks" at St Anne's and a couple of lessons on the "reproductive system" in biology, I'm totally ignorant. Of course, my Christian upbringing has made it abundantly clear "fornication" is a cardinal sin. Everybody at school regards me as the perfect student, always polite and well behaved, conscientious to the extreme and a high achiever. Well, this can be my little secret...

Michael is wandering around my bedroom intrigued by my wall posters, the collection of dolls and the feminine knick knacks on the dressing table. He's making silly faces at me as he expresses surprise at certain items he picks up. I'm not sure whether he's making fun of me. It's time to try some seduction.

I sit on my bed and invite Michael to join me. He's hesitant to do so, and appears embarrassed but with my gentle encouragement plonks himself down next to me. We're not touching so I put out my hand and find his. Darkness might help and I switch off my bedroom light and rely on the two glowing red bars of my radiator to provide sufficient light to see what we are doing. The warm glow makes my bedroom look romantic.

'Do you like my bedroom?' I whisper.

'Yeah, it's pretty,' he replies.

'Would you like to kiss me properly, Michael?'

Michael turns towards me but I can't interpret the strange look on his face. Is he shocked at my forwardness? Is he unsure how to respond? Is he going to turn me down? Is he scared?

'Michael?' I gently stroke his cheek and feel the roughness of his unshaven face. He's still looking at me, seemingly undecided. He needs more encouragement. Taking his hand, I bring it up to my breast to feel the softness of me. Suddenly he responds. Clumsily, he jumps on top of me flattening me against the bed while his hands start roving all over my body. I've lit a fire and now I need to control it somehow.

'Wait a minute, Michael. Wait, let's do this...'

'Get your gear off. Come on, hurry...'

He jumps off the bed and is frantically trying to unbutton his flies. I sit up wondering if it matters to him in this sudden urgency whether or not I remove my nightie. Now Michael is struggling to undo his belt to drop his trousers.

From nowhere there's an almighty crash of thunder that sounds as if it's immediately above our house. It freezes us both. Next, I hear my panicky mother calling out at the top of her voice.

'Are you alright Betty, dear? Are you alright?'

'She's coming in, Michael. Quick, get under the bed, hurry.'

Michael doesn't need a second warning. With his trousers down around his ankles, he gives them a frantic hoist and scrambles under the bed. I have just enough time to pull up my blankets and feign sleep as my mother bursts into my room without bothering to knock and switches on the light.

'Oh Betty, what an awful clap of thunder!'

Whatever mum says next is inaudible because a second thunder clap, almost as loud as the first, shakes the house. Mum runs over to my bed and embraces me. I think she's more scared than I am.

'Good heaven's dear, your nightie's wide open and your heater's on! Are you cold?'

'No, mum, I'm fine thanks.'

'What an awful storm. The BBC weather forecast said to expect storms tonight but it came so suddenly!'

'I'm not a baby mum; you don't have to worry about me. I can cope with storms.'

'Can you darling? Storms don't worry you father either. Once a mother, always a mother, I'm so sorry to...' The rest of the sentence is again lost as a third crash of thunder surrounds us.

'I think I can smell cigarette smoke. You haven't started smoking have you Betty?'

'Of course, not mum. You're imagining it. Now you'd better go back to dad.'

'Yes, I suppose so. He'll never get back to sleep now, he's such a light sleeper.' She bends over and gives me a motherly kiss. 'See you in the morning then.'

'Sure mum. Goodnight.'

She moves across the floor to turn off my heater, then leaves the room after turning the light off.

Now the rain is cascading down so it's difficult to hear anything else. Michael crawls out from under my bed, still fumbling to pull up his trousers and fix his flies. He's clearly shaken by what has just happened and how close we were to being caught. He wants to leave.

'Thank God you didn't leave any clothes lying about that mum could have seen,' I whisper, as a few minutes later we make the precarious journey back down the stairs and along the passage to the back door. We have a quick kiss and he disappears out into the rain. A moment later, I'm tucked up warmly in bed, wondering what things might have been like had mother nature not been so uncooperative.

# PART 2
## (1963)

# 26.

# Glenis Brindleton

I'm so proud of my daughter! Betty began her Bachelor of Science degree at Oxford University, as she had always planned, and has sailed through her subjects. She was awarded two university medals at graduation; one for the most outstanding female student and a second one for physics. The annual Hamilton-Rose prize for physics is given to the student achieving the highest-grade point average in physics during their three years of undergraduate study. Betty consistently recorded distinctions or high distinctions in every subject. We always thought she was clever but now she has been recognised by none other than Oxford University as being brilliant. So brilliant, in fact, that following an extra honours year she has been immediately enrolled to commence her doctoral studies. Oxford, it seems, is desperate not to lose her extraordinary talents.

My husband, David, is less enthusiastic about Betty's successes than I am. Whereas, he's delighted with her academic achievements, he's highly critical of her lapsed Catholicism. Betty has made no effort to conceal her change of heart and, if challenged by David, will happily argue with him about her reasons for rejecting the institution of the Roman Catholic church. It hurts me awfully to hear them arguing and I do my best to defuse these situations. Whenever Betty comes home nowadays, I try to organise things in such a way that they don't have time together. At the moment it seems to be working. When matters were at their nadir, David even threatened to never allow Betty to live under our roof again.

There's another complication too. Over the years, Betty has kept up some sort of a relationship with Michael Brain, the teacher trainee David banned from our house four years ago, ostensibly because he denied having any Christian affiliation. Betty rarely divulges information about her university boyfriends but I know she has had several during her four undergraduate years. No boyfriends have ever been brought home, however, and when I ask why, I always get the same answer, 'Dad wouldn't approve of them.' I find this so sad; David's dogmatism is isolating us.

I'm definitely broader minded than David. To be honest, knowing the people my daughter is mixing with is far more important than whether or not they hold the same set of values as we do. It would be a dull old world if we all thought and believed exactly the same things. Variety is, supposedly, the spice of life. Personally, I'd welcome Betty's friends to our home but I know this would lead to a major falling out with David. Who knows where his anger might take him? Separation, or even divorce, could eventuate. I still love my husband in many ways and I don't want to end up in such an awful scenario.

Betty has been advised her doctoral studies are likely to occupy at least three more years of her young life. So far, David has been prepared to continue to support her financially. Betty won a scholarship to Oxford, which covered most of her accommodation and tuition fees during her undergraduate years. We only needed to top up her finances to provide sufficient money for her to spend on personal items and socialising. Now she's embarking on further studies, Betty will need additional financial support. So far, David hasn't baulked and is still supporting her with some spending money but I'm worried if the two of them get into more arguments, he will change his mind. I'm doing my best to keep things moving along smoothly, although David has occasionally grumbled about having to continue to support a daughter who has disappointed him in so many ways.

Betty comes home every few weeks and usually stays for a couple of nights only; I think she's fearful of having another major blow up with David. Perhaps wisely, she doesn't want to overstay her welcome, although I'd love her to stay much longer. Last time she was with us she confided in me that she had taken a part time job as a waitress at an Oxford restaurant three evenings a week. 'Surety mum, in case dad stops paying for my extras.' Probably, a sensible move.

I'm increasingly concerned about my husband's health; he's become more tense and stressed recently. I fear David is heading towards a nervous breakdown due to overwork and an inability to relax. I have tried, unsuccessfully, to get him to take some holidays. Several times I've selected a quiet guest house in the country or at a seaside resort and have even offered to do all the bookings, the packing and the driving. All he has to do is say "Yes." But he never does. He's quick to find fault nowadays and becomes irate about the silliest things. One day he'll complain the toast is not dark enough, another day he doesn't like what I'm wearing or the house is too hot, too cold, or too drafty when he gets home. Talk about walking on eggshells!

One positive is my increasingly close friendship with Dorothy Hardvale. You might expect us to have drifted apart once our girls graduated from St Anne's back in 1959 and went their separate ways, however, the opposite has happened. I guess we are both lonely in different ways. Dorothy has never fully recovered from the loss of her husband in such a cruel way; and I mourn the loss of a husband that I once had but now seldom recognise.

I have to admit, we two women get together from time to time when we are feeling down and crack open a bottle of decent wine and get quietly pissed. It's amazing how cathartic this feels. We share our problems unashamedly, as our inhibitions evaporate. This weekend, David will be away at a medical conference in Colchester. Apparently, if he wishes to continue practising as a GP, he must do a refresher course every year. What better opportunity for Dorothy and I to get together for one of our "nights." She'll be coming round for dinner at six and will stay the night to recover. Two of Dorothy's children have already flown the nest and her youngest, Derek, is sleeping over at a friend's place so she doesn't have to worry about being away for a night on the booze.

*   *   *

It's July and we have been enjoying a spell of delightfully warm weather. On a couple of days, it has even clocked 100 degrees Fahrenheit, which is considered a heatwave in England. What a contrast to earlier in the year when we suffered a vicious winter. We had four months of bitterly cold weather. There was snow on the ground until April and around Kent the sea actually froze over. For many weeks lakes, ponds and canals were so deeply frozen that huge numbers of people enjoyed ice skating. Even some of our waterfalls froze!

Dorothy and I are relaxing in the shady part of the garden enjoying a cheese platter and a glass of white wine. It's peaceful here, no sounds of the incessant traffic out on the main road just the cheerful chirping of our feathery friends. A robin with a handsome red breast lands on the edge of the birdbath and looks at us curiously. 'Perhaps he wants some wine?' Dorothy suggests. The robin's response is to suddenly dive into the water and start a frantic washing routine that empties out half the water. When its ablutions are finished there's much shaking of its feathers before it takes off and disappears into the branches of a golden ash.

We chat about some of the events of the year. The last time we had done anything together we went to the cinema to see Cliff Richard in the musical "Summer Holiday." We are still young enough to swoon over his good looks and smooth voice. But there's a new musical sensation in Britain, a group out of Liverpool called "The Beatles." Their debut album, "Please, Please Me" was released in March and has been a huge success. A few weeks ago, the Beatles hit number one on the British charts for the first time with their single, "From Me to You." This new group of four young lads looks destined for a great future.

Next, we discuss politics. We're both from a similar political background, conservative. Usually, we agree on political matters. A couple of fascinating events in the last few weeks has had everybody's tongues wagging though. The first is the Profumo Affair.

'What do you make of this Profumo business, Glenis?'

'Oh, it's awful. Profumo's the Secretary of State for War for heaven's sake, yet he's been sleeping with this Christine Keeler. I know he's denied any wrong doing in the House of Commons but the recent police investigation has shown he was lying. He's guilty alright!

'Yes, this Keeler girl is a real tart. Apparently, she was previously a topless show girl at a night club in Soho and has been sleeping around all over the place. And...she was a centre page nude in the Tit Bits magazine.'

'Worse than that, she was friends with this Russian fellow, Ivanov. Have you heard about him?'

'A little bit, but tell me more...'

'Well...Captain Ivanov is a Russian, who, at the time Profumo was having an affair with Keeler was working as the Soviet Naval attaché in the Russian Embassy in London. He was definitely a Soviet spy but MI5 was on to him and thought it might be able to persuade him to become a double agent and work for us. He'd been sleeping with Keeler as well. Can you imagine the pillow talk?'

'Dorothy...do you ever wonder whether your Tom was caught up in any of this spying business?'

'Nah! I'm sure I would have picked up on something if that was the case. I can assure you the police at the time gave me a thorough grilling and, in the end, went away convinced there was nothing untoward like that happening.'

The two friends help themselves to another glass of wine and share more cheese and crackers. The wine is starting to loosen their tongues.

'Now, Dorothy, we are immersed in another lot of scandals with this Kim Philby bloke. Who would ever have thought that five undergrads at Cambridge University would be persuaded to become Soviet spies? It's absolutely shocking!'

'I agree. Perhaps it's a good thing he has finally defected to Russia.'

'I've been reading about Philby in "The Times." He has been a double agent for the Soviets since 1934 and gave away British and American secrets to them throughout World War II and right up to 1951. It seems "The Cambridge Five" were all arts students. Philby, himself, only gained a second-class honours degree in economics and history.'

'I think university students who study the arts are particularly susceptible to becoming communist or fascist sympathisers. I'm so glad Betty's studying science and isn't at Cambridge.'

'My dear, Oxford might be just as prone to this sort of thing as Cambridge, you know.'

'I doubt it, Dorothy. Pass me your glass please and I'll open another bottle before we have dinner.'

# 27.

# Lucy Entwistle

I have been taking advantage of the pleasant warm summer weather to hang out a load of nappies. Little Graham will soon be having his first birthday and I'm wondering how best to celebrate. Perhaps a small party with a few friends and immediate family would suffice? If the weather is promising we might go down to the park to the swings and the see saw. Graham loves going there. We'll need an alternative plan if the weather is inclement. This house is not spacious and the rooms are small. We will struggle to squeeze even ten people indoors. I must remember to talk to Malcolm about my ideas when he gets home from work.

I love motherhood (most of the time). Malcolm and I courted for eighteen months before Malcolm finally proposed and we married just over two years ago. When Malcolm graduated as a primary/secondary teacher from Culham College for Schoolmasters he applied to Local Education Authorities (LEAs) all over the country. This is what you have to do to land a teaching position in the state school system. It's a flawed system though because the best socio-economic LEAs, where the best schools are and the parents are most affluent, get first pick. Naturally, most newly qualified teachers want to be employed in the best parts of the country. Inevitably, the best LEAs employ the pick of the bunch and the next best get the next best batch of teachers and so on. You can see what happens... the least desirable LEAs end up getting the dregs. This, then, is a self-perpetuating form of class distinction. In an Ideal world the best, most inspiring teachers, should be being appointed to the worst schools in the worst areas in the country.

Anyway, Malcolm attended a series of interviews with LEAs up and down the country and ended up being offered an excellent position at Oxford North Primary School, a couple of miles from the centre of the famous university town. He's been there for two years now and loves it. I was thrilled that Malcolm ended up going to Oxford because my closest friend, Betty Brindleton, is studying there. Although we have pursued very different careers, Betty and I remain great friends and we catch-up regularly. It's amazing when you think about it; I'm happily married with my first child, Graham, while Betty lives it up as a university student attending all sorts of wild and sometimes debauched parties. The stories she tells me are hard to believe! How we've changed. I used to be the extroverted one and Betty the introvert. Now, I think she is far more outgoing and adventurous than I am!

I did well at my secretarial college learning typing, shorthand and the secretarial skills necessary to run an office or work as a personal assistant. As soon as I finished my training I was snapped up to work in an accountants' firm called "Sinclair, Walls and Sinclair." I did well there until Malcolm and I moved to Oxford. For a year I worked as a secretary for Professor Arbuthnot in the faculty of Medicine. Once baby Graham came along I had to leave but the money I had earned over the previous three years really helped us set up our home. We can't afford to buy our own place yet, partly because Malcolm had to go into debt to cover the cost of his two years of tuition and accommodation fees at Culham. I don't think he has ever forgiven his father for refusing to pay his contribution towards his teacher training.

Malcolm arrives home at half past five and if the weather is pleasant, we take Graham out into our pocket-sized garden at the back of the house to have a play on his rug. He lies there contentedly shoving everything within grasp into his mouth and then throwing the items away again. Malcolm seems happy with the ideas I've had for Graham's first birthday.

'Who should we invite, Malcolm? The limit has to be ten to be able to squeeze into our very small house.'

'Well, family first, you, me and Graham. Your mum. Then there's your best friend Betty. As far as I know, she's still going out with my good pal, Michael, so perhaps he can come too. That makes six people. Who else?'

'What about your parents, Malcolm?'

'I don't think so, darling. True, they're showing more interest now they have a grandchild. Mum, in particular, wants to see more of Graham. But dad and I are not ready to meet up again. Give it a bit more time...'

'That's really sad, Malcolm. How about we invite Graham's two uncles, Rodney and Derek then?'

'Excellent thinking. And, to make up the ten, we must invite Graham's God parents, Jasmine and Doug.

'Consider it done. I'll make all the arrangements.'

Little Graham gave a sudden gurgle of contentment.

'See Malcolm... Graham agrees with the guest list.'

# 28.
......

# Michael

It's over four years since Betty and I started going out together. I'm madly in love with her but she blows hot and cold. I don't know how many times I've proposed to her but she always either laughs it off or says, limply, she might think about it. We lost our virginity together in her back garden the very next time I visited her at three o'clock in the morning. I think we were just really curious and wanting to find out how to do it. After that, we managed a few more sexual liaisons before she went off to Oxford to start her science degree.

Before she left, I remember pleading with her to remain my girlfriend while she was at Oxford and suggesting we should start thinking about marriage. She scoffed at the idea and told me not to be stupid. She told me I only had a teenage crush on her and I would soon get over it. She'd enjoyed the sex, she said but there was nothing serious or lasting between us. All she had wanted from me, she claimed, was some sexual experiences before she went to Oxford. This exploitive admission was deeply hurtful.

I did my best to stay in touch but it was difficult. Betty didn't want me following her to Oxford and soon it became clear she had found someone else. I wrote or rang every week. She would take my calls but never bothered to reply to my letters. Then, a few months later, out of the blue, Betty said I could come and visit her in her "digs". It transpired that her boyfriend had left her and now she wanted to make it up with me. We had some amazing sex that weekend. Betty had learnt a thing or two from her recent boyfriend. For a short time, she even convinced me that I was the one and that we were made for each other. It didn't last.

Soon, another university boyfriend arrived on the scene and she lost interest in me again. I knew I was in love with Betty and I remained steadfastly faithful to her. There were several pleasant girls I met from time to time but I resisted the temptation to ask any of them out for a date. This on/off relationship with Betty continued until I graduated from Culham at the end of two years and started applying for teaching positions. Twice more during my two years of teacher training Betty invited me to come to Oxford and stay with her for a weekend. It was the same each time. Betty would apologise profusely; tell me she was stupid to have fallen for these other men and that I was the only true partner for her. Making up was marvellous and briefly we seemed madly in love again.

Determined to pursue Betty until she agreed to marry me, I applied only to the LEAs in and around Oxford. Limiting my options like this was not a sensible thing to do. For six months I was unemployed and could only pick up the odd day of teaching here and there when a teacher was away or off sick. Finally, I landed a full-time job at a comprehensive school, teaching subjects that were not my specialties, in a rundown school ten miles out of Oxford. I was prepared to do this, however, so I could be near to Betty.

Betty's science graduation was a marvellous day. Sadly, I felt obliged to stay completely out of sight of Dr and Mrs. Brindleton. They didn't even know I was there! Graduating students were permitted to have three people attend their graduation ceremony. Because Betty was a prize winner, she was allowed an additional ticket. Lucy Hardvale received the third ticket and covertly I scored the fourth. The four of us were supposed to sit together for the ceremony but that couldn't happen. Instead, I exchanged tickets with somebody else who was sitting on their own at the very back of the Great Hall who wanted a better seat. There was no way I was going to spoil the day by sitting next to Dr Brindleton! I was so proud of Betty. She received a wonderful reception when she went up to receive her two university prizes at the end of the ceremony. She looked strikingly beautiful resplendent in her new graduate gown, stole and mortar board.

Outside the Great Hall there was a magnificent manicured lawn out of bounds to everybody until the day of graduation. Graduates and their visitors were then permitted to pose on this sacred piece of lawn for photographs. Once these were done, the ropes and signs were quickly re-erected and only the groundsman could then step on the hallowed lawns for another year. From a safe distance, I watched Betty being photographed and interviewed by the local media. How I longed to embrace her! I managed to catch Betty's eye for one brief moment before she eventually disappeared with her parents. Doctor and Mrs. Brindleton had booked a room for the night at the fashionable Ashmolian Hotel where they were to enjoy a posh celebratory dinner. Morosely, I made my way back to my lonely flat a few miles out of town. From memory, that night I dined lavishly on baked beans on toast.

Shortly after midnight I was awakened by the ringing of the telephone. It was Betty. She was back in her "digs" and feeling lonely. Would I like to join her for the rest of the night? Half an hour later, I knocked discretely on her door.

The door opened a few inches, enough to reveal a smiling Betty clad in a flimsy nightie.

'Come in, Michael.'

We enjoyed a long embrace and a loving kiss.

'You were wonderful today, Betty. I was so proud of you.'

'Thank you, Michael. I was so pleased you came, even though you had to remain persona incognito.'

'Did you have a great celebratory dinner with your parents?'

'Yes, but I wished you could have been there.'

'Sadly, that's never likely to happen. I don't measure up to your dad's expectations for his special daughter.'

'Would you like something to drink? Coffee? Tea? You know we're not allowed to keep alcohol on the premises?'

'No, I'm fine thanks.'

Betty moved over to her bed. I watched, transfixed, as slowly she slipped the nightie over her head to reveal her ravishing naked body. She let the nightie fall to the ground and stood in front of me, a full and perfect figure.

'I've got condoms if you didn't bring any, Michael.'

I couldn't help my eyes roving up and down Betty's body. Her figure was fuller now that she was twenty-one and so perfectly proportioned. tantalisingly My erection was desperate to be eased.

'No, I haven't any.'

Betty turned and bent over her bedside table showing me her luscious slender bum. She riffled around in the top drawer for a moment before finding a Durex which she held up in front of me, tantalisingly.

'Come on then, Michael. Let's celebrate my science degree properly.'

Betty lowered herself on to the bed and lay on her back all the time watching me intently. Slowly, she bent her knees up and parted her legs to show me her very special place.

'No, Betty! I don't want to,' I blurted out.

Stung, Betty sat up and glared at me. 'What's the matter with you, Michael? You've never hesitated before. Come on, don't be silly. You know you want it. Are you too tired or something?'

'No, I'm not tired. I'm sick of you just calling me up like some sort of a sex slave to satisfy your sexual desires whenever you don't have a boyfriend handy. You just use me!'

'Michael, that's an awful thing to say. You've told me many times you love me and want to marry me. Now, when I'm begging you to make love to me, you reject me. If you really love me, come and show me.'

'I'm sorry Betty. I'm not prepared to go on playing second fiddle to your various other boyfriends. I've always been faithful to you. I've only ever slept with you and that's because I love you, and you only. How many other men have fucked you on that bed? Come on, tell me Betty? You might be clever and brilliant but you don't have a bloody clue about love and emotions.'

Angrily, Betty grabbed her nightie and pulled it over her head.

'Get out, get out! I don't ever want to see you again. Don't even try to contact me, Michael. Go on, clear off, leave my room at once...'

\*   \*   \*

I'm feeling totally miserable and depleted as I drive back through empty city streets. Sleep proves impossible as I restlessly and repeatedly think through what has just happened. I know I was mean and nasty to Betty to refuse her sexual desires but I'm really pleased that, at last, I've made a stand. At least Betty may now understand my situation a little better. For a very long time she has known I wanted to make a commitment to live the rest of my life with her, as her husband and the father of her children. So far, my undying loyalty has meant little or nothing to Betty. She has been totally consumed by her studies and pursuing the promiscuous life open to students at Oxford who wish to live that kind of a lifestyle.

When Betty and I have had the occasional weekend together, she always assures me she loves me and sometime in the future she will seriously consider marriage. She gives me hope, then smashes it when I discover she's sleeping with some other man. Perhaps Betty's over-sexed? Is this some kind of documented medical condition? If we ever do get married, does it mean she'll be having extra-marital affairs all the time? As her husband, could I cope with such unfaithful behaviour? So many questions but, no answers.

When I was doing psychology at Culham we studied a section

on mental disorders. I remember reading about nymphomania; uncontrolled sexual desires experienced by a very small percentage of women. It's rare. Some research links it to ailments such as dementia, Parkinson's disease and bi-polar disorders. There's no way Betty suffers from any of these illnesses so I think her sexual activity is a craving for attention and a yearning for a loving relationship. Perhaps she feels inadequate in some way? Perhaps she just enjoys sex and is hypersexual?

Next morning I open my briefcase and remove the thirty history assignments from the students in class 2F. I've promised to get these back to the students when I next see them on Monday afternoon. I'm tired though, from lack of sleep, and find it hard to concentrate. Betty and I parted company last night angry and frustrated. It's the first time we have had such a horrendous falling out. Now, I'm uncertain what to do next. One thing I do know is that this situation can't be allowed to fester for long; I need to at least talk things through with Betty and get back on pleasant speaking terms. I can't see her this morning because she's going to have lunch with her parents but I can call around this evening when her parents will have left. I reach for the next history assignment in the pile and start to read and correct.

I've marked about half the pile of assignments when my phone rings. It's Betty!

'Michael, I'm ringing to apologise for my behaviour last night. I don't want us not to be good friends so I hope you can forgive me?'

'Thanks for ringing Betty. I had a sleepless night worrying about everything and was planning to come round to see you later this evening.'

'It's all my fault Michael. I really wanted to make love last night and was so angry that you rejected me. You made me feel disgustingly ashamed of myself, but I deserved it.'

'Well, Betty we've been seeing each other, on and off, for over four years now and we don't seem to be going anywhere. You know

189

I love you and I want to marry you, but you don't reciprocate. If you were really interested in a permanent relationship, you wouldn't be sleeping around all the time and would remain faithful just to me.'

'Yes and no, Michael. I do love you and one day we'll settle down together but you have to understand also that I believe in free love. If I like someone and want to sleep with them then that's what I'll do.'

'That's not free love, Betty, that's free sex.'

'Yes, I suppose it is. I can still love you Michael even though I'm having sex with other men.'

'I don't know that I can accept that, Betty. I'm not a religious person, but I do respect the sanctity of marriage, the belief that parents make better parents if they only have sexual commitments to each other. All other sexual unions must be excluded.'

'That's very sad Michael because I don't believe that monogamy is natural. We all have strong sexual needs and are far happier if we express them. Limiting that expression to just one person throughout your entire life is simply asking for trouble. It's unnatural. Many married couples have other secret liaisons on the go. Then, when it's discovered, they usually divorce, which is awful for any kids. If there was free love in the first place this misery wouldn't happen. Look at most of the animals in the world. They copulate at any time and with as many of their own species that are available. It's free sex out there and remember we are animals too.'

'Yes, but surely Betty we are superior to other animals because we have higher functioning brains and can think rationally. I don't believe many of the great philosophers and religious leaders would agree with you.'

'One day I'll be happy to marry you Michael, and hopefully bear your children, but don't expect me to have no other sexual liaisons. Perhaps you'd be happier yourself, if you enjoyed free sex like I do. Then, there would be no tensions when we do eventually marry. Think about it, Michael.'

'I don't want to share you with others. It's like giving away pieces of birthday cake.'

'Well, Michael, those are my conditions. I'd love to keep seeing you and having beautiful satisfying sex. It's up to you, though. As they say, the ball is in your court. Now I must go, or I'll be late for Mum and Dad's lunch.'

# 29.

......

# Malcolm

Tomorrow is Graham's first birthday. Lucy has bought him a cute blue suit to wear and nearly everything is in readiness. Everybody has promised to come so there will be ten of us falling over each other in this small house. It's a sixteenth century cottage with tiny rooms, low ceilings and a narrow winding staircase to the two bedrooms and bathroom squeezed in upstairs. We even have an attic! The wooden floors are uneven and creak mercilessly but the place is cosy and romantic. Originally the cottage would have been thatched but some years ago the landlord replaced the thatching with grey slates. Removing the thatching was unpopular in the village since the villagers were proud of their heritage and wanted to preserve it. The outside of the cottage is painted white with cute small windows made up of small interlaced window panes. Lucy and I love it here and wish we could buy the cottage.

Lucy has enjoyed preparing for Graham's party. There's a birthday cake with the requisite single candle as well as a small red car sitting on an icing road. Graham loves cars, or "brm-brm" as he calls them. There's even a small toy cottage that looks a bit like ours. We are chuffed to have two new gramophone records to play as background music; Cliff Richard and the music from "Summer Holiday" and the Beatles LP "Please, please me." There are light and dark blue balloons festooned around the lounge room and Graham's birthday presents are wrapped and ready. In the morning

Lucy will only have to make the sandwiches, warm up the sausage rolls and bring out the shortbreads and other yummies. Sadly, rain is forecast for tomorrow so we'll have to stay indoors.

We retire to bed early and spend time chatting about who's coming and how well they are likely to get along together. Our visitors are young with the exception of Lucy's mum, who is middle-aged. It will be particularly interesting to see how well Betty and Michael get along. We understand Michael will be bringing Betty in his brand new red Mini Cooper "S". Graham will go bonkers when he sees it!

Betty and Lucy still meet up for a coffee every few weeks. Betty is rightly proud she can now write her name as "Miss Betty Brindleton, B.Sc. Hons (Oxon) and is even prouder she was invited by the university to undertake studies for a Doctor of Philosophy (PhD) in nuclear physics. It seems Betty can't get enough of the world of scientific research and is madly enthusiastic about immersing herself in her studies for the next three years. There's little doubt, Betty is destined for a brilliant academic career.

Naturally, Lucy is full of praise for her friend's academic achievements but is increasingly perturbed by Betty's other exploits at Oxford. Betty has been alarmingly candid about her "love life" at the university. She openly boasts to Lucy about her attitude towards free love and how she's convinced that everyone would be much happier if they followed her free love philosophy. It seems every time they sit down for a coffee together; Betty has another boyfriend she's sleeping with. Lucy knows for sure there have been at least six men she has heard about and there may well be more. Lucy doesn't wish to appear a prude in front of her friend so she avoids being critical and just listens. On one occasion, Betty even asked Lucy whether she and Malcolm might like to join the movement and enjoy the delicious fruits of a free love life.

Whenever Lucy inquires how Betty is getting along with Michael, she receives the same sort of response. 'Oh, we're fine.

We get together every few months and enjoy ourselves in the bed and out.' If pressed to make a further comment Betty follows up by assuring Lucy that she and Michael will probably live together permanently one day, but she's enjoying herself too much to worry about that now. 'Michael knows I believe in polygamy and if he wants to live with me, he'll have to accept that. I'm trying to get him to widen his horizons and discard boring old monogamy.'

*   *   *

Graham's first birthday party is a roaring success. There are no major mishaps. The attractive wrapping papers around the birthday presents are soon ripped off, chewed and discarded by the excited one year old, who relishes being the centre of attention. It's a miserable day weather-wise and everyone stays warm and snug indoors. Graham and grandma Dorothy bond nicely. All too soon, it's time for the guests to leave but not before Graham is taken outdoors, under a large umbrella, to admire Michael's bright red "brm brm."

# 30.

## Betty

It's the start of the new academic year and I'm on my way to a special seminar held in one of the tutorial rooms reserved for post-graduate students. My supervisor, emeritus professor Sir Peter Meirs, has insisted I attend as it will be an induction for the dozen or so students in the department of physics who are commencing their doctoral studies this year. I'm so thrilled to be a member of this elite group of scholars.

Emeritus professor Sir Peter Meirs is a formidable man in his seventies who, it seems, has been a senior academic in the physics faculty since time began. When I was first summoned to his study, I remember feeling fear and excitement in equal measure. Fear because professor Meirs has a reputation for being ruthless and intolerant of any student that doesn't come up to his high expectations and excitement because I knew I was to work with one of the most brilliant British physicists of the century. The professor was recognised as the leading researcher, advocate and promotor of the nuclear industry in Britain.

Emeritus professor Sir Peter Meirs turned out to be nothing like the pre-conceived image I had in mind of a physics professor. He was dapper, wearing a suit and tie with a brightly coloured kerchief erupting from his breast pocket. Clean shaven, without spectacles and looking fit and sun-tanned, he rose and extended his hand to me as I entered his space. He moved like a man half his age and reminded me more of a successful business man from Fleet Street in London.

Well over six foot tall, his hand-shake all but crumpled up my fingers. With a broad, welcoming smile, he waved to a chair. I sat, wishing I had dressed more smartly and waited for him to speak first.

'This,' he announced, in a booming voice, 'is a momentous occasion.'

He paused to allow me a moment or two to ponder just why it was 'momentous.'

'Why is that, sir?'

'Because young lady, I have supervised many a doctoral student over the years but never a member of the fairer sex.'

'Oh, I see,' I responded, slightly embarrassed.

'My heartiest congratulations to you. This faculty has only awarded six PhDs to women since its foundation more than a couple of hundred years ago. I hope you will be the lucky seventh.'

'Thank you, sir. I can assure you; I will do everything I can to be that lucky seventh.'

He placed his hands together, palm to palm, reminiscent of Durer's famous etching.

'Now, let's drop this "sir" stuff from the outset. When we are working together kindly address me as "Peter." When we are in the public domain, however, it's always "Professor." Understood?'

'Yes sir, I mean...Peter.'

He laughed, then started grilling me on why I was interested in *nuclear* physics and what aspects of the field most fascinated me. We covered a lot of ground in the next thirty minutes, with the professor outlining a number of possible areas of inquiry, some of which had not occurred to me before. I came away from this initial meeting exhilarated and in awe.

*  *  *

It's ten to three and I'm arriving at the designated seminar room early. There are three young fellows sitting there already and we introduce ourselves. Soon a few others hurry in until there are ten of us. Not surprisingly, I'm the only female in the group. Shortly after three, a much younger member of the academic staff sails into the room, apologises for being late and introduces himself as associate professor Erin Dennis, coordinator of the doctoral neophytes for 1964. For the next fifteen minutes we are asked, in turn, to formally introduce ourselves. I'm conscious of being the only female present and that this has already created extra interest from several of the men. Women physicists are, indeed, a very rare breed.

Perhaps because I'm a woman, I was asked to start the round of introductions. I think it went well enough and now I can sit back and concentrate on hearing from the others. One young man has particularly caught my attention. He is one of the last to speak and I listen intently.

'Good afternoon, everybody. My name is Jason Stenhammer and I graduated with first class honours from the University of Exeter last year. Naturally I'm thrilled to be accepted into this doctoral program here at Oxford. My areas of interest include...'

I can't believe how handsome this guy is. He's sitting opposite me so I have a full-frontal view. The face is perfectly symmetrical with a strong clean-shaven jaw, a neatly trimmed moustache, brown eyes and wavy hair. He simply exudes confidence and his gorgeous smile I find quite dis-arming. Jason is in the wrong place; he should be in Hollywood. I'm so absorbed with his good looks that I barely take in what he's saying. I've had a few men friends over the last three years but none compare with Jason in the looks department. He has finished his introduction now and there's polite applause. Jason is looking straight at me. I can't help it but I hold his gaze for several seconds. I'm used to men making eyes at me; however, this guy is something really special. I simply can't keep my eyes off him.

Once the introductions are over, associate professor Dennis

talks for half an hour about what we can expect over the next three years or so; the challenges, expectations, pitfalls and thrills. It's a useful session. Finally, we are invited to join him for afternoon tea in the adjoining room where quite a spread has been laid out. We senior students are being treated like Royalty.

Like magnets, Jason and I come together. The chemistry is sizzling. I have never met such an exciting man. He tells me he has an appointment to go to shortly and invites me to come to his apartment at seven this evening to have dinner with him. How could I possibly refuse? His apartment is less than a ten-minute walk from my digs.

\*   \*   \*

Before leaving for Jason's apartment, I prepare carefully. I put on one of my most engaging dresses, apply my make-up tastefully, select a suitable bottle of red wine and place a full packet of condoms in my handbag. I have a feeling these may be needed!

I can't get there fast enough. Seldom before have I felt such physical urges. As I'm hurrying along, I keep reminding myself not to throw myself at Jason, to observe proper decorum, to let him take the initiative and make the moves. I don't want to appear too eager, like some kind of cheap slut. After all, until today we two had never even met. I need to play it cool and calm down.

Nevertheless, when I arrive at the front door I'm breathless with anticipation and have to stop and compose myself. To the side of the main door are four names written onto small pieces of cardboard and enclosed in glass frames displaying who it is that resides on each floor. There it is. Floor three … Jason Stenhammer. I press the bell button and wait to use the speaker. I don't have to wait long before a crackly voice comes down the line.

'Is that you, Betty?'

'Yes, it is Jason.'

'Welcome! My apologies for the lack of a lift. Just come up the stairs to the third floor and I'll be waiting for you.'

There was a loud click and the heavy front door opened a few inches. As calmly as possible, I made my way up three flights of stairs and stood on the landing in front of Jason's door. Before I could knock, the door opened and there stood Jason with an adorable welcoming smile.

'Come on in Betty, welcome to my bachelor's pad.'

'This is so kind of you Jason, especially when we have only just met.'

I place my bottle of red on the table.

'It's my pleasure. May I take your coat?'

I turn and can feel his hands gently easing my coat off.

'I like your dress, Betty'

'Thank you.'

'Now, something to drink?'

Within a few minutes we are comfortably seated at his small dining-room table that Jason had laid before I arrived. He pours us each a glass of my red wine and then places a bowl of steaming hot soup in front of me.

'Mulligatawny,' he smiles, 'spicey meat, straight from the Indian sub-continent.'

'Top quality goat meat no doubt, Jason?'

'Of course, nothing but the best.'

Jason impresses me with his culinary skills, unusual in a man and we enjoy a three-course meal while we polish off my bottle of red. I'm beautifully relaxed. Jason insists on leaving the washing up for him to do in the morning and pours me a generous glass of tawny port.

We sit together on the couch but the port is never touched. We both know what we really want and soon retire to Jason's bedroom. It's a night I'll never forget. We needed the full packet of condoms!

\*   \*   \*

It's a week later and I'm now living at Jason's apartment. All my gear is here and I have relinquished my student digs at the university. I hope this sudden move is not premature. Jason and I are getting along incredibly well and enjoying passionate sex. I seem to have forgotten all about poor old Michael Brain because I'm totally infatuated with this man.

We have both commenced our doctoral studies and are working on the selection of a suitable topic for our research. In a few weeks we will appear individually before the Faculty's Board to defend our chosen topics. It's an event that strikes fear into the hearts of all neophytes.

One of the amazing things about Jason is his abiding interest and knowledge of current affairs. He is, as they say, a mine of information. Of course, being doctoral students in the rapidly emerging field of nuclear physics is about as exciting as it gets. There's so much happening in the world. The "Cold War" continues unabated and everyone is living in a shadowy state of anxiety. Low level fear is part of everyday life nowadays and everybody has to develop their own coping mechanisms. Here in Britain, as a fully-fledged nuclear power, it seems we are often appearing in the world news headlines.

On April 6th Britain signed the Polaris Sales Agreement with the United States which will eventuate in the building of nuclear submarine facilities at Faslane Naval Base on the River Clyde in Scotland. A week later, seventy thousand protestors descended on London from Aldermaston to demonstrate against the development of nuclear weapons. In June we had the Profumo Affair with Christine Keeler. Shortly afterwards, Kim Philby was named as the third man in a spy ring of Cambridge graduates who, for many years, had leaked British and American secrets back to the Soviet Union. It is now known Philby recently defected to Moscow. You only have to look at these sorts of news events to realise the world of nuclear physics Jason and I are moving into is a potentially dangerous one!

# 31.

# Dorothy

When Tom was still around there were five of us living in this house. Now there's two. Lucy is happily married and residing in Oxford. Rodney has signed up with the British Army and is undergoing initial training, or "square bashing," as he calls it at Catterick in Yorkshire. He expects to serve for five years minimum. That just leaves little old me and my youngest, Derek, who is in his penultimate year at school. Derek has surprised me. He has matured, become a conscientious student and will be doing his "A" levels next year with the intention of going on to a university. He has left his run a bit late but is a determined lad when he sets his mind to something. Derek might still make the grade. If not, he plans to go to a teachers' college.

The house is too large for the two of us and in another eighteen months it could, conceivably, be only me rattling around here on my own. I'm thinking of selling up and moving into a far smaller house or even a flat. I've been going through long neglected cupboards and places in the house so as to throw out, or donate, unwanted stuff. This morning I dared to trespass on Tom's old domain, the garden shed. In nearly fourteen years, I've never done more in Tom's shed than pick up a garden tool and later return it. Each time I've been in the shed, however, I've been conscious there are many other of Tom's things there, but I've never had the time, or inclination, to look around properly. That all changed today.

Inside two hours, I heaved and dragged about half of Tom's things outside into the fresh air and then divided them into three piles. Pile one was scrap, the second pile was objects to be kept and the third pile was made up of items to give away to neighbours or the Salvation Army. Everything was covered in a thick coat of dirt and dust so the next job will be to clean and shine.

Cleaning out Tom's shed proved a surprisingly nostalgic experience. Many of the items I could still directly associate with my ex-husband; the wheel-barrow and tools he used to build the retaining walls in the back garden, the hammer he wielded when erecting our paintings, even the half empty bag of grass seed he had used for the front lawn. In one of the cupboards I discovered a couple of old photo albums. One was from his own family before we met, but the second album was particularly interesting. He had kept a collection of black and white photos taken on his Brownie camera during our courting days. Wow, did this bring back some memories! There were photos of us at Brighton Pier, on Brighton beach, rambling in the Lake District, sightseeing in numerous places. I appeared in nearly all the snaps. There was also a very revealing photo of me getting changed into my bathing costume in the sand dunes somewhere. I never knew about that one!

It's amazing how photographs can transport one back to happier times and places. Although Tom only appeared occasionally, the pictures served as a powerful reminder of our earliest times together. As I thumbed through our old photo albums I inevitably started to cry.

After fourteen years the heartache is still there. Why Tom did you leave me? We were so happy, or so I thought. Was it another woman? Did something terrible happen to you? If so, how come nobody has ever found your body? Your disappearance must surely have been pre-meditated because you arranged for me to receive a cheque every month which I am so grateful for. If you are still alive, why haven't you ever come back to see me? How could you have walked out on the kids like that?

By the end of the morning, I've shed more tears than I have for a long time.

\* \* \*

Lucy, Malcolm and little grandson Graham came to visit last weekend. Usually, I drive over to see them in Oxford but they said they wanted to get out of their house for a change. I love having them to visit and can't spend enough time with bouncy, giggling Graham. On Saturday afternoon we took Graham down to see the ducks and moor hens. He was an absolute delight and chatted happily away in his own baby gibberish most of the time until sleep overcame him. On the way home I asked them about Betty.

'Do you still see Betty?'

'Oh, yes mum. Probably once a month she comes over for a meal and a catch-up. She adores Graham and always brings him a rattle or a little toy or something. Spoils him rotten.'

'How's she going with her studies?'

'Really well, as far as we know. She's most secretive about what she's studying though. We've tried to get her to explain what her research is, but she won't tell us anything. She always says we wouldn't understand, even if she did tell us.'

'And that's rubbish,' Malcolm chimes in. 'I keep telling Betty that a scientist must be able to explain to us lay people what it is they're doing. If she can't explain why her research is important then why would anyone want to go on funding it? That's what we teachers do...we put complex concepts into easy, simple every day English for our pupils to understand. I even volunteered to help Betty do that.'

'It's no good, mum. She just says its "hush hush" and refuses to talk about it.'

'I reckon she's researching nuclear power, nuclear weapons or nuclear submarines,' adds Malcolm.

'Perhaps then, she's bound by the Official Secrets Act? If she is, she's probably right not to say anything.'

'Betty might be silent about her research mum, but she's very open about her love life.'

'Oh, really?'

'Yes. She's incredibly loose with her morals. She's living with this new bloke now who's also doing his PhD in nuclear physics. She moved into his apartment a few weeks ago. Although she's not explicit, she reckons it's the best sex she's ever enjoyed.'

'And that's saying something because she's been sleeping around for more than four years at university,' adds Malcolm.

'Have you met the latest heart throb?'

'I have,' says my daughter, 'he's a knock over handsome looking fellow.'

'Isn't it strange how Betty has changed? At St Anne's she was a quiet, demure kid. She used to cling to you like a limpet Lucy because she was scared of going anywhere on her own.'

'True. You wouldn't believe how university has changed her, mum. She's into free love and all that stuff now. She really believes this is how we should all be living. I'm surprised she hasn't propositioned you yet Malcolm?'

'Well, as a matter of fact, she has tried three times already Lucy.'

For a fleeting moment Lucy looks shocked, before she realises her husband is pulling her leg.

'She's lucky she hasn't fallen pregnant.'

'Betty's on the pill. I don't know how she manages to get the pill when she's single, but she does.'

'What about poor old Michael? Where does he fit in with all this?' I ask.

'He says he still loves Betty and is waiting for her to settle down and get over this silly stage in her life.'

'Betty told us she invites Michael to come and have a "dirty" weekend, as she calls it, every few months and this keeps him happy,' Malcolm remarks.

'That's really disgusting!'

'Actually,' Malcolm interrupts, 'Michael has recently told Betty he's not going to have any more "dirty" weekends with her. He feels she's just using him.'

'Oh dear, I feel so sorry for Michael. Do you think he'll finally walk away from Betty?'

'Who knows?' Lucy and Malcolm respond in unison.

'She doesn't deserve him,' Malcolm adds.

We have arrived home by now and it's time to get afternoon tea for my three lovely visitors.

\*   \*   \*

Two days later, I'm sitting inside "The Copper Kettle" waiting for Glenis Brindleton to join me for morning tea and a catch-up. It's one of those foggy days that casts an eerie spell over everything. Actually, I love these kinds of days. Everything becomes impressionistic and reminiscent of the works of the many famous artists who so relished these conditions. Without much effort, I can recall the magic artistry of such famous impressionists as Turner, Renoir and Degas.

After a few minutes, Glenis looms up like a ghost out of the fog and enters the café. She removes her gloves and starts rubbing her hands vigorously to warm them up, at the same time looking around to see where I'm seated. On seeing me, her face lights up and she makes her way over to the table for two I've booked tucked away in a corner of the room. We exchange niceties, look over the menu together and order. Both of us are increasingly conscious of the battle of the bulge, so we order modestly; Glenis asks for raisin toast, while I select a small éclair. Nothing beats a shared pot of Earl Grey tea for two.

We spend a few minutes tut-tutting about last month's great train robbery, whereby an audacious gang stole no less than 2.6 million pounds from a Royal Mail train. The worst robbery in living memory Glenis assures me.

Glenis, as always, is looking prim and proper. She's wearing a sharp blue suit, little jewellery or make-up and has managed to retain some semblance of the neat figure she has had ever since I first met her. However, she seems nervous today as if there's something on her mind. It's not long before she speaks about what's worrying her.

'Dorothy dear, we've been friends for quite a few years now. Would you mind if I shared something private with you?'

'Of course not, that's what friends are for.'

'I'm not sure how to begin because what I've heard may just be malicious rumour-mongering.'

Glenis stops to pop a piece of well buttered raisin toast into her mouth and wipe her fingers.

'After mass last Sunday, this lady, who I barely know, came over to speak to me and told me boldly and spitefully she had heard Betty was one of a student group of "free lovers" residing in Oxford. The woman even had the audacity to ask me how I felt about this. Of course, I reacted strongly and told her that she must be mistaken. My daughter, I assured her, had been brought up as a good Catholic girl and would never be a part of such debauchery. Thankfully, David didn't hear the woman. He was talking to someone else at the time.'

'And how did she take that?' I ask.

'She shrugged her shoulders and said something like, "I just thought you might like to know." I mean the cheek of the woman! Before I had a chance to say anything more, she turned around, waltzed off and began chatting to someone else.'

I took another sip of my tea and tried to think of something appropriate to say. I knew only too well that the woman who had confronted my friend so crudely, was absolutely right.

'Anyway Dorothy, this woman's unfortunate comments have been playing on my mind ever since and now I'm wondering if there might be something to worry about after all. Now, your daughter's living up in Oxford, so I'm wondering if she's heard anything? There may be some sort of a group but I can't imagine sweet Betty being a part of it.'

I put down my cup of tea and reached for Glenis's hand. She looks at me inquiringly, urging me to respond.

'Glenis dear, I think there may be some truth in what you've heard.'

'Oh no, surely not?'

I squeeze her hand gently and hesitate before I continue, trying to find the right words.

'Lucy and Betty meet up in Oxford every few weeks for a catch-up and I'm really sorry to tell you that Betty is quite open about her radical views. She *does* believe in this free love business. I'm really surprised you haven't heard anything about it before?'

Glenis removes her hand from mine and holds it in front of her face as if she's going to cough or vomit. There's a look of fear in her eyes and she seems incapable of speech. I sit patiently, wishing I could get up and give her an almighty hug but that's hardly acceptable behaviour in a respectable restaurant. Eventually, Glenis finds her tongue.

'I can't believe it. My little girl is into "free love" or whatever it's called. Is this when people have no qualms about sleeping with anyone they like?'

'I'm afraid so, Glenis. Lucy has told me a little bit about it. According to this radical group, it's more natural and healthier mentally and emotionally to sleep with anyone you like and to have no restrictions. Some of the group are still prepared to marry, but both spouses in such a marriage are expected to be open to free love at all times. I hasten to add, Lucy and Malcolm are most definitely not involved.'

Glenis is aghast. She has abandoned her piece of toast and seems close to tears. She forages around in her handbag until she finds a handkerchief that she pushes about a few times under her nose. With teary eyes she looks helplessly at me and shakes her head.

'I still can't believe it,' she repeats, 'how am I ever going to tell David? It will kill him!'

'Perhaps it would be wise not to tell him then?' I suggest.

# 32.

# Doctor Brindleton

My last patient for the day has just left my surgery; a young man with venereal disease of all ailments! Regretfully, I'm seeing more of these sexually transmitted diseases nowadays. I put it down to the more promiscuous ways of the younger generation and easy access to the contraceptive pill. I also suspect there's a widespread drifting away from the teachings of our Lord, resulting in greater hedonism. Fewer people are attending churches and hearing the word of God so we now have rebellious, disaffected groups of young people such as "Teddy Boys" and "Skin Heads" wreaking havoc in our largest cities.

Looking at my watch, I see it's already twenty-five to seven and I'll only just make it home in time for tea at seven. Mrs. Sanders, my receptionist, leaves promptly at five o'clock so tonight it's my job to close up surgery and check everything is safely put away. Mrs. Sanders, dear lady, has been with me for many years but she's almost seventy and has told me several times she wishes to retire. Finding a suitable replacement for her is just one more problem I have, on top of all my other worries.

It's difficult to isolate a particular problem as being paramount; it's more a combination of several challenges. I'm finding running this practice, on my own, increasingly stressful. When I feel stressed, I tend to become short tempered with my patients and, in a few cases, they have left my practice and gone elsewhere.

Often the reason for my impatience is the stupidity of the patients. There's an increasing number of people who are obese, others have irresponsible attitudes towards their prescribed medications, then there are children with medical issues resulting quite simply from parental neglect. How, I might ask, am I supposed to help people who won't help themselves?

I'm also worried about my own health. I'm working long, unforgiving hours and seem to tire more easily. A fatigued doctor starts to make mistakes and I know I have made a few howlers in recent years. So far, touch wood, I've been able to get away with the occasional incorrect diagnosis, error in treatment, or failure to keep up with the latest recommended procedure for certain conditions. One of these days, however, something may go seriously amiss and I may end up being struck off the register. What an awful disgrace that would be!

I'm also aware my marriage is in the doldrums. I hardly know what Glenis gets up to these days because I'm so busy. I'm certainly not much support for her. When I get home, late in the evenings, I'm too exhausted to have any meaningful conversation. I guess I've allowed myself to get into a rut. I can't remember the last time I took Glenis away for a holiday. I even forgot our wedding anniversary this year! Apparently, it's our twenty-fifth coming up next so I had better make an effort to do something special for that.

My daughter, Betty, worries me too. With an IQ of over 130, which I believe qualifies her for membership of Mensa, I always knew she was gifted and I'm delighted to see that, so far, she has realised that potential. To have been accepted into a doctorate at Oxford University is quite something. No doubt she has a bright future ahead of her in the British nuclear power industry. But relations between Betty and myself are horribly strained. The fact she rarely comes home to see us nowadays is a sure sign of that tension and when she does deign to visit, none of us can relax. Like many of her generation she has forsaken her religious upbringing. I have no idea what, if anything, she believes in these days. I'm deeply concerned she has forsaken her faith.

These negative thoughts are churning around relentlessly in my brain as I drive along the fifteen-minute route back home. It's almost totally dark when I pull into our garage, find my bag and make it indoors. My day has been troublesome enough already but as I remove my coat I'm confronted by a tearful Glenis, who, I can see, is in quite a state. What's happened now? Glenis is a resilient sort of a woman and it takes something substantial for her to break down. I escort my wife into the lounge, where I settle her down in her favourite armchair and bring over a sweet sherry, a treat I know she enjoys.

'Now dear, what's this all about?'

'It's Betty.'

'Is she okay?'

'No David. I wouldn't be crying like this if she was okay, would I?'

'I suppose not, dear.'

Glenis took an uncharacteristically generous gulp of her sweet sherry and sat up straight in a supreme effort to compose herself.

'Betty's...Betty's... sleeping with a man. They're not married. In fact, she's been sleeping with several men.' At this point, Glenis broke into a whimper and buried her face in her handkerchief.

'My dear, how do you know this?'

'I...I... heard a rumour and then Dorothy confirmed it as true when we met for morning tea today.'

'And how on earth would Dorothy know about such things? It's probably just silly malicious gossip.'

'I don't think so, David.' Again, Glenis was overwhelmed by tears.

For the next five minutes I listen carefully to my wife recounting, in some detail, what has transpired. She tells me first about the rude woman at church last Sunday and then about her meeting today with Lucy. According to both these sources, Betty is championing and practising "free love" between consenting adults. Of course I don't believe a bar of it. Betty may have given up going to mass and allowed things to slip somewhat but to suggest she has suddenly become some sort of sexual pervert or loose woman jumping into bed with men, is quite preposterous.

'I'm sorry, Glenis, I think what you have told me is a load of claptrap. Bunkum! Betty wouldn't do sordid things like that. She may have strayed from her faith somewhat but that kind of behaviour is abhorrent and she would never stoop so low. You should never have listened to this sort of rubbish in the first place.'

'Oh David... how I wish I could be as confident as you are. Dorothy wouldn't have told me about it if she wasn't sure. Much as I hate to say it, I think it *is* true.'

'Nonsense. We can settle this matter once and for all.'

'How?'

'I'll ring Betty tonight. We have her telephone number. I'll tell her we've heard some nasty rumours and just want to warn her this kind of claptrap is circulating. I'm sure she'll be most anxious to tell us it's a total fabrication. No need to worry, my dear. Now, what's for dinner?'

\*   \*   \*

After dinner, my usual practice is to help Glenis with the dishes and then retire to the lounge to read "The Times." Tonight, however, I head for the telephone stand in the hallway to ring Betty. When I ring her number, a strange woman answers. She tells me Betty moved to a new address several weeks ago. Thankfully, my daughter left her telephone number with the lady so I try this new number. Betty answers.

The brief conversation that ensues leaves me shattered. Betty openly admits to living with several men over the last few years and then has the audacity to start outlining what she describes as her "life philosophy." I can't bear to hear another word and slam the phone down. I'm weak in the knees and need to sit down lest I faint.

After a few minutes, I'm a little more composed and the dizziness subsides. I feel strong enough to go into the kitchen to speak with my wife. Glenis is still busy there with the dishes but on seeing me comes over quickly, takes my arm and leads me to the nearest kitchen stool.

'David, you look awful. You're as white as a sheet. What's happened?'

'I've just rung Betty. It's all true! The rumours are correct. She's admitted everything!'

'Oh David, how awful!'

'The worst thing is she doesn't see anything wrong with her new way of thinking; in fact, she seems proud of it!'

'What can we do, David?'

'Not much. I'm going to write Betty a strongly worded letter tonight, reminding her of her upbringing and expressing my disgust at her abhorrent behaviour. Furthermore, I'll stop our regular payments into her bank account forthwith. I see no reason for continuing to support her financially. She may be clever but she's amoral!'

'Oh David, what if she falls pregnant?'

'Then she's on her own and will have to deal with the stigma and disgrace attached to having a child out of wedlock by herself.'

'Could you perhaps prescribe her some contraceptive pills?'

'No way, that would be tantamount to complicity.'

'Oh David, I'm so sorry it has come to this. I know you have a lot on your plate already, and this is just one more thing to deal with.'

I manage a weak smile and move to the study to start composing my letter to Betty.

*33 Hatters' Lane*
*West Dryton*
*Oxfordshire*

*1st September, 1964*

*Dear Betty,*

*To say that my telephone conversation with you this evening was a shock is to put it far too mildly. Your mother and I are at a total loss to understand how it is that you have fallen in with such a group of radicals. No philosophy can ever legitimise the kind of behaviour you are currently practising. What you are doing is not only wrong; it is contrary to all accepted belief systems. I earnestly hope you will see the error of your ways and return to the acceptable mores of a respectable society.*

*In the meantime, you leave me no option other than to cancel the monthly allowance we have been providing you with over the last four years. I shall be contacting Lloyds Bank first thing in the morning to instruct them to discontinue payments into your bank account, effective immediately.*

*It is a sad state of affairs when my only daughter, brought up in the loving arms of the Roman Catholic Church, rejects its teachings and instead turns to such Satanic ways.*

*Your mother and I earnestly pray you will return to your senses soon and we can once again welcome you back to your home in West Dryton.*

*Your heart-broken father.*

# 33.

# Glenis

After doing the dishes, I retire to the lounge and turn on the television. David is usually in the lounge in the evenings too but tonight he's in his study composing a letter to send to Betty. We have only had TV for about six months but I have to admit I find it good company when I'm left to my own devices, which is all too often these days with David at work and Betty at University. The BBC is showing the tail end of the news bulletin. Harold MacMillan, the Prime Minister, is quite unwell and there's speculation he may not be fit enough to continue. There's also mention of the Beatles again. Their latest song, "She Loves You" has rocketed to the top of the UK charts.

However, I'm too worried about Betty to concentrate on what's showing on TV. I switch the television off and go to the study to see how David is going with the letter he's writing to Betty. I'm just in time, he's about to put the letter into an envelope ready for posting. I chide him gently and remind him that this is supposed to be a letter from us both, not just him. I think he gets the message because he passes the letter across to me to read. In my opinion it's too strongly worded and unforgiving. Furthermore, I have been totally left out of this whole letter writing process. When I politely express these views, David shrugs his shoulders and insists Betty must understand we have no tolerance of her disgraceful behaviour. Once again, I reluctantly accede to his wishes. The letter is placed in its envelope ready for posting when David leaves for work in the morning.

I certainly don't condone my daughter's new found philosophy but I'm fearful David's letter is such strong condemnation it may cut Betty off from us completely. I'm sure if I received such a letter from my parents, I would not wish to visit them. It would become too difficult. I'm still Betty's mother after all and I want to be there for her if needed. What if she falls pregnant? Who can she go to for loving advice and support during those challenging nine months? And again, when the baby is born, she will need a mother's wise counsel. My fear of severing any contact with Betty is so great I determine to do something about it. When David is at work tomorrow, I'll make a point of ringing Betty to have a meaningful mother to daughter talk. If I do this tomorrow, I can speak to her *before* David's unforgiving letter reaches her.

David seems spent and is muttering about needing to go up to bed. I offer him an Ovaltine before he retires but he declines my well-meant gesture, irritably. My husband and I seem to be gradually drifting apart as the years go by. It's so sad. I'm sure couples have to *make* marriages work; however, David rarely does anything to bring us closer together. There are no cuddles, no special treats, no romantic getaways, not even the occasional night out together to a film or dinner. I do what I can to make his life pleasant. I cook meals he enjoys, handle all the housework, so he doesn't have to do anything at home, I show an interest in his work and generally just try to be good company. But this has to happen both ways. As they say, it takes two to tango. David is almost fifty and I'm forty-eight. At our ages we should still enjoy sex but I doubt David can even remember what that is!

Something else has been worrying me about David. They're just little things but they seem to occur more and more frequently. I've not mentioned anything to David about them yet and I don't know whether he's even aware of them himself. For now, I'm just observing. I hope it's just me being over-anxious and there's nothing really to be concerned about. The whole matter crystallised in my mind one evening when I watched a Panorama TV program about something I had not heard about before called, "dementia."

The first dementia-like behaviour I noticed with David was occasional items turning up in strange places. Quite often David loses his spectacles, something that many of us do, but twice they have turned up in the refrigerator. We have an attractive carved wooden bowl on the hall stand which is where we have for many years left our house keys and the keys for the cars. David's keys go missing all too often nowadays and then we have to go hunting all over the place to find them, while he becomes increasingly agitated. His keys have turned up in the downstairs toilet, in our bedroom, on book shelves and once in the biscuit barrel of all places! I have also noticed how David is at times lost for words. It can happen suddenly mid-sentence. It frustrates him no end and often makes him angry. Usually, I can supply the word he is so desperately seeking but that annoys him too. So, I never know whether it's better to give him the word he badly wants or hold my tongue. Of course, this could all be the result of extreme tiredness but I'm starting to wonder whether it's something more.

Repetition is also becoming a weird phenomenon. David will sometimes ask me the same question several times before he leaves for work. I answer each time, as clearly as I can, but either he doesn't hear me or it doesn't register. Yesterday, for instance, David asked me three times whether I had bought a birthday card for his sister, once when he got out of bed, before I gave him his breakfast and then again as he was about to leave for work. Being a doctor, David is always fastidious about washing his hands and rightfully so. Sometimes he will go to the bathroom more than once to wash his hands before dinner. A couple of days ago he complained that the hand towel in the bathroom was wet and should have been put out for washing. The towel was unpleasantly wet because he had just used it three times in quick succession. Three times he'd been to the bathroom to wash his hands!

If I'm right, and David *is* suffering from early-onset dementia, I wonder what, if anything, I should do about it? My husband is assuredly familiar with the plethora of signs of dementia and must have diagnosed some of his elderly patients with the complaint over the years. Is it possible that David recognises the early indicators of dementia in others, but doesn't see it in himself? Perhaps he *does* detect the symptoms in his own mannerisms but simply chooses to ignore them in the forlorn hope they will, in time, go away. Anyway, for the time being I decide to do nothing except continue to monitor David's behaviour.

*   *   *

Next morning I can't get David off to work fast enough, I'm so keen to talk with Betty. I make sure his car keys are in their correct place and hand him his usual picnic lunch. It's a typical drizzly English day, gloomy and miserable. It looks like the sun has decided to take the whole day off. I make sure David has his umbrella with him because he'll have house calls to make later in the day. As soon as his car clears the driveway, I phone my daughter at her new number. It rings repeatedly and I'm about to hang up when a sleepy male voice answers.

'Hello...Jason here.'

It had not occurred to me that the boyfriend might answer the phone, which is silly of me.

'Er...hello, Jason.'

'This is Betty's mother here. May I speak to Betty, please?'

There's no response from the other end, although I can hear breathing.

'Well, she's still asleep,' the voice mumbles, 'we had a big night last night.'

A number of images flash through my mind as I try to imagine what "a big night" might mean. Was it a party? A bit too much to drink? Perhaps it was a night of unremitting sexual pleasures? Or, God forbid, perhaps it was all three!

'I really would like to speak with her please. Would you mind?'

'Wait a minute,' is the abrupt reply.

I sit by the phone for several minutes, waiting patiently. I'm about to ring off when there's a quiet voice at the other end.

'Mum...?'

'Yes, it's me dear. How are you?'

'Okay, thanks,' comes the guarded reply.

'If you have a little time, I was wondering if we can have a bit of a chat?'

'If you're going to start lecturing me, the answer is NO!'

'Certainly not, dear. It's just a mother to daughter sort of thing.'

'Mum, if you're going to start telling me about the birds and the bees, you're four years too late.'

'No, of course not dear. I just want to tell you that even though your dad is very upset about this free-love thing, I want you and me to stay in touch. You're my daughter and whatever you do, I will still love you and try to help whenever needed.'

'Thanks mum. I'm sorry dad is so narrow minded about these things. To be perfectly honest, Jason and I get along famously. We're both studying nuclear physics and greatly enjoy each other's company.'

'Will you marry him?'

'I'm not sure I believe in the institution of marriage, mum.'

This comment takes my breath away. It's contrary to everything I have ever believed in. For a moment I'm speechless.

'Mum, are you still there?'

'Er...yes...yes, I am, dear. But... what will you do if you ever want to have children?'

'I don't have to be married to have kids, mum. I might still settle down with dear old Michael one day and let him be the dad.'

'What does Michael think about that?'

'I think he's okay with it.'

'So, will you then stop this free-love business?'

'No way. I really enjoy having intimate relations with special men. That won't stop if I have kids.'

'But, how will poor Michael feel about that?'

'It's up to him. If he wants to sleep around, that's fine by me, because I will be. In fact, I'll be encouraging him. Sometimes we might even enjoy a threesome or a partner swap.'

Once again, I'm lost for words. This whole concept about free-love is so totally foreign to my strict Catholic upbringing.

'Threesome? What's that?'

'Oh, come on mum. What do you think? It's three people having sex together.'

I can't believe I am hearing my daughter speak positively about such depraved behaviour. I've heard more than enough. Once again, I'm almost lost for words.

'Okay. Well... I guess I'd better go now, dear. Thank you for talking to me about these things. I have to admit I'm shocked but please keep in touch. Despite your strange ideas, I'm still your mother and I'm so much wanting to know how you are doing. It'll be best if I ring you, I think?'

'Yes, I agree. Thanks for the call, mum. Bye...'

And she's gone. I wander in a dazed state back to the kitchen, where I make a much-needed cup of tea. I take my cup into the lounge and start coming to grips with the extraordinarily frank and revealing conversation I've just had with my only daughter.

## 34.

# Jason Stenhammer

'How was your mum?'

'Okay, trying to get used to our ways. I was very up front with her and just about blew her mind with some of our ideas. At least she wants to stay in touch which is more than my dad wants.'

'Will you go down to visit them?'

'I don't think so. If mum wants to meet up she'll have to come to Oxford. I'm not sure my dad would even allow me to visit them anymore. He's turned against me, big time.'

'That's a pity. What are you up to today?'

'I'm still trying to refine the topic for my thesis. Peter Meirs has given me some interesting papers from a recent conference of British and American nuclear physicists at which they investigated the most likely future directions for the industry. Really fascinating stuff! I want to make sure my research aligns with what these top scientists are predicting.'

'Sounds good, Betty.'

'And you Jason? What are you doing today?'

'It's Thursday morning so I'm off to see my mentor.'

'Jason, who is this guy you meet up with every Thursday morning? I know he's not your PhD supervisor.'

'Correct. He's also a nuclear physicist but he's working on some top-secret stuff and is forced to keep a low profile.'

'Does he have a name?'

'Of course, but I'm not allowed to divulge his name.'

'Why ever not?'

'His work is so hush hush the authorities don't want anyone, except a very select few, to know where he's working or what he's doing.'

'Really? How come you're one of the "very select few" then, Jason?'

'I can't explain that to you right now. Sorry. I know this all sounds very covert but there are good reasons for it. Leave it for a couple of months and I may be able to take you along to meet him. Then all can be revealed. No promises, but it's possible.'

'I'm going to try to work out who this clandestine character is. I reckon there are only about fifty British nuclear physicists in the whole country so by a careful process of elimination I might be able to come up with a name.'

'Possibly... but who said he was British?'

'Oh, I see...that makes it far more difficult then.'

'Give me a kiss before you go.'

Betty is a sensuous lass and she willingly comes over and embraces me. Her hand reaches down to my privates where she rubs me teasingly.

'How about we have another early night tonight?'

'Betty, you're impossible to satisfy!'

'I know and it's a lovely problem to have.'

She laughs and with a cute little wave lets herself out the front door to make the short walk across to the college library.

Betty is amazing in bed. I've slept with a few girls, but none compare. She loves to take the lead and is *so* adventurous. I've never had sex like it. My delightful challenge is trying to satisfy her sexual appetite.

I check my watch and realise I have only half an hour to drive out into the country to rendezvous with my "mentor," the person Betty is now desperate to meet.

# 35

## Lucy

A couple of days ago Betty rang to ask if it would be convenient to come over for a cupper and a chat. Being largely tied to the house with little Graham, I always welcome her sporadic visits. She's coming over this afternoon in about half an hour. I've been a bit mischievous though, and unbeknown to Betty have invited her old heart throb, Michael, to join us as well. Michael's school is only ten minutes' drive away so he can come over straight after school finishes and be here shortly after three o'clock. Unfortunately, my Malcolm has soccer training after school today and won't arrive home until after five.

Betty doesn't talk about Michael, unless I actually ask her how he is. I think she's still keen on him but she's still having too much fun sleeping around to want to settle down and have a family with him. I feel so sorry for dear Michael because he's totally devoted to Betty. As far as I know, he hasn't had any other girlfriends and is patiently waiting for Betty to come back to him. It's going to be interesting to see how the two of them get along this afternoon.

I think Graham has started teething. The last couple of days he's been uncharacteristically grumpy and I've noticed there's some redness around his gums. He appears happy enough at the moment though, playing with the saucepans at the bottom of the kitchen cupboard. I've baked some ginger biscuits and they're smelling absolutely beautiful. Time to get them out of the oven. The front door bell is ringing which is excellent timing. I'm hoping to have a chat with Betty on her own before Michael turns up.

My friend is looking in the peak of health and we enjoy a long embrace. She drops to the ground and starts playing with Graham while I attend to the biscuits and organise the tea things. Ten minutes later, Betty and I are sitting at the table drooling over my surprisingly tasty biscuits.

'You're looking so well, Betty.'

'Thank you. It's the heady mix of carrying out challenging exciting research and enjoying scintillating sex that does it,' she beams.

'Well, I guess I have one of those two, though I miss out on the academic stuff,' I laugh.

'My PhD work is moving along so well. Yesterday, I appeared before the professorial board with my thesis proposal and, amazingly, they really liked it. They asked a few searching questions and even gave me a couple of useful suggestions. Now I'm actually starting my research proper. Money won't be a problem as the university covers that side of things.'

'I'm so pleased for you, Betty.'

'As you know, Jason is doing his PhD in a similar field and we constantly exchange views and bounce ideas off each other. When we get tired of the science, we jump into bed and let off steam.'

I don't approve of Betty's theories about free love and offer no comment. Betty takes my silence as being tacit approval because her next remark astonishes me.

'*You* should try it, Lucy. You and Malcolm could make up a foursome with Jason and me. It would be lovely. You'd be amazed how exciting it is. Come on, why don't you give it a go?'

I was spared giving Betty an answer by the sound of the front door bell. As expected, it was Michael. I had told him Betty would be here, although Betty was unaware Michael was calling in. It was good to watch the pair embrace warmly and share a quick kiss. Michael had confided in me earlier that he and Betty hardly ever saw each other these days. He was quite candid about it. He told me he didn't want to spend time with Betty while she was living with someone else. Amazingly, he claimed he still loved her and wanted to marry her one day and be the father of Betty's children. I could never be so tolerant myself. I deliberately left them together chatting and busied myself next door changing Graham's nappy and having a little play with him. When I returned, they were arguing.

'It's time you grew up Betty and stopped all this free love experimenting. Four years you've been sleeping around with anyone who takes your fancy. Many people believe you're behaving like a slut, which is precisely what you are doing...'

'Bullshit Michael! You're just jealous of all the fun I have. If you had any balls, you'd follow my lead. I'm no slut because I select carefully who I sleep with. What's more, I'm totally convinced if everyone accepted free love, we'd all be far happier. There'd be no awful rapes anymore and we'd be able to follow our natural sexual urges. Don't try and tell me Michael, that I'm the only woman in the world who appeals to you physically? There must be thousands of other lovely women out there *you* would like to sleep with if only you weren't trapped by your own silly, outdated, middle-class values.'

'That's crap, absolute crap Betty and you know it! Of course, I find other women attractive. It's partly because of that, that the institution of marriage was established thousands of years ago. If you want to give children a stable, trusting, loving upbringing they need a devoted mother and father and not to have a never-ending string of so-called "lovers" coming and going all the time.'

'Now *you're* talking rubbish Michael. If you had ever read a bit of anthropology you would know that many societies across the world bring up their children amongst an entire community of attentive adults. Think of African villages, for example. When a child is born, the whole village helps look after that child. The child has many "aunts" and "uncles". The nurturing role is shared by most of the villagers, not just the biological parents. In fact, an African child may well grow up to be far better adjusted than children in our small and very limited nuclear families in the west.'

'That may well be the case Betty, but I don't think the parents sleep around all the time. In many societies, men simply won't marry a girl if she's not a virgin. Most fellows here in the UK would prefer to marry a virgin.'

'Twot! Absolute twot! Most girls in this country have lost their virginity well before they marry.'

'What evidence do you have to back up that statement, Betty?'

'Let me explain where I'm coming from Michael. I'm an adherent of the liberal philosophy that seeks complete freedom from state regulations and religious teachings with regard to my personal relationships. We all have a right to enjoy sexual pleasures and the laws of a country, or the preachings of religious people, should never be permitted to impede that. Freedom to love, unconstrained by stifling religious dogma, or the antiquated laws of a country, is what I totally believe in.'

'So, where do you stand then with marriage?'

'In many cases marriage is nothing more than the annihilation of the woman. In most marriages women are considered to become men's property. Look at the pledge that's taken by the wife-to-be during the Christian marriage ceremony... Women have to agree to "love and obey" their husbands.'

'Yes but that's all changing.'

'Not much, Michael. Certainly not in the Islamic world, perhaps slightly in the Christian world.'

At this point, I coughed discretely, and let the two combatants know I was standing in the doorway waiting for things to calm down. It worked. They both looked at me rather sheepishly and held their tongues. My well-meaning attempt to bring the two back together again had failed dismally. The awkward silence held, while I refreshed their cups and passed my biscuits around again.

Betty and Michael went their separate ways shortly afterwards. Nothing had been resolved. Betty left as determined as ever to continue to observe the tenets of her liberal philosophy of free love. Michael walked out feeling despondent and probably regretting he had bothered to come.

When Malcolm returned home shortly after my visitors had left, I explained in detail what had transpired. Together we agreed we would politely decline Betty's invitation to join her and Jason in a foursome if she ever asked again.

# 36.

# Malcolm

It's hard to describe how fortunate I am to have found Lucy and how happy she has made me. Our deep love for each other has blessed us with Graham, a beautiful healthy child. It's all the more amazing when I look back on my past; adoption, war, falling out with my parents and the extreme financial struggles I had to endure when my father refused to honour the government's means test. Today, I enjoy a rewarding job as a teacher and adore my loving family.

The end of 1963, my second full year of teaching, was notable for several reasons. Lucy and I celebrated our second wedding anniversary in October when we went to the cinema to see the second James Bond film, *From Russia with Love.* Plenty was happening in politics too. Harold MacMillan, the British PM, resigned because of ill health and was replaced by Alec Douglas-Home who had to renounce his peerage to take the position. The event that shocked the world, however, occurred on November 22$^{nd}$. John F. Kennedy was assassinated! This was one of those surreal times when everyone remembers exactly where they were when they heard the awful news.

Lucy and I are renting our cute little cottage just outside of Oxford. On my meagre teacher's salary, it will be years before I can afford to put down an acceptable deposit to purchase our own house. Quite rightly, Lucy wishes to stay home while Graham is little and we are planning another child to keep him company.

There will be no additional money coming in from Lucy for a few years yet.

Last week we saw an interesting advertisement calling for teachers to go out to work in Australia. My pay here is ridiculously low. For instance, during the summer holidays I can work in a Schweppes bottle factory doing repetitive manual work for forty hours a week and earn more there than I do as a fully qualified school teacher! That's not fair, especially when I stayed on at school for two extra years to do my "A" levels and then spent two more years studying at Culham College for Schoolmasters.

The Australian advertisement appeared on Independent Television (ITV) and featured a muscular, sun-tanned young Australian guy standing on a vast empty beach wearing only a swimming costume and a mortar board. He was beckoning and saying, 'Come and teach in Australia.' I saw the same advertisement in the office of the Local Education Authority (LEA) last week. The advertisement went on to state that teachers were required all over Australia and the journey would cost no more than ten pounds per person. Applications from qualified teachers had to be made through Australia House in London.

Lucy and I discussed the possibility of migrating to Australia the first time we saw this advertisement. We are definitely interested. What do we have to lose? We are young and fit and open to adventures. Who wouldn't jump at the chance of travelling to the other side of the world for a measly ten pounds? And, what about all those wonderfully enticing sun-drenched golden beaches? The greatest drawbacks? Leaving behind the country we love and family and close friends. In my case, family is not so important since my relationship with my parents is tepid at best. It's different for Lucy though. She's close to her mother and her two brothers who have both now matured into likeable larrikins.

After much thought, Lucy and I decide to go ahead and apply to Australia House and see what happens.

\*   \*   \*

Two weeks later, an official looking letter arrives from the Australian High Commission in London. The letter explains I have been placed on a list of candidates to be interviewed on the fifteenth of January 1964 and spells out what I must bring: passport, proof of vaccinations and my teaching qualifications. The letter also provides more details about the emigration process. If accepted, I can anticipate leaving Britain within six months, either by air or sea. The expectation is that I will teach in Australia for a minimum of two complete years. When my two years are up, I may choose to stay in Australia or return to the UK at my own expense. If I decide to return *before* completing two years of teaching, I will be required to repay the Australian Government a proportion of my travel expenses to Australia. This all sounds perfectly reasonable and I immediately agree to present myself at Australia House on January 15th. Lucy and Graham don't have to come with me.

Shortly before Christmas the three of us set off for Ovingdean down on the Sussex coast to visit my parents. Their semi-detached house is too small to accommodate us so we have booked into a bed and breakfast place about half a mile away. To be honest, staying elsewhere is better for everyone, seeing that matters are still strained between us. Of course, my parents dote over Graham and he happily laps up their attention.

The main purpose of our visit is to break the news that we may be emigrating to Australia. I don't expect this news will concern my father much but my mother will be deeply saddened.

Lucy spoke to her mum about our decision last week. Dorothy Hardvale was surprised but quick to see the benefits for our young family and possibly, one day, for herself. Now that her three children have almost flown the nest, Dorothy is looking to find satisfying work and new challenges. Work might be more attractive in sun-bathed Australia. Perhaps, she hinted, she might think about migrating as well!

Driving from Oxford to Ovingdean is a long journey and Graham soon became irritable, confined as he was in such a small cramped space. The weather was lousy too, so stopping to give Graham a stretch and a play along the way became a difficult challenge. We travelled through rain and fog in equal amounts and it was horribly cold. We passed two or three accidents en route and by four o'clock in the afternoon it was already getting dark.

Shortly after five we parked outside number 65 Elvin Road, Ovingdean, the quiet street where my parents are spending their retirement years. Their welcome was pleasantly warm and within a few minutes Graham had completely forgotten how cranky he'd been all day and was happily rolling about on the floor being tickled and cooed over by my mother with Lucy in support. This left me to the mercies of my father.

The two of us retired to the kitchen where tasty smells emanated from the oven. 'Toad-in-the-hole,' confirmed my father. Awkwardly, we sat at opposite ends of the small kitchen table.

'Beer?'

'Yes please.'

'As you know, I only keep Guinness.'

'That'll do fine, thanks.'

Dad busied himself for a moment pouring out the stout and cleaning up where he spilt some. Then he placed half a pint in front of me. He had aged since I last saw him. More stooped, less hair and additional furrows across his brow. I didn't think he had a healthy pallor and he had certainly put on weight while losing muscle tone. He was only sixty-five!

'It's good to see you, old boy,' a strange term of endearment he often used.

'Are you and mum keeping well?'

'As well as can be expected.'

We both took a mouthful of our beer and I decided now was an appropriate time to raise the matter of our possible emigration to Australia.

'Dad, I have some news that may surprise you.'

I noticed the firming of the mouth and the slight tensing of his frame which I had seen on earlier occasions when something he thought he might not like came up during our conversations.

'A teacher's pay in the UK is poor, to say the least, and is not likely to improve soon as far as I can see.'

'A pity you didn't join the Armed Services. You would have done much better there.'

I ignored his dig. He was right, of course, although the officers' fixed income he had retired on had done him few favours.

'Lucy and I have little hope of purchasing a house for many years on my humble salary.'

I could see my father was anxious to see where I was heading with this conversation.

'As you know son, your mother and I have nothing to spare. Nor will there be much in the will. We are living frugally. If I die first everything will go to help your mother.'

'Yes, I realise that. Anyway... Lucy and I have decided to apply to emigrate to Australia.'

I took another mouthful of beer and watched for my father's reaction. He was never given to showing his emotions and again maintained an almost inscrutable expression on hearing this news. I waited patiently for a response. When it came, it surprised me.

'An interesting lot those Australians. Did you know you have some cousins out there?'

'No, I didn't.'

'The Carmichaels. Rachel Carmichael lives in Sydney and then there are some Entwistles too.'

'That's interesting.'

'I went to Australia on long service leave many years ago. It's a big country.'

'So... what do you think of our decision?'

'Well, you've stuffed things up here pretty damn well. Perhaps a new start "down under" would be to your benefit.'

I took that as being tacit approval.

# 37.

......

# Betty

It's early Sunday morning and I'm in bed, half awake. A few minutes ago, I heard the milkman doing his rounds in his funny little electric van that's completely silent except for the gentle hiss of the air brakes. The milk vans are supposed to be so quiet they never wake people up. This may well be true; however, our milkman is an over enthusiastic whistler and wakes us up anyway with whatever tune has taken his fancy each morning. Today, it's tunes from "My Fair Lady." I recognised *Get me to the Church on Time* and then *I Could Have Danced All Night* as he walked back to his van. Rumour has it, they are making a film of this famous musical to be released sometime next year.

Jason is still slumbering peacefully. I know it's going to be horribly cold getting out of bed so I snuggle back down again and start giving some thought to the meeting I have tomorrow with my supervisor, Emeritus Professor Sir Peter Meirs. He wants me to update him on the literature review I've been working on for the last six months. It's been fascinating work. I think I've read every relevant conference paper, book chapter and journal article that's ever been published. Nuclear physics is such a dynamic field that new research findings are being released virtually every week from the handful of countries that are the world leaders. My French is reasonable and I can handle their publications but research coming out of the USSR is a different matter. The Soviets are reluctant anyway to tell the world everything they are working on and there's the language barrier too. Fortunately, Sir Peter has a Russian contact who escaped from the Soviet Union a few years ago who, for a handsome price, translates Soviet publications for the English-speaking world.

The first two chapters of my thesis will be devoted entirely to my review of relevant literature. Peter Meirs wants to see how I intend to structure this review and what emphasis I'll be placing on the various major research centres around the world. My main task today is to develop a plan, together with a rationale, for why I believe it to be the most efficacious way of presenting the review. Quite a challenge!

Jason stirs but thankfully remains asleep. It's gradually getting light and my mind switches to thinking about my parents. Poor old mum, I shocked her to the core when I told her candidly about my attitudes towards sex and having multiple partners. The day after I explained things to her on the telephone I received dad's letter. Sadly, it was exactly what I expected from him. Good riddance! it's his problem, not mine. I know what I want out of life. If it doesn't sit well with my father, too bad. He may come around to accept things in time but I rather doubt it. He's a dyed-in-the-wool conservative. He'll probably cut me out of his will, not that that really worries me. At least mum wants to stay close and I appreciate that. Jason and I are careful about avoiding conception. He even pays 50% of the cost of my contraception pills. Unless something goes freakishly wrong, I won't need mum's assistance with pregnancies and babies and all that stuff for many years yet. I'm still only twenty-two.

And then there's dear old Michael. I love him to bits but he's such a stick-in-the-mud. He's trapped in the old-fashioned way of thinking that a man and a woman should marry and remain sole partners for life. How totally boring is that? You can't tell me normal healthy men and women are not attracted to many members of the opposite sex. Tragically, for hundreds of years most societies have sought to virtually criminalise our natural desires to have intimate relations with others and have forced marrying couples into unnaturally restricted and limited sexual lives. Is it any wonder many marriages break down because one or both partners are "unfaithful?" I'm all for free and fulfilling love with whoever we want, provided the other party consents. I don't want the state, or the church, or anyone else to dictate to me what I can or can't do in bed.

I don't know what to do about Michael. He's like a devoted, faithful hound dog hanging around me in the hope I will one day change my views. I've told him I have no intention of jettisoning my free love philosophy and have urged him many a time to change *his* thinking. I've lost count of the number of times I've invited him to join Jason and me or, better still, go out and sleep with some other pretty girls he likes. He would be much happier if he could overcome his old-fashioned mores and give free expression to his sexual desires. Alas, apart from sleeping with me, his attitude remains immutable. I know he wants to marry me, to possess me, to have kids with me. Perhaps, one day in the future, I may moderate my thinking but I'm enjoying life too much presently to even think about it.

Jason is waking up and rubbing his erect penis seductively against my backside. Now his hand is coming over hungrily seeking my clitoris. No point in resisting. All my good intentions for planning my literature review will have to be put on hold.

\* \* \*

Fulfilled, we lie naked under the covers together. I'm vaguely aware it's past eight in the morning. It's daylight and a weak sun is hovering just above the window-sill unsure whether it has the energy to rise up any further. It's tempting to fall asleep again in the warmth of the bed with my man at my side. However, Jason is annoyingly alert and wanting to talk.

'Betty…'

'Umm...'

'Do you remember me mentioning a colleague of mine, another nuclear physicist who's been helping me with my thesis like a sort of a mentor?'

'Yes, of course. I've been trying to fathom out who he is...'

'Well, he's really keen to meet you.'

'Really? Why?'

'For professional reasons only. He's old enough to be your father, so I don't imagine he'll be wanting to jump into bed with you, even though nuclear physicists are an explosive lot.'

'Ha ha...'

'I was telling him a bit about your research and he reckons he's working in a very similar field to yours and might be able to help. What he's doing is top secret stuff and protected under the Official Secrets Act, 1939.'

'Umm...sounds interesting, Josh. But who is this guy? I'm sure I must have read some of his work in my research at some time.'

'I doubt it.'

'Why?'

'The vast majority of the research going on around the world is out there and freely available in the public domain. However, a handful of countries at the cutting edge of exciting new discoveries obviously have vital secrets they're not prepared to divulge. It's all about competition; commercial and strategic. It stands to reason. If you can get ahead of your rivals you want to keep those crucial findings secret for as long as possible. Britain, like its competitors, has a small core of top nuclear scientists working in such a clandestine manner. My colleague is one of them.'

'Wow, that's amazing. But why does he want to meet me? He won't be able to tell me anything if it's covered under the Official Secrets Act.'

'I don't really know. Perhaps he'll advise you to stay away from something if he's already researching it.'

'Anyway, I guess it would be good to meet him. What's his name?'

'Sorry, I've told you before, I'm not allowed to reveal that.'

'Golly, this *is* secretive business!'

'Sure is. Shall I go ahead and organise a meeting then? I can drive you there.'

'Where does he live for God's sake?'

'Here in Oxford.'

'Sounds intriguing! Have a look on the calendar and see what time you can arrange with your Dr Mystery.'

# 38.

# Dorothy

My motivation to prepare the house for a possible sale has increased markedly following Malcolm and Lucy's disclosure that they are applying to emigrate to Australia. A number of things now seem to be falling into place. Rodney loves his life in the army and already has his sights set on promotion after only a couple of months of service. Derek's studies are progressing well and he will sit his "A" levels in less than twelve months' time. Of course, I won't disrupt his studies by selling the house before his examinations are out of the way. If Lucy and Malcolm do emigrate, I may follow them out to Australia. I would love a fresh start far away from England's desultory weather. If the boys are happy here and Lucy and my adorable grandson leave for "Down Under" then selling the house and following them out would seem my best option.

Two days ago I received a distressing letter from Lloyds, my bank. The letter was short and to the point. It appears there is some kind of an arrangement whereby the wonderful monthly cheques that have been coming ever since Tom's sudden disappearance will cease next year when Derek turns eighteen. As soon as I received this letter, I telephoned the bank and demanded to speak with the bank manager. He simply confirmed the situation and indicated there was nothing he could do to help. Legally, he said, parental support was only required until the last of my children turned eighteen. Again, I urged him to tell me where the money had been coming from. Who had authorised the monthly payments and how could I make contact with that person. It was all to no avail; the bank manager refused point blank to answer my questions. When I asked to speak to a more senior bank executive in head office, he simply dialled the number and passed the phone over to me. A man with a posh Queen's English accent told me, politely but firmly, there was nothing Lloyds Bank could do to help. He kept saying, 'the matter is confidential, madam.'

The approaching cessation of the monthly cheques is another reason to sell the house. The money from the house sale, wisely invested, should keep me comfortable for years to come.

Another worry involves my good friend Glenis. Ever since I had that morning tea with her and broke the news to her about Betty's unusual sexual activities, the poor lady has been a wreck. She's clearly depressed and rings me frequently to have a moan or ask my advice. Some of her crack-pot schemes for trying to change Betty's behaviour are bizarre and I have had difficulty dissuading her from following through on them. Recently, she told me she was going to ring the Vice-Chancellor of Oxford University and ask him to throw Betty out of Oxford if she didn't stop her debauched behaviour. I finally convinced Glenis that Betty was an adult and what she chose to do in her personal, private life was nothing the VC could or should, influence, unless it was a criminal act. Another time, Glenis wanted to employ private detectives to kidnap her daughter. Glenis even approached the Mother Superior at the Saint Assisi Convent in Oxford and asked her to take Betty in as a boarder. Apparently, the Mother Superior was only able to offer some prayers to alleviate the situation.

At the same time as Glenis was coming up with these crazy ideas, she continued to ring her daughter frequently to maintain what she termed, 'motherly contact.' No wonder Glenis was troubled. On the one hand she was trying to keep in touch, but on the other hand she was busily attempting to undermine her daughter. David, her husband, was no help either.

I did my best to present a more positive view point to Glenis, emphasising Betty's brilliance and how proud they should be that Betty was destined to be an outstanding nuclear physicist. Quite possibly, Betty might one day even become internationally famous.

We only have the one GP in West Dryton, Doctor David Brindleton, husband of my friend Glenis Brindleton. David has been in the village for many years and has always been our family's doctor. He helped bring my children into the world and was strongly supportive when Tom left me. Records of every appointment, ailment, medication and procedure any of us has received over the years would be safely stowed away somewhere in his extensive medical filing system. Receptionists have come and gone but Doctor Brindleton has stayed on and it seems as though he has been with us forever. Obviously, we have been happy with his care or we would have sought another GP from the district around us.

I certainly don't want to be the harbinger of more bad news for Glenis but I'm wondering if David Brindleton is suffering from some form of early dementia. Last week I had occasion to see Doctor Brindleton at his surgery. Nothing serious, just a nasty corn that needed to be removed. I think it must have been almost a year since I had last visited the good doctor but this time there were some worrying traits. When I walked into his surgery he looked at me blankly, as if he had never seen me before. Then he referred to the file sitting on his desk that the receptionist must have placed there and his face lit up.

'Ah...Dorothy, how lovely to see you again.'

Strange that he didn't immediately recognise me when I've been his patient for about twenty-three years during which time he has probably examined, prodded, stitched or treated virtually every part of my anatomy. The next thing he said nearly floored me.

'And how's Tom these days?'

I must have reacted like a stunned mullet because he immediately realised he had said something wrong and reddened with embarrassment. I honestly don't think he could still remember what had happened fourteen long years ago and how he had done so much at the time to help me overcome my anger and anguish. Could it be, I wondered, that dear Doctor David Brindleton was losing his capacity to recall important events? Anyway, I recovered quickly and mumbled something in reply before explaining why I had come to see him.

Corns are reasonably easy to handle but can take ten minutes or more to remove depending on their size and position. Mine was on the instep of my left foot and becoming painful, particularly if I wore high heels. The doctor asked me to lie on my stomach on his examination table and he set to work. He seemed to be managing fine but our conversation worried me. He asked how the children were, a perfectly normal sort of question since all three were also his patients. I answered him briefly with a salient fact about each of them. A couple of minutes later, he asked me the exactly the same question again! What's going on? Wasn't he listening? Surely his short-term memory isn't that bad?

One other matter *really* concerned me. My bare feet were sticking out over the end of the examination table so the doctor had easy access to my troublesome corn under the bright light of his angle-poise lamp. I was wearing a pretty dress. Twice I felt his ungloved hand move slowly up my legs. He only went as far as my knees but it was more than enough to alarm me. Never before had I had reason to think that Doctor David Brindleton behaved anything but professionally. I couldn't be absolutely sure what he was doing so I just lay there motionless hoping like hell he wasn't going to go any further up my legs. He didn't. Was this some sort of absent-minded careless movement or something more sinister?

When I arrived home, I consulted our edition of *The World Book Medical Encyclopedia*. Dementia was listed but it referred me to Alzheimer's Disease. Loss of short-term memory was cited as the most common and severe symptom. There was no mention of abnormal behaviour that might explain Doctor Brindleton's roving hands though. So, I remained unsure what to make of my visit. If I hadn't already had the unpleasant task of telling Glenis about Betty's doings in Oxford, I would have outlined my concerns about her husband. Surely, *Glenis* must have noticed the memory problems and the repeated questioning? Perhaps she's so preoccupied with her worries about Betty she's ignoring her husband's symptoms? I have heard of people who refuse to believe something that's blatantly obvious to everyone else. Poor Glenis, I feel so sorry for her.

# 39.

......

# Jason

The "mentor" I visit most Thursday mornings is my special coordinator. I cannot disclose his actual name for reasons of security. Let's just call him "Norman." Norman first approached me when I was finishing my honours degree. It was very casually done. He sat next to me one day in the student canteen at lunchtime and we began chatting. It was soon apparent he was some kind of a nuclear physicist although, he stressed, not a member of the academic staff at Oxford University. Norman told me he was doing research for a private company, British owned and financed, and was currently head hunting a few carefully selected young Oxford educated student scientists to join the company. I had been recommended to him.

Doctor "Norman" was middle aged, approximately six foot tall and still in excellent shape. It occurred to me that his sturdy build was no fluke and that he must follow some robust fitness routine; regular gym perhaps? Maybe he was into one of the martial arts? Norman was an engaging sort of fellow with a relaxed, easy manner and was an excellent conversationist. I suspected he wore a wig or a toupee, but if so, it was such a brilliant fit that I couldn't be sure. He sported a full beard that made him look rather like King George V. I liked him immediately. By the end of our lunch Norman had told me enough about the company he worked for to excite my interest and I agreed to meet him for lunch the following Thursday so he could tell me more. He suggested we meet at a small café nearby and assured me he would put next Thursday's meal on his company's expense account.

Not surprisingly, *Le Bijou* promoted French cuisine and next Thursday I enjoyed an excellent meal which made me realise just how humdrum university canteen food was. Norman was in no hurry over lunch as he explained how he sometimes travelled around the country meeting, interviewing and in some cases employing new young university-trained researchers for his company. What surprised me was the high level of secrecy surrounding the organisation. Norman was unwilling to reveal any details and I emerged from our lunch meeting not knowing the name of his company, the nature and range of its work or even the name of the CEO. According to Norman, the British Government had set the company up some years ago to carry out highly sensitive research into the application of nuclear physics together with related fields. All the company's work fell under the umbrella of the Official Secrets Act, 1939. Norman promised me the starting salary was the highest any young person like me could expect to earn anywhere in the country and that superb fringe benefits were also available. I have to admit I came away from *Le Bijou* that day, elated. All this could be mine if I was fortunate enough to be one of the very few to be selected.

Next Thursday, Norman and I met again, this time at the "Stoat and Badger" an upmarket pub a little way out of town. Norman came armed with photographs. Two were of a splendid country house set in spacious gardens somewhere in the UK and proudly flying the Union Jack. Norman indicated this building was the company HQ which attracted the maximum levels of security. Other photos depicted two well equipped laboratories, where scientists worked with their backs to the camera so there was no way of identifying them. Finally, which I found really enticing, were some photographs of luxury apartments that company staff occupied and all paid for by the company. In one of these I saw a young married couple with a small child watching television, a picture of domestic harmony. Norman assured me the company would provide high quality off-campus student accommodation for me if I went ahead with my doctoral studies and also decided to join the company. It sounded almost too good to believe.

Next, Norman outlined some of the difficulties I would encounter working for the company and asked me to consider these carefully before deciding to make a formal application. On top of the list was agreeing to work under the conditions and limitations of the Official Secrets Act, 1939. This meant I would never be permitted to disclose the nature of my work to anyone, including my parents, relatives, friends or partners. Secondly, I would have to agree to undertake whatever work was assigned to me by the company even though that work might be something I did not expect or wish to be involved with. I must also accept that failure to rigorously observe the Official Secrets Act to the letter of the law might result in imprisonment as a traitor of the realm. In addition, I must provide evidence I didn't have a criminal record and must maintain this perfect record whilst in the employ of the company. Finally, I must supply three character referees for the company to contact.

We arranged to meet again the following Thursday. If I accepted these conditions, and Norman believed I had the talent the company was seeking, I would then be handed an application form.

\* \* \*

Once again, we met at the "Stoat and Badger." Norman preferred this location because we could remain virtually incognito and stay as long as we wanted without being hassled. He had already found a quiet table that was well lit and didn't wobble about too much on the uneven floor.

'Shall we eat first?' he greeted me.

I never say 'no' to a good feed and as soon as Norman confirmed the company would pay, I ordered extravagantly. The cost of my two-course meal together with drinks, didn't worry him. We ordered at the bar then spent a few minutes with 'small talk,' before Norman got down to business.

'Now Jason, have you brought all the paper work I asked for?'

'Yes, it's all here.' I pulled out a wad of papers from my brief-case and laid them out on the table for him to check. Norman went through my papers carefully asking a few questions as he did so. Thumbing through my passport he seemed surprised I'd only been abroad once, a school trip to Italy when at high school.

Our main course arrived, delivered by a glamorous girl with a delightful figure but rather too much make-up for my taste. She dropped a fork next to my chair and in the act of picking it up gave me a tantalising glimpse of her perfectly rounded breasts.

'Sorry sir, I'll get you another one,' she pouted, giving me the sweetest of smiles. A moment later she was back and placed a clean fork down gently on my left side with another of her disarming smiles.

'Is there anything else I can get you, sir?'

I resisted saying something that might not have been polite and the attractive waitress left us leaving a waft of pleasant perfume behind.

'Looks like you're a bit of a ladies' man, Jason?'

'Not really, Norman.'

'The highly secretive nature of our work requires the company to know who you are in a relationship with. We cannot afford to take any risks. It's a matter of maintaining tight security. There are real dangers if we ever employ staff who are sleeping around. The fairer sex, remember, are most adept at procuring secrets during pillow talk.'

I took this last remark on board, as I chased some elusive green garden peas around my plate.

Norman took a sip of his wine. 'Jason, I need to take all your papers with me to photocopy them. Are you happy for me to do this? I promise I'll look after them.'

'My passport too?'

'Yes. I'll bring everything back safely next Thursday. We can meet here once more for lunch. In the meantime, let's get this application form completed.'

Norman produced a two-page document that asked all the standard questions. There was nothing unusual. Regrettably, it provided no further information about the company I was hoping to join. I filled the application in before our desserts arrived, delivered once again by the waitress with the looks to die for.

I was nervous about leaving my passport with Norman. However, the opportunity to land a job with his company was simply too good to miss. The last thing I wanted to do was upset Norman in any way, thereby perhaps jeopardising my chances of joining the secretive company. For me, it was well worth the risk.

Norman and I left soon afterwards. I looked in vain for the pretty waitress on my way out but she was nowhere to be seen.

# 40.

# Michael

Today's my birthday and I'm twenty-four. Although Betty and I are no longer an "item," we've kept in touch and I'm still hopeful one day she'll come back to me. It's five years since we first met and we have kept one delightful tradition going; the two of us go out to lunch together to celebrate each other's birthdays.

We have arranged to meet at "The Carfax," a small restaurant snuggled in behind the twelfth century Carfax Tower. We both arrived early and took the opportunity to climb the challenging stairs to the top of the tower from where we enjoyed a wonderful vista of many of the thirty-nine splendid Oxford University colleges.

'Isn't it amazing!' Betty exclaimed. 'Do you realise this is the oldest continuously functioning university in the whole English-speaking world and the second oldest in the world?'

'I knew it was very early.'

'Nobody knows for sure when it was established as a seat of learning, but it really took off during Henry II's reign.'

'Oh, and why was that?'

'Many naughty English scholars used to duck over to a university in Paris to study up until 1167 when Henry II banned the practice. So, from 1167, Oxford University blossomed.'

'Oxford preceded Cambridge then?'

'Sure did. There was a violent dispute in 1209 between the university's students and the Oxford townsfolk. Some of the academics got fed up and decided to up sticks and find somewhere else, more peaceful, to do their teaching and research. These disgruntled academics subsequently set up a new university located where there's a bridge that crosses the Cam River. And so it was that "Cambridge" was founded.'

'Come on Betty, look at the time, we must go. I booked our table for midday.'

A few minutes later we were comfortably ensconced in "The Carfax" each studying a menu. I told Betty not to worry about the expense and to order what she fancied. She was looking her ravishing best and I felt sudden surges of jealousy towards the man she was currently sleeping with.

'Are you still living with Jason?'

Betty coloured prettily and took my hand. 'Yup, he's a big help with my studies, Michael. We bounce ideas about. He's also doing a PhD in nuclear physics you know?'

'Yes, I did know.'

'So, we have a lot in common.'

'Betty, you've never told me anything about your research. Can you explain it to me in simple English?'

The waiter arrived and took our order. I looked expectantly at Betty, waiting for a response.

'Okay, have you heard of nuclear fusion?'

'Nuclear fusion? I don't think I have. I've heard of nuclear fission though.'

'Yes, everyone knows about nuclear fission. Fission is about splitting atoms apart to create nuclear power. Fusion is the opposite; it's about joining atoms together. The theory of nuclear fusion has been around since 1934 when Sir Ernest Rutherford posited the idea that energy could be produced by converting hydrogen into helium. Nuclear fusion mimics the reaction that powers our sun where immense energy is created by the fusion of two atoms of hydrogen to make helium. As the atoms join, a single neutron spins off, the reaction creating a massive surge of energy. Hydrogen is the most abundant element in the universe. If we can find a way of controlling the conversion of hydrogen into helium, we can solve all the world's energy needs for ever. And what's more, it's far safer.'

'That's amazing, Betty! Do you think it's really a possibility?'

'Well Michael, I wouldn't be devoting the next three years of my life working on the problem if I didn't believe it was achievable, would I?'

'I suppose not. Has anyone got close to doing it?'

'Five years ago, late 1958, scientists working on the Zeta project at the Harwell Nuclear Power Research Station near here, claimed they had achieved nuclear fusion. It was heralded around the world as perhaps the greatest discovery of all time. Tragically, they had to backtrack, their announcement was premature. The so-called break through could not be replicated and the Zeta project, rather unkindly, became known instead as the Zeta fiasco.'

'Wow, how disappointing! And are you working on nuclear fusion, Betty?'

'Sure am. I'm trying to look at the problem afresh. I'm convinced that nuclear fusion's going to be possible sometime in the future. Whoever succeeds first will be in possession of an incredible civilisation changing resource.'

'Are there other scientists working on the problem?'

'Of course. I know of at least five teams of nuclear physicists outside the UK who are beavering away at the challenge.'

'You could become incredibly famous Betty, if you achieve a major breakthrough.' I reached out and held her hand to give it a squeeze of admiration.

Our main course arrived and we stopped talking so as to devote our undivided attention to the tempting repast before us. Ten minutes later, our immediate appetite satiated, we resumed our conversation.

'So, how are you proposing to create the world's first successful nuclear fusion, Betty?'

'That, my dear man, is *my* secret.'

I thought about this for a moment and then realised, with a jolt of fear, that the kind of work Betty was engaged in could be highly dangerous. Not just because of the danger of scientific experiments going wrong and killing or maiming the researchers, but also because unfriendly, unscrupulous states would be desperate to access the findings of her research. Brilliant as Betty was, she had naively entered a field of internationally important investigation and her personal safety could well be in danger. With the so called "cold war" raging, what was being done to protect the woman I loved from harm? It would be the height of stupidity to assume the Soviets, for example, were not enormously interested in the work Betty was undertaking.

'Betty, are you worried about your personal safety while working on nuclear fusion?'

'Not really. Living with Jason is a big comfort. He's very worldly and protective of me. Jason is in the same situation as me, working on potentially explosive, excuse the pun, research. We both fully appreciate the dangers. If one of us comes across anything, even slightly suspicious, we share it.'

'Could it be dangerous for your health experimenting with fusion though?'

'Not if we take the necessary safety precautions. Next year, I'll be staying at Harwell for weeks at a time while my preliminary findings get tested in their labs.'

'But what about the Russians, Betty? They must have agents working over here? What about the Profumo affair and people like Kim Philby defecting to Moscow only last year? You're working in a highly sensitive, volatile field of research and I'm worried about you.'

'You're so sweet, Michael. I do appreciate your concern but Jason and I can look after each other very well thanks. Oh goodie, here come our desserts.'

\*  \*  \*

I came away from our lunch date worried. Betty seemed to have a remarkably laissez-faire approach to the potential dangers of the work in which she was engaged. She may well be right about Harwell Research Station and the efficacy of the safety precautions employed there, but far more dangerous in my view was the possibility she might get caught up in some nasty political intrigue. She was a sitting duck for Soviet spies operating in the country. In fact, she may already be under their surveillance! The more I thought about it, the more worried I became. I still adore Betty and don't want her to come to any harm.

This Jason fellow Betty has shacked up with must be well heeled. The only time I had occasion to visit Betty at the apartment she shares with Jason; I was blown away with the place. Spacious and well appointed, it enjoyed lovely views over the ancient dreamy spires of Oxford. Situated up on the third floor, it certainly wasn't the sort of "digs" associated with most financially struggling university students. Jason must have wealthy parents, I concluded. No wonder Betty finds Jason an attractive man to share her bed with; sex as well as the comforts of a luxury apartment must seem irresistible.

I toyed with the idea of alerting the local police to the fact that two PhD students researching nuclear fusion lived at this particular address. Perhaps the police could keep an eye on the place? However, I soon realised the police would just laugh at me and do nothing. Police are far too busy to waste time watching an apartment merely on the whim of a young bloke like me. After all, I have absolutely no evidence to support a request for them to provide police protection.

There is something I can do on my own, though. Betty and

Jason's apartment is just off the main road I take every day on my way to school. I decide to start leaving for school five or ten minutes earlier and spending the extra time hovering around their apartment. I can do the same on my way home after school. This practice will at least help to ease my mind. Some days I'll park my car nearby and walk around to the apartment; on inclement days, I'll remain in my car and drive about the place. Hopefully, I won't be noticed. So, next week, I'll start my own private detective work.

# 41.

# Doctor Brindleton

These commercial salesmen annoy me. I've just had one here during my lunch hour (I'm far too busy to see them any other time) and they're becoming more and more aggressive with their sales pitches. This young whipper-snapper simply wouldn't take "no" for an answer. He ranted on about all the benefits that would accrue to my practice if I changed over to his particular brand of medication for treating hypertension. All the accepted brands do the same thing and lead to identical results anyway. This bloke reeled off half a dozen commercial benefits I would enjoy if I switched to his products and a whole lot more if I gave him exclusivity. The "bribes," because that's what they are, included six months' free supply of pens and pencils, a new stethoscope, a fancy instrument for measuring hypertension, as well as a reduced purchase price for the first six months and a couple of other things I can't remember.

The young salesman left only a few minutes ago but already I've forgotten what some of his "bribes" were. I really don't know why my memory keeps letting me down so badly. I have no problem recalling things that happened years and years ago; it's only my short-term memory that's creating difficulties. Anyway, it's time for lunch. Glenis made me some sandwiches so I'll pop into the little room I have next to my surgery and retrieve them from the fridge. It's handy having this extra room where I can have my lunch alone and in peace. There are always patients in the waiting room, so I try to avoid going out there at lunchtimes. There's a comfortable easy chair in my small escape room and I can peruse the mail while enjoying something to eat.

However, when I open the fridge door, I discover to my annoyance, my lunch is nowhere to be seen. I'm sure I brought it with me to work today. Perhaps I'm mistaken? Perhaps Glenis didn't give me any sandwiches? God forbid, maybe I left them at home? Or in the car perhaps? I'll go and check whether they're in the car. But where are my car keys? They're not in the bowl where I always put them. Oh gosh, I must be going mad. One thing I do know is that I'm starving and *need* to eat. I know... I'll go and see if my new receptionist knows where my lunch is. A cute little thing she is, very pretty, but I can never remember her name. I wrote the name down somewhere so I could address her correctly. But now I can't remember where I wrote her name down. Oh well, I'll just go out and ask her if she knows what's happened to my lunch.

The pretty little thing fusses around me like a mother hen as soon as I tell her I've mislaid my lunch. She assures me I *did* bring my lunch to work today and that it was in my usual blue picnic box. Together we look in the fridge, around the reception desk, in my cupboards and even double check whether it was left in my car. All to no avail. Joan, or Jan, or Jean, or Jenny, suddenly gives a little squeal of delight. 'Here it is,' she laughs, 'it's in your waste paper basket! How did it end up there?'

I look at my picnic box in some confusion. How could my lunch box have ended up in there of all places? My receptionist is adamant she didn't place it there and politely suggests I may have put it there myself absent mindedly when I first arrived early this morning. Things turning up in strange places has been happening a lot recently. I simply can't explain it but it's rather unnerving.

My receptionist settles me down in the back room with my blue picnic box and turns up a few minutes later with a freshly made pot of tea. She's a delightful little thing. I really must try and remember what her name is. Between mouthfuls I glance quickly through the day's post that the receptionist has opened for me. It's the usual tedious stuff: bills, advertising material, a couple of letters from grateful patients and a Brighton postcard from a patient who is in the process of moving there. The Brighton postcard reminds me of the card we received yesterday from Betty.

My daughter rarely comes home nowadays, instead she sends us postcards or rings occasionally. I don't like this arrangement but relations between Betty and me have deteriorated to such an extent that it's better we don't meet face to face. When I wrote to Betty to advise I was no longer prepared to pay her the monthly allowance, I expected a furious reaction. To my great surprise, she didn't react at all. Glenis went to Oxford later to visit Betty and returned with a probable explanation; Betty was living with a wealthy fellow student and didn't need our money any more. It seems she's living in sin with her sinful partner paying for her everyday living expenses. I suppose, if she's going to continue to pursue this kind of immoral life, perhaps it's not quite so bad if she simultaneously benefits financially. In my book though, this sort of an arrangement might be regarded as little more than a high-class form of prostitution. I have no intention of welcoming my daughter back into our home while she lives this disgraceful life.

Betty's postcard mentioned she was progressing well with her research into nuclear fusion and that she would be spending some of her time at the Nuclear Power Station at Harwell. I'm gradually becoming accustomed to the idea that in three years' time there will be two doctors in this family, a doctor of medicine and a doctor of science.

My wife is becoming a worry to me as well. She's far too lenient towards Betty and anxious to remain in touch either by telephone or by visiting her in Oxford. I have told her I strongly disapprove of these regular attempts to make contact with Betty. We should be presenting a united front, thereby demonstrating our unequivocal disapproval of Betty's lack of morals. Glenis always used to obey my wishes but nowadays she increasingly does what *she* wants and ignores my requests. I have even had to remind her of her marriage vows when she promised to "love and obey" her husband!

It's not just Glenis's disobedience that concerns me. Of late, I've been finding her behaviour more and more irritating. She's becoming a "nagging" wife. I have no idea why. Perhaps her personality is changing with the menopause? She never gives me a moment's peace in the mornings when I'm getting ready to go to work. It's as though she thinks I'm incapable of getting ready on my own. She spends the entire time fussing about. Have you got your hat? Have you remembered your blue lunch box? Can you find your car keys? Did you clean your teeth? Did you remember to put your wallet in your pocket? It's as if she thinks I'm a small child going off to school who can't be trusted to do anything on their own. It's much the same when I arrive home dead tired at the end of the day. Never ending questions; have I done this... have I done that... Sometimes I can't stand it any longer and I snap back.

I'm not sure what I'll do if Glenis' behaviour gets worse; there's a limit to what a person can put up with. When I snap back at her, she quietens down for a short time, but after a few minutes she starts up again. Sometimes there's an expression of pity on her face, it's almost as though she's feeling sorry for me! I'm beginning to wonder if she's displaying early signs of senility. Of course, I'm not her doctor; it would be unprofessional of me to be her GP. However, one of these days, I might ring Glenis' GP and ask him to check Glenis over for signs of early-stage dementia. Come to think of it, I don't remember who is her GP nowadays. It may be a female doctor. Anyway, I must remember to follow it up one of these days.

I've heard of married couples that separate, or even divorce, when one of them becomes so unwell with dementia that the other person cannot cope any more. We certainly haven't reached that dire stage yet, but things do appear to be progressing that way. A nursing home for Glenis would be my choice, eventually. As a strict Catholic, I could never entertain the possibility of a divorce; that would never be an option. For the time being I'll just continue to carefully monitor poor Glenis's behaviour.

# 42.

# Glenis

Dorothy has been a tower of strength for me over the last few weeks as I try to come to terms with Betty's crazy ideas and my husband's emerging health problems. Today, Dorothy is coming over to play Scrabble. I have the lounge nicely warmed up for us and a yummy afternoon tea ready. There was a light fall of snow this morning and more is forecast this evening.

A well rugged-up Dorothy arrives a few minutes late and is delighted to come into my warm and cheerful lounge where the Scrabble is already set up. We decide to enjoy afternoon tea straightaway.

'Well Dorothy, how's your young family?'

'All going well, thanks Glenis. Lucy missed her monthly period though and suspects number two is on the way.'

'Oh, that's fantastic, Dorothy. Perhaps you'll become a grandma a second time over?'

'I hope so. What about Betty? Is she still living with this Jason fellow?'

'Unfortunately, yes. Although he's got plenty of money and she's living in style. She's a kept woman it seems.'

'Interesting. Where do you think Jason gets his money from?'

'I wish I knew. I asked Betty that very same question but she doesn't know either. Apparently, Jason comes from a large family with no money to spare. His father was a council worker who worked on the roads and his mother died in childbirth with their fifth child. The source of his money is a real mystery. He has this lovely apartment that must cost heaps to rent and stylish new furniture to go with it.'

'Perhaps he has a wealthy uncle or Godparents? Or did he win the football pools in a big way? What about premium bonds?'

'I have no idea, Dorothy. All I know is that he can afford this splendid apartment and has plenty of money left over for their daily living expenses.'

'I hope you won't mind my saying this Glenis dear, but you don't suppose it's illegal money, do you?'

'God forbid, I hope not. Betty's been living with Jason for some time now so you'd think she would have seen something suspicious by now if he was going out and robbing banks or raiding jewellery shops.'

Dorothy laughed and helped herself to a second chocolate biscuit.

'And what about that pleasant young lad, Michael? Is he still interested in your daughter?'

'I believe so but only from a distance. Not surprisingly, he doesn't approve of Betty sleeping about the place either. I think he's devoted to her and still hoping Betty will come to her senses, leave Jason and come back to him. Of course, David will never approve of Michael.'

'And what does Betty think about going back to Michael?'

'Hard to say. She's certainly fond of him. Just being "fond" of someone is hardly the foundation for a strong marriage, though.'

'Tell me honestly, Glenis, did you ever sleep with anyone else before you married David?'

'Good heavens, no. I've always strictly followed my faith and fornication is one of the deadly sins. I was scared of even kissing a boy before I married David. What about you Dorothy?'

'Well, I have to admit, there was one man I had sex with before I married.'

'Oh, dear Dorothy. Did he force himself on you?'

'No, not really. I guess I encouraged him to an extent. At the time, I was madly in love with him and desperately wanted to marry him. One night we went back to his place, rather drunk, and he started getting amorous. I was terrified he would lose interest in me if I didn't submit to his advances. I lost my virginity that night.'

'And did he lose interest in you after that?'

'I'm afraid so, yes.'

I was shocked to hear this from my best friend and saddened too. I didn't know how to react. Rather limply, I asked Dorothy if she would like another cup of tea.

*   *   *

Next morning, after I managed to get David off to work, I walked down to the railway station to catch the only train bound for Oxford that stops to pick up passengers in West Dryton. Betty knows my train pulls in to the Oxford Station at 11.21 and has promised to meet me and take me out to lunch. She's always reluctant to take me back to her apartment in case Jason doesn't want me there. I've brought my camera to photograph the interior of her luxurious apartment to show David and Dorothy how decadent it is. I'm hoping Betty will relent and let me in for a few minutes. Her apartment is only about ten minutes' walk from the station.

Yesterday's snow has all but disappeared, leaving only a few sheltered places up against the bare hedges and fences where it persists. It's bitterly cold though, with icy pale blue skies and a stiff northerly blowing directly from the North pole. Sheep are huddled together amongst the trees or around bales of feed scattered by farmers. Frosts have turned the grass brown and the trees stand stark and naked. One cluster of tall trees has become the nesting place for a flock of noisy rooks and their nests stand out against the skyline like blobs of black paint. Despite it being winter there's a raw beauty about the countryside and I wouldn't want to live anywhere else.

We steam into the university city on time and I brace myself for the frigid air that will embrace me as I alight onto the platform. I gather my coat around me, pull on my gloves and tighten my woollen scarf. I can see my daughter waiting on the platform dressed in surprisingly little for such cold weather. Young folk believe it's more important to show off their youthful figures than be comfortable. I'm relieved to see she looks well.

Betty welcomes me warmly and tells me she's booked a table at the "Elephant and Castle", a pub that dates back to the sixteenth century and only half a mile away from the station. It's too cold to dawdle and we make our way briskly towards the pub with the steam from our breathing blowing out behind us in short-lived puffs. Our table is booked for a quarter past twelve so Betty takes me into the ladies' lounge to have a drink before the meal. She gets me an apple juice and brings back a fancy drink for herself. When I ask what she's having, she tells me rather wickedly, it's called a "Bloody Mary." My face must have registered mild shock at such an uncouth name. Laughing, Betty assures me she is not making it up. This particular kind of drink is, indeed, known as a "Bloody Mary."

'Mum, it's a mixture of vodka and tomato juice with a dash of Worcestershire sauce. It looks rather bloody so takes its name from Mary, Queen of England. She's reputed to have burnt nearly 300 religious dissenters at the stake. The name is quite fitting really.'

'I see.'

'How's dad?'

'Much the same. Certainly no better, and his forgetfulness is getting worse.'

'Now, mum, I have some good news.'

My immediate thought is that Betty is pregnant. Like it or not, David and I are going to be grandparents.

'I'm earning a salary already.'

'Really? But you're not working. You're only a student still.'

'True, but this company is paying me a sort of a retainer. They are most interested in my work and are going to offer me a full and very generous salary as soon as I graduate. In the interim, they are happy to pay me a half salary to ensure I will stay with the company once I become Doctor Brindleton.'

'Well darling, that's fantastic news! What's the name of the company?'

'Sorry mum, not allowed to disclose that. It's hush hush. All I can tell you is that it's a British company engaged in research into nuclear fusion.'

'It all sounds very secretive, dear?'

'Well, it is. If we can crack the last remaining barriers to nuclear fusion, we want to keep that know-how safely here in the UK. It'll be worth millions and millions of pounds. The whole world will be desperate to have access to this newly developed technology.'

'How exciting! What does Jason think of this?'

'He's in the company too. That's why we have such a lovely apartment. He signed up with them about six months ago. It was Jason who introduced me to the recruiting officer because he knew my research would also be of great interest to them.'

'Oh, I see. So... that's how he's got all his money?'

'Yes. Time for lunch mum. Now I'm an earning girl, I'll pay for you.'

'That's very sweet of you.'

We enjoyed our meal. Betty paid the bill and left the waiter a handsome tip. We wrapped up and walked out from the warmth of the Elephant and Castle to face the elements again. Betty hurried off to see her academic supervisor, leaving me with an hour or so to kill before my train departed.

\* \* \*

I was annoyed Betty wouldn't allow me back into her apartment to take a couple of photographs for fear Jason would be disturbed. There was nothing to stop me taking a photo of the exterior, however, so I set off, on foot, to do just that.

It was bitingly cold as I made my way down the street. I stayed close to the shops whenever I could to enjoy the occasional wafts of hot air emanating from their open front doors. The sky was darkening. Snow had been forecast for the afternoon and the glowering clouds were streaming in from the north. Shoppers were well rugged up as they hurried about their business, many with red noses and weepy eyes. Fearing an imminent snow storm most were homeward bound.

Betty's apartment was not far along the next street so I ignored the threatening weather and pressed on. I rounded another corner and in a couple of minutes was standing on the pavement on the opposite side of the street from Betty and Jason's apartment. The pavement was not tree-lined here and I had an unrestricted view. I fumbled around in my handbag, found my camera and took a couple of reasonable photographs.

It was then I noticed a young man standing a few yards further along the pavement well rugged up in a blue duffle-coat and matching coloured balaclava. His hands were thrust deep in his pockets while he stamped his feet trying to keep them warm. There was something familiar about him, although I wasn't sure what. Several times he glanced in my direction as if suspicious of *my* behaviour. I decided to take one last photograph; a close-up of the front door which was a cheerful red colour and I stepped out onto the road to get the door better framed. When I walked back to the curb the man approached me.

'Excuse me, are you Mrs. Brindleton?'

I looked up and found I was looking into the face of Michael Brain, the young man who had been Betty's boyfriend, on and off, for the last five years or so.

'Oh, hello Michael. What are you doing standing out here in this freezing weather?'

'I guess I could ask you the same question, Mrs. Brindleton.'

'I'm just taking a few snaps of my daughter's place to show my husband and our friends. Are you waiting for them to come home?'

'No, not really. To be perfectly honest, Mrs. Brindleton, I'm worried about Betty and what she's getting herself involved in.'

Michael looked at me inquiringly, hoping perhaps I could enlighten him.

'Oh, why?'

'Did you know she's been signed up by some mysterious secret organisation who wants access to her research work?'

'I only found that out today, Michael.'

'Well, I may have been reading too many crime novels but I'm suspicious about what she and her boyfriend have signed up to. It sounds distinctly dodgy to me. You know what they say; if it's too good to be true, then it probably is.'

'Oh dear, Michael. Only a little time ago I was thrilled to hear Betty was earning a salary. Now you're suggesting it's all dodgy! How do you know?'

'I don't know for sure Mrs. Brindleton. I'm still in love with your daughter, despite your disapproval, and even though she's now living with Jason, I still care about her.'

'That's very commendable, Michael. But what use is it standing out here in this freezing weather? Are you watching their place or something?'

'Well yes, I am. I may be wasting my time but I feel a bit better if I stay in touch with their comings and goings. I drop by for a short time each day when I go to work and then again after school. They don't know I do this, so please don't say anything to Betty, will you Mrs. Brindleton?'

'You can trust me, Michael. But have you ever seen anything interesting?'

'I've only seen one gentleman visit occasionally. I know he's visiting them because he rings their bell for the third floor. A middle-aged bloke, smartly dressed, usually wearing a Burlington coat and a dapper hat. I've no idea who he is. Perhaps he's Jason's father?'

'Well, I'm sorry I can't help you, Michael. Please let me know if you find out anything interesting. Now, I have to go; I have a train to catch.'

'I certainly will Mrs. Brindleton.'

I turned and headed for the railway station, just as the first large feathery flakes fluttered down around me.

This peculiar chance meeting with Michael had put me on edge.

# 43.

........

# Lucy

Yesterday, my GP confirmed I was pregnant with our second child. Thrilled with the news Malcolm and I called in the baby-sitter and left little Graham with her for the evening so we could go out and celebrate at our favourite cosy restaurant. No alcohol for me, although Graham quietly enjoyed a pint. We are hoping for a girl this time but will be happy, of course, with whichever comes along. Malcolm and I spent the first part of the evening discussing how best to accommodate this welcome addition to our family and what we needed to do to prepare.

Before our desserts came out, Malcolm started telling me about a chance meeting he'd had with Michael. Apparently, they had both attended the same Inservice course for primary school teachers and when the day was over decided to go out together for a quick drink.

'I feel terribly sorry for my old mate, Michael.'

'Why darling?'

'The guy's still very much in love with Betty, but she doesn't want to have anything much to do with him.'

'Perhaps he should give up on Betty altogether then? There are plenty more fish in the sea.'

'He can't. He's still infatuated with her, despite the fact she's been shacked up with this Jason fellow for over six months now.'

'It must be five years he's been keen on Betty. I wouldn't wait that long for anyone.'

'Not even if it was me, you were waiting for?'

'No, not even for you!'

'Anyway, Michael started telling me about what he does almost every day when he goes to work and again when he's coming home.'

I took another mouthful of my sticky date pudding and waited for Malcolm to continue.

'You'd never guess what he does?'

'Handstands in the main street?'

Malcolm ignored my facetious remark.

'He spies on Betty's apartment.'

'What on earth for? He could get into trouble with the police for doing something stupid like that. Isn't it called invasion of privacy or some such thing?'

'Malcolm's worried about Betty and some secret company she's signed up with. It turns out she's already being paid a salary. He reckons this company is actually buying access to her research findings.'

'What's wrong with that? Betty's a brilliant student and her research work must be cutting edge?'

'Exactly! But nobody knows anything about this company! Who are they? The company claims to be a British organisation but Malcolm has his doubts. The company's shrouded in secrecy. How does anyone know it's a British company? You know there have been several cases over the last twenty years with the USSR trying to access top secret British material. Remember the "Cambridge Five?" Then there was the Profumo Affair, Christine Keeler and all that stuff? Can't you see why Malcolm's worried?'

'Well, I suppose so. What's Malcolm going to prove though, standing around outside Betty's apartment for half the day?'

'I think he feels he's keeping a protective eye on Betty. He's also watching to see if any other people visit the apartment.'

I chase the last bit of sticky date pudding around my plate and savour the sweet taste for the last time.

'Are there any visitors?'

'Only one, some middle-aged bloke.'

'It's hardly effective surveillance if Malcolm is only there at the same time every work day, is it?'

'I guess you're right.'

'Let's pay the bill and, Mr. father-to-be-a-second-time, you can take me to bed and show me again how you managed it.'

Giggling mischievously, I left the restaurant arm in arm with my lover.

\* \* \*

I had a phone call from Betty the next day. After I shared the wonderful news that Malcolm and I will be welcoming a second child in about seven months' time, she asked me to meet her for coffee and cake at Fortes, an expensive classy establishment frequented only by those who are happy to part with a few pounds. Fearing the high cost, I hesitated. Betty must have sensed this because she immediately promised to pay. I had only been to Fortes once before. I remember it as a dressy place and went to check I had something decent to wear. Little Graham has a nice new outfit, so he will be fine. This will be an excellent opportunity for me to quiz my best friend about this mysterious company with whom she has, allegedly, signed up.

At the entrance to Fortes, I'm made welcome by a janitor clad in a smart black suit and top hat. 'Welcome to Fortes madam. Do you have a reservation?' I assured the gentleman I was meeting a Miss Betty Brindleton who had booked a table and with an expansive wave of his arm and a broad smile he ushered me in through the doors, 'We are expecting you, madam.'

I was immediately struck by the springy dark plum-red carpet, an indication of its depth and quality. The large precinct was bathed in a pleasing subdued lighting with each individual table displaying a lantern-like object in the centre. While I was taking in the overall ambience, a well-dressed lady appeared and inquired if she could escort me to my table. I asked to use the rest room first and she gave me directions. Five minutes later, with a clean Graham, she met me again and conveyed me to a table for two in the middle of the restaurant where there was already a high chair provided. I settled my son in and found him a dinky toy to play with. He was happily making his "brm brm" sounds when Betty arrived.

I was struck by how well dressed she was. Betty looked the part of the successful young female professional about town. A solicitor perhaps? Possibly a business woman? Nobody would suspect she was but a humble university student. We hugged and I complimented her on her appearance. I was pleased to see she still blushed when praised. Graham dropped his toy on the floor and began to wail. A moment later we were finally settled and ready to order.

'Now, Lucy darling, I'm paying for this little shindig.'

'That's very good of you.'

'Well, I'm no longer a kept woman. I have an excellent salary, considering I'm only a student.'

I played dumb and pretended I didn't know about her "job." This way, I thought, I might glean more information than Michael had managed to extract from Malcolm. As I was waiting for Betty to tell me more, a man with a goatee beard and a distinct limp arrived and made himself comfortable a couple of tables away from us. I thought it odd that he was on his own. Everyone else in this expensive restaurant had one or more people at their table to socialise with.

'That's amazing Betty. Is it a part-time job?'

'Well, yes and no. The company has explained they really want the benefit of my brains as well as unfettered access to my research findings over the next few years. They're so keen to not let anyone else make use of my findings that they have put me, and Jason, on the payroll immediately. I guess you could say they have purchased exclusive rights to our expertise and findings.'

'That's *so* exciting Betty. May I ask how much they are paying you?'

'Lots! I'm not allowed to tell you the actual amount. However, Jason and I are now comfortably off. We're going to buy a car soon. Jason signed up with the company six months ago. That's why we have been able to afford such a lovely apartment.'

'Betty, forgive me asking you this, but how do you know you can trust this secretive company?'

'We have all the proper contracts and guarantees. They always pay our salaries on time. All they want at this stage is for us to update them on our research. We've met the CEO too; a very likeable Englishman.'

The man with the goatee beard, two tables away, was starting to make me feel slightly nervous. Several times he glanced over to our table and appeared to be listening to our conversation. Who was this guy? Was he just a lonely man wanting company, or did he represent something more sinister? For the rest of our time in Fortes I did my best to keep half an eye on him without seeming to do so. Graham was wriggling in his high chair and, like any small child, making noises from time to time which may have been annoying the man with the goatee, yet I couldn't help feeling uneasy about him. Betty had her back to the man and was totally unaware of his presence.

Betty has matured remarkably since entering Oxford University. No longer the shy, uncertain lass who began her studies four years ago. She now presents as a sophisticated young professional woman. Slim and well dressed, her poise and bearing are typical of a confident person who is going places. I just hope she and Jason know what they are doing and not being blinded by the generosity of this mysterious company that is sponsoring them.

The man with the goatee is still watching us as we make our way out of Fortes.

# 44.

# Betty

I'm on my way home after another session with my
supervisor, Professor Peter Meirs. He's happy with the
way my research is coming along and even made a couple
of helpful suggestions. Before leaving, I took the opportunity to
tell the professor about the company that has recently employed
me. His immediate and strong reaction shocked me!

First, the professor claimed not to know anything about a
clandestine British company engaged in high level research into
nuclear physics. Next, he told me firmly to have nothing more to
do with the company which he described as being "bogus". He
became even more alarmed when I told him I had already spent
time outlining my research to a director of the company. To cap it
off, Peter Meirs informed me my research was not mine to share
with anyone else. Oxford University, he stressed, held the copyright
on any student work undertaken under the supervision of Oxford
University's academic staff.

According to Professor Meirs, I have done the wrong thing by
even talking to the company's Chief Executive Officer. When I was
genuinely unable to disclose the name of the CEO, my supervisor
shook his head in disbelief. He was clearly displeased and accused
me of being "totally naïve." My working relationship with my
esteemed supervisor has always been comfortable and productive
since my research commenced. Now, I'm fearful our relationship is
seriously damaged, if not completely fractured. It doesn't take much

imagination to predict what might happen next. Professor Meirs is very likely to decide not to continue as my supervisor. The worst-case scenario will involve being hauled up before some university disciplinary board and given my marching orders. My research and future career as a nuclear physicist are now in jeopardy!

As I'm nearing our apartment, I realise Jason is in the same boat as me. Our generous salaries, the splendid apartment we have been enjoying for months are under threat. The company that is employing us will have to speak to the university's hierarchy and some sort of an understanding will need to be reached. Everything has suddenly become horribly messy. Hopefully Jason is at home so I can break this news to him. Together, we can spend the evening deciding what we can do to try and ease the situation.

A cold wind blasts me as I turn the corner and start the final hundred yards to the red door that is the welcoming entrance to our block of apartments. I pull my scarf tighter around my neck in a vain attempt to keep out the cold. As I do so, I'm vaguely conscious of a shiny black car pulling into the curb a few yards ahead. Two well-dressed young men jump out and head my way.

'Excuse me madam, are you Miss Betty Brindleton?'

Surprised, I stop and look up into the face of a tall athletic man who asked the question.

'Yes, I am. Why?'

I must have looked anxious because the second man jumped in immediately.

'Please don't be alarmed. We are from Internal Security and just need to ask you a few routine questions.'

I looked from one to the other thinking this was some sort of silly mistake. Why on earth would Internal Security, whoever they are, want to question me? I laughed nervously.

'What do you want to ask me?'

'It's of a confidential nature, madam,' replied the taller of the two, 'It's not something we can discuss out here on the street. We have a room available at the police station.'

It has always been drummed into me that a young woman should never accept lifts from strangers. Several thoughts crowded my mind. Are these two men genuine? How do I know they are who they say they are? Can I trust them? If Justin is home, perhaps I could ask him to come with me? How do I know these two fellows are not just clever rapists? It's all too much, too suddenly. I don't know what to say. I stayed rooted to the spot, frightened.

As if they'd been expecting my hesitation, my caution, both men delve into their inside jacket pockets and fish out some sort of an ID which they flash in front of me as if this is all that's needed to settle any lingering doubts I may have. I'm not convinced and surprise myself, when I ask, 'May I have a better look at your IDs please?'

Now it's the men's turn to look surprised. Presumably a quick flash is usually sufficient and people come along meekly. The taller man lets me have a closer look at his ID. I see the name "Thomas Asswave" and in smaller writing, "Internal Security Officer." It looks genuine.

'Are we going to be long?' I ask.

'Hopefully an hour will suffice, madam. We will, of course, bring you back here when we are done.' He smiles pleasantly.

Reluctantly I nod and start to move towards their car. The two men are the height of good manners and open the rear door for me. I slide in and find myself in what appears to be an unmarked police car. There's some kind of two-way radio system next to the driver's seat and a couple of official looking police files are lying next to me on the back-seat. The taller man offers me a cigarette which I politely decline. He lights up and we move off.

As we make a one-hundred-and-eighty-degree turn, I'm thrilled to see Michael Brain watching the whole proceedings from the other side of the road. I feel comforted that someone who knows me has witnessed my departure in this mysterious black car. Michael has been paranoid about me of late and sometimes hangs around outside our apartment. He says he's worried about me and wants to keep an eye on things. Sometimes I feel his attentions are creepy but this afternoon I'm delighted he's present.

The two men exchanged a couple of comments but didn't speak to me. Five minutes later we pulled into the car park of the Oxfordshire Police Station and inwardly I sighed with relief. Again, the men were courteous. They opened the door for me, called me madam and led me through a long corridor to an office at the back of the station. We passed several other police on the way. The shorter man pulled out a bunch of keys and unlocked a door.

The office was spartan. There was a table in the centre with two hard backed wooden chairs on either side. A large metal filing cabinet was the only other piece of furniture. A black telephone, a pen and a wad of paper lay on the table. Thomas, the taller man, apologised for the unfriendliness of the room and explained it was only occasionally used for interviews. He then introduced his colleague as Fred Sneddon and the three of us sat down at the table with me facing them both. The polite, respectful mood was maintained. Thomas opened proceedings.

'First of all, our apologies for not giving you any warning that we wanted to speak with you and then having to whisk you off in the way we did.'

'Yes, it was all rather dramatic,' I agreed.

'As you already know, we are from Internal Security. It's our responsibility to investigate matters of concern raised by members of the public with regard to a range of national security issues.' Thomas paused for a moment to let this sink in. Then Fred took over.

'This afternoon our department was contacted by Sir Peter Meirs, worried there may have been a breach of national security. He cited you, madam, and a gentleman by the name of Jason Stenhammer as the potential offenders. Sir Peter stressed the urgency of this matter, believing you and Mr. Stenhammer may have already divulged some nationally important research findings.'

Both men were now staring at me accusingly. The atmosphere in the room changed abruptly and I'm feeling far more nervous. Apparently, what Jason and I have been innocently doing has created problems for Internal Security. Being described as a "potential offender" did not sit well with me.

'The wise course of action for you, madam, is to tell us everything you know about this company that's employing you. If you cooperate fully with us, we may be able to make things easier for you. Do you understand?'

'Yes, I do.'

'Tell us about Mr. Stenhammer.'

For ten minutes I told the two men everything I knew about my boyfriend while they asked probing questions. I told them how we met, what he was like and how he encouraged me to follow him and also sign up with the company that was paying his salary and providing our apartment.

'Miss Brindleton, where do you think Jason's loyalties lie?'

'What do you mean?'

'Has Jason ever done anything that made you suspect that his loyalties may not be first and foremost with Britain?'

This was the question that made me realise what these Internal Security men were really driving at. Jason and I, were under suspicion for passing information to a foreign power. Until now, this idea had never even occurred to me. I had been happily discussing my research findings with the CEO believing him to be the CEO of a top-secret British agency. Internal Security were now forcefully suggesting otherwise. Next, their questions focused on the CEO.

'How many times have you met this CEO?

'Five, perhaps six times.'

'Are other people present?'

'No. Only the first time when Jason came with me to make the introductions.'

'Has the CEO ever told you his name?'

'No.'

'So, how do you address him?'

'I call him "sir."'

'Where do you meet?'

'We always meet at a pub.'

'Which one?'

'It's called "The Red Fox."'

'How often do you meet?'

'Perhaps fortnightly. If I have any exciting new findings related to my research then we meet more urgently.'

'Describe the CEO to us. What does he look like?'

'Middle aged, fit and healthy, definitely British, he speaks the Queen's English. He's strongly built. Plays squash I know, because he brought a racquet with him once. He's quite good looking with a full head of hair although it could be a wig. He has a full beard and dresses smartly.'

'Are there any distinguishing marks? A scar perhaps? A mole? Gold plated tooth? Anything that could be helpful?'

I pictured the CEO in my mind's eye for a moment or two but could think of nothing in particular that might distinguish him from others. The men asked several more questions about the CEO's appearance until satisfied they had an accurate description.

'When are you planning to meet the CEO again?'

'Next Wednesday for lunch.'

'Good. What time?'

'One o'clock.'

'At the "Red Fox" again?'

'Yes.'

'On your own?'

'Yes.'

'Miss Brindleton, we believe your so-called, CEO, is a Soviet agent and that you and Jason have been well and truly manipulated.

This puts you both in a most unenviable position; open to the accusation of working with the Soviets. We are going to offer you the opportunity, however, to make amends and avoid any action being taken against you. Are you interested?'

'Of course, I am. I had absolutely no idea what I was getting myself into. I must have been hood-winked, Jason too...'

'You need to understand, Miss Brindleton, we are yet to be convinced that you are merely a naïve innocent party in all of this. There are extremely serious consequences should we determine you have knowingly and willingly cooperated with the Soviets.'

# 45.

.......

# Jason

This afternoon I finished my research studies early and walked down to Bill Bryce's second-hand car dealership which is only three blocks away. Betty and I have decided to purchase a decent second-hand car. A colleague recommended Bill Bryce's dealership as having a wide range of good quality vehicles. He purchased his car there and felt they gave him an "honest" deal, something that seems rare amongst second-hand car merchants nowadays. This is the first dealership I've visited so I'm new to this game.

Most of Bill Bryce's stock is on display out doors and potential customers are encouraged to wander around. One salesman has already approached me offering to assist, but I discouraged him by saying I was "looking only" and definitely wouldn't be buying today. The cars appear outwardly to be in good condition and proudly display their respective signs informing customers of the model, year of release and asking price, together with a sales pitch such as "genuine bargain" or "too good to miss" or "one owner only." I slowly wandered around viewing Austin/Morris 1100s, Vauxhalls, Minis, a couple of Triumph Spitfires, even a few Renaults and Citroens. As I approached a silver Jaguar, I noticed a couple of smartly dressed young men observing me from behind the next row of cars. I've just ditched one over-enthusiastic salesman. Surely, they're not sending two my way this time.

The silver Jaguar is the best car in the yard but also comes with the highest price tag. I walk round to the rear of the car and suddenly, without warning, the two men who were observing me a moment ago, are standing on either side of me. I now realise they are considerably larger than I am and both look menacing.

'Jason Stenhammer?' asks the one on my left.

'Yes, that's me.'

'We're from Internal Security,' adds the man on my other side. 'We're taking you in for questioning.'

'What the hell for?'

'You'll find out.'

The man on my left wafts an ID badge in front of my face and firmly takes hold of my upper arm. The other man fastens onto my right arm. I'm given no choice in the matter as I'm propelled along between the rows of cars. I'm literally frog-marched towards a black sedan parked on the road side.

This is all very sudden and I'm tempted to yell out for help. The men have anticipated my thinking, however, and one of them growls, 'don't even think of calling out. It will only make it worse. Keep your mouth shut and everything will be explained shortly.'

I decide to take the man's advice and allow myself to be hustled into the back seat of the waiting car. Once ensconced in the back seat with the door slammed shut, I speak up.

'I want to know what the bloody hell you think you're doing. You can't pick up people in the street like this, it's not allowed.'

'It is allowed, if someone is suspected of treason.'

'What on earth are you talking about?'

'I suspect you know *exactly* what we're talking about.'

'This is crazy. I've got my rights as a citizen, and I demand a solicitor.'

The men ignored me and started discussing which was the best route to take. It was soon apparent they didn't know Oxford well and were unfamiliar with the one-way system in the heart of the city. After taking a couple of wrong turns, we ended up at a police station. I was bundled out of the car and taken to a Nissan hut set up behind the car park. At some stage the hut's interior had been divided into a string of small interview rooms linked by a narrow passage-way. It was poorly lit and smelt musty. There was nobody else about and I was roughly ushered into the first of the uninviting rooms.

The interview room had nothing to commend it. It was cold and damp. Three metal chairs were stacked up in the corner of the room and a small wooden table, not much larger than a school desk, occupied the centre of the room. The place hadn't been cleaned for a long time; cobwebs hung about the dirty window and in the corners of the room. What looked like mouse droppings were scattered across the floor.

'Jesus, this is a bloody awful place,' exclaimed the older of the pair. 'See if that gas heater works, Basil.'

The man called Basil produced a cigarette lighter. After a couple of tries the gas heater leapt into a row of blue flames and then coloured red as it started to emit more warmth. The three dusty chairs were roughly assembled around the table and I was ordered to sit on one of them. Basil pulled out a packet of "Players" and offered them to the older man and then, grudgingly, to me. We both declined whilst Basil lit up and began to fill the room with blue smoke. Finally, the older man spoke again.

'My name's Harry Carpenter. I'm a senior investigator with Internal Security. I apologise for the state of this place but it's the best we could get at short notice. My colleague here is Basil Trelawney.'

Basil gave me an unfriendly nod and drew heavily on his fag. He was a squat man with small beady eyes and a mop of unruly hair. I could imagine him as a weight-lifter or a wrestler with his meaty sausage-like fingers. Not someone to mess with. He sat with his legs crossed while the fingers on his left hand tapped repeatedly on the table as if a tune was humming repeatedly through his brain.

Harry Carpenter was a very different kettle of fish. Tall, fiftyish with a receding hairline, he was clearly the brains of the pair and had probably enjoyed a private school education. There was nothing thug-like about Harry, his long, well-manicured fingers were like those of a pianist. He wore horn-rimmed glasses that annoyed him intensely because they stubbornly refused to stay in place for more than a minute or two. Harry settled himself down, removed his tiresome spectacles and for the first time looked me straight in the eyes. He appeared to be assessing me before he spoke.

'Mr. Stenhammer, I believe you're a doctoral student?'

'That's correct.'

'What are you researching?'

'Nuclear fusion.'

'In simple English, explain to us what your research is aiming to achieve.'

I spent the next five minutes outlining my main hypothesis and describing the research methodology I was employing. I think Harry understood the gist of what I was saying but the lights didn't come on for Basil. At the end of my explanation, I felt I must challenge the motivation of these two men.

'I've outlined my research to you. Now, I think I'm entitled to know what this inquisition is all about?'

'Earlier today, Internal Security received an urgent request to look into your activities and those of a lady by the name of Betty Brindleton. It has been alleged the two of you have been passing on confidential and highly sensitive material to an unknown person, or persons who may not be friendly to the West.'

'What!' I exclaimed, 'where's all this rubbish coming from?'

Harry rummaged about in the top inside pocket of his tweed jacket and produced a scruffy envelope which he referred to.

'An eminent scientist... Sir Peter Meirs.'

'This can't be right. He's my academic supervisor, for heaven's sake!'

'Well I can assure you, this assertion is being treated as a breach of security and at a dangerously high level. Four of us have travelled up from London today as a matter of some urgency. Our two colleagues are interrogating Miss Brindleton while we speak with you.'

'Betty's my girlfriend,' I blurt out, 'what's happening to her?'

'She's answering their questions as we speak.'

'But...this is stupid...there's nothing for you to be alarmed about!'

'On the contrary, Mr. Stenhammer, we beg to differ. Perhaps you would like to tell us who, apart from your academic supervisor, you have been discussing your research findings with?'

'Betty, my girlfriend and a few fellow research students. This is normal practice and is encouraged.'

'Indeed...' Harry re-positioned his errant spectacles again, 'and... who else?'

'My employer.'

'And who is that?'

'I'm not at liberty to say.'

'Why the bloody hell not you tosser,' interjected Basil, vehemently.

'Answer the question please Mr. Stenhammer.'

'I only speak to the CEO.'

'A man or a woman?'

'A male.'

'Does he have a name?'

'I don't know his name.'

'Doesn't that strike you as being odd, Mr. Stenhammer?'

'No, because it's a British company, based here in Oxford and protected by the Official Secrets Act of 1939.'

'Really? Well... it might interest you to know that the company is so secret nobody else in Britain has ever heard of it. It seems the only people who know about this company are you and Miss Betty Brindleton.'

'That's nonsense. I don't believe you.'

'You better bloody believe it mate,' Basil chimes in again, angrily.

'Sir Peter Meirs is unaware of its existence,' Harry adds. 'Surely, if this is a legitimate company working in the field of nuclear fusion, an eminent scientist like him would know everything about it?'

'Well, I can't explain that.'

'That's not good enough Mr. Stenhammer. We are holding you for further questioning on suspicion of illegally imparting confidential material and contrary to the Official Secrets Act of 1939.'

'That's preposterous. You have no right to hold me on such a ridiculous trumped-up charge.'

'Handcuff him please, Basil. I'll arrange for Mr. Stenhammer to be held in the overnight cells here tonight. Then I'll exchange views with our colleagues who have been interrogating the young woman before deciding our next course of action.'

For the first time in my life, I was handcuffed and led away to an overnight police cell.

# 46.

.......

# Michael

I must have been doing my morning and afternoon surveillance tasks for a couple of months and I suppose I have seen Betty once a week if I'm lucky. The urge to join her as she walks along the road is all-consuming. The first few times Betty didn't seem to mind if I joined her and she was highly amused when I explained I was there to keep an eye on her. She scoffed at the idea that she was in any sort of danger. One afternoon I crossed the road to join Betty as usual, but things went horribly wrong.

'Hi Betty, I love your new dress.'

'Do you,' she retorted, angrily.

'Oh! Have you had a bad day?'

'Yes, I have. And seeing you isn't helping!'

I fell into step beside her. The least I could do was try and cheer her up. I'd had some good news at school that day and decided to share it. I thought it might help to lift her mood.

'Guess what happened to me today, Betty?'

She stopped abruptly and turned to face me. She was furious.

'Michael, you're a bloody pervert! Have you got nothing better to do than hang around outside my place half the day spying on me? There's something wrong with you! You're fixated! Are you some sort of a sex maniac? Fuck off!'

With that, she broke into a trot and virtually ran to the red door at the entrance to her block of apartments. I stayed rooted to the spot, speechless. Never before had Betty spoken to me so viciously. What she had said was hurtful and unfair and my mood plummeted. There was no point staying any longer. I made my way back to my car parked down the street in a half hour parking zone only to find I had over-stayed by ten minutes and incurred a hefty parking fine.

As I drove back to my lonely little flat, I tried to make sense of Betty's angry reaction. What had brought it on? I honestly didn't know, but I longed to spend some time with her to help her deal with whatever was troubling her. Most likely her research was not progressing as well as she hoped. Perhaps her on-going problems with her parents had erupted again. Then, with a sudden leap of hope, I wondered whether she and Josh had had a major falling out. Maybe it was a combination of all these things. Whatever the reason or reasons, I feared Betty would never be sharing it with me. Furthermore, she had made it abundantly clear she wanted me to back off and leave her alone. Yet, I was still worried about Betty's safety and what she was getting herself involved with. In the end, I resolved to continue watching her place but not speak with her. In a week or two she would most likely be over her problems and then, maybe, I could resume my short impromptu chats.

\* \* \*

It's almost three weeks since Betty's unexplained fiery outburst. I still watch her place most mornings and afternoons on my way to and from school but have resisted crossing the road to talk to her on the few occasions I have seen her leave or return to her apartment. Each time I see Betty I feel agitated. I love her dearly still and cannot imagine a future life without her in it. Most of my friends think I'm crazy and have advised me to move on. None of them waited five years for a girlfriend to accept them. My parents think the same way and have gently tried to persuade me to look for a new partner.

Mum and dad think Betty has behaved very badly towards me. I suppose, eventually, I may have to accept everyone's well-meant advice but I'm not prepared to give up just yet.

One afternoon I was standing in my usual spot in the shade of an ancient elm tree that marked the entrance to a small park. It was conveniently located almost opposite Betty's home. The tree afforded pleasant shade in summer time and limited protection from the wind and rain of winter. Over the months I had come to know the squirrels that cavorted about in the branches of the elm or careered across the lawns. I even knew where the birds' nests were, which ones were still occupied and which ones deserted. A couple of times I had even picked wild mushrooms growing in the lawns.

I had become quite well known to a few folks. The council gardener, responsible for looking after the small park, would always come over for a quick chat about the weather or to complain about people who dropped litter in "his" park. Then there were the regulars who would be hurrying off to work or walking back home in the afternoon. One old dear would stop without fail on her way back from the shops. She always seemed to be dressed in the same clothes and carried the same shopping bag which was never more than half full with perhaps a loaf of bread, a cabbage or a handful of potatoes. She explained small, frequent shopping trips were the best way to manage her arthritis.

On this particular afternoon, the gardener had just finished telling me he had planted fifty tulip bulbs in his best garden bed in readiness for Spring, when I noticed Betty rounding the corner at the end of the street on her way home. Every time she suddenly appeared like this, I felt my heart rate leap and had to resist the urge to run over and give her a hug and a kiss. It was almost a month since Betty had snapped at me so cruelly and I reckoned by now it could be safe to run across the road again and engage her in conversation. As always she looked so desirable with a cute pony tail and a mini skirt that showed off her legs to full advantage. High heels gave her that magic poise that accentuated her shapely figure. For a brief moment I recalled the few weekends we had shared together when she gave me to believe she might be in love with me.

As Betty came down the road, I lost sight of her for a moment, as a shiny black limousine glided past her and pulled in to park right in front of her apartment's red door. I watched intrigued as two men sprang from the vehicle and hurried towards Betty. Within seconds they were talking earnestly to her and I could see Betty looked worried. I considered running across the road and intervening; Betty might at least be grateful for my moral support. I was too late, however. Within half a minute the men opened the car's back door and appeared to order Betty to get in. She was clearly reluctant to do so, but obeyed. The car's engine must have still been running because without a moment's delay, it pulled out and with a screech of its tyres turned 180 degrees and headed off in the opposite direction where it was obliged to stop at the traffic lights.

It had all happened so quickly. Who were these men and what did they want with my beautiful girl? My gut feeling was that they were police which meant Betty must be in trouble for something. If so, the men would be taking her to one of the three or four police stations in town. I raced to my car to try to follow the black limousine so I would know to which police station she had been taken. I was concerned, however, that there was nothing to indicate it was a police vehicle and the men were not wearing police uniforms. Another possibility, that didn't bear thinking about, was that she had been kidnapped. Perhaps these men were rapists and seeing an attractive woman walking along the street alone decided to jump her; an opportunistic crime. If this was the case surely Betty would have resisted strenuously, screamed and put up a fight. Another possibility was the men were from the mysterious secret British company paying Josh and Betty's salary and providing their apartment for free. Maybe this was the way they did business?

I jumped into my car and followed the black limousine. I was too late though and had to watch helplessly as the black car moved off through the lights when they turned green, leaving me stranded at the lights as they went back to red. If it was a police car, I had lost contact and didn't know where it was headed. Now I would have to drive around the four Oxford police stations and ask at each one whether Betty Brindleton had been brought in for questioning and, if so, on what charge.

It took me over an hour. None of the police stations had any record of a young woman by the name of Betty Brindleton being wanted for questioning or being signed in. At the fourth and last station, I formally reported what I had witnessed. The policeman on duty dubiously took down the rather flimsy details I could provide. Understandably, he was unsure how to report the incident. Was it a kidnap? Was it a missing person case? He even suggested it might have been nothing more than a couple of her male friends picking her up to go to a party. He didn't seem to think there was anything that could be done that evening and advised me to get in touch next morning if I was still worried.

## 47.

# Malcolm

A short time ago, I ended a long phone call with my friend, Michael. He was in quite a state. Apparently, Betty, who he still dotes over, had been taken in for questioning by Inland Security officers. After a couple of hours of interrogation, they had driven her home to the apartment she shared with her boyfriend, Josh Stenhammer. When they dropped her off the two officers told her Josh was being held overnight and not to expect him home until sometime the next day. Predictably, Betty was very unhappy. Unhappy about being taken in for questioning, unhappy that she was suspected of passing secrets to Soviet agents and then finally arriving home to an empty apartment and hearing of Josh's prolonged imprisonment.

After being held at the police station for a couple of hours Betty badly needed a shoulder to cry on. At first, she thought of Lucy, but it was about the time that little Graham was probably being put to bed, so she changed her mind and rang Michael instead. She had been feeling bad about the way she had treated her old boyfriend some weeks back, and this call would also give her a chance to make-up and be friends again. Michael was hugely relieved to hear from her and explained how he had spent time going around the various police stations trying to find her. Now it was Michael's turn to seek a sympathetic ear.

Once Michael finished outlining what had happened to him over the last few hours, the two of us settled down to discuss what it all meant and what could possibly be done to support Betty. It was a long phone call and I was glad Michael was paying. Lucy realised our conversation was important and kindly volunteered to put Graham to bed and read him a story, which was my job usually.

Michael and I agreed on almost everything. From the outset we had been uncomfortable about Betty and Josh meeting up with some mysterious, nameless CEO to report on progress with their nuclear fusion research. For us outsiders, it sounded distinctly dubious. We were even more concerned when we learnt that Jason, and later Betty, were receiving salaries from this so-called British company and that the luxurious apartment was also part of the deal. In our own ways we had both stressed caution to Betty and asked her to find out more about the secretive British company. Betty was, however, full of confidence and assured us Jason had months ago done the necessary checking and cross checking. She was, she said, perfectly happy to trust Jason's judgement.

Michael and I also agreed it was extraordinary Professor Peter Meirs had not been informed of Betty and Josh's connection with this company. Was this because the pair had been warned not to let their supervisor know? Was it a deliberate deception? If so, it seemed tantamount to guilt. Had the company insisted their academic supervisor be kept in the dark? If this was the case it made the whole bizarre story even more sinister.

Next, Michael and I turned our attention to what would happen as a result of this debacle.

'If these Inland Security guys believe Betty and Josh have a case to answer, then the situation is dire,' ventured Michael. 'If, in fact, the company is bogus, or Soviet controlled, they are in deep shit and will end up doing time. It'll probably be the end of their PhD work. Betty, for one, will be totally shattered. All she has ever wanted to do is scientific research.'

'There has to be some sort of court of law,' I added. 'They can't be put away without a proper trial in front of a beak or a full jury.'

'Who knows?' added Michael, 'infringements of the Official Secrets Act maybe be dealt with behind closed doors. That way they can protect against more sensitive material getting out.'

'Yes, that sounds plausible. So Michael, is there anything we can do to help Betty right now?'

'Not much. She has promised to keep in touch with me and tell me of any new developments. Betty's been ordered to report to the central police station tomorrow at mid-day for further questioning. By then, Inland Security will have compared Betty's story with what Josh has told them.'

'How long can they legally keep Josh locked up?'

'Twenty-four hours, I think.'

'Michael, do you think we should be trying to find a solicitor for Betty?'

'Not yet mate. Hopefully it doesn't come to that. I don't have the money for those guys anyway.'

We ended our conversation there. Too many unknowns...

# 48.

## Dorothy

I've just heard from Lucy. They are all well and bub number two is coming along according to plan.

Her reason for ringing was on behalf of her best friend Betty, who, it appears, is in a spot of trouble. Lucy didn't go into details but it seems Betty may have fallen foul of Internal Security for being too free with her research findings. Lucy and Malcolm think Betty may soon be in need of a good solicitor, which is why they have just contacted me.

Tom and I had a close friend, Libby Johnson, who is a solicitor. Even though Tom left me all those years ago, Libby and I have ever since remained firm friends. We lock horns on the tennis court regularly and get together for a good "natter" from time to time. Like me, Libby is a widow and has never re-married. Her husband died of leukemia at the tragically young age of thirty-five leaving her two children to bring up on her own. So, we have much in common.

When Tom disappeared there were a number of legal matters that needed urgent attention. A husband suddenly disappearing without trace is virtually unheard of and I was confronted with a number of legal matters that I had no idea how to handle. There were dealings and arrangements to be negotiated with the police, Tom's workplace, Internal Security, the bank, the taxation office, social security and various other instrumentalities. With three children under seven, I simply couldn't cope. In stepped my friend, Libby Johnson. Only twelve months' earlier she had been through a batch of legal problems after the loss of her husband.

Libby rescued me! I don't know what I would have done without her support and legal expertise. I struggled to meet her professional costs and expenses though and she ended up doing some of my work pro bono. I could never repay her except with my unstinting friendship and sometimes helping with her two children. Lucy and my two boys knew her as "Auntie Libby" and always enjoyed a happy relationship with her. Hence, Lucy's request to sound out "Auntie Libby." According to Lucy, Betty might be in serious trouble and in need of someone like Auntie Libby, now a barrister, to provide some professional help. To be perfectly honest, now that Libby is a senior barrister and extremely busy, she will be horrendously expensive.

Later that evening I rang Betty's mum, Glenis. It would be good to have a catch-up. At the same time, I might find out whether they had heard anything about Betty's predicament. I knew matters were still horribly strained between Betty and her parents and thought it unlikely. I was right. I didn't even mention that Betty could be in trouble. Doctor Brindleton would go off his head if he knew the unfortunate girl was now in strife with Internal Security.

At least, if it became necessary to employ Libby Johnson, I knew the Brindletons could afford her substantial fees.

# 49.

......

# Doctor Brindleton

Glenis and I went to nine o'clock mass this Sunday. It was not a good decision. Normally we take it easy on Sunday mornings and attend the eleven o'clock service. Apart from the struggle to get there on time, the nine o'clock mass is the one where that dreadful woman came and spoke to me about Betty and her adoption of all those sinful ideas of free love. I shudder every time I think about it. The cheek of the woman! I believe she actually enjoyed telling me how my one and only child had fallen from grace. The most awful thing about that brief conversation was that it turned out to be true. Betty unashamedly practices and proudly boasts about this disgusting form of debauchery. I really don't know what the world's coming to!

I warned Glenis to avoid the woman if she was at mass today. Then, when we were taking our seats a few minutes before mass, I suddenly spotted her. The nasty woman was sitting on the opposite side of the aisle, wearing a tarty looking hat, and in the company of a man I had not seen before. I dug Glenis in the ribs and pointed the woman out. Glenis gave me a knowing nod.

The Catholic church at West Dryton is small and serves the faithful in our village and its immediate environs. Our numbers have been slowly declining over the years and there has even been talk of combining the two masses in the future. Today's congregation numbered around a hundred and I calculated that if we moved quickly enough at the end of the service, we could shake

Father O'Bryan's hand and be out the church door and away before "that woman" had time to approach us.

As soon as the service ended, I hustled Glenis out of the pew and together we made our way smartly down the aisle towards Father O'Bryan who was already dutifully standing at the church door to farewell his parishioners. I thought we had done well, until from nowhere, came that awful chirrupy voice.

'Good morning, Doctor Brindleton. I'm so pleased you are here today.'

My heart sank. I knew that voice only too well. Where had she suddenly materialised from? I turned and offered her the curtest of nods I could muster. Then I swivelled around and studiously ignored her as we approached Father O'Bryan.

'Doctor Brindleton, please spare me a moment of your precious time after we have greeted Father O'Bryan.'

'Yes, of course,' I mumbled, frostily.

As soon as Glenis and I had made our salutations to the elderly Father O'Bryan, we headed briskly down the narrow path towards the wooden lych gate at the entrance to the church grounds but the wretched woman ran after us.

'Doctor Brindleton...Doctor Brindleton...you promised me a moment of your time...'

There was no escape. In trepidation, I stopped and turned. Glenis, fortuitously, saw a friend nearby and moved off leaving me to face the woman on my own.

The woman, accompanied by her much taller male friend, pulled up next to me with a satisfied smug look on her face.

'Thank you so much for waiting, doctor,' she smiled sarcastically, tidying her hair at the same time. 'This is my partner, Arnold,' she beamed. Arnold and I shook hands.

'Do you remember me doctor? I'm the lady who passed on some interesting news to you about your daughter some weeks ago,' she looked at me, expectantly.

'Yes, I think I do,' I responded, with a deep sense of foreboding.

'Well, I'm often up in Oxford and I have contacts there. I'm a Tupperware sales lady, you see. Perhaps your wife might be interested in hosting one of my Tupperware parties one day?'

'I doubt it,' I replied, as forcefully as possible without sounding too rude.

'Anyway, I thought you might not have heard that your daughter's been in trouble with the authorities. It was all over the Oxford Mail yesterday.'

The woman, I could see, was relishing this encounter. She looked up at me keenly to observe my reaction. I immediately thought of Betty's perverse ideas about free love. Had Betty now been trying to seduce someone important? Had she been caught out and exposed in some ghastly sexually embarrassing orgy? Was there a scandal brewing about her living with a married man? Instinctively, I crossed myself and braced to hear what horrors this woman was determined to reveal.

'I don't think you've heard about it doctor, have you?'

'No... I don't think I have.'

The woman seemed more than pleased to hear this and lent forward conspiratorially, lowering her voice as she did so. Her partner moved closer too, worried he might miss out on whatever juicy morsel of scandal she was about to impart.

'It's the law, doctor. She's been arrested by the special police for breaking the law. Her boyfriend was also arrested. He's still in prison, but they let your Betty out.'

'Arrested? What on earth for?' I blurted out.

'Secrets doctor. The paper said she's been giving secrets to the Soviets. Special police came up from London to deal with the matter. I can't remember what the police were called...interior police, or something like that. Her boyfriend's up on the same charge. They reckon if they're found guilty, they'll be put away for years, maybe life!'

I felt suddenly weak in the knees and nauseous. I feared I was going to faint. I needed something to hold on to and staggered a few paces further down the path to prop myself up against the wooden lych gate. Through my fog, I was vaguely aware the woman was speaking again.

'Are you okay doctor? There's a seat in the gate if you need it.'

The woman's partner took my arm and sat me down on one of the bench seats built into the lych gate. And there I remained for several minutes until someone told Glenis I was unwell. She came hurrying over and I was conscious of several other people fussing around me. After a few minutes I felt a little better and it was collectively agreed I could now go home as long as Glenis did the driving. As we left the church grounds, I remember looking back to see where that dreadful woman and her partner were, but they had disappeared.

* * *

I said nothing as we drove home. Glenis kept looking my way to see whether I was okay and remained strangely silent too. I realised I must be suffering from slight shock. Feelings of dizziness, fainting and weakness were typical symptoms. Less easy to recognise was a drop in blood pressure, the most concerning symptom when a person is in shock. I placed a hand on my wrist to gauge my pulse rate; it appeared to be more rapid yet weaker than usual. I knew I would need to take it easy when we reached home.

Glenis was kindlier and more cooperative than usual after she sat me down in my favourite armchair. In fact, she couldn't do enough to help. Gone was the bossy woman who pestered me constantly every morning before work, checking I had everything. This was the Glenis of old, wanting to please and happy to do whatever I asked. I was tempted to ask my wife for a stiff whisky but knew that, medically, this was not recommended. I settled for a good cup of freshly brewed tea instead.

Glenis, I could tell, was worried about me. My bit of a turn had shaken her too. Soon, however, I felt the warmth of the tea calming me down and I smiled pleasantly at Glenis.

'Thank you my dear. I expect you'd like to know why I had a bit of a turn this morning?'

'I imagine it was that awful woman again?'

'Yes, you're right, although it was not so much the woman, per se, but the message she conveyed.'

I took another mouthful of tea, and feeling even better, requested a couple of sticks of Kit Kat; one of my favourite treats. Glenis obliged, returning quickly, anxious to hear more.

'So...did she have some more news of Betty?'

'Yes, and it's not good. You had better sit down dear and I'll tell you everything. Then we must decide what's best to do.'

It didn't take long to repeat the news from "the woman" and to answer a couple of questions Glenis asked.

'Now of course, Glenis, what this woman has told us may not be strictly accurate. I wouldn't be surprised also, if she's not given to using a bit of hyperbole. We need to verify what the woman is claiming has happened to Betty. For example, the woman was babbling on about the "Interior police" and I don't believe this country has such an organisation. What this means, my dear, is that you need to telephone Betty as soon as possible and get her side of the story. It may not be nearly as bad as the woman is making out. Sadly, Betty and I are hardly on speaking terms so you'll need to make the call.'

'I think that's an excellent idea, dear. I'll ring her now. Would you like another cup of tea before I ring?'

I accepted a second cup of tea and enjoyed my second stick of Kit Kat while Glenis made her call. Sometime later I awoke to find Glenis back in her armchair and keen to tell me what had transpired.

'Oh, sorry my dear. I must have had a little nap. Did you get through?'

'Yes, she was home and I had a good chat. The woman had it basically correct and it does sound serious, dear.'

'I was afraid that's the case.'

'Let me see if I can summarise what Betty told me. It was not the "interior police" who detained Betty and her boyfriend; it was "Internal Security." The boyfriend, Josh, was held for almost twenty-four hours and Betty thinks the authorities are far more worried about him than her. Josh has been working for the company six months longer than Betty and it was he, not Betty, who was given the apartment rent-free. According to Betty, she and Josh are under suspicion for supplying confidential material to the Soviets. It seems the company that had been paying them both a salary is a bogus company. Believe it or not, the company is actually thought to be a front for Soviet agents collecting information about the latest British research into nuclear fusion.'

'Oh, how dreadful! What have we done, Glenis, to deserve such a daughter? First, she comes out as some sort of a sexual deviant and now she's been caught passing confidential research findings to the Soviet Union. It can hardly get any worse!'

'I think you might be exaggerating a little, dear. Nothing has been proved yet with regard to the Soviets; it could all be a massive mistake. More than ever, Betty needs all our love and support to help her through this.'

I didn't share Glenis's optimism.

# 50.

......

# Jason

I 'm home at last, exhausted and emotionally spent. The
lovely Betty is fixing me a drink and something to eat.
The food I was given in the police cells was lousy. Thank
God I endured only twenty-four hours in captivity. I don't think
I could have coped with much more.

The two men who had first taken me in for questioning, Harry
and the unsavoury Basil, left me after half an hour with a cup of tea
and a biscuit, making sure I was safely locked in. To my surprise,
two other men returned a little time later and took me across to
Interview Room 4 located in the police building itself.

The older of these two new men introduced himself as Dave
Worsborough and spoke with a slight speech defect. His face had
been somewhat re-arranged and I guessed he'd been either a boxer
or a rugby player in his younger days. One ear was mangled giving
him what is sometimes referred to as a "cauliflower ear." At some
stage his nose had been badly broken too and left flattened so he
looked like a bulldog. Dave appeared to like his misshapen visage
though and used it to promote a tough-guy image. Even his hands
were solid with thick wrists and sausage-like digits. A scar above
his left eye completed his brutish looks.

The younger man I found far more impressive. He was well dressed,
spoke with a public-school accent and sported a small, neatly trimmed
black moustache. A pair of glasses gave him a bookish appearance and
I guessed he was some sort of university graduate. His right eye-lid

had a disconcerting, uncontrollable twitch, which, after a few hours of interrogation became highly irritating. Dave referred to him as "sir" or Nigel. I never discovered his surname. It was clear that Nigel was the brains and the senior of the pair. Perhaps Dave's role was limited to roughing up anyone who was uncooperative whilst Nigel was conveniently out of the room?

I was to get to know Interview Room 4 intimately over the next twenty-four hours. As interview rooms go, I reckon this one was at the more comfortable end of the spectrum. A newish rectangular table was placed up against one wall together with a modern recording system and four reasonably comfortable matching chairs, two on either side of the table. A double window looked out over a car park below. The room smelt as though it had only recently been painted or perhaps it was a strong disinfectant? A metal radiator punched out heat from a centralised system from time to time. The only other object in the room was a standard issue photograph of her Majesty Queen Elizabeth II who smiled down graciously on whatever transpired in Interview Room 4 as, no doubt, she did in all other official interview rooms.

I won't bore you with the countless questions and answers that went back and forth for many hours. Instead, I'll summarise what happened.

Nigel and Dave focused on the man I called "Norman," the CEO who had met me for several lunches as he lured me in to sign up for his company. They wanted every detail I could provide; what "Norman" looked like, where we had met, what he wanted to hear about, the enticements he offered. Then they moved on to our regular Thursday "mentor" sessions at which "Norman" and I had discussed developments in nuclear fusion research. "Norman," I told them, was a nuclear physicist with more than sufficient background and knowledge to interact meaningfully with me.

A number of obvious gaps in my knowledge seriously perplexed them. They found it hard to believe that I knew nothing about "the company" and had never met anyone else from "the company" other than the mysterious man I referred to as "Norman."

I don't know how many times we went over and over the same ground. As I fatigued, the more confused I became until I was unsure what I was telling them. After a few hours, Nigel and Dave handed over to another pair of interrogators, Harry Carpenter and Basil Trelawney, the same two men who had interrogated Betty.

At some stage I was served an evening meal; a mug of tea, an almost cold meat pie with a pile of overcooked vegetables and a large green apple. Unappetising as the meal was, I wolfed it down since I was ravenous. After the meal was cleared away I was subjected to yet another battery of questions from Nigel and the ugly looking Dave, who had returned for a second innings. Finally, around eleven o'clock, I was led away to an overnight lock-up call. It was basic. There was a toilet in the corner, a small sink and a bunk with a worn mattress, a grubby pillow and two or three folded army blankets. It was all I could do to collapse on the bunk, fully clothed, and pray I'd be allowed the luxury of a full night's sleep.

I was woken at seven to the sound of keys rattling in the lock and the call, 'breakfast'. The door swung open and a burly constable eyed me over carefully, decided I wasn't dangerous and then placed a tray on the end of my bunk. 'Get that into ya...' and he was gone. My second meal in captivity was no better than the first; a mug of insipid tea, a bowl of tepid, solid porridge with a blob of brown sugar in the centre and another large green apple. The porridge was barely palatable but I ate it to give me the strength to keep going. I had no idea how long I was going to be held, although I vaguely remembered reading somewhere that you could not be held for more than twenty-four hours without being formally accused of committing a crime.

Dave and Nigel reappeared around nine o'clock and escorted me to their unmarked police car. They wanted me to take them to the small cottage about half an hour out of Oxford where I had been meeting Norman for my regular mentoring sessions. The cottage was being rented by the company. I had seen little of the interior except the sitting room that doubled as an office, a small bathroom and a poorly stocked kitchen. Norman had told me nobody was living there but it was a handy place to have out in the country for small meetings and the storing of files. I never met anyone else at the cottage. Betty only met Norman in one of the Oxford pubs.

As Dave drove us to the cottage, following my navigating instructions, Nigel began to open up. After questioning me for many hours and comparing my responses to those provided by Betty, the four interrogators had now decided how they were going to proceed. They had come to the conclusion that "Norman" was indeed a Soviet agent and that he had cleverly deceived Betty and I into believing we were working for and being paid by a British company. Betty and I had been duped. They found it difficult to believe that we had been so easily taken in. 'Naïve, academic twits' was how Nigel described us. According to Internal Security there was no British company and the salaries Norman was paying us were being funnelled in by the Soviets.

Their plan now was to meticulously search the cottage to gather evidence that would hold up in a court of law. This had to be done in such a way that Norman wouldn't notice someone had been through the place.

A few minutes later we pulled up outside Norman's limestone cottage. A second car pulled in behind us bringing Harry Carpenter and Basil Trelawney and two other plain clothes police.

The cottage had previously been a farm house, built most likely for a farm labourer and his family back in the eighteenth century. The garden had been neglected for years, although some mature trees remained and the surrounding limestone garden walls were still intact. The house needed a paint job. Norman had told me the last occupants, an elderly couple, had vacated the house about two years ago. Presumably, Norman had had access to sufficient Soviet funds to re-wire the place and update the plumbing so everything was back in good working order. Norman had also ordered a large load of firewood that was neatly stored in the shed behind the cottage and provided the heating when required.

# 51.

# Lucy

Malcolm is always late home on Thursday evenings following football training. More often than not he's covered in mud and smelling sweaty when he blows in around seven o'clock. I'm not complaining though, because he resists going down to the local with most of the boys in the team who pine for a few beers. It's mostly the single lads that frequent the pub.

Whilst Malcolm is in the bath, I receive a phone call from my good friend Betty; I rarely get a call from Betty at this time in the evening. She tells me something really serious has come up and she wants our opinion on what best to do. She says it's something she can't talk about over the phone. It sounds mysterious and ominous. Anyway, she'll be arriving in an hour or so. I warn Malcolm to get properly dressed and not appear only in his pyjamas. I manage to settle Graham down to sleep a little early.

Shortly after eight o'clock Betty is at the front door. She gives me the longest and most heartfelt hug ever and is clearly deeply worried about something. For a moment I wonder whether I should be offering her something a bit stronger than a tea or hot chocolate. I take her coat and offer her a seat by the fire. Malcolm, appropriately dressed, joins us.

Over the next ten minutes Betty pours out her heart and soul. She tells of her sudden accosting by men from Internal Security, the horrific hours of questioning and her eventual release. She outlines what happened to Josh and how they are both suspected of being informants to a Soviet agent. Betty is convinced she and Josh have been innocently drawn in by a man named Norman to reveal their latest research findings in nuclear fusion. As doctoral students at the cutting edge of developments in the field, they became easy prey for the wily Norman who professed to be the CEO of a clandestine British company. Now, she feels awful about her and Josh's naivete.

'That's an extraordinary story, Betty. I can understand how you feel dreadful about what has happened.'

'Didn't you ever suspect this Norman guy was not what he seemed to be?' asked Malcolm.

'Not really. Josh had signed up with him months before so, naturally, I thought everything was above board. I trusted Josh and I trusted his judgement.'

'But the fact everything was so hush-hush must surely have made you wonder? A secret company? A CEO who wouldn't reveal his real name? You being paid a handsome salary just to pass on the latest information you have on nuclear fusion? Surely, you must have had some suspicions?' Malcolm persisted.

'Yes, I did wonder at the start but Norman was such a likeable man. Almost immediately I felt comfortable with him. He was like a father figure for me. You know about all the problems and disappointments I've had with my own father, don't you? Well, in many ways the friendly, supportive Norman was everything I wanted in a father.'

'Was there anything, anything at all about Norman that made you suspect he was a Soviet agent?'

'Absolutely not. He's as English as an Englishman can be.'

'Spies can be incredibly clever,' remarked Malcolm, 'they can be very difficult to catch out if they have been well trained. I've heard that they are even taught the nursery rhymes of the country they are spying on.'

Betty laughed. 'Well, if Norman is a Soviet, he's brilliant. I think if he *is* a Soviet agent it's more likely he's an Englishman who has been persuaded to spy for the Soviets.'

'That sounds more feasible; a British traitor!'

'Anyway, these guys from Internal Security have given me an opportunity to redeem myself. It sounds dangerous though and I don't know what to do. I have to let them know by ten o'clock tomorrow morning whether I will assist them or not.'

'Intriguing,' says Malcolm, 'tell us what's on offer.'

'Tomorrow I'm due to meet Norman for my fortnightly lunch date. We are meeting at "The Red Fox." He pays for the meal and drinks from the company expense account and I brief him on the latest research I've come across in the last couple of weeks. Sometimes, I give him photocopies of papers I've come across or papers presented at conferences. Anything that's hot in the world of nuclear fusion. He even refunds me the cost of the photocopying. He's so knowledgeable and often asks searching questions. Norman even brings along a small battery-operated tape-recorder which he leaves on the table while we are discussing scientific matters.'

Betty pauses to finish off her hot chocolate and lick her fingers after finishing a ginger-snap biscuit. Malcolm and I wait patiently to hear how Betty can earn her redemption.

'The guys from Internal Security want me to go ahead and attend the lunch as normal. They haven't told me what they're going to do, but I'm sure they will arrest him there. It could be dangerous though! It's possible he'll resist. There could be a brawl in the restaurant. God forbid, there could even be a shoot out!'

'You've got to do it Betty,' Malcolm jumped in, straightaway, 'if this Norman guy has been passing all your stuff back to the Soviets, it's your duty to help get him caught.'

'It's all right for you to be brave and heroic Malcolm, you don't have to actually be there and face the music. What do you think, Lucy?'

'Oh, I don't know. I think I'd ask them to arrest him as he's coming into the pub.'

'Yes, but remember, they don't know who Norman is. They will have to wait for him to sit down at my table to know who their target is.'

'It sounds horribly risky, Betty. I don't think I'd be game.'

So, Betty left the house with two contrary opinions, one strongly in support and one urging caution. No doubt she would have a sleepless night before contacting Internal Security in the morning with her decision.

# 52.

# Michael

Having drawn a complete blank on the afternoon of Betty's abduction by two strange men in a black limousine, there was little more I could do. I tried ringing Betty's apartment several times but to no avail. The phone simply rang out. Jason, I concluded, must be away or out all evening. I had reported Betty's possible kidnapping at the last police station and given them a detailed description of the woman I loved. The policeman had asked what my relationship was to the missing person. Was I the husband, a relative or her boyfriend? When I couldn't claim to be any of these, I think he viewed me merely as a jealous admirer verging on the obsessed.

Needless to say, I barely slept that night. Betty had quite literally disappeared. In the short fleeting sleeps I did manage, I dreamt about Betty across a string of places and situations. I saw her on the side of the football pitch in West Dryton, at home with her parents, sneaking out to meet me in the dead of night just before her "A" levels. There were beautiful memories of enjoying birthday lunches together, meeting Betty with her close friend Lucy, and of course, best of all, making passionate love during the few magic weekends we had shared together.

I was up early next morning as usual. There was no longer any point in watching Betty's apartment from across the street. However, I could start ringing her apartment again. I waited until seven o'clock and telephoned and was thrilled to hear a sleepy Betty answer.

'…Hello…Betty here.'

'Oh Betty, thank God. You must be at home. Are you okay?'

'…Yeah…I'm okay. It's good to hear from you Michael.'

'I've been so worried about you, Betty. I saw you going off in that car yesterday and tried to follow. I thought you were headed for a police station, so I checked them all out but none of the stations had any record of you being brought in. That got me *really* worried!'

'I was at a police station but I was not being interviewed by the police. That's why the police had no record of me coming in. The two men who picked me up were from Internal Security. It seems that Josh and I have made a terrible mistake by getting mixed up with this secret company.'

'As you know, I was worried about the company from the outset. I'm just so relieved to know you are safely home.'

'Josh is still being held by Internal Security and I'm home on my own and feeling pretty awful. Do you want to come round? I can cook up some bacon and eggs if you want…'

'I'll be there in half an hour.'

\*    \*    \*

Betty was fully dressed when I arrived. Yesterday's drama had certainly taken its toll. She gave me a long and loving hug and didn't want to let go. Tears streamed down her face until she hurried to the bedroom that she shared with Jason to find a clean handkerchief. Her pent-up emotions poured out as she ran through the frightening experiences she had suffered since her abduction. Despite her progressive views about free love, her doctoral studies in the field of nuclear fusion, underneath it all, Betty was still a vulnerable young woman. My heart went out to her. I listened and empathised as best I could. Eventually, she was finished telling her story and together we retired to the kitchen to cook the promised eggs and bacon.

'Michael, I do want your advice please about something the Internal Security guys have asked me to consider. I went round to see Lucy and Malcolm last night to ask them what they thought I should do. I have to come to a final decision this morning. Internal Security want me to ring them with my decision before ten o'clock. Josh is not here so I can't ask for his advice.'

I felt a stab of jealousy that Betty would go to Josh for his opinion before mine. At best, I was only a second string to her bow. If I hadn't rung her this morning, she may not have even bothered to ask my opinion.

As we enjoyed our poached eggs and crispy bacon, Betty outlined the proposal the Internal Security men had put to her. They wanted to know if she would be prepared to meet Norman for their regular fortnightly lunch today as if nothing had happened. Although they hadn't said it in so many words, Betty was sure once the two of them were enjoying lunch, Norman would be apprehended.

Betty had some misgivings about the whole idea. Believe it or not, she confessed to liking Norman. She described him as a kindly fatherly figure she had grown to trust. Betty enjoyed their time together. Norman, she said, was highly intelligent, could converse on her level, and at the same time was fun to be with. She still found it hard to believe Norman was considered to be a Soviet agent interested only in the data and research findings she and Jason were feeding him. He seemed such a lovely guy and British to the core. Betty still clung to the hope this whole business was a ghastly mistake and there really was a legitimate secret British company.

'Michael, what do you think I should do? Malcolm said I should cooperate with the Internal Security fellows but Lucy was less sure. It could be dangerous she thought. What happens if everything turns violent? Somebody could get badly hurt. There could even be guns!'

I took a moment before answering.

'Betty, I know you get tired of me saying this, but I'm in love with you. The last thing I would ever want is for you to get hurt. But these guys from Internal Security are specialists in handling these kinds of situations. I'm sure they would deal with the matter professionally and do everything possible to avoid any violent confrontations. I think you owe it to Internal Security to cooperate. This is a chance for you to clear your name and get back on side with Oxford University, your academic supervisor and friends and family. You could even end up being regarded as a bit of a hero.'

'You are so sweet, Michael. Thank you.'

# 53.

# Dorothy

Today I rang Libby Johnson's chambers to ascertain whether she would be interested in defending Betty Brindleton, should it become necessary. As might be expected, Libby was in court but her personal secretary politely took down the few details I provided about the case and promised to ring back after she had had time to speak to her boss. I made sure the secretary also knew that Libby and I were long lasting friends.

Over the many years Libby and I have remained friends we have managed to find time to meet and chat at tennis, Christmas drinks at her place, birthday parties for her and my children. The bond has stayed strong despite the fact that financially we are miles apart. I still struggle financially, whereas Libby Johnson's career has taken off and she's now a comparatively wealthy woman. This discrepancy in our two fortunes has never been an issue and I'm so thankful to Libby for this.

I have to admit that for some time now I have had an ulterior reason for continuing my close friendship with Libby. It's her younger brother, Andrew.

Andrew is a fascinating character who lives life to the full and loves to tell of his adventures to anybody prepared to listen. He has a delightful sense of humour and has everyone laughing almost as soon as he speaks. Quite simply, he's a naturally funny man. Andrew is a dentist and tells endless amusing anecdotes about his unfortunate patients. No names are ever mentioned, of course.

When not inflicting pain on his reluctant clients, Andrew is thrill seeking. He's in his mid-forties but shows no signs of slowing down. His pursuits include mountain climbing, skiing, speleology, orienteering and even shooting the rapids in flimsy little boats. There are probably other death-defying activities he engages in that I have yet to hear about.

Andrew is single. According to Libby, he has had many close shaves when he's fallen passionately in love with some gorgeous young thing, but when it comes to the crunch he's always pulled out at the last minute. So, there have never been wedding bells. Libby reckons Andrew is not prepared to give up his life of risk-taking in order to settle down and become a stay-at-home father. The call of the wild outdoors is simply too strong and Libby has given up ever seeing her brother settle down to a more sedate married life.

Andrew gets along well with everyone; even his sore patients like him and come back for more. He's particularly a favourite amongst women, who are attracted by his good looks, daring life-style and enormous sense of fun. I'm no exception. Whenever I've been in Andrew's company, I return home elated and feel I can take on the world again. Slowly, but surely, I have been falling in love. This is the complete opposite to every one of Andrew's previous affairs when he's fallen head over heels with some woman, fated her madly for a few weeks, then tired of the lass and ended everything as abruptly as things had exploded at the start of the relationship.

Andrew's sister, Libby, has witnessed the deepening affection growing gradually between us over the years. She likens it to certain weather events. The numerous sudden and intense romances in Andrew's life she dismisses as his storms. There's thunder and lightning, it's loud and frightening but each storm passes quickly and is soon forgotten. Our growing attachment, however, is different, more like the slow and beautiful coming of the dawn. The growing light and deepening colours give promise of a bright new day to come.

Libby is sure she's right about the developing romance and resolves to do something to gently bring things to fruition. So, when Libby's secretary informs her that I would like to come and see her she immediately arranges for half an hour of her precious time to be blocked out. She advises her secretary we will take tea together in her chambers at three o'clock.

\*   \*   \*

Libby's chambers, located in the main street, are shared with five other barristers. They are housed in a handsome four-storey eighteenth-century sandstone edifice, replete with a grand double-door entrance and a short flight of well-worn steps. It's an imposing building, appropriate for those who are the guardians of the law. Libby is waiting for me, together with a splendid silver tea set and a packet of Bath Oliver biscuits. She stands to welcome me and promises thirty minutes of her valuable time.

After the usual niceties, I explain Betty's plight and ask Libby whether she would be interested in defending her. Perhaps wisely, Libby does not commit but offers to consider the matter carefully. She admits it would be an interesting distraction from the normal petty crime cases she handles on a regular basis.

'Dorothy, you and I have been good friends for many years now and I have something confidential I would like to discuss with you.'

'I guess you're right. It must be fifteen years since you saved my bacon over Tom's sudden disappearance. I still feel I'm in your debt for all you did then for me and the three children.'

'Well then, I'm going to offer you the perfect way of repaying that debt, Dorothy dear. More tea before I go on?'

'Yes please, and another of those yummy biscuits, if you don't mind.'

'I'm not sure how you are going to take this, but I can assure you it is well intentioned.'

Libby has me intrigued. My first thought is that she is going to offer me a job working in her administration office. She knows that now the children have flown the nest I'm looking for some interesting employment. What Libby comes up with, however, is a total surprise.

'Dorothy, do you realise my brother, Andrew, is very fond of you?'

I laugh, 'Andrew is everyone's best friend and exudes bonhomie to everybody he meets.'

'True, but I think he has more bonhomie to exude in your direction than any other.'

I must have looked puzzled.

'Oh, come on, Dorothy, haven't you noticed the way he looks at you, how he pays special attention to you? He even bought you a handsome birthday present this year.'

I felt myself blushing. It's true, I have always found Andrew an attractive man. If ever I was to re-marry, it would be to someone like Andrew. He possesses so many qualities I admire in a person: integrity, empathy, energy, good humour, courage, generosity. However, I'm still legally married and there's no way I can divorce a "missing person" which is why I have never seriously entertained the thought of marrying again. Besides, I'm forty-four and close to menopause.'

'So what?'

'Oh, Libby...your brother is a wonderful human being and I have always admired him greatly but he's mid-forties now and has never been married. He's not the marrying type. He enjoys his wild adventures too much to want to be stuck with a wife. He's never short of young female company if he wants a bit of sex. It's laughable to think he would be interested in an old bat like me.'

'You're wrong Dorothy.' Libby looks over her glasses with that fierce stare she has developed as a barrister whenever she wants to refute a statement. 'You're quite wrong, my dear. Andrew, despite all his bravado, is keen to settle down and lead a quieter life.'

'That maybe so, but there's no shortage of attractive younger women who could give him a family. He's certainly not too old to be a dad.'

'Ah...that's where you're wrong dear. Firstly, he only has eyes for you. I think he's in love with you and its time you reciprocated.'

'But Libby, it would be a miracle if I could bear children at my age.'

'Andrew doesn't want kids.'

'Why ever not?'

'Okay, I'll let you into a little secret. Andrew *can't* have kids.'

'What?'

'This is in strict confidence, you understand?'

'Yes, of course.'

'A couple of years ago Andrew had an unfortunate accident while rock climbing. You may remember he was in hospital for a week or two?'

'Yes, I do remember.'

'Well, that accident, apart from giving him a broken leg, also smashed his genitals.'

'Oh gosh, poor man!'

'The result is not all bad. It has left him impotent but he can still enjoy intercourse. It's a case of having lots of fun with no results. He fires empty blanks. Now you can understand why younger women wanting children would probably not be interested in him. As you know, Andrew is an honest man and would never deceive someone into believing he could make them pregnant.'

'I see...thanks for telling me.'

'Well, dear its time you thought seriously about your own future. You're not getting any younger but you're still a fit, attractive, active woman. Dentists are very well paid but they want more than just pulling teeth. Now, if you'll excuse me, I have a defence brief to prepare for tomorrow morning.'

I left Libby's chambers with an unexpected new spring in my step.

# 54.

......

# Glenis

Not surprisingly, I slept little on Sunday night. When I did sleep, I had recurring visions of Betty, dressed as a poor Soviet peasant lady, sweeping the roads of Moscow with a birch broom. Next, I saw a long row of massive billboards displaying huge head and shoulder photographs of Soviet female heroes. These heroes wore drab dark clothing and smiled proudly, because pinned to their buxom bosoms were the bright red ribbons of the Star of the Soviet Union medals. In the centre of the row was Comrade Betty Brindleton.

At some stage during this nightmarish time, I determined I must take the first train to Oxford and visit my daughter. I had no idea what, if anything, I could do to help. It was, I suppose, a mother's instinctive reaction. If your daughter's in trouble, then get to her as soon as possible to provide moral support, if nothing else.

As usual, I had to wake David at six-thirty. He's always at his grumpiest when I wake him and a Monday morning waking is the worst of them all. He snarled at me like some dangerous beast suffering from a nasty injury and bent on revenge. I laid out his clothes on the end of his bed while he relieved himself in the bathroom. While I was tossing up which of his wide selection of ties would go best with his paisley shirt, David blundered out of the bathroom looking as though he'd been pulled through a bush backwards.

'You still here?' he grumped.

'Yes, dear. I'm just putting out your clothes for you, as I always do.'
With a grunt, he wandered over to his bed and dropped his pyjama pants in front of me. Normally, he had the decency to wait until I had left the room. A large flabby white backside revealed itself. Then, as if to scare me off completely, he turned to show me his flaccid penis dangling uselessly between his legs. I couldn't remember when I had last seen David's privates, let alone enjoyed any activity in bed. For several years now we had slept in separate bedrooms. Hastily, I selected a suitable tie and threw it at my husband before hurrying from the room.

Over the last few weeks, David's suspected dementia seemed to have plateaued. Despite my suggestion that it might be a good idea to be checked out by a specialist he had chosen to ignore me. It would be so helpful if I could obtain a reliable diagnosis and *know* what I was dealing with. I have mentioned my concerns to Glenis and Betty who were both sympathetic and agreed he should be seen by a specialist doctor. They felt it was my responsibility to see this happened.

Today, David and I went through the same awkward situations that happened every morning. I checked he had everything ready to take to work, David asked numerous repetitive questions and appeared not to be able to recollect my answers. In the hour or so before he finally left, he became increasingly angry with me. Everything I did, quietly and unobtrusively, annoyed him further. Today, he couldn't even remember where the inside door to the garage was. When I gently guided him in the right direction, it was all too much and he exploded.

'Get your bloody hands off me, you pervert. First, you're poking around in my bedroom when I'm naked, now you're smooching up to me as I'm going out to get the car. What's wrong with you woman?'

I'd had enough. I burst into tears and stood there feeling helpless and totally rejected. David was not the man I had married; his very personality had changed. I watched helpless as David opened the door to the broom cupboard, realised this was not the way to the garage, slammed it shut, and glared at me as he found the correct door. But he had one more parting shot as he left.

'Glenis, you're some sort of a sex maniac. Book an appointment with a psychiatrist. If you don't, I'll do it for you!'

He stormed out.

\*   \*   \*

As soon as David was on his way, I dressed for town and walked to the bus stop. My Oxford bus pulled in at the stop nearest Betty's apartment at three minutes past ten and a few minutes later I arrived at the familiar red door. I was about to enter when two beefy men came lumbering through the open red door blocked my way. The men were carrying out Betty's radiogram. I asked what was going on and was told Mr. and Mrs. Stenhammer were leaving (the removalists had wrongly presumed Josh and Betty were married). I hurried up the stairs and found Betty flinging the last of her clothes into a couple of large cardboard boxes. She had half expected me to turn up, she said. Betty needed another ten minutes to finalise things and suggested we then go out for a morning snack and she would explain everything. We ordered raisin toast for two and large Ovaltines at the Lyons Corner Shop.

'Whew, I'm glad to get that done,' declared Betty. 'We've lost the apartment and have to move. We've also lost our salaries. The company was a total fraud!'

'What's happened?'

'The guy we called Norman almost definitely is a Soviet agent. They arrested him on Wednesday while I was having lunch with him.'

'How awful! Are you okay?'

'Yup. I was terrified at the time. Internal Security wanted me to go ahead and meet Norman as usual. I thought there could be shooting or at least a fight but everything went remarkably peacefully.'

'Oh golly, dear, it sounds terrible!'

'We had just finished our soup and were waiting for the mains when three men from Internal Security quietly approached our table from different directions. The one who came up behind Norman simply put his hand heavily on Norman's shoulder, bent down and in a very soft voice told him not to move because he was under arrest. Then he told Norman to stand up very slowly and put his arms in the air. Norman did exactly as he was told. Before he left, he looked down at me and apologised. He was the perfect gentleman right to the end. Then the four of them left without any fuss. Half the people in the restaurant didn't even know anything untoward had happened.'

'Wow, how dramatic! You were so brave, dear.'

We paused our conversation for a moment as the lass arrived with our raisin toast and glasses of Ovaltine.

'On Saturday I had to have another meeting with a couple of the Internal Security fellows. It only lasted ten minutes or so, but what they had to tell me was unbelievable.'

I looked at my daughter anxiously and wondered what was coming next. Betty had already been through ordeals that many people would not have been able to cope with.

'Go on dear, tell me what they said.'

'First of all, they confirmed they were one hundred percent certain Norman was an Englishman who had been working for the Soviets for years. Internal Security had known for a long time there was a highly effective and quite brilliant spy operating somewhere in the country. For years this person had been successfully passing secrets back to Moscow. Every time they thought they were closing in on this mysterious person, he would elude them. He kept changing his name, moving to a new location, changing tactics and adopting different techniques and codes for relaying his information back to Moscow. However, like almost all such agents, eventually they run out of luck or make a mistake.'

'How exciting dear, do go on.'

'You know, I really liked Norman. He seemed such a great guy, almost like a father to me. It's a terrible shock to discover he's really a brilliant spy who the authorities have been hunting for years. It's hard to believe he's a traitor. A few years ago, if found guilty, he would probably have received the death penalty.'

'Well, they've got him now, thank goodness.'

'Next, they said we had to get out of our apartment pronto and Jason and I would no longer receive our salaries. Apparently, everything was being financed by the Soviets. Jason and I, it seems, have been living the good life for months on the Russian rouble.'

'So where are you two moving to?'

'I'm going to a small flat on my own. Internal Security have arranged it for me.'

'Really... Internal Security are prepared to get you a flat? Why?'

'To thank me for my cooperation but also to keep an eye on my safety for a month or two until they are sure there won't be any reprisals.'

'Are they paying?'

'For three months only. Then I have to find the rent myself. It won't be easy if I no longer have a salary coming in.'

'Perhaps we can help with the finances, dear?'

'That would be marvellous, mum. Then they told me something else that was extraordinary. I was totally gob smacked!'

Betty's story was already amazing. It was hard to imagine what else might be coming. I licked the last of the butter off my fingers and waited.

'It's about Josh. He hasn't been released.'

"Why ever not?'

'The security guys believe he also signed up for the Soviets and was working on me to get me to join them.'

'Betty that's awful! Did they ever ask you to join?'

'Definitely not. But who knows what might have happened in a few months' time?'

I gasped and put my hand to my mouth. The thought that my sweet, innocent daughter might so easily have become a traitor, a Soviet agent, a criminal of the worst type, was almost too much to take. I sat there in stunned silence.

'I've got to go mum. I need to supervise the arrival of my gear at the new apartment. I'll ring you tonight with my new phone number and address.'

'Okay dear. I'll pay the bill.'

'Thanks mum,' and Betty hurried off.

I stayed for a short time alone, thinking over all that Betty had told me. Now, I was worried about how much of all this I could pass on to David and how he would react.

# 55.

......

# Dorothy

Since enjoying afternoon tea with Libby Johnson in her chambers, I've given a great deal of thought to what she had to tell me about Andrew. I must admit I've been increasingly aware of Andrew and have noticed how he often seeks my company when we meet socially at a tennis afternoon or at someone's "do". Until now though, I've thought nothing more of it; believing we are just good friends who enjoy each other's company. Andrew makes me laugh. Sometimes the humour is at the expense of his long-suffering patients, sometimes it's at his own expense when describing some fiendishly difficult challenge he encountered on one of his crazy adventures. Could Libby be right? Is there the potential for our friendship to blossom into a full-blown romantic relationship?

After my bath last night, I stopped for a moment to look at my naked body in the long bedroom mirror. I hadn't done this for an awfully long time and was pleasantly surprised. My breasts were firm and I still looked fit and slim. Playing tennis regularly, at least once a week, has kept me in good condition. I may be forty-four, but I've kept my good figure. Yes, I tell myself, I'm still a physically attractive, desirable woman. Of course, what a person looks like is *not* the most important consideration, but it sure helps.

I saw Andrew stripped down to his swimming togs at a pool party last year. He's a ball of muscle, not an ounce of surplus fat. It's no wonder the young women are so attracted to him. I think he's forty-five but could easily pass for ten years younger. Maturity, a sense of fun, personality, substantial financial assets and good looks are a winning combination. It seems extraordinary that such a desirable man could be seriously interested in having a relationship with an older woman like me.

If Andrew and I do get together, what are the ramifications for my children? What will they think once they are over their initial shock? It's not as though they're going to be deprived of a vast inheritance; there's only the house which I was planning to sell anyway. And then there's Tom. We are still legally a married couple. What happens in the eyes of the church and the laws of the country when one person in a marriage seeks a divorce as a result of the long-time disappearance of their partner? And what about Andrew's family? As far as I know, he has never married or fathered a child. I'm sure he's slept with a number of women, although that is supposition. Would his family welcome me? At least I know his sister, Libby, is on my side.

The strangest thing is that Andrew, if he's really interested in courting me, hasn't invited me out on a date. Why? Surely, such an extrovert wouldn't be shy or embarrassed to ask me out? Or perhaps, this whole "affair" is merely wishful thinking on Libby's part? Could this whole business simply be a figment of her imagination? Libby has a happy fulfilling marriage herself so it's quite conceivable she wants to set her brother up with a permanent partner before he gets too ancient.

To be perfectly honest, I would love to have a relationship with Andrew. Eventually, after a couple more days of mulling it around, I decide to go against the conventional mores and be the one to take the initiative. I'll invite Andrew out on a date. But I'll expect him to pay!

\*   \*   \*

Inviting Andrew out on a date is not as easy as it sounds. He's a busy man. When time away from work permits, he's usually off with his mates caving, diving or hiking long distances through rugged countryside. He told me recently he has most of his weekends and the next annual holidays booked out for months ahead. My invitation will have to be for a date during the working week; the theatre perhaps or one of those Ingmar Bergman films they are showing in Oxford? Dinner at a decent restaurant would be great too. There are, of course, museums, art galleries and public lectures but I have no idea if Andrew is interested in such activities and anyway, they are rarely open in the evenings. I procrastinate for several days and then begin to doubt whether this crazy idea of inviting Andrew out on a date is a wise move. He's such an independent sort of person; he might resent a woman like me being so pushy. In the end the whole tricky dilemma was solved for me. The phone rang on Wednesday evening and it was Andrew.

'Hi Dorothy. Do you have a spare minute?'

'Andrew, for you, I have more than a spare minute,' I said and then regretted my rather flippant reply.

'Good, I have a proposal for you.'

'Really?'

'Yes, really. What are you doing two weekends away?'

'Playing tennis at the club.'

'Can it be missed?'

'Well, I guess it depends whether I get a better offer?'

'A group of us are going caving over the weekend and we need a chef. I've heard glowing accounts of your culinary skills and so I'm offering you the job. The pay and conditions are exceptional and we will contribute generously to your superannuation. What do you think?'

'Crickey Andrew, this is all a bit sudden. Where are you going? Have you got all the gear and food organised?'

'We're going to explore some caves that have only recently been opened up for speleologists. It's about an hour's drive away.

Our usual chef has a broken leg and we're desperate for a quality replacement. All you have to bring is a sleeping bag and a change of clothes. We are sleeping in rustic cabins with log fires. The kitchen is surprisingly well equipped. We have power, a large fridge, an excellent cooking stove and more pots and pans than you can poke a stick at. You'll love it!'

'I don't have a sleeping bag...'

'No problem, you can share mine....no seriously, I have a spare one you can use.' There are a couple of women in the group so you can bunk down with them.'

'What's the rat situation like?'

'Rats? Plenty of 'em. We catch 'em and stew 'em up. You can cook rat...ratatouille can't you Dorothy?'

'Ratatouille is a vegetable stew, you ignoramus.'

'I stand corrected. It'll be lovely to have you along, Dorothy. It'll make my weekend. I'll pick you up at five on the Friday evening. No need to cook on the first night, we'll eat out at a pub nearby.'

'You will remember to bring the spare sleeping bag won't you Andrew?'

'On the contrary, I'll do my very best to forget, then you'll have to share with me.'

I giggled flirtatiously, then instantly thought better of it.

'If the chef doesn't get a good night's sleep, then the meals will be deplorable,' I responded.

'Okay, I've got the message. See you at five in two weekends time,' and he was gone.

My worries about how best to foster a deeper relationship with Andrew abated. Spending a weekend in such close proximity with the man (but not in Andrew's sleeping bag!) should go a long way towards furthering our interest in each other. Not exactly a "date," but getting closer. Now, to start working out what clothes to take...

# 56.

......

# Lucy

Mum rang last night. She said she has some amazing news to give us but wants to come to Oxford this Saturday morning to tell us about it, in person. She didn't want to talk about it over the phone. Strangely, she asked me to also contact Betty so she can hear the news as well. Malcolm and I have been trying to guess what mum's big news is. Perhaps she has had a terrific offer on the house and is going to sell soon? Or maybe something exciting has happened for one of my brothers, Rodney or Derek? Are they getting engaged? Why, though, is it important to have Betty in the house to hear the news? It's mysterious but exciting at the same time. Mum expects to arrive around ten o'clock I have been running around tidying up and making fresh scones.

Betty arrives a bit before ten. She's still full of the story of how she lunched with Norman and his sudden arrest by three Internal Security men. She had been terrified there might be a massive scene; a brawl, or even a shootout. In the end, everything went amazingly smoothly, because Norman offered no resistance and accepted his situation like a gentleman. Betty was not impressed, however, that she was left to pay the bill for their lunch!

Mum arrived a few minutes late due to parking difficulties. After a few happy minutes playing with Graham, she was seated and ready to give us her "amazing news". We sat around the kitchen table spreading strawberry jam and cream on our still warm scones.

I think mum was enjoying keeping us in suspense.

'Well folks, I have some incredible news for you.'

'Come on mum, don't keep us waiting any longer.'

'Yesterday, at lunchtime, I was contacted by the Oxfordshire police. They were very polite and asked me if I would be prepared to come to the police station to help them with the identification of a person. They said they would send a car to collect me and would bring me home afterwards. When I asked what this was all about, they wouldn't say. Anyway, the car arrived at about three o'clock with a nice young man as the driver. He told me we were expected at the police station by four o'clock.'

'All very hush-hush then mum?' said Malcolm.

'It was. I could tell it was something important because when we arrived at the police station I was met at the door by a senior sergeant and taken to a comfortable waiting room. I was offered a cup of tea and shown where the ladies' bathroom was located. Police stations are usually horrible, unfriendly places but they were clearly keen to make me welcome.'

I offered mum a top up of her tea and another scone but she declined both. She was anxious to continue her story.

'Next, I was taken down the corridor to meet the Chief Inspector in his spacious office. We shook hands and he introduced two other men who he said were from Interior Security. I can't remember their names, but they were pleased to see me.'

'Did you say the two men were from Interior Security?' asked Betty, looking puzzled, 'are you sure it wasn't Internal Security?'

'Yes Betty, I think you're right, dear. Yes, my mistake. The two men were from Internal Security. They were dressed up in smart suits and looked very important.'

'Go on mum. What happened?'

'One of the men, the tubby one, told me they had someone they wanted me to meet but they warned me it might be a shock. Of course, I immediately thought of my Tom, who left me so many years ago. I couldn't contain myself and I blurted out "Is it my husband, Tom?"'

'Oh mum, how exciting! Was he alive or...?'

'He was alive. To cut a long story short, they escorted me to a cell down in the basement and there, sitting on a bench behind bars, was Tom. I almost fainted. It was definitely him. He greeted me and smiled. I was so taken aback I just stood there speechless. Tom spoke to me in a friendly voice, almost as if we had never been apart. He was full of remorse and kept apologising to me and the children.'

'Oh mum, what a shock!'

'It was, dear. I had so many mixed emotions. This man had been my devoted husband for nine lovely years before he simply disappeared one day. I didn't know whether to yell at him and tell him how cruel it had been for me and his children or go in and embrace him.'

'So, what did you do?' asked Malcolm.

'After a couple of minutes, the men gently led me away. It was awful. Tom was shouting out that he loved me and how sorry he was about everything. When we returned to the inspector's office, they told me seventeen years ago Tom had become a Soviet agent. He had admitted everything. His few contacts knew him as Norman.'

My mother stopped for a sip of her tea and a chance to recover her composure. Clearly this whole business was still horribly raw. She had a short cry before continuing.

'The men thanked me for my cooperation and went on to explain Tom was likely to get life for treason. In due course, after his case had been through the courts, he would be kept in a maximum-security prison somewhere in Britain. I would probably be allowed to visit under strict security protocols if I wished.'

'If it's any comfort to you,' said Betty, 'I found him to be a lovely man, friendly and kind.'

This was too much for mum and she broke down again. For the

next hour the four of us asked numerous questions, cheered mum up and asked each other what all this meant for the future. As Tom's daughter, I felt strangely removed from the whole sorry business. The long time since I had known my father had slowly expunged any feelings I still had for him.

# Epilogue
....................

D octor Thomas Entwistle, nuclear physicist and Soviet agent, was interrogated for many hours over the next two days. He gave little away and remained a gentleman throughout the exhausting ordeal. On the morning of his third day in detention, he was discovered writhing in pain in his cell. Rushed to hospital it was soon realised he had deliberately ingested a powerful dose of some toxic substance. He died later the same day. Tom would have known he must take his own life. Failure to do so would mean his extermination at the hands of the Soviets as soon as it could be arranged. Although thoroughly body searched, Tom had somehow still managed to smuggle in the necessary draft.

Tom's interrogators did manage to piece together a few facts before his demise. While working at Harwell's Atomic Research Station he had been lured into the Soviet web through a combination of generous bribes and promises. When he first disappeared, he had travelled to Moscow on a falsified Soviet passport where he spent over two years learning Russian and the art and science of spying for the KPG. Tom was then smuggled back into Britain where he successfully infiltrated certain universities and research institutions that held valuable information related to research into nuclear fusion. He frequently moved addresses and changed his name and appearance. The KGB regarded him very highly and he had received a number of Soviet medals and citations.

With Tom's passing, Dorothy no longer had to worry about what had happened to him, or wonder whether she could legitimately marry again. She was a great success on the caving trip as the chef and a few months later married Andrew at a large wedding in Oxford. She later enrolled in a dental assistant's course and now works for Andrew as one of his dental nurses. She sold the house well and lives with Andrew in his large rambling home on the outskirts of Oxford. Andrew still enjoys his wild adventurous weekends but now has Dorothy to keep an eye on him and cook him delicious meals.

Lucy and Malcolm went on to have three beautiful children. The poor teachers' salaries in Britain encouraged them to migrate to Australia where they settled down happily in Adelaide. Their kids are sports mad and as brown as berries. Dorothy no longer feels the need to migrate to Australia, but visits every few years with her husband Andrew.

For Betty, the terrifying experience of being so closely associated with a Soviet agent was a massive wake-up call. The interrogators detained Josh as a suspect for several months before finally releasing him. He abandoned his research into nuclear fusion and ended up as a public servant working in Birmingham.

Betty eventually returned to the ever-faithful Michael and before the end of the year they married at a quiet ceremony in a registry office. Glenis attended but not her husband. Michael and Betty have since had two children. Betty completed her PhD and was immediately accepted for post-doctoral studies at Oxford University. Within ten years she was an Associate Professor in the Faculty of Science at Oxford University. Sadly, nuclear fusion has never been achieved but Betty is forever hopeful.

Betty never wavered in her support for free love. Micheal very reluctantly accepted the situation. Betty certainly moderated her sexual behaviour out of respect for Micheal and their marriage. Once the children came along Betty found she had less time and energy to seek out other partners and her marriage almost normalised. Her extra-marital affairs became less and less. They are still married and are a happy family unit.

Doctor David Brindleton struggled on for a few more months until his position as a general practioner became untenable. Glenis looked after him devotedly for a few years at home until his dementia became too challenging for her to manage. David is now in a nursing home in Oxford and receives holy communion every fortnight when the Catholic priest visits. He never remembers having received his holy communion though and complains bitterly as only David Brindleton can.

www.ingramcontent.com/pod-product-compliance
Lightning Source LLC
Chambersburg PA
CBHW031947130726
47904CB00012B/292